Of Marytrs
And Marigolds

Aquila Ismail

ISBN-10: 1463694822

EAN-13: 9781463694821

Library of Congress Control Number: 2011911858

CreateSpace, North Charleston, South Carolina

For my parents

MAPS

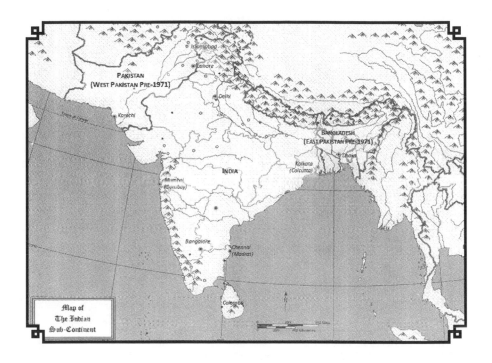

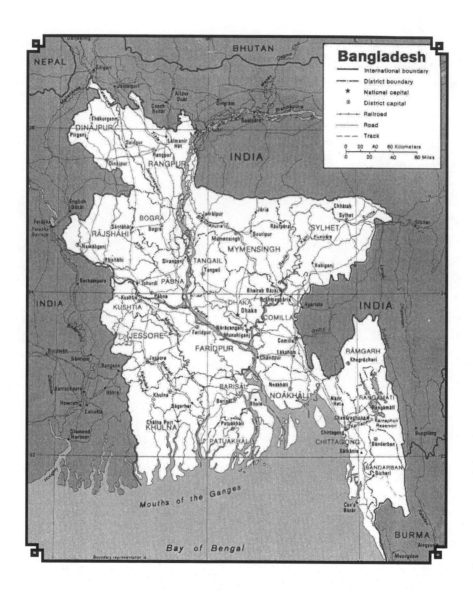

Bid me farewell, my brother!

I bow to you all and take my departure.

Here I give back the keys to my door

...And I give up all claims to my house.

We were neighbors for long,

But I received more than I could give

Now the day has dawned

And the lamp that lit my dark corner is out.

A summons has come...

"Farewell," by Rabindranath Tagore

Note: Tagore's poem 'My Golden Bengal' is the National Anthem of Bangladesh.

February in the golden land is a misty melancholic month. The air redolent with the fragrance of delicate orange stemmed white shefali flowers awakens memories of past heartaches. Perhaps, this is why the shefali is also known as the flower of sorrow. The days are crisp and the nights filled with love and longing. The forty-four rivers that criss-cross the land, unreplenished by melting snow in the Himalayas or by the monsoon rains, meander sluggishly as if reluctant to meet the salt of the sea. Small grey mosquitoes begin their life cycle at sunset and gorged with human blood end it at daybreak. Clusters of tiny greenish white *raat ki rani*, the queen-of-the-night, blossoms in the dark, sending forth a heady scent, attracting snakes and spirits of young women who have died at childbirth. When the mist of the morning clears yellow-ochre butterflies and four winged orange dragonflies flit between the asters, dahlias, pink and mauve sweet pea vines on bamboo trellises, and gaily swaying cosmos, all brought to this land by British colonizers nostalgic for the smells of English gardens. Orange-yellow marigolds overflow their beds and amid the haunting strains of *"my brother's blood splattered on the twenty-first, can I ever forget,"* are offered to six martyrs to the mother tongue of the golden land.

The flood of dew was still fresh on the broad-leaved grass that soft February morning in 1972 when Suri was herded out of her house in Mirpur, a suburb of Dacca, by soldiers of Bangladesh. Forty-nine days earlier, East Pakistan, the eastern part of the land created for the Muslims of India in 1947, had become Bangladesh, the golden land, the land of those whose mother tongue was Bengali. All those whose mother tongue was not Bengali had no claim to this golden land whatsoever.

That morning, the tidal wave sweeping three hundred thousand men, women, and children into the Indian Ocean, the Pakistani General's orders to kill three million Bengali 'sons of bitches,' the Bengali Liberation Front's massacre of Urdu-speaking women in a jute mill in Chittagong, the scorching of the earth in Dacca with the blood of Bengali intellectuals one day before the December War was won by India and lost by Pakistan, were all part of the past year. And the past cannot be undone even by God.

So that misty February morning, with the fragrance of the shefali blossoms wafting in the air, driven from her home, Suri sat in the mess of the afterbirth of Bangladesh, born after nine months gestation just like the human fetus, her white dupatta wrapped around her lithe body like a cocoon, when a voice gurgling with elation swept over to her.

"A man! A man! Trying to hide among the women, eh! *Haramjada*! Bastard!"

The rest of the sentence was lost within the sounds of braying laughter. Suri raised her head from her knees and looked in the direction the laughter was coming from. A soldier, oiled hair slicked back, dark thick moustache covering his upper lips, bayonet in hand stood a few feet away. A sudden chill overwhelmed her. Was this the same impatient soldier who, last night, unhooked the gold hoop in her ear and pulled it out, tearing her earlobe? The red splotches of blood were now indistinguishable from the red flowers printed on her white qameez.

Suri's heart threatened to burst as she watched the soldier bend forward and, with the dull silver blade of his bayonet, bear down the black and gold edged red sari wound tightly around the face of a skinny woman. He stretched his arms, tugged at the ends of the sari entwined in bony fingers, and unraveled the covering from the head and shoulders.

"Come and see this…come and see this woman with a moustache…come quickly," he jeered.

2

His hands reached out to the sari-clad man's crotch, and the braying laughter boomed out again. "She has the jewels as well… hehehe!" he sneered at the terrified young man.

Several soldiers stopped rifling through the bundles carried by women when they left their homes and headed toward their comrade. A soldier bounded over, arms flailing, crushing the white flowers among the green grass and grazed Suri's toes with his heavy army boots. She winced, withdrew her bare feet further into the small circle of her haunch and legs, and shifted closer to her mother and sister as if to fuse with them into one round heap. The soldier grabbed the sari-clad man's hair and pulled him up. The young man's palms came together in the universal sign of mercy; his eyes opened wide, his Adam's apple bobbed up and down, and his quivering guttural voice floated over the field.

"Forgive me…forgive me…I just wanted to be with my mother. I have done nothing to you. I am not from among them…I am just a poor man…"

As the soldiers dragged him out, his sari trailed behind in a swathe of red with streaks of black and gold. An old woman followed the soldiers to the edge of the field near the trees. Several soldiers surrounded him. The first kick with heavy army booted feet landed on his stomach, and the skinny man doubled over. The old woman clung to the man, but a soldier pried her away. The woman pleaded, cried, and wept and grabbed the knees of first one soldier and then another.

"She must be his mother," Suri told herself.

The young man still pleaded, "Sirs, I am not a *Razakar*. I did not volunteer to help the Pakistan Army…I am just a poor man…I am not from among them…"

"What is he saying, Suri? Do you think he is from the alshams-albadr?" asked Suri's mother, her Ammi, sitting next to her in the dew-drenched field.

"Apa, he looks like those men who rode around in the jeep with rifles day before yesterday," Suri's younger sister Munni remarked. They had seen the jeep speed by from their bedroom window.

"Maybe, Munni, we don't know," Suri replied.

"But, Apa, remember they shouted Pakistan *Zindabad*..."

"They're so stupid. Why are they still shouting slogans of long life for Pakistan? Don't they know this is now Bangladesh? Stupid! Stupid! Stupid! And because of them all of us in Mirpur are suspected of having guns and rifles in our houses."

"But the soldiers who barged into our house last night were not interested in weapons. They wanted money and jewelry..." Suri's mother interjected.

"Ammi, stop it! I don't want to talk about last night."

"Oh! God, I'm sorry, beti," Ammi replied.

"The way they are beating him, that man will die!" Suri's voice trembled as she made the remark.

They heard the soldiers berating the young man. "Then why are you trying to fool everyone by wearing a sari?"

"My mother told me to. I am her only son...please let me go. I will go with the men..."

A soldier's boot landed on the young man's back, and he lunged forward. Suri turned her face away. She did not want to see if the soldiers were going to thrust their bayonets into his chest, like they did to four Urdu-speaking Pakistani prisoners, just days after the December War ended. At the sight of bayonet thrusts deliberately missing the heart so that the spectacle, held in Dacca Stadium, could be prolonged, the air was said to have resounded with cries of five thousand men, women, and children: "*joi...joi...* long live...long live Bangladesh!"

"But that was just a rumor—it had to be!" Suri told herself.

When the pleading and screaming ceased, Suri mustered enough courage to look in the direction of the trees. She could not see the young man but the soldiers looked pleased. One by one they spat on the spot where the young man lay. Perhaps he was facing the serene February sky with his mother trying to stop the blood trickling down her son's temples with her white sari. When the blood dried on the cloth, it would not be easy to wash off!

Then an almost absurd thought occurred to Suri: This stupid man should have worn the red bordered yellow sari, and then he would have been safe. Perhaps, the red, black, and gold had given him away. For was it not in February that girls in red bordered yellow saris, carrying marigolds in their anchals, walked barefoot over the grass to the martyrs' memorial and offered obeisance to the six young men martyred to the Bengali language on the twenty-first day of February in 1952. Last year Suri too had worn the traditional yellow and red cotton sari when she went with her Rumi to pay homage to his cousin, Lal bhai, who was one of those martyrs, shot in the head by the police as he cycled through the old city to his work as clerk in Dacca High Court. But seventeen days still remained to that anniversary! So the notion that a yellow sari would have saved the young man whose blood now coloured the white flowers on the green grass was probably just a silly thought, Suri concluded.

While Suri's mind conjured up the past, the women in the field whispered to one another, intoned verses from the Quran, the verse of Prophet Jonah as he repented in the belly of the whale: "with Your mercy I look for Your help, followed by, I was a sinner and hurt others, forgive me." By reciting the Quran, they hoped to invoke God's mercy in this mist of despair and helplessness. Sekina, their neighbor, who had moved from the southern port city, Chittagong, to Mirpur after that March night when General Yahya ordered the massacre of Bengalis, sat near them. Sekina's family had migrated from Surat in India and chosen to settle in Chittagong in the early years of Pakistan.

Sekina's baby was not yet weaned. This was a good thing, for there was no food for anyone. She suckled the baby, hiding him under the part of the orange and green sari that was draped across her bosom, while her sister-in-law, the beautiful Naima, virginal in white, soothed her five-year-old niece. Suri's older brother Sadi had promptly fallen in love with her as he did with every pretty girl he saw.

After dealing with the man in the sari, the soldiers turned their attention once again to the women in the field. They were not taking any chances with letting an Urdu-speaking male resident of Mirpur escape by hiding among the women, and so they needed to check faces and other things that defined womanhood. One soldier picked up the end of Suri's dupatta with his bayonet.

"What is this? Being bashful...let me see."

Suri quickly removed the white dupatta covering her shoulders and bare dusky arms. The soldier tapped first one bosom and then another with his bayonet, nodded, and smiled as he proclaimed that Suri was indeed not a man. Through blurred eyes, she saw the same soldier stop in front of the very pregnant Saleha, put his hands up her shirt, and run his palms over the swollen belly.

"Another Bihari bastard to take care of, we will deal with him as well, ehehe!" Saleha was an Urdu-speaking Pakistani, but the soldier referred to her baby as a 'Bihari', as if the child was from the Indian state of Bihar.

Saleha sobbed aloud as the soldier went up to Sekina and picked up the sari end to see what she was hiding.

"Boy or a girl?"

"Girl!"

"The baby is not a girl...why is she lying?" Munni whispered.

"Be quiet," Ammi scolded her.

Before the soldier could check if what the mother said was true, his eyes fell on Nuru sitting nearby. Nuru's mother worked for Suri's family and lived in the quarters next to the kitchen. She had gone home the night before with her good-for-nothing husband.

"What is this boy doing here?" the soldier roared.

Realizing that he was the object of the soldier's attention, Nuru took off as fast as his bowlegs could carry him. The soldier chased him through the sea of women and disappeared behind the houses. A few minutes later he came back grinning and smiling. Perhaps, he was pleased that he had managed to send Nuru off to join the men gathered at the crossroad. The chase had made him forget about the baby.

That February morning when the sun had begun its daily ascent, Suri's father, her Abbu, had gone out to the front veranda of their house to see if the morning newspaper had been delivered although he did not expect that it had. He walked with a stoop for the pain inflicted in his chest by the soldiers late last night was still fresh. Suri's father had not gone to his office ever since Sheikh Mujib was set free from prison in West Pakistan and returned to Bangladesh, his liberated golden land. Abbu's colleagues advised him that it was better for him to stay home and wait for the change in government postings that were to take place soon. "We are saying this for your own good Mr. Haq!" they added.

Since the days of Indian and Pakistani fighter jets maneuvering and dodging in dogfights over the skies of Dacca in December, Suri's family had slept downstairs on mattresses dragged down from the beds upstairs and lined up each night in the long drawing room. Initially this was to enable better observation of the blackouts, but now it felt comfortable to be near each other. They even managed to tie mosquito nets to latches and knobs of the doors and windows opening into the room. The small grey mosquitoes made it impossible to sleep without these nets at this time of the year.

During that December War, at first the sounds of explosions and gunfire could be heard in the distance. As the Indian troops circled Dacca and tightened the noose around the city, the sounds came closer and closer. In the night, the explosions were more clearly audible, and when the tracer shells lit up the sky with phosphorescent glow, Sekina's pet rooster sounded the call for sunrise. Everyone laughed at it being tricked. Those were the only light moments that month.

For some reason, the mosquito nets, the white sheets, and the colorful satin edged blankets that Ammi had brought back from Karachi, the city by the sea in West Pakistan, when she went to visit her brother and mother, had infuriated the four Bangladeshi soldiers who crashed into their house the night before that February day.

"Look at these Biharis. Look at their gall! Even now they live like kings," they growled.

Abbu, was inconsolable after the soldiers had rampaged through the house.

"All of you forgive me. Suri, Munni, Sami, please forgive me...I could not protect my family. Where is my Sadi?"

"Be thankful Sadi left Mirpur! God knows how your son might have reacted when the soldiers hit you. He is so hotheaded. They would not have liked it!"

"I should have realized after March last year that there would be more trouble and should have sent all of you away to Karachi ...

to your brother...I should have insisted," Abbu wailed, " I should have known after what happened in Chittagong and Khulna in March."

"Ji," Ammi comforted her husband, "we are from here. All our children were born in East Pakistan..."

"Now it is not East Pakistan," Abbu interrupted her, "It is now not the land of the Muslims. It is Bangladesh...the land of the Bengalis."

"But we came here right after Pakistan was made, so we belong here. Do not torture yourself. We have so many friends. They will make sure nothing happens to us."

"None of that matters now. We are not accepted as Bengalis... we speak Urdu and anyone who helps us will be branded as well," Abbu said.

Through the night Suri's father wept. Eventually exhausted and emotionally spent, the family dozed off in a huddle. As soon as Suri fell asleep, her friend from Chittagong, the green-eyed Haseena, appeared from the dark recesses of the room and sat down beside her on the mattress. She spoke to Suri in whispers, "You know, I am cursed with the odor of congealed blood."

"How did this come to be?" Suri asked.

"I lay under the dead bodies of fifty-seven women in our house by the Karnaphuli River..."

"When?"

"In March when General Yahya began to kill Bengalis in your city the fighters of the Liberation Front took all the Urdu-speaking men away and all the Urdu speaking women in the mill took refuge in my house..."

"Why?"

"The Liberation Front...those fighting for the freedom of the Bengalis wanted revenge for what the General had done in Dacca to their people. All these women took refuge in my house, and three men came in and fired bursts from their machineguns at us..."

Before Haseena could finish her sentence, Abbu's panic-stricken voice pierced through the somnolence. "Get up! All of you! Get up! Everyone is out in the streets. We must leave the house."

"Run, Suri…the fighters are here…" Before Suri could stop her and tell her that it was okay, that this was not March of 1971 but February of 1972, Haseena disappeared into the receding darkness.

From out on the veranda that February morning, Abbu had seen some people walking in the streets. This was strange for no one even went to the bazaar anymore. Absolutely nothing had come in from the city for a week now, while for the past month fresh vegetables, meat, and fish were only sporadically available in Mirpur bazaar. Abbu went to the black metal gate and looked over it to the left and then the right. Not just a few people, but many were passing by in twos, threes, fours, and fives in an unending stream. He ran back into the living room and woke everyone up.

"Come on, we need to go out quickly." He shouted, "The soldiers are here again. We must go out before they come into the house again."

Suri jumped up, her heart pounding. She ran to the living room window. Parting the heavy dark curtains, she looked over the boundary wall and saw Bangladeshi soldiers disembarking from trucks that had stopped in the street outside their house. Fear gripped her, and she backed away from the window, sat down on the dark maroon sofa, and tried to calm down. She heard her father again shout at them to hurry up and follow him out the door.

"Everyone is outside. Do you want the soldiers to come in and drag us out?"

"Abbu, please do not make us go out. Let's just lock the doors and hide in here. I don't want to go out. Ammi, please let us just stay inside." Suri was shivering. The episode last night with the soldiers had been the most frightening in her life.

"If we do not go out, they will come in and force us out," Abbu replied.

"Ji, they have already searched our house and will not come in again," Suri's mother tried to reason with him.

Munni grabbed Suri's waist and clung to her. Suri's younger brother, Sami, got up and began to fold the mosquito nets. Even in this time of panic, he wanted everything to be neat and tidy.

"Everyone is out there. I can see Doja sahib and Harris...Let's go. Hurry we must go immediately!"

Suri mustered enough courage to look out the window again. She saw Ghousia and her pregnant older sister Saleha, who had come to her mother's house for the baby's delivery, walk by. They lived down the road.

"But why should we leave our house?" Ammi continued to argue.

A loud clanging sound outside followed by shouts of "Come on out...Hurry up! Do you Bihari bastards think we have all day," shook them up.

Now there was no way they could stay inside the house. There were soldiers outside the gate.

"Shall we take something with us?" Ammi asked.

"Do you think they will not search us if we carry anything with us?" Abbu's voice quivered as he said this. "I cannot stand it if they touch us again. Whatever they take from the house can be re-placed once things settle. Let's just go out and see what happens."

As the five of them stepped out into the cool misty February morning, Tonto, Sami's dog of indeterminate pedigree, thought he was being taken for a walk and wagged his tail vigorously as he nuzzled his master's hands. The one-opaque-eyed Nuru with the bowlegs ran out and stood in front of Ammi.

"Begumsahib, do not leave me," Nuru pleaded.

"Where is your mother?" Ammi asked the boy.

"She went home with Baba last night. She said she would be back soon."

"Why did you not go with her?"

"I did not want to go with him. He beats me after he drinks *tarhi*." Nuru was in tears.

"Tell your mother to make tea and some rotis for us when she comes back..." Ammi began to instruct Nuru. "We will be back soon." Seeing Nuru's crestfallen face, she added, "No matter, come with us."

"Should we lock the front door?" Ammi directed her question to Abbu.

"No, they will only break the door down if we do."

The Bangladeshi soldiers last night had really frightened Abbu. He was not taking any chances of encountering them in his house again. Much rather be out in the open with neighbors. But not all the neighbors were in the streets that morning. Mr. Jalil, who lived across the road, had taken his family back to his hometown Tongi in the outskirts of Dacca to visit relatives. The neighbor from the house down the road had left to visit his brother in Joydebpur twenty-two miles to the north.

Abbu still clutching his aching chest, wearing the grey check lungi and white muslin kurta he slept in, walked toward the cross-road where a small crowd was gathering. The soldiers who lined the road directed Suri, Munni, and Ammi to go to the other side. Sami held on to Ammi's hand and walked with them. A soldier pulled him away and hit him in the back with his rifle butt.

"This way...come this way...you son of a pig..."

Tonto growled and lunged at the soldier. He did not like any-one laying hands on his master. The soldier aimed his bayonet at Tonto. Ammi quickly came between them. "It's okay...its okay," she calmed Tonto and, turning to Sami, stroked his back, "Go, beta. Listen to me. Go with Abbu. Everything will be okay."

Just ahead on the road, the Nepalese family who lived on the far side of the block was heading toward the crossroad with each member of the family holding one end of a string cot. On it was a life-size bundle wrapped in a white sheet stained with blood. As they approached the crossroad, the soldiers gestured that the cot be left on the side and the women move across the road. When they resisted, a couple of soldiers took hold of the cot and pushed it to the ground.

Mrs. Doja, who had helped Ammi and her best friend, Mrs. Ahmed, take care of poor crazy Rajabi in the fatal throes of birth-ing in the T&T Officers' Colony near New Market where they lived before shifting to Mirpur, came up to Ammi from behind and asked if she knew what was happening.

"I don't, Bhabi...I don't...I think...I hope it is just to search for weapons. None of us have any, so it won't take long...God will take care of us all." Ammi pointed toward Mrs. Doja's son who was walking ahead of them and asked, "Why does he have a bandage on his forehead? Is that blood on it? What happened?"

"Bhabi, when the soldiers came into the house last night, he challenged them, so they beat him up brutally."

"Thank God Sadi is away. He would have done the same, and the soldiers would not have liked it," Suri whispered to Ammi.

Nuru managed to escape notice by dint of his nimble moves and mingled with the women headed across the street spurred on by a line of soldiers. They were forced to go past three lanes and then to the field where the night's load of moisture had wet the clothes of women who were already there, sitting on the grass with soldiers standing guard over them.

The separation of men and women troubled Suri. Was there something else afoot? But what could it be? She dared not voice her misgivings, for just as one did not talk of nightmares for fear they might come true, whatever demon was swirling around would become real. So sitting amidst the wailing of hungry babies, and sleepy children protesting at being woken up so early, she instead turned her thoughts to her Rumi, so gentle with dreamy eyes. She had last spoken to her Rumi a week back and demanded that he come to see her.

"I will soon," he said.

"Why have you not come all these days?" It had been an eternity since she saw him last.

"I will, soon." He repeated.

"Moti would have been really happy with his new country?" Moti was Rumi's best friend.

Rumi ignored her question about Moti and instead announced that he had told his mother that he wanted to get married as soon as he graduated next year.

"To me?" She was surprised. This was the first time marriage had been mentioned in the two years they had known each other.

"Of course to you…who else can I think of marrying?" Rumi was irked. Suri could imagine him flicking the mop of hair from his forehead.

"I don't know…with all this talk of us not being of this land, everything does seem a little unreal!"

"What is 'us,' Suri?"

"Obviously those of us who are Urdu speaking! You know we are all called Biharis now," Suri answered.

"Listen. I don't ever want you to say that again. There is no your people and my people. You and I are the same. I love you, and that is all that matters. I want to hold you and kiss you right now."

Her heart ached as she recalled their first kiss, tender and a little clumsy.

"Even though now they say that I am not of your people?" Suri insisted.

"Don't be silly. This is all nonsense. There is no your people and my people. All this will pass soon…"

Why was Rumi repeating the "no my people and your people" refrain?

Perhaps, he was trying to convince himself.

Perhaps, she had imagined the whiff of apprehension in his voice.

Then the damned Alshams and Albadr men rode around in their jeep shouting slogans of long life to Pakistan, and the phone lines in Mirpur went dead, cutting off this settlement from the city.

When the soldiers were convinced there were no more men hiding among the women, they went back to herding the steady trickle of women and girls, still descending from both the area where Suri's house stood and the area of the government quarters on the other side of the main road.

"All of you bitches sit down!" the soldiers ordered again and again.

The grey tarred main road to Mirpur, a housing area in the suburbs of Dacca where Suri's Abbu had built his house four years back, ran along the far side of the green field. Across the road was the large *eidgah,* a field reserved for community Eid festival prayers. On one side stood a mosque made of woven bamboo cane walls and thatched roof. It was almost invisible under the profusion of purple morning glory giving it a surreal spiritual appearance. Sooner or later that mosque would be converted into a concrete domed structure. Beyond the *eidgah* smaller quarters for staff employees of the government were visible through the mist. The side of the field opposite the road was lined with the *jamun* plum and mango trees. These would bear their burden of fruit in late April but were now covered in shades of light and dark green foliage. Interspersed among the trees, were bushes with red tart berries and mimosa shrubs with leaves that shyly closed when touched.

On the left side of the field was a shallow pond in which pink and white shapla lilies blossomed during the monsoons. The shapla lily was declared the national flower of Bangladesh just days after its green, black and gold flag was first raised in the campus on the 3rd of March last year.

This pond had become part of a great still lake during the floods that submerged the land after the tidal wave swept away villages in the lower deltaic plains in November 1970. The main road to Mirpur was completely inundated cutting off the suburb from the city. The families here took their cars or walked to the edge of this lake and then crossed over in little black boats that emerged overnight on the shores. Some residents worried that they could be completely isolated from the rest of the city by cutting off this road. But then why would anyone want to do that? The floods lasted for a couple of weeks and soon everyone forgot the excitement it caused.

While the women waited for the weapons search to be completed, the sun traversed halfway across the sky. A white car drove up the main road and stopped near the houses on the right, and a man emerged from the backseat. He was of medium height and wore a chocolate brown shirt, black pants, and ray ban sunglasses. Along with two other men, he walked up to the women and surveyed the crowd. Suri recognized him. When she had first seen him on campus, Rumi said that he was Sheikh Mujib's son. The soldier, who seemed to be in charge, ran up to him and engaged in animated discussion at times pointing toward the women and at others to the right where a bus was just visible behind the houses. Then the man walked back to the road and to the right toward the crossroad. About half an hour later, a green and white bus loaded with passengers came into view as it speeded up on the main road, heading toward the city.

"Who are those people on the bus, Ammi? I cannot make out." Suri nervously gripped her mother's arm.

"That bus...that bus is carrying them. They are on that bus. I know it. Suri, Munni, this is the last we will see of them."

"What do you mean, Ammi? Not so loud!" Suri scolded her mother.

"Your father and my Sami are on the bus...I know it."

"How do you know Abbu and Sami are on the bus?" Suri felt her heart denying what the head knew to be true.

"I know," Ammi cried out. "Who else but all the men gathered at the crossroad are on the bus? They are being taken away ...This is the last we will see of them...say good-bye to them...say good-bye...God be with them."

"Ammi, please don't say that." Munni's plump cheeks streaked with tears.

"This is not possible! Where would they be taking them?" Suri asked.

"I don't know." Ammi repeated, "My son, my son, God be with them." She sobbed uncontrollably.

"Ammi, why should this be the last time we see them? They are probably being taken for questioning or something," Suri explained to her mother.

A second bus passed by. A woman sitting near the trees stood up, let out a loud wail, and hit her forehead with both palms. Other women stood up, and a collective lament rose from the field. One woman screamed, "Where are they taking my husband?" Another said, "What will they do with my son?" "God will protect them all." "Sisters...let us pray together for their safety." "What will happen to us?" "They will shoot us and throw us in a ditch...that is what will happen." "No! I do not want to die!" "Sisters, please recite the Quls and God will have mercy on us."

A third bus sped up on the road, and then a fourth, and finally a sixth.

The soldiers rushed in and shouted at everyone to shut up. The Sheikh's son came back, cast his eyes over the women, smiled, and laughed. The spectacle of hysterical women amused him. The soldier in charge gestured toward the trees, and the Sheikh's son skirted the wailing women and stopped with his hands on his hips on the spot where the young man lay on the ground. He directed some soldiers to pick him up. Part of the red sari was still tangled in the askew arms, so the soldiers gathered it in a bundle and placed it on the man's stomach. The mother tried to follow and was stopped. She fell to the ground. The Sheikh's son walked around the women back to the car and drove off.

Suri huddled up again with her mother and sister. There was no need to weep and cry. Everyone would be brought back after talks with officers of the new government. Suri was sure of this. Ammi's cheeks were wet with tears, and she was in no condition to accept that there was a perfectly logical explanation for taking the men on the bus. Had she seen Tonto running alongside the buses? Suri was not sure. How far could he run? He was an old but clever dog. He would turn back, go to the house, and wait for Sami. The bus was probably taking them to some government office for consultations and would bring them back as soon as it was over. Ammi was upset, so she was making such dire predictions. Maybe they were to sign some paper to be able to remain in Bangladesh. But then what was the need to take them out of their homes? A whisper of suspicion passed through Suri's heart.

The women in the field wailed and lamented and then fell silent.

As the day passed the trickle of women coming into the field ended. The day slowly came to a close, and the buses did not come back. The soldier in charge looked at his watch again and again, as though he too was waiting for the buses. The sun began its rapid descent, and the deeper darker sadness of dusk began to gather over the *jamun* plum and mango trees. At last as though tired of waiting, the soldier in charge shouted out orders, "Stand up… stand up…all of you *khankis*…you whores! Leave the field and go back to your houses. Go home…go to your homes now!"

Other soldiers repeated this order throughout the field.

They were letting them go! Everything would be all right once they were home, even if the soldiers had called them whores. For them, it was probably just a figure of speech. They must have finished searching for weapons. They could not have found any.

16

"Ammi, Suri Apa, let's go home! I am hungry." Munni tugged Ammi's hands.

Ammi did not seem to care. But everyone in the field prepared to leave, so she got up as well. She gripped Suri's wrist with one hand and Munni's with the other and walked across the lanes toward their house. As they came within sight of it, they saw some men sitting in the upstairs balcony. The veranda light had not been switched on, and it was getting darker. As the shefali blossoms prepared to flower in the night, Suri thought she saw a grey snake with shiny white underbelly on its branches, just like the one she had seen in her school one winter morning almost a decade ago. But this time it was just shadows playing tricks. Nuru was leaning on the balcony, and his father was with him looking toward the women making their way home.

Suri's voice trembled with fear as she asked Ammi, "Who are all these men in our house?"

"I cannot recognize anyone other than Nuru's father," Ammi answered, "but he is not supposed to come inside the house. Why has Nuru's mother allowed him inside the house. He's such a trouble maker."

"I don't think it is a good idea for us to separate and go into our own houses without our husbands," Sekina, who had walked alongside, said.

"What should we do then?" Ammi asked.

"We must stay together."

All the houses were shrouded in the increasing darkness.

With Ammi still holding on to them, Suri and Munni headed toward the *eidgah* to see what the other women were doing. When they crossed the field, they met with many more women. The crowd swelled as they walked toward the lanes to get to a house that would give them the best protection and keep them safe in the night. Most of the homes were locked. The owners were probably in the crowd, but too afraid to open their doors. Perhaps, they too felt it was better to stay elsewhere. The streetlights had still not come on, and it was difficult to see where they were heading.

The crowd split as they entered the lanes. Eventually, Suri, her mother, and sister and the other women with them found a house,

which was not locked. This was probably because it was an unfinished building, but it was deep enough inside the lanes to be out
of reach of anyone who might want to find them. They walked into
the house and up the stairs into an empty room. The house was
cold and damp with bare unpainted walls. The floor was dusty, and
there were no doors or windowpanes, just square and rectangular
openings in the walls. The moon had not yet risen to relieve the
darkness. As the room filled with women, they sat down on the
floor and waited for dawn, so that at the first hint of daybreak they
could return to their homes.

The first light to strike the room was not the misty soft rays of
the February sun but the cold hard beams of flashlights, careening
over the women, looking them over.

II

It was another cold and damp room that Ammi referred to when she proclaimed, "I spent my honeymoon in the waiting room of a small train station with the rain incessantly raising an awful din."

Ammi's eyes twinkled and her shoulders shook with gaiety whenever she mentioned those early days when she had arrived in East Pakistan from Poona in India. Her mother's words never failed to embarrass Suri. How could Ammi talk of her honeymoon so openly? But that is the way she was.

One week after Ammi's wedding, on the fourteenth day of August in 1947, as dark clouds rolled in and with flashes of lightning and rumblings of thunder sent forth large drops of slanting rain across the tropics, England cleaved two republics from its colony in the triangular Indian subcontinent: Pakistan, the land of the pure, with two parts, East Pakistan and West Pakistan, lifting away from the body of India, the land of worshippers of gods and goddesses.

That setting of the sun on the British Empire lit a fiery blaze that burned through the landscape of new beginnings and kept alight an ember, perhaps, of regret for twenty-five years. Regret at the tearing asunder of Mother India and the hope that one day she will be restored. During that deluge six million people, among them Abbu and Ammi, trudged across newly drawn borders, from India and Pakistan, to get to the land of their faith.

In the year before this cleaving, Abbu trained for his engineer's job in the telecommunication services in Bombay. There he met Ammi's older brother. They became good friends, and he asked

Abbu to spend a few days in his home in the adjoining city of Poona, the monsoon capital of the Bombay Presidency.

Abbu would explain, "I could not go back to my home in Patna for it was too far away so I accepted his invitation." Poona and Patna were on opposite sides of the subcontinent, almost eleven hundred miles apart. "And lucky for you I did not go home, right?" Abbu would tease Ammi. "And let me tell you when I first saw her she was sixteen and pleasingly plump."

And Ammi would say, "I fell in love with your father the minute I laid eyes on him."

At these words, Sadi would cringe, but for Suri it was all so romantic.

"How could you fall in love when you had seen him for the first time?"

"Your father was such a serious young man with his round glasses," Ammi would giggle, "and I liked his wavy hair."

They were both so shameless, showing their feelings the way they did. But that is the way they were.

After crossing the border from India into East Pakistan, Abbu and Ammi took the train to the northeastern city of Sylhet where Abbu was to take up his post as junior engineer in the telephone department. Sylhet, with its picturesque rolling hills, tea gardens, and the Surma River flowing gently by, was the resting place of Hazrat Shah Jalal, a messianic saint. His shrine by the river served as the place of pilgrimage for people of all faiths.

"I knew about this revered shrine before I came to Sylhet," Ammi said. "My father had once taken us to the shrine of Nizamuddin Auliya in Delhi. The Auliya gave Shah Jalal, who is buried in Sylhet, a pair of pigeons to release in the land that he decided to settle in…" Ammi never tired of telling her children of all places of reverence that she had visited.

Abbu would invariably intervene, "I don't want you filling the heads of the children with all this talk about saints and Sufis and the like. I don't believe in all this shrine business…"

"I don't either," Ammi would respond, "but if a man is good and has brought out goodness in the hearts of others, I think it is okay to revere their shrines. Besides the shrines of Sufis became the place of worship of both Muslims and Hindus. I love this concept."

"But people think that these men are divine and will provide their worshippers a shortcut to heaven…"

"If others think like this, it is not the fault of the saints," Ammi would say. "I think we should respect everyone who makes the world a good place to live in!"

The saint was sent by his teacher to Hindustan, as India was known before the British rulers renamed it after the River Indus, with a handful of earth and instructions that he should settle in the place where the earth most closely matched its color and smell. This brought him to the banks of the Surma River. As for the pigeons given to him by Nizamuddin Auliya, these prolifer- ated in huge numbers around the shrine, especially since it was considered a sin to kill them.

"But listen to this hypocrisy. If the pigeons cross the river, it is all right to take shots at them," Abbu teased Ammi.

"Ji, please don't make fun of everything sacred." Ammi never referred to Abbu by his name. When speaking about him to her children, she called him "your father" and "Ji" when talking to him directly.

"Sacred! Please…these were human beings. Granted, they were good people, but we don't have to worship them."

"We should not worship them, but we should certainly respect them," Ammi responded. "Now where was I? Yes! In the shrine's fish tanks, I saw the largest fish I had ever seen. These were witch- craft followers of the king that the saint helped defeat…"

"Don't be silly. These are only old catfish, nothing special about them." Abbu could not resist another dig at Ammi's beliefs.

"Then why did no one eat them?" Ammi asked.

"Probably because the fish were so old that the meat would be tough…" Abbu replied.

"No, no, you are wrong. These are symbols of the fight between the forces of good and evil, and when a fish dies, it is ritually buried."

"All I know is that many from Sylhet town migrated to England." Abbu believed only in the tangible. He knew much about the

British Empire that ruled over his land for two hundred years and never missed a chance, especially at the dinner table, to narrate the various anecdotes he kept stored in his memory.

"When I was in Bombay, I loved to walk on the beach and sit by the grand Gateway to India monument." And then he would commence his history lesson. "The gateway was built in 1911 to commemorate the visit of their majesties to the dominion. But really it was Calcutta that provided the first entry to the British…"

After Sylhet, Abbu was posted to Kushtia in the west-central part of East Pakistan.

"A few weeks before you were born in Kushtia, Suri," Ammi said, "we heard of the troubles in Dacca University and the shooting down of students by the police."

"The Governor-General, Mr. Nazimuddin, made the announcement that Urdu was to be the national language of Pakistan in January 1952…" Abbu said.

"Ji! What I do not understand is this?" Ammi interrupted him. "Khwaja Nazimmuddin was the nawab of Dacca. Granted his descendants were Kashmiris. So why did he make such a policy?" The title of "nawab" or 'Lord' was bestowed on persons by the British in lieu of the services rendered to the Empire.

"He was the head of the country at the time, and perhaps, in those early days…Remember it was only five years since Pakistan was formed, no one was sure what was to be done. Mr. Jinnah died just one year after he got us our country, and he had announced that Urdu and only Urdu would be the national language of Pakistan. Liaquat Ali Khan, our first Prime Minister, was assassinated just four years after independence. It was really chaotic," Abbu explained.

"I see!" Ammi remarked, "the nawab could not renege on what the founder of the nation had proclaimed."

"Still they should have thought things through." Abbu continued, "Bengali spoken in East Pakistan—and they were the majority in Pakistan—had a more ancient history than Urdu."

"Ji, maybe Mr. Jinnah wanted Urdu to be the national language because in India it was considered to be the language of the Muslims," Ammi asserted.

Such explanations irked Abbu.

"Language is not decided by religion but by region."

Still it was true that Urdu contained many words from Persian, the court language of the Mughals, and Arabic, the language in which the Quran was revealed. It also assimilated the Turkic language of the Ottoman Empire. So Urdu had within it the three great Islamic empires: the Mughals in Hindustan as India was then known, the Safavids in Iran, and the Ottomans in Turkey. And when the British Empire was set up in the subcontinent, Urdu was influenced by English as well, and in fact, it saw its real flowering in Fort William College in Calcutta under the patronage of the Empire.

Abbu called Suri his koel, for he had heard one cooing when the sun rose for the first time in her life. The bird was heralding the blossoming of the mango tree in the courtyard of their tin-roofed house. With the ivory white flowers sending forth fragrance reminiscent of the lily-of- the- valley, Abbu held Suri in his trembling hands. There were no hospitals in the town, and Abbu's sister-in-law could not come for the delivery as she was pregnant herself with her fifth child. Apparently she had one each year, and Abbu referred to them as models for the year, just like cars. That was his idea of a joke!

When Ammi went into labor in the dead of night, a few days before she thought she would, Abbu panicked. He ran to the office in the attached building in front of the house, woke up the *chowkidar*, gave him his cycle, and told him to ride like mad to the midwife's house and make her come with him. The midwife was not to be rushed. She refused to come perched on the gateman's cycle and had instead set out on a bullock cart. These carts made of bamboo poles laid side by side with cross bamboo strips held in a flat surface and woven cane half-tube cover in the middle had large wheels on either side which creaked loudly when moving. By the time the midwife arrived in the creaking cart, Suri had slipped out of the dark interior of her mother's womb. No one really remembers if the womb is dark, but it must be! Abbu handed over the birthing to the midwife and stepped out into the courtyard. As he wiped the nervous sweat trickling down his brows, to calm his nerves, he lit his first cigarette of the day.

The two-year-old Sadi slept through the entire drama of Suri's birth.

Kushtia was a river port set up by the Mughal Emperor Shahjahan, who had also built the famous Taj Mahal in memory of his wife. "And the empress was called Mumtaz, just like your mother…" Abbu made this comment whenever the Taj Mahal was mentioned.

"That is so romantic, Ji. Imagine the emperor's devotion and love for his wife that he hired those masons and craftsmen from all over India to build this mausoleum to her memory," Ammi would invariably respond.

"You do know that his wife died giving birth to his fourteenth child. He literally loved her to death…" Abbu laughed heartily at his joke much to Ammi's annoyance.

"Ji, please be careful of what you say in front of the children…"

"He also cut off the fingers of artisans…"

Ammi would not let him finish the sentence.

"Not true…It was the muslin weavers whose thumbs were cut off so they could not weave any more of the fabric than what was decreed to belong only to kings. In any case it was not Shahjahan who did this but his father, Jahangir. And you know that the muslin woven in Dacca was unsurpassed…"

"Do you know that one of Jahangir's commanders named Dacca, Jahangir Nagar, and the original name is based on the temple of goddess Dhakeshwari. Anyway," Abbu would continue, "Kushtia became important only after the indigo planters set up trade here and established a railway connection to Calcutta."

"Maybe that is why blue is my favorite color?" Suri would try to veer away from a topic that had been discussed many times before.

"No, I think it is because your mother dressed you in blue all the time—it's her favorite color. Now where was I? As I was saying, these white traders were really cruel and made the people pay heavy taxes and imprisoned and tortured any farmer who dared to resist. Then the Indigo Resistance Movement began."

A strange tenor overtook Abbu's voice whenever he talked of, and it was often, this first political resistance initiated by Gandhi, the guru of nonviolence. It was almost as though he was somehow connected to the movement because it began near his birthplace in Bihar. The indigo farmers in the area refused to pay taxes to the government, and when no amount of suppression worked, the masters had to give in and pass laws banning all torture and exploitation of the farmers.

"You know that Buddhism originated in Bihar..." Abbu would add.

"We do...we do..." Sadi would roll his eyes and try to put an end to what was to be another history lesson.

"As did Jainism..." undeterred Abbu would continue.

"Tagore spent a part of his life in Kushtia," Ammi would add, "and India adopted one of his poems as its National Anthem." She often tuned in the radio to hear *Rabindroshangeet,* the songs whose lyrics were written and set to music by Tagore himself.

But it was the early days after the cleaving, when she came to the new country as a bride that Ammi loved to talk about the most. Her wedding ceremony was hurriedly arranged because Abbu had to go off to East Pakistan to take charge of his posting. Ammi wore a peach colored sari with borders embroidered with silver thread and a peach choli with short puffed sleeves. Suri loved the outfit and had tried it on many times, although the blouse was far too loose for her.

"I have kept it for you, my sweet! But you will have to put on some weight before I let you get married."

Ammi was such a tease.

"What did Abbu wear for the wedding?"

"You know how your father is about dressing. He wore a three-piece suit and looked really elegant. The others were so envious that I was marrying such a well turned out man."

"Did Abbu get the sari for you?"

"No, what did he know what a bride wears? His brother had already gone to Pakistan with his family so they could not come. My mother and brother made all the arrangements. It was a small affair and we only invited a few people. My best friend Manjula came with her mother and father. She was not very happy that I was to go away."

"Did you stay in touch with Manjula?"

"Very infrequently, the postal system was not yet fully functional. After Sadi was born I became very busy then you came along."

"But why did you and Abbu come here and Nani and Mamoo go to the other wing?" Ammi's mother and brother had chosen to go to West Pakistan in 1947.

"At the time it did not matter really where we went as long as it was Pakistan. They thought it would not be difficult to settle as they knew Urdu, and there was a greater cultural affinity of sorts. Besides Poona was closer to the western wing while Bihar was nearer the eastern part."

Even in East Pakistan Ammi did not miss a single Indian film shown in the local theaters. Never one to pass an opportunity to rag Ammi, Abbu would ask how she could tolerate these silly films with the heroes and heroines running around the trees bursting into songs a dozen times at least during the three hours the films ran.

"At least I admit I like films. You're such a hypocrite. Remember you told me your favorite song was from a film that had Dev Anand as hero? And his song *Hai apna dil to awara…* my heart is a vagabond…really!!"

"And yours was that silly one from the film about the spirit roaming around—what was it called? Mahal!" And for good measure he would add, "You even learnt to speak Urdu from these films."

"Yes, I did! Although we spoke Marathi at home, Urdu was the language of the Muslims and so we knew it." Marathi was the language most widely spoken in Bombay and Poona.

Once Sadi asked Ammi if Marathi was his mother tongue since she, his mother, spoke it.

"Don't be silly now, Sadi!" Ammi chided him. "Your mother tongue is Urdu."

III

Every April when the mango blossoms in the tall trees around the pond at the back of their red brick house in Narayanganj changed to delicate green ovoid fruits, no one could resist its lure. Abbu had been posted to Narayanganj, a river port town ten miles south of Dacca, after Kushtia. Sticks with hooks at the end were used to pick bunches of fruit before the mango ripened. The fruit was then peeled, sliced, mixed with salt, and consumed with eyelids drooping as the tongue twisted in contact with the tartness of the unripe fruit.

Among the trees by the pond, one tree housed a female evil spirit, who wanted all the mangoes for herself, or so Mali bhai, the gardener, said when he wanted to scare the children away from picking the fruits. Ammi did not allow the children to call anyone older by their names but to add *bhai* or brother after it. Mali bhai with his fierce moustache and intense dark eyes would sound dire warnings about female evil spirits calling them *churails*.

"The *churail* sitting in that mango tree can see all of you. So take care. If she likes one of you, she will take you away."

"But the *churail* can see us when we play there? We are still here," Suri and Sadi would argue.

"You are lucky that she has not taken a fancy to you. But all of you had better be careful. If you annoy her by throwing stones at her tree, she may cast a spell on you and your eyes will squint and your tongue thicken and…"

When he was sure the children were frightened out of their wits, Mali bhai would relent in his litany of the dire consequences of annoying the female evil spirit and tell them of the antidote.

"Each time you look at the mango tree, spit and beg the *churail* to leave you alone."

"We would have to spit a lot because the tree is just there and we see it all the time?"

"Okay! So spit once a day at the tree when it is laden with fruit and that will do."

Mali bhai was good at making things easy for the children. And in any case, the evil spirit was supposed to be around only during the mango season. One night Suri thought she heard the rustling of leaves when the air was otherwise still. When she told Mali bhai about it, he explained that it was the evil spirit dancing among the mangoes for one last time just before the last fruit dropped off the tree.

"Does she go away then?" Suri asked in a voice tinged with apprehension at the permanence of the spirit's abode.

"Yes!" Mali bhai replied.

"Where does she go?" Suri asked.

"She just disappears."

"To where?"

"To nowhere!"

"What is nowhere? She has to go somewhere." Suri insisted on a reply.

"Okay, okay, she lives in the banyan tree for the rest of the year."

There was not much comfort from the fact that the spirit flew off to banyan trees, for there was one such tree Suri and Sadi crossed twice each day while walking to and from school.

Soon after coming to Narayanganj, Abbu decided that in order for his children to go to a proper school, meaning one that taught in English, he would have to take matters into his own hands. All official work in Pakistan was conducted in English and not the proclaimed national language Urdu.

Abbu gave education a great deal of importance. He was the first person from his village to matriculate from high school, he would often tell them, and education was the only reason he was able to move to the city, get a university degree and join government services in the telecommunication department. It had not been easy for him to accomplish these achievements. His father died when he was a few months old, and the only income was the small grant given to his mother by the village headman. Abbu's father was his accountant. Abbu's mother passed away when Abbu was a student at Patna University in Bihar.

"See, my brother quit school and could not be bothered, so there was no other option for him but to join the police department at an early age."

With its river port and large jute and cotton mills on the banks of the Sitalakhya River, Narayanganj was an important posting for Abbu, and because he held the sanction of telephones in his hands, Abbu had much clout. He consulted with his friends from amongst the owners of the Adamjee Jute Mill, which was the largest jute mill in the world, as well with the owners of the Dawood Cotton Mill. These friends from Gujarat settled in Burma before moving their assets to East Pakistan on the request of Mr. Jinnah. Several businessmen of the city were Ismailis from Bombay, followers of the Agha Khan, while others were Marwaris from Rajasthan, the land of the dancing peacocks. All were commandeered to the cause, and together they established a board, appointed the Scottish wife of an English officer of Burma Oil Company as head teacher, and set up the school in a large rented house located on the main road leading out of the city. Suri and her best friend Shelly were in the same class with ten other boys and girls, all children of government officials, businessmen, and doctors of Narayanganj. Sadi was in a class ahead of Suri as was the plump fair Indira, who was a Marwari and smelt of delicious pickles.

On the days that it did not rain, Abbu's rule was that they walk to school. Whenever Sadi rebelled against the long walk Abbu would tell him, "Do you know that each morning I had to walk four miles to go to the nearest school? I left at daybreak to get to my classes and walked back in the afternoon at the end of the school day…"

"How far is our school?" Sadi asked.

"Your school is not so far. It is only a mile or so away."

Sadi did not believe him. He was convinced that it was at least ten miles or more. "Did you not have rickshaws to take you?" Suri asked.

"There were no rickshaws in the village. Only bullock carts. So it was better to walk. Right, Suri?" This would remind Suri of her first bullock cart ride.

Abbu had taken the children along on one of his inspection tours to the towns around Narayanganj. After disembarking from the motorboat that had taken them down the Sitalakhya River, on to the Dhaleshwari River to Munshiganj, Abbu hired a bullock cart to get into town. Suri sat on the cart with her legs dangling over the side and the skin on one of her thighs caught in the narrow space between the poles, and she screamed and cried. Abbu put his square blue checked handkerchief under her legs for the rest of the journey. To make her forget the pain, he picked a handful of green shrubs growing in the fields around, laden with pods that enclosed the succulent soft green gram and gave it to her to eat for the rest of the journey. It was delicious. Of course Ammi could not resist some anecdote connected to it. "There was this king who loved good food. When he was overthrown by his brother and put in prison the highest form of punishment that was thought up was that he be allowed just one kind of food. The loyal cook advised the king to ask for gram because hundreds of different kinds of dishes could be made from the gram, *halwas*, fragrant rice *pulaos*, and when soaked and mixed with sliced onion, green chilies, and lemon, it made a delicious salad…"

Unlike Abbu, who usually talked of history and politics, the tales Ammi narrated on balmy soft winter afternoons were of her childhood. She would sit in the courtyard on a wooden *takht* shelling pine nuts that her mother, the children's Nani, sent from West Pakistan and tell her stories.

"Now you see one day Manjula and me decided we would do this…and Zaheda Apa wore that…my father took us to the bazaar and we ate this…the best *bhelpuri* ever was to be had from so-and-so's stall in…"

Each year Nani sent them pine nuts, walnuts, almonds, raisins as well as grapes and apples as these were abundantly grown in

West Pakistan. Ammi, in turn, would send her mother baskets of lychees, bananas, and pineapple. The gifts were sent to and fro by the PIA flights. In those days it took the large Dakota aircrafts over seven hours to fly over India between Dacca, the capital city of East Pakistan, and Karachi, the capital city of West Pakistan. Karachi was also the capital of the entire country of Pakistan and lay along the coast of the Arabian Sea. If Ammi and Nani had exchanged these gifts by shipping it across the Indian Ocean, it would have taken a week or so to get from Karachi to Chittagong port opening into the Bay of Bengal in East Pakistan, then to Dacca, and ultimately Narayanganj and vice versa. The fruits would certainly have spoilt by then.

On those soft winter afternoons, while waiting for the congealed coconut oil to melt so that she could oil her own and Suri's hair, some of Ammi's stories were based in Hyderabad Deccan, where she had spent part of her childhood. Her fez-wearing father, who was a postmaster, was posted here from Poona for a number of years. She talked of seeing the Golgumbadh mosque in Bijapur.

"Do you know it has the second largest dome ever built?"

"Which is the largest?" Sadi had asked.

"I think it was in that country where the Pope lives....ask your father the name."

"St. Peter's Basilica in Rome," Abbu would tell them.

Ammi's father had also taken them to Golconda, famous for its legendary diamond mines. The Darya-e-Nur diamond now among the crown jewels of Iran was found here, as was the Hope diamond.

"There is a curse on the diamond..." Ammi had said.

"All nonsense," Abbu retaliated, "the curse was invented to increase the mystique of the diamond."

Ammi also told them tales of the ultimate do-gooder Hatem Tai and made up long unending stories of the exploits of the black sheep of a family who was made to sit in the mosque intoning, "allahallah." After several coincidences when he found lost items belonging to the people, everyone in town thought he had been bestowed the gift to solve crimes by God for taking His name with such fervor.

Each school morning the route Sadi and Suri took to school went past the makeshift shops just outside the main gate of their compound. These shops sold odds and ends like pots, pans, blow-pipes for stoking fire, curved knives called *baithis, daos* or meat cleavers, and cake molds for rice and lentil *pithas*. Once past the shops Suri and Sadi would walk along the wall of the government boys' school that adjoined the compound. A left turn took them past the red brick courthouse and the large looming banyan tree. Its canopy of branches and leaves reached all the way to the other side of the road. Perched on the branches were large numbers of crows, and after the mango season, the female evil spirit lived there as well.

When they approached the tree, the two would make a dash past the dense covering with their school boxes on their heads to not just outrun the spirit's evil eye but also to avoid being hit with white liquid crow excrement. If they were not quick enough, the hot goo could land on either Suri's green pleated tunic and white blouse or Sadi's white shirt and navy blue half pants and worse on their head. The smelly white excretion was really messy. Although some thought that such an event foretold good fortune, for the one on whom it landed, neither believed it for even one minute. When Sami was old enough to go to school, the three would compete to see who reached the other end first. Running on his spindly thin legs Sami was always way behind.

Every time the city got a new Deputy Commissioner, the shops outside the compound wall were swept away in an effort to clean the city, but these invariably sprang back up a week or so later. This Ammi said was because once the Deputy Commissioner's palms were greased he looked the other way.

"Why would he look the other way when someone gets his palms all oily with black grease?" Suri asked Ammi.

"Really, Suri, you are such a stupid girl. It means he was given *ghoose*," Sadi replied.

"Don't use words like that. It's not nice. Where did you learn the word?" Ammi would scold Sadi. It was not clear whether she meant the word *stupid* or the word for bribery or both.

The banyan tree was the abode of other spirits as well. With long dark silky hair and feet turned backward, these spirits had to be appeased by offerings of *rasgullas,* the round white syrup dripping sweets usually sold in baskets made from dried leaves. On encountering one, the trick was not to look at the feet, for then the heart would stop beating with fright. Their perpetually pregnant teacher, Mrs. Khan, who used to be Miss Daphne, had a sister who, on her way home after a late night shift from her work as telephone operator, stopped at a shop under a banyan tree to buy *rasgullas* for her teenage son. As she walked out, a hand with beautiful slender fingers cupped to receive an offering was thrust out from behind the trunk. Her sister ignored the obvious message and hurried on. The spirit with flowing long black hair and outstretched hands began to follow her, floating on air. As her sister looked back, her eyes fell on the feet, which were, of course, turned the other way round. Frightened out of her wits, she ran all the way home to find her teenage son waiting for her dressed up in female clothes, with bangles on his wrist, lipstick on his lips, and rouge on his cheeks. He told his mother this was how he wanted to dress from now on.

When Abbu heard this story, he quipped, "And the moral of the story is: avoid sweet shops under banyan trees at night, especially if you have sons!"

"Ji, but these are really the spirits of women who have died when pregnant…She must have placed a curse and that is why the son dressed like a bride, I think…"

Abbu ignored Ammi's feeble attempt at explaining the phenomena and added, "Or give the sweets to the spirit and buy some more. This is good for the sweets seller's business," Abbu chuckled.

If it started to rain in the morning, and it invariably did during the monsoons, Abbu did not enforce his rule that the children should walk to school. Abdul Ghani, the cook, protected from rain under his black umbrella would summon a rickshaw from the road and Suri and Sadi would rush from the veranda in front of the living room to sit on the plastic covered red or blue patterned seats. With the school bags placed at their feet, a plastic sheet covering their legs, and the convertible hood of the rickshaw over their heads, the ride would take longer than walking; the men pulling the rickshaws had to work really hard against the driving rain. The rickshaw ride did not always prevent Suri and Sadi from getting wet. Often the chain would slip, and since the tools and spares needed to repair it were stored under the hard seats, they would arrive in school wet and dripping. They never told Ammi about this. It was such fun getting wet!

During the monsoons that extended for almost four months, the ponds and rivers overflowed the banks. Small guppies were found even in rain puddles, as were thousands of black tadpoles. The delicate *hilsa* fish bred in abundance in the rivers. The blooms of the shapla water lilies lent their pink and white hue to the landscape. Guavas, pomellos, and pineapples filled up baskets in the bazaars. The croaking of frogs reached a crescendo just before the rains and was most audible in the sultry nights competing with the jhingoors going "jhing, jhing, jhing" without pause. An occasional snake undulating in the floodwaters that sometimes reached the steps of the courtyard of their red brick house or a frog frantically pumping its skinny legs as it swam to dry ground filled anyone who saw it with awe. Large red ants that rendered real pain with their bites emerged from washed over holes and lined the edges where the wall met the floor. Black insects with transparent wings lay siege to floors, and if the stinkbugs were disturbed, the air was saturated with the pungent smell of rancid almonds. Gardenias spread their tender aroma and the heavily scented globular yellow-green kadam flowers nestled among the broad leaves and tickled the fingers when picked.

When the rains let up for the day, the peanut seller made his rounds with hot roasted peanuts in woven cane baskets carried on the head cushioned by the rolled up all-purpose square *ghamcha*-scarf. The *jhaal-muri* seller put the scarf around his neck with the ends tied to the two handles of the large box filled with puffed rice and containers of sliced onions, green chilies, and thick yellow mustard oil. All the ingredients were placed in a tin, given a good shake, and doled out in cones made from pages torn from old telephone directories.

After the monsoons, and sometimes before, cyclones formed in the Bay of Bengal. When one made landfall, the cyclone alarm was sounded. Doors and windows were shut tight and kerosene lanterns made ready for the night. The howling wind and rain was terrifying. After the winds died down, everyone emerged to sights of dead crows lying between felled trees, electricity and telephone poles toppled over and tin sheets torn from roofs strewn on the streets.

"Once I saw a man cut in half by a flying tin sheet," Mali bhai sounded the warning to keep everyone indoors.

"That is nonsense!" Abbu scolded him.

"No, sahib, it is true…my cousin's brother-in-law saw one man being cut in two with his own eyes…"

"It's always someone's brother-in-law, is it not…"

"No, sahib, I swear it is true…"

It took days to clean up the mess. The smell of kerosene lanterns was the smell of cyclones.

The Sitalakhya River was visible from the roof of the red brick house, and it ran in a long ribbon parallel to the compound. Black-hulled steamers, black wooden boats, motor launches and barges stacked with bundles of jute, the golden fiber, plied on the silty water all year round. River dolphins arching over the water were a common sight.

The statue of the mother goddess Durga was submerged in this river after completion of the *puja* rituals held right after the monsoons. A large platform with a colorful canopy over it was erected each year at the end of the street near the compound. It held the statue of the goddess with her serene smile and ten weapons in her ten hands seated on a throne with her feet resting on a tiger's head. The worshippers placed sweets, coconuts, and flowers at her feet. The large pink woody-smelling flowers placed at the goddess's feet were courtesy of Mali bhai, who was a devotee of mother Durga. The white *dhoti* clad bare-bodied priest offered everyone the special white soft milk sweet *sandesh* on pieces of plantain. Through the air filled with the smoke of burning frankincense the mother goddess smiled on all who stood before her regardless of faith.

This river also received the replicas of the mausoleum of the martyrs of Karbala. On the tenth day of Muharram, called the martyrdom month, almost fourteen centuries ago the first martyrdom of the Levant occurred when access to water and everything else was cut off in the desert. On this day, the day of Ashura, the Prophet's grandson and everyone in his retinue including women and children were killed by the army of Muawiya, the governor of Syria. The martyrdom was commemorated by the believers with special processions of shiny replicas of the mausoleums called *tazias*, some multistoried and so big that several people were needed to carry them, others small enough for a child to hold. All were elaborately decorated with gold and silver tinsel paper with the fringe created by folding the paper and cutting out triangles and diamonds.

An Ashura procession passed by the compound each year. The families living there took chairs up to the roof of the red brick house to watch the passage. Ammi made sure there were jugs full of almond and milk sherbet served to everyone. All the children were given colorful sticks wound with silver lace and green paper to twirl around and simulate the fight between the pious and the impious. Sugar-coated gram sweets, in green cloth pouches decorated with silver tinsel, were distributed to everyone to snack on while watching the procession.

The mourners in the procession chanted the names of the martyred grandsons of the Prophet while beating their chests followed by men flagellating themselves with metal chains. Behind them came the white horse representing the martyred grandson's horse, and men carrying tall sticks with silver palms at the ends, symbolizing the palm of Fatima, the daughter of the Prophet. Everyone could feel the energy of battle with the drumbeat and loud chanting. Finally at sundown the *tazias* were submerged in the waters of the Sitalakhya River.

On the fifteenth of Shaban, the eighth month of the Islamic lunar calendar, Shab-e-Baraat was celebrated. This was the night when a Believer's destiny was said to be recorded. Ammi would force Abbu to go to the graveyard to offer prayers to the dead. He invariably protested but would relent when Ammi told him, "Ji, we are a part of all mankind, so go and pray. It will be good for you."

Sadi would be given the task of distributing to all the neighbors the traditional *halwa* sweets cut in triangles and diamonds in platters covered with green cloth. Mali bhai was in charge of placing small earthenware lamps with oil-drenched wicks along the walls and the window ledges to light up the night and hand out the ration of sparklers and firecrackers. Abdul Ghani thought it was his prerogative, being in-charge of the kitchen to light the clay pots called pomegranates, filled with inflammable powder that created a fountain of fiery sparkle, as well the cone-shaped brown paper wrapped chilies that spun around in a swirl of fire. The only firecrackers the children were allowed were sticks with colored paper covered balls of powder at the end that, when struck against a wall, caused sharp snapping sounds. As for Ammi, she would undertake the nightlong vigil of prayers with the other women of the compound. Suri would stay up as long as she could, repeating the holy verses that she had learned by heart while the grownups recited from the Quran. This was more in the spirit of competition than any concern for the sins committed. She had to be able to boast that she had stayed up longer than her best friend Shelly.

Indira, Sadi's Marwari classmate, celebrated her birthday each year in school. All the students would gather in the central court-yard and be given gifts, cake, and sweets. Once her parents invited the whole school to their large house by the river, and everyone sat on the floor on long white sheets with red tablecloth spread in the middle and ate from plantain leaves. There was no meat or fish but plenty of rice, lentils, yoghurt, pickles, and curdled milk sweets.

"All the other children have their birthday parties at home, and the entire school is never invited," Ammi grumbled when the children came home from the party. "Mrs. Campbell should not have allowed the children to go to Indira's house."

"Indira's father has given substantial funds to the school," Abbu offered by way of explanation.

"I don't believe this. Back in the old days, we always referred to their clan, the Marwaris, as being very stingy."

Abbu clicked his tongue. "They are not stingy and have several large businesses right here in this city."

"But," Ammi replied, "That is neither here nor there. It is wrong to use the children to show gratitude for whatever anyone gives to the school. The next time I will not allow my children to go," she said in a stern voice.

IV

There was no next time. Indira left soon after that birthday celebration. It was 1958, and Pakistan had come under the rule of Field Marshal Ayub Khan. Her people, being of the Hindu faith and thus deemed loyal to India, were not welcome in the land of the pure any more.

Abbu came home from office unexpectedly at ten to tell Ammi that he was going to the headquarters in Dacca.

"You already had your monthly meeting, so why are you going again?"

"I just got a call that I need to be in the headquarters within two hours." Then in a worried voice, Abbu added, "Mumtaz, the army has taken over the government."

"What do you mean?" Ammi asked.

"It means that the government has been dismissed and the Chief of the Army has taken over. And he has proclaimed himself to be a Field Marshal…"

"Can he do this?"

"You mean become field marshal?"

"No, take over the country?"

"Not really! He cannot do either! But when the politicians fight among themselves and pull each other down, this is what happens!"

"So what if we do! It is our right," Ammi said.

"We Pakistanis have had how many? Eight, or is it ten prime ministers in ten years. Is that not a bit too much?"

"Still we should decide…"

"I don't have time to talk now." Abbu cut short the discussion. "I have to take the ten-thirty train and will be back in the evening. I think the head office wants to make some changes in the administration or something. We will see…"

All day Ammi fretted, "We may have to leave this house…we may have to go elsewhere…We might go to Dacca…you'd like that, won't you, Suri?"

"Yes! But I like it better here," Suri answered.

"We have to leave some time. This is not our own house…" Ammi told her.

Abbu came back with news that he was to stay in his present posting in Narayanganj for the time being. But there were to be some changes on the top.

"What changes?" Ammi asked.

"I think people will be brought in from West Pakistan to take over some key posts, and some people from here will be dismissed. The Army bureaucracy does not trust Bengalis."

"Will Mamoo come here? That would be really great." Sadi loved Ammi's older brother who had recently visited them.

"No, no…Sadi, let me talk to your father…Why would people be dismissed…?" Ammi again asked Abbu.

"They say it will be on charges of corruption. But I think there is more to it."

"Abbu, will the field marshal take over the school as well? I want Mrs. Bennett to be dismissed. She punishes everyone…" Sadi chimed in again.

"She only punishes those who do not behave and do not do their work…and no, he will not take over the school," Abbu told him.

"Please, Sadi, let me talk to your father…Ji, does the takeover by officers from West Pakistan mean that you and the others will be sidelined?"

"Could be! At least for now, that is. I don't think they trust those of us in East Pakistan too much. They know that we in East

Pakistan are in the majority and can demand the right to govern Pakistan. They are afraid of this and want to keep us suppressed."

"That is so stupid."

"It is, but that is how it is."

"Who is this Ayub Khan anyway?" Ammi asked.

"He is the Defense Minister," Abbu answered. "Our Prime Minister, Mr. Muhammad Ali Bogra, made the mistake of appointing a general from the army as a civilian minister..."

"I wonder why he did this."

"There seems to be no logic, especially when Mr. Bogra is a Bengali. Maybe he wanted to curry favor with the army."

"Rather stupid if you ask me!"

Abbu went once a month to attend planning meetings at the head office in Dacca. Often the family joined him in the afternoon, taking the train from the station across the road from the compound. On the way, the train passed through rows of paddy fields with water shimmering among the green stalks, *paan* fields covered on all sides by woven cane enclosures, and brick-making yards with furnace chimneys belching smoke. The last station before pulling in to Dacca was near the mysterious and dark Baldah Botanical Garden.

"Tagore was inspired by the camellias here when he wrote his song of the camellia," Ammi would say almost every time the dark red and moss green walls of the garden came into view.

"We know, Ammi...we know..."

"And Tagore called the land of his birth the golden land," Ammi would continue undeterred. "And he wrote those beautiful songs to the gardener...All his songs are so beautiful." She would sigh.

This botanical garden, bequeathed to the city by a Hindu philanthropist Narendra Roy, was almost mystical with orchids, lilies, camellias, and a plant that was supposed to bloom once in hundred years. No one living had seen a bloom yet. The one time they went inside the garden Suri was awestruck when, standing on the edge of the central tank, she saw the sun's rays catch a school of flat silver moonfish that thrived in the dark still waters. The bright flash briefly lit up the gloomy surroundings.

Abbu would be waiting for them at the Dacca station. They would walk across a level crossing on to Jinnah Avenue and head straight to the Gulistan Cinema Complex for lunch at the Chinese restaurant Chu Chin Chow. The entire complex was owned by the Dossanis who were Gujarati businessmen. After lunch, they would head to the Gulistan Bookshop, which sold all the comic books in the world. On every trip Abbu let them choose two each. Sadi would buy *Superman* and *Batman*, Suri *Little Lulu*, *Bugs Bunny*, *Snow White and the Seven Dwarfs*, *Little Red Riding Hood*, and *Jason and the Argonauts*. Abbu got his monthly copies of *Reader's Digest* and *Life* magazines. The books Ammi read were not usually available in East Pakistan, so Nani would send her a bundle of Urdu novels by Razia Butt and A. R. Khatun and copies of the *Urdu Digest* each time someone visited.

Then they would cross over to the shops alongside the Dacca Stadium where Ammi would choose a sari or two and then invariably go to an elaborately decorated specialty *paan* shop that belonged to a family from Lukhnow, where the ritual of *paan* eating was almost an art. *Paans* were dark green heart-shaped edible leaves that grew on vines. Ammi would buy two highly flavored plump triangles, filled with areca nuts, catechu and lime paste, and potent aromatic chewing tobacco for her friend, whose face seemed to be in an eternal pout as she tried to hold in the red *paan* juice. When this friend spoke, she raised her chin and pursed her mouth so that the juice did not spill out. Sometimes, in spite of all the effort at preventing it, the person in front was sprayed with red dots. Whenever Ammi saw this, she would tease her friend by humming,

"*Paan khaye sainyaan hamar*...my beloved eats paan, with his dusky face and red lips, and his muslin shirt splattered with red dots..." All this added up to how handsome her beloved was.

"Stop it, Mumtaz," her friend would reply. "Have you seen my beloved?"

"Yes, and he is quite the man."

Always one to try what was forbidden, once Suri sneaked a triangle from Ammi's friend's pouch. No sooner had she begun to chew the purloined item, she vomited out not only the leaf concoction but all her food as well and felt really queasy for hours. The *paan* was filled with *zarda* aromatic tobacco. Sadi teased her for days, but Ammi thought it better to let Suri learn her own lesson from the experience.

Most other *paan* shops were small stalls that also sold cigarettes and the very popular rolled tobacco leaf *bidhis*. A thick slow-burning jute cord was usually hung on the side so that customers did not need to use matches.

Sometimes Abbu would take all of them to Ramna Park in the heart of Dacca. They would sit near the lake for a couple of hours, lounging around on the grass. In the summer months, the bokul blossoms lying on the grass would scent up the air with their strong cloying fragrance. Garlands of dry bokul blossoms were sold as garlands by little boys wandering the roads. Not many could stand the heavy scent, and even bedbugs pervading mattresses were repulsed by the smell when handfuls were put under to keep them away.

On each trip Abbu would save the best for last. The day would end when he indulged Ammi's sweet tooth by going to the Baby Ice-Cream Parlor, where ice cream was served in glass goblets and eaten with straight-edged spoons in a colonial lifestyle manner.

Whenever they went to Dacca, Abdul Ghani, the cook, would go to one of the two Narayanganj cinemas, Metro and Diamond, to see matinee showings of Indian films. One day he came back fuming and raging. "Begumsahib, these films are all fakes. They are trying to fool all of us!"

"What's the matter, Abdul Ghani?"

"That villain, the devil, was killed in the film I saw last month, and again this month the same man is back. It is all a fraud, and I am not going to another film and waste money on fakes."

No amount of explaining helped, and Ammi solved the problem of the cook's entertainment by telling him to see the morning showings of English films in the new theater Asha, owned by Shelly's father, in the hope that he would not recognize the same actor playing different roles. But there was another problem. He loved the MGM lion.

"Begumsahib, that *baagh* is very good. He goes 'roar...'" Abdul Ghani would roar again and again and again, and all this had to be borne with patience on Ammi's ruling that he was too good a help to let go just because he insisted on showing the children how the lion roared.

The only visible manifestation of the martial law that Abbu said now ruled over their lives was that all the shops outside the gate of their compound were closed down. Within two months, these shops sprouted up again, first in ones and twos, and then the entire road was restored. Martial law quickly failed to frighten people into following the law, or as Ammi asserted, it had tasted the fruits of looking the other way.

The dark, mustachioed, formidable, plump Mrs. Bennett, whom Sadi wanted dismissed by the Field Marshal, wore long dresses that skirted over her knees. She was the scourge of all the boys in the class. She and several other teachers in school were of Anglo-Indian descent and every Sunday went to one of the two churches in the city to pray. Any boy who transgressed her rules was punished with zinging raps on the palms with a wooden ruler. The girls were afraid of her as well, as she could be scathing in her disapproval.

Their teachers, Mrs. Rumbello and Mrs. Maha, were sisters-in-law and hated each other. Miss Helen was pretty and wore gaily colored frocks pinched at the waist by broad black belts with shiny buckles. She had cropped hair, thick eyebrows, and wore pink lipstick on her full lips. She conducted the pt classes in the small courtyard, taught the girls how to swing with the hula-hoop, and organized picnics to Sonakanda and Sonachura forts. These two old quadrangular red brick forts were built by the Mughals to guard the waterways in Narayanganj.

Miss Helen also took charge of all the rehearsals for the annual concerts held each year after the final examinations. Once she directed Suri's class in a musical about a silly chicken called Henny-Penny, who while taking a walk one day, thought the sky had fallen on her head. Miss Helen played the music on the school piano and designed the costumes with Turkey-Lurkey, Chicken-Licken, Goosey-Loosey wearing jump suits in the colors of the characters they were playing, and caps in the shape of the respective beaks. Mrs. Campbell liked the performance so much that she arranged for it to be shown to the ladies of the Burma Oil Company Club in Dacca.

The cast and Miss Helen were taken there in a bus, and at the end of the musical rendition of the saga of the sky falling, they were treated to delicate triangular cucumber sandwiches and thin pieces of fruitcake served on china plates lined with lace paper doilies. The children drank lemon squash, while Miss Helen and the other grownups sipped tea from delicate white with blue flowers china cups. What a colonial experience that must have been! Ammi did not sound pleased when she made the remark.

"If you had your way, you would keep the children at home and let the *moulvi* sahib teach them." Abbu was referring to the religious teachers who taught the Quran.

"That's not true. But we have our ways. Why do we have to be like those who made us their slaves?" Ammi answered.

"They did not. Look, if they had not come to this land, I would have never been able to get out from under the yoke of the village headman."

"That's not true. I think we would have been quite okay without the two hundred years of slavery."

Abbu shook his head. Most likely there was no answer to Ammi's assertions.

Ammi had insisted that Abbu arrange for a *moulvi* to come every alternate day to teach the children to read the Holy Quran. Abbu chose one who was really old and could not see well. He taught from memory and expected Suri and Sadi to learn by rote. Often during the incantations of *"Bismillahisrahamanirrahim…* in the name of Allah,"* Sadi would sneak away, and Moulvi sahib would be none the wiser. In addition to his other afflictions, he was quite deaf. Ammi said Abbu as usual wanted to subvert her attempt to teach the children reverence for Islam.

"Well! I did the best I could." Abbu would feign innocence.

Moulvi sahib knew all about djins and spirits. One djin, according to him, dwelt across the pond that lay behind the boundary wall of the courtyard. Almost the year round the pond was covered with thousands of floating hyacinth plants with thick green tubular stems and leaves supported above the water surface by long spongy bulbous stalks. Single spikes of purple pink flowers periodically turned the pond into a vivid shade of lavender. Twice a year men with their lungis bunched up into loin cloth arrived with long bamboo poles and picked up the hyacinths, several at a time, making large round floats. These mounds would turn brown and saturate the air with the rank smell of rotting vegetation. Ammi would have to suffuse the house with fumes of burning frankincense to keep the stink away. At these times the house would smell the same as the tent set up for the Durga puja that Mali bhai celebrated with those of his Hindu faith in Narayanganj.

The djin in question lived on a pole on the roof of the police barracks surrounded by tall trees. It watched all the moves that the children in the compound made, or so Moulvi sahib said.

"It is only a ceramic insulator!" Ammi did not like the children being afraid.

"But djins can assume any form or shape," Moulvi sahib countered.

Each year on the last day of Ramzan, the Muslim month of fasting, everyone climbed up to the roof just after breaking the fast. There they would peer at the sky to spot the barely visible thin crescent that heralded the end of fasting and the commencement of the Eid feasting.

On Eid day, Abbu, Sadi, and Sami dressed in white muslin kurtas and straight cotton pajamas, and Abdul Ghani in white kurta and lungi would take rickshaws to the main city mosque for community prayers. Suri and Ammi would bathe and put on their new Eid clothes and wait for them to return. One year when Suri was five and incapable of making what-to-wear decisions, Ammi had a *gharara* stitched for her to wear on Eid day. These pajamas with pleated flares at the bottom were made popular by Miss Fatima Jinnah, the sister of the founder of Pakistan; Ammi adored her for being so active in the freedom movement. Clad in her *gharara,* Suri went along with Abbu and Sadi to the mosque. Suri was the only girl in the congregation, and the imam conducting the prayers did not like this very much. According to him, the mosque was a place for men only. Perhaps, sensing that she was unwelcome, Suri held on tight to Abbu's hands throughout the prayers and the long sermon. She did not even let go when after the sermon Abbu embraced everyone around him once, twice, thrice. This was the first and last time he took her to the mosque. Not that she wanted to go either!

When everyone returned from the prayers, a special Eid breakfast was served. The main offering was the s*heer qorma,* a special vermicelli sweet made in milk boiled with almonds, raisins, pistachios, and dry dates. This was the taste of Eid day if days had taste. Guests would pour in immediately and the first to come were usually the men who worked for Abbu. Then his friends would pay their Eid visit. The vermicelli and small fried *kababs* were served to all the guests. The scent of oily fragrant *attar* pervaded the air.

In the evening, it was the turn of the women to visit one another. Ammi always wore saris, white cotton with red or black or green borders in the day, and in the evenings gaily colored silks and chiffons, which Nani sent every Eid from Karachi. She would tie her hair in a bun with a flower on the side and rim her eyes with kohl. Suri usually wore frocks, blue in color mostly, made from glittery silk or lace material, matching ribbons in their hair, and white court shoes.

The second Eid of the year, the Eid-ul-Azha, was celebrated two months and ten days after the first Eid to commemorate the sacrifice rendered by Prophet Abraham. The few times that Abbu succumbed to social pressures to offer the ritual sacrifice, a goat was slaughtered and hung up on the branches of the guava tree to be chopped up. Abbu did not like this second Eid, although it was supposed to have a higher rank purportedly because it entailed sacrifice. It was considered to be a greater sacrifice if the goat or the cow had been brought up in the household and then slaughtered. Abbu did not find this ranking very logical.

In fact, the whole sacrifice itself was not understandable because at least one-third of the sacrificial flesh was kept by the person who bought the animal, one-third given away to friends and acquaintances, and the remaining to beggars who came door to door to collect meat. Everyone generally had a good time with the feasting. The only exception was the sacrificed goat. Abbu was against this need to kill animals to commemorate something that took place hundreds of years ago. After a couple of times, he abandoned the ritual and said to hell with what everyone thinks!

The guava tree under which the goat was slaughtered grew at the entrance of their large colonial-style red brick house with formal and informal gardens on one side of the compound housing the telephone exchange and residence for the officers and staff. A green wooden gate led into a long walkway of green grass at the end of which grew profusely flowering shrubs of large pale pink woody smelling flowers. Alongside these lay dense jasmine bushes spread over bamboo trellis with small white flowers filling the air with soft exotic perfume. In summer, the beli shrubs bore their fragrant blossoms. The formal laid out garden was on the left. In the winter and spring months as Mali bhai moved from flower bed to flower bed, loosening the earth and pulling out weeds, the children followed him as he recounted the tale of what Gul said to Bakauli and in the answer lay the mystery of the universe. Then there was the tale of the prince whose heart resided in a parrot held in a gold and diamond cage, and the evil vizier who failed for the umpteenth time to kill the parrot.

"Why in a parrot and not a crow?" Suri would ask.

"Because the crows are cunning and the parrot is gentle and beautiful…"

"Won't the crow protect the heart better?"

"But the parrot is more beautiful…"

"So…"

"So the prince cannot keep his heart in an ugly crow and then put it in a golden cage, can he?"

"Why not?"

"Listen! Do you want to hear the story or what…?"

"Don't listen to her Mali bhai…so what did the vizier do next?" Sadi was exasperated at such lines of questioning by Suri.

"I would keep my heart in a hawk, and by the way, crows are not ugly…"

"Why would anyone care about your heart? And shut up and listen," Sadi had said.

This was not a good story as far as Suri was concerned. The green parrots were enchanting, and no prince had any business keeping his heart in one, thus exposing it to so much danger! All birds needed the sky to soar in.

The branches of the guava tree were a favorite perch for the children during the long summer afternoons when they were supposed to be taking their afternoon nap. The doll maker, who lived in the quarters behind the red brick house, would come looking for her sons and would assail Suri, "No one will marry a cripple... come down before you break your arms and legs and your head...!" The doll maker never said the same about the boys.

"Breaking her head would not be such a bad idea now..." Sadi would butt in.

But he was really upset when Suri got an awful gash on her forehead while taking the shortcut to the doll maker's house through the storage yard that was full of poles and large wheels of cable. A sleek, brown mongoose with intense dark eyes, darting across the path brushed Suri's legs. As she leapt to one side to avoid it, she hit her head on the ends of a stack of poles.

Sadi went with her to the government hospital to get the wound stitched by Doctor Wahid. He was a family friend and lived in Dacca, commuting the ten miles every day to Narayanganj. Sometimes his wife would come with him to spend the day with Ammi. The Doctor's wife always wore dark red lipstick, had red roses in her hair, and drew a black veil across her nose in the presence of men. If she did not want to draw attention, then she should go easy on the red and black which is so beguiling, Ammi often commented. She did not like the idea of hiding one's face.

"Why does she cover her face in front of Abbu?" Suri had asked

"She covers her face because they are Qadianis," Ammi explained, "Their imam is supposed to be Mehdi, the long-promised messiah to the Muslims. He decreed that women must do so in keeping with Islamic traditions."

"But we are Muslims, and you don't cover your face?"

"We are not as fundamentalist as them. Our Prophet preached moderation, and that is what we follow," Ammi explained. Then she added, "But if their imam brings solace and goodness in the hearts of his followers, it is enough."

Suri's first trip to Karachi to meet Ammi's family occurred soon after the mongoose incident. There on Clifton Beach, Suri encountered another mongoose in a snake-mongoose fight. What a terrifying sight it was. The poor half-drugged black snake fought valiantly with the vicious brown mongoose. Blood dripped from the mongoose's mouth when it finally killed the snake. The man who staged the fight petted and stroked the mongoose and did not bother to even collect and dispose of the dead snake. It was horrible, and to think they had to pay to see this ugly scene.

That was their first trip to West Pakistan together. Ammi needed to be with her family in her time of sorrow. Her fourth child, a baby girl, died of pneumonia complications when she was just eight months old. Abbu sent Suri, Sadi, and Sami to Shelly's house while the burial rituals were undertaken. The next day he took all of them to the graveyard on the outskirts of Narayanganj along the road to Dacca. A small mound of earth with a black cage over it marked the place where the baby lay buried. Ammi's eyes were swollen and red from weeping. She told the children to say a prayer for their sister each time they passed the graveyard. "She will go straight to heaven if you do." She added.

"Not that she needs it," Abbu commented.

"Ji, please…"

"But she was too little to need redemption," Abbu insisted.

"All human beings are sinners…"

And before Abbu could say anything more, Ammi began to cry. "But she was so little. Can you not argue for once…"

Abbu put his arms around Ammi's shoulders, apologized for his insensitivity, and offered to make a permanent concrete structure over the grave.

"No, no. Never do that. It is a sin. Graves should never be made permanent. Three hundred souls are to rise from each grave on the Day of Judgment."

Abbu, with great self-restraint, did not respond.

Attached to the red brick house were the kitchen and the quarters for the cook on one end of the back courtyard. Every day Ammi, sitting on a small low wooden stool, supervised Abdul Ghani as he lit the wood stove and stoked it by blowing through a tubular metal blowpipe. She would put together the main meat or fish curry and leave him to make the rest of the meal. All the spices were ground on a stone slab, and Abdul Ghani never tired of boasting that no one could make a finer paste. The round coriander seeds, the long cumin seeds, the hard pieces of turmeric that had to be pounded to smaller pieces before grinding, peeled pieces of ginger and garlic were each ground separately with just enough water to make a thick paste. The last spice on the slab were dried red chilies because the hot flavor would otherwise overwhelm the other spices.

Every day Abdul Ghani made rice, lentils, and the vegetables as well as round soft rotis, and on special occasions like Sunday breakfast, parathas. Ammi was used to eating bread in her mother's household in Poona rather than the boiled rice that was a staple in East Pakistan, so both were served at meal times. Whenever Shelly's mother made her special *hilsa* fish curry with mustard seeds, she would send some for them. Ammi made sure that all the thin delicate bones from the flesh were removed before eating for these could easily lodge in the throat. If that happened, then mouthfuls of boiled rice had to be swallowed to dislodge the bone and this took all the joy out of eating the delicious fish.

Abbu's heavy smoking was always a point of contention, and in spite of Ammi's oft-repeated admonishments, he did not give it up, smoking at least three packs of Gold Flake or Capstan cigarettes a day. Often he would make his own cigarette in a square metal boxlike contraption that he brought back from his year-long training in England where he was sent by the government in the summer of 1960. With pursed lips and great concentration, Abbu would place the box with both flaps open on his lap and wedge a cigarette paper peeled from a wad into the roller at the junction. On it he carefully put a line of tobacco taken from a flat round tin lined with crinkled paper. Then the top flap of the box was slowly moved upward in an arc as if the box was being shut. As the flap moved inward, the cigarette rolled out. The edge of the paper was licked and the tube of tobacco sealed in.

Once Ammi caught him making Sadi lick the ends of the paper and gave him hell for trying to introduce her son to smoking at such an early age. She did not know that Suri had been given the opportunity to lick the paper as well, and no one was about to tell her.

V

Soon after Abbu returned from his training in England, some strange misgivings arose between him and Ammi. It started soon after a friend Abbu had met in England and who was in Narayanganj on vacation began to come over in the evenings with his sister. He would sit with them for hours in the living room. Ammi thought it so tedious to chat with them every evening and often left to resume supervision of the children's homework and dinner. There was nothing unusual about friends coming in the evening, but sitting indoors was a drastic change from Abbu's usual evening sojourns in the front garden with friends and colleagues.

"Ji, this is a bad example for the children," Ammi told him.

"I'm just keeping them company. They have so many problems at home," Abbu replied.

"Why does he not go to his hometown in Chandpur with his sister?"

"The poor sister was widowed at such a young age and has no one to look after her, and it is boring in the village for him."

"You took us there last winter, and I thought it was quite a charming place especially with all the date palm trees. Besides what does this have to do with the man bringing whiskey into our house?" Ammi admonished Abbu.

"Mumtaz, it is so hypocritical of you. You don't mind if I drink when we go to the club, but you don't want it in the house." Abbu was an office bearer of the local Narayanganj Club and went every other evening to meet his friends. Ammi would join him only when dinners were organized.

"Yes! I don't want you to drink in front of the children," Ammi responded. "Besides, what does my feelings about your drinking have to do with that woman coming here?"

The widow had dark shiny black hair and often left it loose and wore saris with sleeveless blouses. In her high-heeled shoes, rouged cheeks, and reddened lips, she drew Ammi's ire.

"If she is a widow, then she sure does not dress like one!" Ammi proclaimed with petulance leaking into her voice.

"She is young, and why should she wear white, or is it black, that you women want widows to wear?" Abbu chided Ammi.

"I do not believe in all this white and black stuff. But she comes across as really desperate to hook another husband!"

"Nothing wrong with that, is there?" Abbu said. "We do not condemn widows to isolation, do we? We did that in the village. Hindu widows were shunned and isolated. They were absolutely forbidden to remarry…"

"But the *angraiz* changed that, did they not?" Ammi always referred to the British in the Urdu word for them. "And don't change the subject. Should she flaunt herself as available? Besides, if she wants to look for another husband, why does she spend all her time with her brother and you?"

"Stop it, Mumtaz. Don't be suspicious!"

"I am not! Or should I be? After all, you men profess that you can marry four wives!"

"Stop it…You know I do not believe in those stupid things that some ignorant *moulvis* say!"

"So why are you protesting so much?"

"Stop it, Mumtaz!"

One day Ammi suddenly decided to visit her mother with her children. They took the train to Dacca with Mali bhai and Abdul Ghani minding the luggage and seeing them off at the airport. Ammi's brother met them in Karachi and took them by train to Hyderabad, one hundred miles from Karachi, where Nani lived in a small house given to her in exchange for the one she left behind in Poona at the time of the cleaving. This city was located on the banks of the mighty River Indus, from which the English derived the name for India. Purportedly it was easier for the colonizers to pronounce India rather than the original name Hindustan that connoted that it was the land of the Hindus.

It was hot and humid in Hyderabad. The only cool area in Nani's house lay under the square opening on one end of the ceiling with a wind catcher over it. All the houses in this city had these chimney like structures on the roofs. Nani lived near the Shahi Bazaar, the royal bazaar as it were, in a bustling neighborhood. The city had a different smell than the one in Narayanganj, perhaps, because of the large numbers of one-horse carriages.

Soon after they arrived, Nani and her friend decided to take Suri and Sami out to the bazaar and treat them to freshly roasted gram, sweet *shahtoot*-mulberry, and ice sticks made from crushed ice, covered with sweet syrup and a dollop of homemade ice cream on top. A horse driven *tanga* was hired, but Suri was afraid to climb the teetering platform to the seat, not least because her grandmother and her friend were both women of substantive girth, and she felt sorry for the horse. She would rather have walked. But Nani chided her, "*Challo...darpok...*come on, you coward," and made her climb on to the front seat.

Nani picked up Sami and placed him on the backseat and then heaved herself onto the carriage followed by her friend. Much to Suri's horror, the carriage tilted back to touch the ground, and the poor horse flailed in midair. The driver cursed and tried to get hold of the front leg of his horse and ordered Nani and her friend to get off. The two laughed and laughed as they stepped down, but the driver did not find it funny. None of the other *tanga* drivers agreed to take them, so they had to walk in the heat to the bazaar.

That day Nani bought *palla* fish from the fish market and when she fried it for lunch, it looked and tasted exactly the same as the *hilsa* that Shelly's mother would make for them in Narayanganj. The *palla* fish were caught at the Kotri Barrage as they made their one hundred mile journey from the sea to spawn in the River Indus. The *hilsa* were caught at the mouth of the Bay of Bengal before they returned to the sea after spawning in the Padma-Meghna-Jamuna delta.

Abbu joined them a month later and brought them back to Narayanganj. Apparently Ammi forgave him for whatever he had done. She did take him to task for making the children miss school. And all Abbu could sputter was, "But you took them away, not me."

Abbu was finally made Divisional Engineer in 1962 and transferred to the head office in Dacca. Several months later when his fifth child was put in his arms in Mitford Hospital, he announced that he was going to call her Munni.

"Ji, it's okay to call her that, but we need a proper name for her as well."

"We'll think of that later."

"I want to name her Amina after the mother of our Prophet."

"Okay, okay, but we will call her Munni."

When Suri asked her why Munni had two names and she only one, Ammi said that in many Muslim localities of India the youngest girl was always called Munni, meaning "little one." What about the eldest? They were called "Burhki," meaning the older one. Suri was glad that Abbu had not insisted on calling her that.

In Dacca, they were given a ground-floor flat in one of the four white buildings reserved for T&T Officers in Azimpur Colony. The rest of the colony with innumerable cream colored buildings was allocated to officials of various other government departments. Down the tree-lined road from the colony was the Azimpur graveyard. Here three martyrs to the Bengali mother tongue, Safiur Rahman, Abul Barkat, and Rafiuddin Ahmad, killed in 1952, lay buried. The first two had migrated to East Pakistan from the Indian part of Bengal at the time of the cleaving and the third was from Manikganj. The other three martyrs, including the nine year old Offiullah, were buried in their home towns. Further down was Peelkhana where the Dacca headquarters of the paramilitary East Pakistan Rifles was located.

A new cook, Mannan, was hired, as was a woman, recommended by Mrs. Ahmad, whose husband was a colleague of Abbu. She would come for a few hours every day to do the cleaning and washing. Ammi was horrified when she turned up for work with just the sari covering her pendulous breasts. She immediately went across the road to New Market to get her a blouse and petticoat with instructions that she was to wear them when she came to work. Mannan, whose family lived in the deltaic village of Patuakhali, was quartered in the rooms above the row of garages along with other men, who worked as cooks and bearers for the residents of the colony and did not have their families with them.

Rajabi, who lived under the stairs of the four buildings by some system of turns that only she knew of, also did not wear blouses or petticoats. But no one knew how to make her do so. She wandered around the compound in dirt-clogged sari and rags around her waist. At meal times, she would stand in front of one of the ground floor flats, and no one ever refused to give her food. How she came to live in the colony was a mystery, and no one wanted to take on the "curse of the innocent" by making her leave. The rags around her waist were always stained brown red, and those coming up and down the stairs quickly passed her by. Anyone who teased her or bothered her was severely admonished. She liked the white tube roses that Ammi grew in the small garden attached to the flat, and each time these blossomed, Rajabi would lean over the fence and delicately take a couple of the tubular flowers, put them in her matted stringy hair, and walk off with a smile on her face.

One night Mrs. Ahmad came running to Ammi. "Bhabi…come quickly," she whispered breathlessly.

"What's the matter? You look sick," Ammi said.

"Bhabi, Rajabi is about to give birth, and she is covered in blood." Rajabi was at the time living under the stairs in Mrs. Ahmad's building.

"What?"

"None of us realized her state," Mrs. Ahmad said.

"I don't believe this!"

"Come and see for yourself."

"It's unbelievable!" Ammi was furious. "This is cruel and sinful!"

"What can one say of men?" Mrs. Ahmad answered. "But hurry. We need to do something quickly before everyone hears of it and comes to watch."

"You go to her while I get Dr. Rahman from New Market," Ammi said. "I will call Mrs. Doja and Mrs. Chowdury and ask them to join you."

Together they shielded Rajabi and shooed away anyone who came to look. Doctor Rahman arranged for an ambulance for the writhing and bellowing Rajabi. Ammi and Mrs. Ahmad went along in the ambulance, but neither Rajabi nor the baby survived. Ammi came back late in the night distraught and angry.

"How could anyone do this? The barbarian…it is a sin…Whoever did this will go straight to hell…how can we find out who did this?" Ammi repeated again and again.

"Let it go, Bhabi…How can we find out the man responsible? God will punish him," Mrs. Ahmad responded.

"Why does God allow this to happen?" Ammi asked.

"God only knows!"

Shortly thereafter, the quarters above the garages were converted to a club with table tennis tables and carom boards for use by the residents. The cooks and others were given a set of rooms in the nearby telephone exchange compound.

Abbu did not enforce his walk to school policy in Dacca because the distances were greater and the children did not go to the same school. Suri was admitted to the all-girls school located on Bailey Road, Sadi to the Residential Model School in Dhanmandi, and Sami to Adamjee Boys School in the Cantonment area.

On school days the green and white microbus, one of the perks of Abbu's promotion, took Suri and Sami past the Dacca University buildings. Then a left turn brought them to Mymensingh Road between the racecourse and the Arts Council where a row of krishnachura trees growing on the central dividing island lit up the skies in April with a riot of deep vermillion and orange flowers overwhelming the lime green leaves. The rest of the year, the crooked, twisted grey trunks hid this colorful secret.

After passing the big white Shahbagh Hotel on the left, the microbus took a right turn in front of Sakura Shopping Center. A perfectly domed krishnachura tree grew on the side of this building. The microbus would continue down the road toward the roundabout, with the cream colored Intercontinental Hotel on the right, the green lush Ramna Park adjoining it. In the center of the island at this crossroad grew one large tree and the most exotic orchids protruded from the hook of a branch and the moss covered trunk. Legend was that anyone who touched the blooms was doomed to real bad luck the rest of their lives. So, untouched, the flowers thrived saturating the air around with a sweet exotic smell. The microbus took a right turn at the tree with the cursed orchid along the outer flank of the park, and then a left at the white walled President House, down Bailey Road to the school. After dropping Suri off, the microbus went back on to Mymensingh Road and turned right toward the Cantonment to Sami's school.

One winter morning, Suri entered the school, walked past the shefali tree that grew in a circular flowerbed in front of the gate to get to her classroom so that she could leave her bag at the desk and head for early morning school assembly. That morning they were to offer prayers for Mr. Kennedy, who had been assassinated in America. A heady scent floated out of the carpet of orange stemmed white flowers that lay on the dew-laden grass. While passing the shefali tree, Suri caught sight of a long grey thick-as-her-wrist snake draped over a low branch. When the shock wore off, she noticed the trickle of blood making a red line down the jaw of the snake. The snake was hit on the head with a stick by the school gardener, and when it stopped writhing and the eyes on both sides of the head glazed, it was hung on the branch, on the orders of the spinster, some said jilted, assistant headmistress of the school.

Not content with just placing the snake on the branches of the fragrant blossoms, she stood guard over it as well, as though the snake was in any position to slither away. In her stiff white sari with ends tucked at the waist and silver-rimmed glasses on her nose, the spinster chided the girls as they filed past in their uniform of blue qameez, white shalwar, and royal blue sweaters.

"This is what we found lurking in the hedge, and you girls had better not put your hands in there to get the ball." And with her voice pitched a notch or two higher, she added, "If any of you are bitten by any snake in the hedge, I am not responsible!"

Most of the girls coming in through the main gate turned their faces away from the sight of the shiny white underbelly. Some girls said, "Okay…" Others squealed, and yet others felt sorry for the snake.

"But the poor snakes are more afraid of us than we are of them…." Suri challenged the assistant headmistress. She remembered that Mali bhai had told her that snakes were wary of human beings.

"How do you know? Have you ever faced one?"

"No, I haven't because they probably hide when a human being approaches, and imagine if a ball lands near one it's not going to wait to see what…!"

"Do not argue with me. Go to your class."

"But today we have the big baseball match, so what are we to do?" Suri asked.

"If the ball goes into the hedge, call the gardener to take it out."

It was not right that the poor gardener would have to wrangle with a snake. In any case, if the girl from the orange marigold team swung the baseball bat, and the ball happened to land in the hedge surrounding the playground, then the fielder from the red hibiscus team could not allow a homerun to be made because a snake may be lurking in the hedge. She would put her hand in the deep dark undergrowth and retrieve the ball, snake or no snake.

When Suri told her family about the snake draped on the shefali tree during dinner that night, Ammi muttered, "God help us," under her breath.

"What do you mean, Mumtaz?" Abbu was perplexed at Ammi's reaction.

"It is bad omen to kill snakes…"

"But I thought that was about dreams," Abbu responded. "If one kills a snake…or is it if one sees a snake in a dream…it means there will be some great change in your life or something like that."

"No, no, it means that you have an enemy," Ammi explained. "When we were children, we were told not to even say the word *saanp* for fear one would materialize then and there. We would call it a *rassi* instead…"

"Really, Ammi, that's funny. Calling snakes ropes," Sami giggled.

"Don't make fun of this...if a snake is killed, then its partner exacts revenge even if it takes forever..."

"How does the partner know who killed the snake in the first place?" Abbu seemed to be enjoying the conversation.

"The eyes of the snake keep an image of the killer, and the partner snake sees it and goes after the one who killed it."

"You don't really believe that, Mumtaz, do you?"

"No, I do not," Ammi conceded, "but snakes and creatures should not be killed without reason. It is bad luck."

"Whose luck turns bad, the one who kills the snake or the one who sees the dead snake?" Abbu insisted.

"I don't know. All I know, it is not right..."

"Come on now, nothing will happen to anyone unless one sees it in one's dream...I think!" Abbu had the last word for once.

That night Suri dreamt of snakes, men chasing snakes, one snake chasing her and other snakes curled around the shefali tree. "God help us—we are surrounded by enemies," was Ammi's comment the next morning. Abbu said Suri had dreamt of snakes only because she had seen one and it had stayed in her subconscious mind.

At the regular school assembly that winter morning of the snake in the shefali tree episode, the headmistress led a prayer for the soul of the handsome Mr. Kennedy who had been assassinated in Dallas a week earlier. Some months later, the entire senior section of the school was taken to the United States Information Services building on Purana Paltan Road to view *Years of Lightning, Day of Drums,* a film on the life and death of Mr. Kennedy. The sight of Jackie, his beautiful wife, wearing pink, cradling her husband's wounded head in her lap while he bled to death was so sad. Everyone had wept at the sight of his little son saluting as the coffin passed by.

After the affair of the dead snake on the shefali tree, the rule was that if the ball went into the hedge play was frozen, just like when if someone said "statue," and everyone had to freeze and anyone moving was out. This game was played at all the birthday parties and was quite a lot of fun. The birthday girl made funny faces, stuck out her tongue, opened her eyes wide, and pulled her lips down with the fingers on both sides of the mouth, all to induce some movement in the frozen girls in their frothy multilay-ered lace party frocks with starched cancans. Any girl who moved or laughed or giggled was out, and one who remained a statue longest won the prize of either a long box with six colored pencils or a box with six long white sweet sugar cigarettes stained brown at the end. Dangling the sugar cigarettes from the lips, a girl could pretend to be Audrey Hepburn from *Breakfast at Tiffany's*. Maybe it was these films that made the girls in school do American things like play baseball instead of the more English game of cricket. In any case, smoking the sugar sticks was actually much better than smoking the lighted dry cylindrical stalk of jute, inhaling the smoke, filling the throat with the woody smoke, and then passing it on to a friend. However, unlike with the sugar sticks, while chok-ing on the lighted golden fiber stalk, one felt as good as one who has committed a moral transgression does.

Suri's best friend Shelly also joined the school on Bailey Road and commuted every day from Narayanganj. Najma, Nargis, and the blonde Ghazala who lived near the school, in the walled Ispahani Colony reserved for those whose ancestors were from Is-fahan, Iran, completed the group of Suri's four best friends. They did everything together. None of them liked the Civics classes, not least because they were taught in excruciating detail all about the Field Marshal's Basic Democracy system imposed after his *coup d'état*. Under the complicated five-tier system of government, elected representatives, or 'Beedees' as they were called, made up the body that elected the President. The girls got to witness firsthand how the system worked.

The Field Marshal, confident of his strength and popularity, decided to let the people show their support by holding elections for President of Pakistan in January 1965.

Fatima Jinnah, the sister of Mr. Jinnah, the founder of Pakistan, who lived in her family's rose colored Mohatta Palace near Clifton Beach in Karachi, decided to call his bluff and contest the election against him. Ammi was ecstatic when this happened. In Dacca, Ammi joined the city chapter of the organization that Fatima

Jinnah had set up for welfare work among the refugees who came to the country after the cleaving and now did general relief work. Together with her best friend Mrs. Ahmed, she regularly attended the meetings of the local office and performed tasks like collecting food and sorting clothes whenever a storm or flood ravaged any part of East Pakistan. When Fatima Jinnah announced her stand against the Field Marshal, Ammi and her friend both immediately decided to work for the campaign.

"She is seventy and yet so daring," was Ammi's constant refrain about Fatima Jinnah.

"The Jamaatis are not going to like this." Abbu was referring to the Jamaat-e-Islami, a party of politicians who sought power in the name of Islam. The organization had branches in both East and West Pakistan.

Abbu was not too sure of Fatima Jinnah's chances.

"I know he is going to use the Jamaatis as those in the Army always do," Ammi said. "But we will overcome this stupid notion they spout that women are unfit to lead the government."

After attending a rally in support of Fatima Jinnah in Dacca, Ammi was beside herself with joy. "There were hundreds of thousands of people, and they cheered and cheered this white-haired frail woman in her white *gharara* and dupatta. There were so many people there that I have no doubt that she will win. The crowds called her the mother of the nation."

Thousands of people, many of whom were students, had turned out to see Fatima Jinnah. Hundreds cheered her along the route from Dacca to Chittagong when she went there to canvass ahead of the polls. At each station, the people begged her to speak.

"But you do know that the elections are indirect, so do not have much hope of her winning. The Beedees are in the Field Marshal's pocket." Abbu wanted to make sure Ammi knew how the deck was stacked.

"He will not dare go against the popular will!"

"Just watch! He will. And he will win."

"Miss Jinnah has called the Field Marshal a dictator, and that is what he is!"

"I know that she is holding him responsible for giving away our water rights in the water sharing treaty with India," Abbu said referring to the Indus Water Treaty. "But he has such a big hold on the bureaucracy and the army. Every one of them will ensure that he wins."

"Then this election is meaningless."

Ammi had to accept the outcome when the Field Marshal won in a landslide.

In May, another tragedy struck. A PIA passenger plane crashed near Cairo while on its inaugural flight to the Egyptian capital. Ghazala's neighbor in Ispahani Colony, Jalal Al-Karimi, was aboard the ill-fated flight. As it turned out he survived and heroically rescued five others from the burning debris. One hundred and nineteen passengers, including the beautiful stewardess Momi Gul, were killed.

In September of the same year *Gone with the Wind* was released, and it was a great hit. When Suri got home after watching the Civil War and Scarlet O' Hara trying to survive her travails and loves among the rows and rows of wounded and dead, Sami excitedly told her that the Field Marshal had declared that they were at war with India and the schools were ordered closed. Her mind instantly veered to images of the dead and wounded. However, not much action in this war between India and Pakistan was seen in East Pakistan. All the attacks and fighting took place in West Pakistan, specifically near Lahore. Ammi worried about her brother as Karachi port was also attacked again and again, and he lived in Gizri near the Clifton Beach. During the eighteen days the war lasted, lectures were arranged on civil defense and how to respond to air raids. Sadi and the other boys in the colony were taught to shoot rifles lying full length on the ground aiming at targets trying to hit the bullseye. How this would help if the enemy attacked was unclear, especially when no one owned anything more serious than air rifles. On some days, the girls in the colony were allowed to learn how to shoot as well.

When not practicing the art of civil defense, everyone sat at home and played blackjack and rummy, listened to the radio for news and rousing war songs like, "*Ai watan ke sajiley jawanon...*

Brave soldiers of the nation, my songs are for you," sung by the melody queen Noorjehan from Lahore. And the chorus of "*jhanda uthae obhijatrira door jatrae chol lo* ... with the flag raised the brave soldiers go to fight..." by a group from Dacca. All felt pride in their country and the soldiers defending its soil.

After the United Nations sponsored ceasefire took hold a meeting of the leaders of the two countries was arranged in January in the cold freezing Russian plains of Tashkent to work out a peace settlement. The day after the agreement was reached, the Prime Minister of India, Lal Bahadur Shastri, strangely enough died of a heart attack. The foreign minister of Pakistan, Zulfikar Bhutto, who had accompanied the Field Marshal to Tashkent, disassociated himself from his mentor soon afterward and threatened to reveal the secret deal struck between the two sides in Tashkent. He never did, but his threat to do so, resonated really well in his speeches. He then went full swing into politics, forming a political party with the promise of bread, clothes, and shelter for all and called it the Peoples Party.

"Imagine a *wadera* making a party of the people. He is a big landowner of Sind. What does he know of ordinary people?" Ammi commented when she heard one of Bhutto's speeches on the radio. Hyderabad and Karachi were both in Sind, so Ammi felt she had a right to an opinion.

"And all this talk of revealing the 'cat in the bag' nonsense about the Tashkent deal that he keeps talking about is so aggravating," Abbu added. "No one is talking about how Dacca was left completely vulnerable to Indian attack." The Army generals quoted some silly doctrine of the defense of the East lies in the West, but more likely they did not consider East Pakistan worth defending. The bureaucrats of West Pakistan even refused to acknowledge that the foreign exchange earned by the export of jute grown in East Pakistan was used for development in West Pakistan, and nothing was invested in the eastern part of the country.

"It's so utterly unfair!" Ammi remarked.

"Maybe the six-point demand that the League has put forth will make sure we have more say in the running of the government," Abbu said. The Awami League had by now become the largest and by far the most popular political party in East Pakistan. "I hope the bureaucrats in West Pakistan agree. It will ease much of the tension between East and West Pakistan."

"I hope they do, but I don't have much hope." Ammi did not have much faith in the intelligence of the civil servants. "They will surely not like us in East Pakistan demanding any rights. Just watch what the damned bureaucrats do."

After the war, Field Marshal Ayub Khan, who was now also President of Pakistan, banned the import of films and saris from India, but he did not ban travel. Najma, whose family had come to Dacca from Calcutta at the time of the cleaving, went there every summer and returned with all the latest fashion news culled from the many Hindi films that she saw there. By now the films made in India had progressed from Ammi's favorite black-and-white film *Mahal* about wandering spirits to Technicolor and even Cinemascope, although the heroines still ran around the trees singing of love and longing. Najma was the first among them to wear sleeveless baggy boat neck shirts, known as the sack, tight *churidar* pajamas and slippers with big black-and-white plastic flowers. She copied these costumes from the large-hipped heroines of the hit films she saw on her trips. If a certain outfit worn by a heroine was to be duplicated, the family tailor was paid to see the film and turn out a replica. Everyone poured through the copies of Indian magazines like *Filmfare* and *Femina* that Najma got back from her trips. The most copied heroines were Asha Parekh and Sharmila Tagore, who was the grand niece of Tagore. With her dimpled cheeks, large hairdos, and heavily kohled eyes, she became a popular star when she appeared in the film, *Kashmir ki Kali*, the flower bud of Kashmir, with the green-eyed hero Shammi Kapoor. The song in the film "ohoho…ahaha…*sawan ki ghata chayee*…the clouds of monsoon gather and my heart soars at this sight…" was a huge hit. The Field Marshal could not jam the radio waves, so everyone was familiar with the latest songs from programs like Binaca Geet Mala broadcast on Radio Ceylon.

Nargis dreamt of becoming a famous dancer. She took lessons from a guru to learn the Kathak dance of the Mughal courts and hoped one day to perform live on television, introduced in Dacca and Lahore the year before the war. The first shows on the single Pakistan Television channel were *I Love Lucy* and Larry, Moe, and Curly Joe as the *Three Stooges* and even a science thriller called *A for Andromeda*. Suri and Sami did not miss a single episode of the Andromeda series in which a group of scientists detected a radio signal from a distant galaxy that contained instructions for the design of a powerful computer. Once the computer was built, it gave the scientists instructions for the creation of a living organism, played by Julie Christie. The evil motives of the computer had to be exposed before humanity was destroyed. Of course, human beings prevailed over the machine!

Sadi did not much like his residential school, located in Dhanmandi, a posh area of Dacca, and begged to be brought home each time the family visited him. But Abbu wanted him to learn from the discipline of community living. Sami's school was set up by the same Adamjee family who owned the world's largest jute mill on the banks of the Sitalakhya River.

Sami loved cricket. Ammi's younger brother played first-class cricket in the Eaglets cricket team in Karachi and had even played in England. When he visited them, the seven-year-old Sami followed him around in awe. At the end of his visit, this uncle gave Sami his diagonally stripped official Eaglets tie and he slept with it under his pillow for days.

Suri liked the cricketers better. Whenever matches were played in Dacca, the girls went to the stadium, sometimes even playing truant from school to cheer the home side. They had one and all fallen in love with Mike Brearley, the captain of the English team, when he came to play in Dacca. He was so handsome.

Every school year, the three school teams, marigolds, frangipanis, and hibiscuses, competed for points in sports and academics. There was even competition to see which team did the best rendition of the hymns to the glory of the Prophet. On the day of the annual school *milad,* organized to offer praise to the Prophet, the girls wore white outfits and specially prepared dupattas made by dyeing cotton lengths in orange, yellow, or red depending on the house they belonged to. The fabric was starched, gold lace stitched on the four sides and then scrunched. Incense sticks in special silver containers filled the large *shamiana* tent with a strong aroma of sandalwood mixed with rosewater. Piles of ash from the burning incense made grey blotches on the white sheets spread over rugs for the mothers of the students, who came as guests, to sit on.

The prayer books were placed on cushions covered with red tinseled cloth, and two teachers who taught Urdu, and three senior girls, one from each house, read out from the book on the life of the Prophet. Volunteers sprinkled rose water from silver containers on all the women when they stood up to intone the chant "*ya nabi sallam alaika, ya rasool...*" as offerings of love and greetings to "the One on whom the holy book was divined." When the prayer was invoked asking God to help all those in distress and "keep our pure country safe," some women invariably overcome with emotions wept. Brown paper bags filled with the special *milad* sweets, the doughnut-shaped *baloo shahi*, were distributed to everyone.

The school library was well stocked with all the Kay Tracey, Nancy Drew, Trixie Beldon books, and the girls avidly lapped these up. Then they progressed to *Rebecca, Jamaica Inn, Frenchman's Creek, Far from the Madding Crowd, Jude the Obscure, Wuthering Heights*, and *Emma* borrowed from the British Council library. The library had an auditorium attached to it, and every year the Thespians, a club formed by students of the English Department of the Dacca University, put on plays like *Macbeth, The Importance of Being Earnest*, and *Charley's Aunt*. Najma's brother was an actor in the group, and Ghazala's sister a director, so Suri and her friends were able to attend all the performances.

Whenever Ghazala's cousin, Haseena, came from Chittagong to stay with her, both of them would often come to Suri's house to spend the day. Ammi would get chicken patties and pastries for them from Olympia Bakery in New Market, and after tea they would go to Balaka Cinema to watch Doris Day and Rock Hudson movies. The others would join them, and sometimes Shelly when she stayed with Suri came as well. They saw *Summer Holiday* and *Young Ones* with Cliff Richard three times each. They even used the songs from his films for the farewell show for the matriculating class when it was their turn to organize it. In that series of enacted songs were also included "Que Sera Sera" and "Henry the eighth

I am I am, I got married to the widow next door, she'd been married seven times before, and everyone was a henry, so henry the eighth I am I am." It was so much fun.

Each time she came to Dacca, Haseena invited her friends to the southeastern port city of Chittagong. Lying on the banks of the Karnaphuli River, Chittagong was a busy outlet into the Indian Ocean and almost a hundred miles from Dacca. Haseena's father was senior manager of Ispahani Jute Mill so she could arrange for them to stay in its guesthouse. Just before the matriculation board examination, Suri, Shelly, and fifteen other class friends took up the offer and made the trip. The girls with Mrs. Mushtari, their geography teacher and Mrs. Zohra their Urdu teacher, boarded the train from Dacca Station in the morning. Through the eight-hour journey, they sang Bengali songs "*Majhe dheu behejai*...the waves are high and you winsome maiden make sure you do not drown while fishing," and English ditties, "Oh my darling Clementine," and ate boiled egg sandwiches and bananas for lunch. The train stopped at innumerable stations, and it was evening when they reached Chittagong.

The terrain there was different from Dacca. The low rolling hills covered with green grass and trees crossed with winding roads that led to houses on the slopes were almost picture perfect. The number of trees covering the hills made it seem as though they were entering a rain forest. From the station, they took a bus to Kalurghat by the Karnaphuli River. It took them almost an hour to get there. On the way they stopped at Savoy Bakery on Station Road to buy some cakes and pastries that this bakery was famous for, as a present for Haseena's mother. Haseena met them at the mill guesthouse and invited them to dinner that night in her bungalow that lay a few minutes' walk from there, alongside the wall that separated the river bank from the colony. Her house was big and the garden with a radhachura tree was charming.

The following day the girls took the bus over Kalurghat Bridge that spanned the river and in three hours reached Cox's Bazaar. This beach was almost sixty-five miles long and was located in the southern-most tip of East Pakistan. Mrs. Mushtari said this was the world's longest unbroken beach. At Teknaf, the beach adjoined

Burma. The sea was tranquil and the tide low when the girls went out on the sand. A film crew was shooting on the beach, and the girls naturally went to take a look. Much to their joy, the actor in the scene was the latest heartthrob, the light-eyed Nazir Beg from Karachi, who had settled in Dacca and married his director's daughter. Nazir's head was bandaged, and a red ketchup spot on the temple marked the seeping blood from the make-believe wound. He was mouthing some lines in Urdu. The crew did not let them approach the actor, so they asked around and found out where he was staying. That evening the girls cleaned themselves up as best as they could and took the bus to the motel. Nazir met them outside and was quite friendly and gave them his autograph. Later, when his Urdu film called *Chakori*, after the celestial bird that sings its love for the moon, was a huge hit, the girls boasted for days of how they had seen the shooting and met the leading man. The song, "*kahan ho tum ko doondh rahi hain ye baharein ye sama…*where are you, these days of spring are looking for you…" sung by Ferdousi Begum was so romantic. It was said that Ferdousi Begum had met Nazir Beg in Karachi and had brought him over to Dacca to become an actor. Everyone wondered if she had been smitten by his good looks!

After Cox's Bazaar, it was decided that they would see the Kaptai Lake. The man-made lake formed by the dam was constructed with the help of the American government to tap the force of the river. It was the nearest thing to paradise Suri could imagine. However, the paradise was tainted on learning that when the dam was constructed in 1962, one hundred thousand people were displaced and even the palace of the Chakma king of the hill tracts was submerged in the waters. Kaptai Lake lay en route the Indian state of Tripura on the southeastern border. The Chittagong trip was one the girls would remember for a long time. There was so much they learned about each other in the one week of living together.

The year before that trip Abbu was made in charge of the telecommunication system of the entire northern area of East Pakistan and transferred to the headquarters in Rajshahi. It was decided that the family would not go with Abbu to his new posting, as there was a dearth of good schools in the area, meaning there were no good schools that taught in English. They would visit Abbu during the holidays. Since he was given a house in Rajshahi city, the family had to vacate the flat in Azimpur. It also meant no more microbus to take everyone to school, but rickshaws were always available. Before Abbu left to take up his new position, the family shifted to a small house in Green Road, a part of Dhanmandi near New Market. Dhanmandi had a lake at its center. Doctor Wahid, who still went every day to Narayanganj to work, lived on the right bank of the lake with the head of the Awami League, Sheikh Mujib, as his neighbor.

For the next two years, all vacations were spent with Abbu in Rajshahi. The flight in the Fokker aircraft took about an hour. The headquarters of the paramilitary East Pakistan Rifles was located there, and many of the officers in the outfit were army officers from Lahore. Only a few had their families with them and these Punjabi officers invariably boasted of the mysterious magic, the *jadoo* of this land, by which they meant the dusky Bengali damsels, Ammi claimed.

Rajshahi was famous for its mangoes, lychees, soft silk saris, and the many ruins of palaces and mansions mostly abandoned by Hindu landlords when they left for India after the cleaving. The mango trees were not as tall as those by the pond in Narayanganj that the female evil spirit lived in during fruit-laden summers and the branches almost touched the ground, unable to carry the burden of the hundreds of smooth green oval fruit on long green stems. The lychee trees were tall and bore delicately flavored round green red lychees with white jellylike flesh and dark brown shiny seed at the center.

Once while the family was visiting, some English consultants came to see Abbu and were invited to the house for dinner. They asked if they could be served the jackfruit they had seen in the bazaars. These *kathals* grew on big trees with large oval leaves that, when picked from the twig, exuded a milky white sticky latex like substance. The cook gave the visitors a full display of how the fruit was split and the yellow fleshy bulbs removed. The slippery yellow flesh had a strong smell, and not everyone liked it. But the large brown seeds tasted like chestnuts when roasted on a griddle or on hot coals.

During the two years that Abbu was posted in the north, he took them to all corners of the area under his charge. Usually they traveled by road in a jeep and went all the way up to the borders with India, stopping at various railway towns like Saidpur and Rangpur, so Abbu could inspect the telephone exchanges there. They even took a short helicopter ride to Kushtia, the town of Suri's birth. The telephone exchange was in the same place, but Ammi could not recognize the now concrete bungalow that stood in place of the tin roofed house that she had given birth to Suri in.

They went all the way to Dinajpur. At the time of the cleaving, this district was divided into two with one part in Pakistan and the other in India. As usual, Abbu had his anecdote about the Tehbhaga Movement that flourished there.

"You know *tehbhaga* means three shares. During the movement, the farmers demanded two-thirds of the share of their crops for themselves, and this influenced the tenancy act enacted in nineteen hundred and fifty."

Ammi wanted to see the Mahasthangarh fort of sanctity, so Abbu took them to Bogra. This district was considered the nerve center of the northern area. Mahasthangarh was a place of pilgrimage for Buddhists, Hindus, as well as Muslims. With Ammi's love of the concept of unity of all faiths, she insisted on visiting it twice, as she did the Bhaga Mosque built in 1523 with ornate terracotta walls, and the Phutia Temple Complex with its cluster of old Hindu temples.

All around Abbu's official bungalow were fields of green mustard plants whose light yellow flowers created an aura of gentleness around the house. This was deceptive since the pods of the plants contained seeds that when crushed gave out a hot pungent flavor and the oil that emerged was thick brownish yellow with a strong smell. Some people cooked in this oil, and it was also rubbed on the scalp and was supposed to be good for the hair, but the smell would bring tears to the eyes.

The Padma River flowed close by. The high embankments filled with dense trees were a favorite place to walk in the evenings, and at dusk the trees lit up with the green glow of fireflies. It was all so enchanting!

VI

A large sacred *neem* tree that cast shadows on a life-size blue mosaic mural of Virgin Mary was the first sight that greeted students when they entered the premises of the Convent College in Tejgaon, close to Dacca airport. The mural left no doubt that the intermediate college that Suri joined, after matriculation in 1967 along with the rest of her group, was run by a monastic order. It was, in fact, run by American nuns.

In the first year of college, Suri's best friend Shelly turned sixteen, and since she was the first among them to attain that grownup status, the girls decided celebration of that event would be carried out in grand style. They had enough money between them to eat at the Chinese restaurant near the college and buy Shelly the embroidered jute tote bag she wanted. Everything was set for the evening, and all of them dressed up in their most stylish outfits.

Daisy's boyfriend and a couple of his friends were to join them, as well as the boy who was smitten with Shelly since the days of the intercollege debate meet. There was only one problem; the curfew hours in the dorm began at nine. Once the clock sounded the hour two Alsatian guard dogs were let free by the Sisters to roam the entire perimeter of the college. No one ventured out of the building for fear of being attacked. Daisy informed them that she knew for a fact that the dogs did not attack anyone in white robes.

"Who told you this?" Shelly was not so sure.

"I know. Sister Marian told me herself."

Sister Marian understood that girls will be girls, and she had not exactly been a paragon of virtue when she was young.

"Okay, so we can wrap ourselves in bed sheets to fool the dogs, can we not?" Suri asked. "And we can keep the sheets in Najma's car during dinner."

Now everything was set for the evening.

Suri wore her mauve outfit with white lace ruffles copied from a picture of Twiggy. Of course, Twiggy wore it as a short dress over sheer white leggings and Suri over white pants. Suri was so smitten with the thin leggy model that she even cropped her hair short with a *V* at the nape of the neck. Suri's ears were not her best feature, and she spent considerable time hiding the point of her ears with the small amount of hair left after the daring haircut. Shelly wore a green qameez over white shalwar, a nylon net dupatta clinging to her neck, and her hair in two thick coils over her shoulders. Raka as usual wore a sari. Daisy wore her straight blue shift dress. She was Chinese with the characteristic poker straight hair and each Saturday night slept with curlers so that her hair would be curly for church the next morning, which invariably failed to happen.

When the girls returned to the college, after Shelly's gorgeous fun-filled birthday dinner, both the main gate and the side gate were locked. This was anticipated, so Najma's car was drawn against the wall, and the girls climbed on the front bonnet one by one and dropped over to the other side carrying the white sheets. As soon as they landed they wrapped themselves in the sheets and walked quietly toward the dorm, which was on the first floor in an annex connected to the main building by a walkway. No dogs were in sight.

"I told you the white sheets would work," Daisy announced triumphantly.

"I will believe it only when we get to the dorm." Shelly was worried.

The white ghosts of the convent walked up the stairs and on to the walkway. Then in the light coming through the main door of the dorm, they saw Sister David holding the leash of the two dogs lying unconcerned near the hem of her white habit. Someone had snitched.

"Well! Well! What have we here? More nuns in the convent, right?"

"Sister!...we were just trying to see if your dogs would...in white...it's Shelly's birthday...we're sorry," was what the girls could come up with collectively as explanation.

"I know what you were all up to! Breaking the rules is not acceptable. And going out to meet boys! You are all wicked. We will have to inform your parents."

"Please, Sister, we just went out to dinner...You can ask in the restaurant...we were there all the time...Please do not tell our parents..." the girls mumbled.

"You know the rules!"

"Sister, please we beg you, please, please, please."

Sister David's hard face softened somewhat now that she had reduced the girls to blathering idiots.

"Okay, since this is the first time, I will be lenient with you. See that this does not happen again. But all of you will have to do twenty hours of study room each."

The girls groaned but did not protest. Study room was the most torturous form of punishment. One had to sit in the classroom from six to eight in the evening and pretend to study under the supervision of one member of the duty society, comprised of girls who liked to butter up the nuns. They were sure to be put in separate rooms. Ten days was unbearable. But the fun they had that evening was worth it.

Boys were not allowed inside the college, except as participants of the debates and science fairs, when young men from the counterpart boy's convent college came to the girl's college. These rules did not deter the girls from meeting their boyfriends. It was not as though the no-male-female-relationship policy of the nuns was sacrosanct either. The pretty vice principal of the college was rumored to be in love with a young handsome priest from the St. Joseph's Boys' School located down the road from New Market. When she went away for good, it was said that she had finally cast aside her vows and run away with her lover. It was all such delicious gossip. If nuns and priests could conduct affairs, why were the girls forbidden? So the girls would sneak out to meet their boyfriends. As the attendance in class was strictly monitored and the threshold for tolerance of absence was low, the girls could absent themselves only with parental permission. Many girls became expert forgers of parental signatures.

The laboratories for practical classes were held in a small double-storied building on the left of the main gate with the chemistry labs on the upper floor. The lab assistant, a young man named Samuel, dispensed the acids and other chemicals to the girls who went in for the practical classes. He was a thin nervous sort of man always dressed in white pants, white shirts, and the chemist's coat that everyone was required to wear in the lab. The girls were fond of him, treating him like a kid brother. He had recently converted from Hinduism to Christianity and had come here from Bogra. A large community of Christians lived there and Suri's Abbu had helped get the YMCA a telephone connection. The chemistry professor bullied Samuel mercilessly. If he made even the slightest mistake, the tongue-lashing was unbearable.

"You incompetent fool…who hired you for this? Look, girls, he does not know the difference between sulfuric acid and hydrochloric acid."

Not that the girls knew the difference either, at least not visually. They depended on him to give them the right stuff, and there were never any mishaps. But the professor picked on him relentlessly. The girls could see how the man cringed and bore all this abuse because he was poor and needed the work. They even complained to the nuns, who did not give their concern much attention.

One morning around eight Suri's class was scheduled to be in the lab, but the door that led upstairs, which Samuel opened each morning, was locked. He slept in a little room next to the lab. The girls knocked and pounded the door to no avail. Then someone got Sister David, and even she was unable to get any response. Joseph, the cook and all-purpose helper, was summoned, and he climbed a bamboo ladder to the first-floor veranda. He then broke the glass of a window and entered the lab. A few minutes later

Joseph came down the stairs and opened the front door. His face was ashen, and he looked sick.

"What's wrong, Joseph? Where is Samuel?"

"Sister…"

"What is it?"

"Come with me…"

Shelly could not contain her impatience and slipped past Joseph and ran up the stairs,

"Stop her, Sister…"

Sister David followed. The other girls remained downstairs. Joseph did not go up again.

Shelly came running down, "His eyes are still open…" her voice quivered.

"What are you saying?"

"His mouth…" And Shelly threw up.

In the night, Samuel had decided to end it all by drinking acid. He was still alive when Joseph found him, barely breathing, frothing blood and foam in the mouth. A note found by his side revealed that he was in love with a girl in the chemistry class, and he cursed the chemistry teacher for insulting him in front of her, and because of him, she paid no heed to him. The girls wondered for days about whom he was in love with and thought that he should have stood up to the teacher instead of taking his own life in this awful manner. They would have been on his side. The cold-hearted chemistry teacher exhibited no remorse.

All the male teachers in the college were peculiar, perhaps overwhelmed by the young girls milling around. The physics professor was short, bald, and stammered when a student asked him a question. The senior chemistry teacher walked around talking to a model of the benzene molecule. The tall handsome economics professor was referred to as Samson, maybe, because he had large biceps that constantly threatened to escape the sleeves of his tight shirt. He married a very short student from the BA class. They made quite a pair. Everyone wondered if he picked her up to kiss her!

The male teachers also taught in the boy's convent college located in Motijheel which was the main business center of Dacca. Father Thomas was the principal there, and with his intense blue eyes he looked just like Peter O'Toole. He was a biologist and had been credited with discovering a kind of roundworm nematode. Father Thomas would be summoned to teach that particular topic in biology to the girls who were in the premedical science group. He came to the college on his bicycle with his white habit tucked at the waist and the bottom of his white trousers clipped at the ankles. Some girls who were not even in the science section would crowd into his class. Sister David would come, shoo these girls away, and behave in a coy and sweet manner, not at all like her real dragon self.

"Look at her fluttering her eyes!" "She really wants to impress Father Thomas!" "But he does not even look at her!" were the most commonly heard comments at such times.

The most glamorous girls in the college were those who came with their civil service secretary fathers posted in Dacca from West Pakistan. Usually when these girls joined the college, sometimes in the middle of a term, they behaved in a snobbish and arrogant manner, as though they were somehow superior to the "natives." This attitude, everyone said, was a result of the indoctrination of their fathers who believed somehow that those in East Pakistan were inferior. To be fair, though, after a few weeks these girls would realize their new friends were lots of fun, and they did not want to leave even if their fathers were posted to their old homes. Some, like Usaila, everyone called her Ursula from the James Bond film *Dr. No*, preferred to stay in the dorm for as long as they could. Ammi said she understood why. There was too much emphasis in West Pakistan on appearance and how things looked rather than how things were. Ammi said she had seen this tendency in her own brother's home. Suri, however, knew that Usaila stayed back because she was having an affair with a boy here. Maheen was also from West Pakistan, specifically from Lahore. Her father was a general in the Army and had been in Dacca for some years now. She lived in the Cantonment not far from the college. Maheen was different and not as glamorous with short bobbed hair and freckled face. She was a carefree, energetic tomboy, and fit right in with Suri's gang of friends. Shelly especially liked her and made sure that she was included in all their shenanigans.

During the two years of college, several girls got married. Why they would do so, especially when so young, was strange. But everyone loved to attend the weddings and gossip about what went on afterward. Most of the girls from the college who got married did so to Bengali civil services officers who trained in the Pakistan Civil Services Academy in West Pakistan. Apparently these men favored the convent girls.

Nargis's cousin married before she even completed her first year. Suri, Shelly, and Najma gathered in Nargis's house to dress and go to the wedding in the big white Shahbagh Hotel on Mymensingh Road. They had their hair coiffed and set at the hairdresser's, sitting under the large helmet dryers for what seemed like hours. Suri's hair was still very short, and the hairdresser made a big pouf out of it so she tamped it down as soon as she got to Nargis's house.

The wedding was quite boring except for the fact that the bride fainted on the dais. Nargis said she was faking it to show how delicate she was. It was obvious what she thought of her cousin. What would have been fun was the *gaye hulood*, the yellowing of the body, when turmeric paste mixed with fragrant oils is symbolically rubbed on the bride's skin to impart a golden glow. This premarital ceremony had been skipped because the groom was scheduled to report to his first posting in Islamabad, the new capital of Pakistan. He was to do so within days of graduating from the Academy and therefore had only a week to get married. It took almost five hours to fly to Islamabad from Dacca by the Boeing 707s that the Pakistan International Airlines used.

When Abbu first went to Islamabad for a conference, he came back quite unimpressed with the city. "It looks so derelict and uninviting," he said.

"Obviously what do you expect from a city filled with bureaucrats!" Ammi remarked. "And tell me why the capital had to be moved to Islamabad? Karachi is so much closer to us here." This city by the sea was the center of business activities as well as an important seaport. The ruling elite in West Pakistan said that the capital was shifted to Islamabad because Karachi was too vulnerable to naval and air attack by India, but everyone knew it was because the Field Marshal's digestion was always precarious there.

The people of East Pakistan did not like this move. They had an affinity with Karachi, they could go there by sea, the air route was shorter, and it was more cosmopolitan. But as usual they had not been consulted.

"The new capital is on the side of the Margalla hills," Abbu added. "You know what *margalla* means? The throat of the snake! What a peculiar name."

In the Convent College library, the girls discovered Dostoevsky. Then Sister Marian introduced them to Kazantzakis with *Zorba the Greek* and *Report to Greco*, and it was as if the doorway to a spiritual world opened for them. Sister Marian was the literature teacher and made them read long passages from Bernard Malamud and about humans being meaningless ciphers and hung up art work in the common room with quotes taken from Kazantzakis like, "My entire soul is a cry, and all my work is a commentary on that cry." Also discussed with great enthusiasm were theories of existentialism and Sartre and Camus. Dostoevsky was depressing, but the more depressing the better. *Brothers Karamazov* and the grand inquisition and the odor of corruption were all reviewed too. They read *And Quiet Flows the Don* by Michael Sholokov when he won the Nobel Prize. It helped that Russian books were relatively inexpensive. There were deep discussions, and Suri felt heady whenever she participated in discussing topics like "what did Kazantzakis mean when he said, 'when Charon comes to claim your soul...'" or "is the title *The Medium Is the Massage* actually 'medium is the message,'" etc.

Abbu was posted back to Dacca and placed in an administrative post. Used to more technical work, he did not like this posting. As well he felt that something had begun to change in the attitudes of the hierarchy in his organization. Abbu was a bit disconcerted at this. "Mumtaz, there is some talk of giving good posts to only sons-of-the-soil. And you know what that means? Only people born on this soil and not people like me who came here from India in 1947 are to be considered for good posts."

"It's probably just a bit of frustration against the center in Islamabad. You know how they are, always sending people from the western wing to the highest plum posts. And with the League putting forward its six-point demand for greater say in the government they are getting more and more obnoxious with us here."

"You're right! It's not fair that people who live here and work here all through their careers get short-circuited after attaining the level of divisional heads. We are rarely promoted beyond this or posted to the headquarters as heads of departments. It's not fair. But for those here to take it out on people who were not born here is also not fair. "

"I'm sure it's just temporary."

"I hope so. Otherwise, it would be very frustrating. To create a category among the officers is not good. Look at our situation. Those in the head office classify us as Bengalis, and those from here say we are West Pakistanis because we are Urdu-speaking. It's not good!"

Not too happy with the work, Abbu took leave and began construction of the house in Mirpur. The settlement had recently been opened up for special allotment to government servants. Many of those who had come here at the time of the cleaving readily availed this rare opportunity to own land in the country they had opted for. The house was completed while Suri was still in the Convent College. Ammi planted the krishnachura tree in front of the wall as she did the shefali. They did not have a garden here, but Ammi grew all the seasonal flowers in pots and kept them on the verandas in both the ground floor and the first floor. She grew marigolds in winter, and zinnias lent their shades of pink to summer.

During the weekends when Suri came home from the dorm, the dinner table conversations invariably drifted to the conspiracy purportedly hatched in the Indian city of Agartala against the country by Sheikh Mujib, who headed the Awami League. He had been arrested by the Pakistani government on charges of treason along with several Bengali Army officers. Ammi was convinced it was in retaliation to the six points that the League had set forth to attain greater autonomy from the central government. Shelly's father was now an active League member and fully supported the demands for East Pakistan to have a say in running Pakistan.

"The West Pakistani bureaucrats must have become apoplectic when they saw the demand. What does your father say? He was in the delegation that talked to them," Ammi asked Shelly when she was staying over one weekend.

"Why would they, Chachi?" Shelly replied. "We are only asking for the right to make some decisions for ourselves. See how we were left vulnerable to Indian attack in the 1965 war."

"You know how they are. They think we in East Pakistan don't have the capacity to rule," Ammi responded.

"Why would anyone go all the way to Agartala to conspire is what I would like to know?" Suri asked.

Agartala was the capital of the Indian state of Tripura and lay a mile or so from the southeastern border of East Pakistan across Kalurghat Bridge via Kaptai. From Dacca, it took four hours by road to traverse the seventy-five miles to Tripura state.

"Ayub Khan probably thinks that if he involves India in the conspiracy for East Pakistan to secede from Pakistan, then it becomes treason," Shelly replied.

"It's so silly," Ammi said. "We still look at everything through the prism of Pakistan's enmity with India. Instead of talking to the League the bureaucrats are bullying the leaders to give up their rightful demand to have a greater say in the affairs of Pakistan. We should not yield."

The conspiracy case was built around the charge that some Bengali officers were making 'false' claims that the people of West Pakistan overwhelmingly dominated the military.

"It is not a false claim but absolutely true," Abbu remarked. "Even the paramilitary forces like the East Pakistan Rifles are controlled by them. Remember all the Punjabi officers we met in Rajshahi."

These Bengali officers, it was alleged, had decided to make East Pakistan independent through an armed uprising.

"Of course, before it could actually happen, the conspiracy was detected by the ever vigilant intelligence department of the government and nipped in the bud!" Ammi's voice scarcely hid her sarcasm.

Thirty-five conspirators including the Sheikh had been arrested. The angry officialdom was bent on identifying them as separatists and agents of India.

"Going to prison is very hard," Shelly told her. "A lot of people break under the pressure. But just watch, the Sheikh will not give up."

"He should not!" Suri remarked.

During the trial of the so-called Bengali conspirators, the Field Marshal decided to celebrate the Decade-of-Development in Pakistan. Ammi expressed her consternation when Abbu told her that they had received memos to cooperate in the festivities.

"This is really the last straw! We are being taken for granted. They do not understand that we are going through a painful time with the Sheikh and others facing treason charges…It's almost as if they are sticking their tongues out to us."

"We have been asked to organize seminars to adulate the Field Marshal."

"Who does he think he is, the Emperor of Pakistan? This arrogance is unbelievable."

"They want us to focus on the Second Capital Complex that he is having built in Dacca."

The Second Capital Complex was conceived by the Field Marshal as a monument to modernity and a gift to East Pakistan. The famous architect Louis Kahn was hired to design the entire complex with parliamentary building and offices surrounded by lakes and parks.

"Imagine he is building a second capital in Dacca and a federal capital in a new location in West Pakistan wasting all that money. Why does he not concentrate on the economic inequality between East and West Pakistan? The center does not invest anything here although it takes all the revenues from the export of jute."

Then a sergeant, number seventeen on the list of the accused in the conspiracy allegedly hatched to cede from Pakistan, was shot and killed in prison. The streets of Dacca boiled over, and turmoil ensued. The road in front of the Convent College was blocked, and the girls who did not live in the dorms could not go home till late in the night. News of the shooting spread like wildfire in the city. A furious mob marched to the Secretariat building near Jinnah Avenue, where the conspiracy case was being tried by bureaucrats from West Pakistan, and set it on fire. Those trying the case had to be evacuated secretly.

Faced with the prospect of a massive movement against him, the Field Marshal withdrew the charges. All those put behind bars were released and the next day on February 23, 1969, a huge public reception was arranged for the freed men in the racecourse ground where Sheikh Mujib was bestowed the title of *Bongobondhu,* Friend of the Bengali People.

The protests by the people of East Pakistan against Field Marshal Ayub Khan's rule did not die down with the release of the prisoners. He tried to contain it, but when the people of Karachi also came out against him, he handed over power to General Yahya on March 25, 1969. In his first television address to the nation, this General promised that he would hold elections so that people could make the government of their choice.

"They will never do that…" Ammi hated the generals.

"Maybe they will have to this time," Abbu replied.

VII

"Are you sure it was not because we are from the convent?" Suri had asked Rumi about their first encounter in the Dacca University.

"Initially," he replied, "we wanted to come over and chat up the convent girls because we are convent boys. But really, Suri, I came to see you specifically. I knew immediately that you were the one for me." Rumi was so romantic.

Suri was sitting in the University library with her friends Nargis and Najma when three boys came over to their table and tried to engage them in conversation. They were shushed away, but they persisted and introduced themselves as Rumi, Moti, and Naveed. This was a brazen move especially for Rumi who was quite shy.

"Come on! Was it not your idea to approach the girls?" Suri asked him this each time she wanted to hear him say that he had eyes only for her.

"It was! I saw you from a distance and said to myself that this girl I want to meet."

"You did not know anything about me, so why the interest?" Suri was fishing for compliments.

"You were in animated conversation with your friends, and you looked so lively. I had to meet you. It was just one of those unexplainable desires."

"I don't believe in the 'love at first sight' stuff!" Suri was thrilled at this disclosure but did not want to let on.

"But it is true."

"I don't believe you!"

That first meeting was a disaster as far as Rumi was concerned. Naveed totally dominated the conversation in the library. Rumi had not been able to get in more than a few words through Naveed's monologue of how much he knew about the world. Naveed was from Lahore and lived in the university hostel. He even invited all of them to his large government-owned bungalow in Chittagong and said he would arrange for them to cruise around on his father's boat. His father was the port master there. Naveed was such a showoff, but he did have a fun way of looking at everything. Rumi was sure that Suri had not even noticed him, but she had and was struck by his dreamy eyes. Maybe she too fell in love at first sight but would not admit it.

Something unexpected had occurred during Suri's university admissions process. Her name did not appear on the merit list of those admitted to her department, even though she was placed in the honors list of the Intermediate examination and Najma and Nargis were not. When she went to the administration office to inquire, the clerk told her that her documents were incomplete and that she needed to give proof that she was born in East Pakistan.

"That is a funny request. I was born here," Suri told the clerk.

"I don't know! Your mark sheet says that you took Urdu as your vernacular subject, so how do we know you are not from West Pakistan?"

"I am not, but even if I am so what. We are one country, are we not?"

"Yes! But now we have quota for students from West Pakistan just as they do for students from East Pakistan. Only a limited number of our students are allowed there, so we are going to do the same."

This situation was upsetting. Suri was born at home, so there was no official proof of birth. Nor was there any reason to get one. The problem was resolved by getting an affidavit stating that Suri was born in East Pakistan, but it left a lingering uncertainty. When Sadi joined the university two years earlier, no such demand had been made of him. Ammi thought it was the stupid Agartala conspiracy charges made by the bureaucrats of West Pakistan against the Sheikh that had begun to divide the people. Nothing good would come out of this, she said.

After the first meeting, Suri bumped into Rumi everywhere on the campus, in the administration office, in the bank, in the corridors. It was almost as though he knew where she would be at all times, not that she minded. Nargis observed that they were becoming an exclusive pair, and Suri mildly protested.

A few weeks into the classes, Nargis invited Suri and Najma to go with her to Mymensingh, seventy-five miles north of Dacca, to see a Kathak dance drama choreographed by her dance guru. They left early in the morning with Nargis's mother in her Volkswagen Beetle and were to stay overnight at the government rest house on the banks of the old Brahmaputra River. The lower reaches of this river was sacred to the Hindus. Also Brahmaputra meaning 'son of Brahmo' was a rare male name for a river when all the others in the Ganges River system had female names.

Mymensingh was the birthplace of Nazrul Islam, the rebel poet who now lived in self-exile in Calcutta. His poem "I am the trembling first touch of the virgin, I am the throbbing tenderness of her first stolen kiss...I am hell's mad terrific sea of wrath...I am the rebel eternal..." was a powerful rallying cry for the downtrodden. But Suri especially liked his more melodic song "In this festival of flowers, why is the poet so sad."

The dance drama they had come to see was about the famous love affair between Anarkali, a ravishingly beautiful commoner, and Saleem, the heir to the Mughal throne. The female dancers all wore *peshwaz*, the dress worn by the ladies of the Mughal court, with fitting bodice and pleated skirt, tight *churidar* pajamas, and trailing veils. According to a legend, three and a half centuries ago, the sister of emperor Shahjahan, wearing an exquisite jamavar *peshwaz*, was walking along the ramparts of the Red Fort in Delhi. The fort was lit up with torches and aromatic amber candles in celebration of her birthday. Her trailing veil brushed a candle, and the fire threatened to engulf the princess. Four ladies-in-waiting threw themselves on her to douse the flames. Two died of burns, and the princess almost lost her life. Needless to say the birthday celebrations were a disaster, as was the dance performance in Mymensingh. The lead girl forgot all her cues, and the guru was in tears. Nargis was livid at the lead dancer for causing so much pain to her guru. But Suri and Najma enjoyed the evening because they were unaware of the mistakes.

While Suri was away, Rumi called at least a hundred times. She had not told him of the trip. Ammi, aware of his frantic behavior, asked Suri what was troubling him. She also questioned Suri's preoccupation and the fact that she almost failed in her first class test. Suri mumbled some excuse about group study, but she knew that Ammi was not convinced. Her brother, Sadi, guessed that her conversations on the phone with Rumi were not for study purposes and did not disguise his disdain for whomever his sister was having an affair.

Shelly was thrilled when Suri told her about Rumi. "He is tall and slim with the dreamiest eyes possible. You should see his eyelashes!"

"I have to meet him!" Shelly was in another department, and Suri rarely met her on campus.

"You will, soon," Suri told her.

"Ask him to come to the student center tomorrow for lunch."

"Okay, but I'm not sure Rumi will come. He's quite shy."

"Come on! He did approach you quite brazenly, did he not?" Shelly teased Suri.

"Okay, Okay. I'll see you tomorrow."

The next day Suri waited with Shelly for Rumi to show up at the Teacher Student Center. When Rumi walked in, as usual with his shirt untucked, a thick mop of hair falling over his forehead, and a lopsided gait, Suri's heart skipped several beats, and her face felt flushed. Her entire being soared with happiness, and at that instant, she knew that she wanted to be with him forever.

Shelly teased her afterward. "You should have seen your face. It had such a silly grin."

"Come on. My face was quite composed."

"Really, Suri, you cannot hide your feelings for him. Your eyes were sparkling. I have never seen anyone more in love."

"I am not in love with him! We are good friends!"

"You and I are good friends," Shelly remarked. "You and he are in love."

Suri knew that this was an argument she was not going to win.

Nargis with her doe eyes and fabulous figure managed to break many hearts in those first months on the campus. She blithely flirted, but when she met her army captain at the department's annual picnic in a coconut grove in Joydebpur, she was truly smitten. He was a classmate's cousin and was posted in the Joydebpur Cantonment. A few months later they were married. He had been transferred to the garrison headquarters and wanted Nargis to go with him.

Suri and Najma helped get everything organized for the wedding. The dais on which Nargis was to sit for the prewedding *gaye hulood* ceremony was covered with a yellow sheet that had red motifs printed on it. The bamboo canopy decorated with paper streamers and strings of flowers sheltered the bride from the soft evening sun. Nargis wore the traditional red bordered yellow sari like those worn to celebrate spring, and to pay respect to the six martyrs. Her arms, wrists, hair, and neck were bedecked with garlands of white fragrant beli flowers interspersed with red roses. The married women in the gathering lined up to take turns at first daubing their own foreheads with the turmeric paste, and then doing the same on the bride's forehead, thus transferring the good fortune of women who were blissfully wed on to the bride. This was followed by putting a piece of *ladoo,* the traditional wedding sweet, in the bride's mouth. Widows and divorcees were not allowed to take part in this ritual so that their perceived bad luck would not somehow be given to the bride.

Once the rituals were over, Suri slipped away to join Rumi, who was waiting for her near the gate. They had arranged this rendezvous so that the meeting would be camouflaged by the wedding rituals. Suri felt a little guilty doing this, but she lived for the time she spent with Rumi. They walked over to his house, which was a couple of lanes away, and sat on the patio at the back under the stars. The gardenia bush next to the patio was in full bloom with large smooth creamy white flowers. The fragrance that wafted in the air could only be described as flowing from heaven.

They held hands and kissed. Rumi said that everyone was away, and they were alone in the house. The hour with him passed by in a whirl of exquisite pleasure that bound them forever as one. When Rumi walked her back to Nargis's house, she could not bear to let him go. The next day they met at the wedding reception in the Intercontinental Hotel. With Rumi by her side, and in her orange and gold chamois satin sari, Suri felt like a bride herself. Nargis left for West Pakistan with her husband. He had to resume his duties in the garrison headquarters in Rawalpindi.

After sneaking out that evening, Suri decided to invite Rumi to her house and introduce him to her family. All the lying to her parents was clouding her otherwise perfect love for Rumi. On that first visit he was a bit nervous.

Rumi asked, "How shall I address your mother?"

"Call her Chachi! I call your mother that and relax. I have already told Ammi about you."

On the day Rumi was to visit, Suri wore her blue checked sleeveless shirt over white pants. Such ensembles had become very popular after the famous designer, Pierre Cardin, changed the uniforms of the PIA hostesses from white shalwar and green qameez to form fitting A-line tunics and slim line trousers. Suri's slightly wavy hair had grown to shoulder length by now, and she got Munni to straighten it by running a warm iron over it. When Rumi arrived, he was greeted by Ammi and taken to the drawing room. The pink and magenta zinnias in the flowerpots made the day look as festive as the feeling in Suri's heart. Ammi asked Rumi about his studies and his family.

"My father was a judge of the Dacca High Court, and now he practices law," he said.

"Where are your parents from?"

Suri was surprised at this question.

"They're from here, Ammi!" A whiff of annoyance crept into Suri's voice.

"I am only asking this because Rumi speaks very good Urdu," Ammi said. "I meant no offense."

"None taken Chachi. My mother and uncle studied in Delhi, my uncle is a graduate of St.Stephen's college. Both are great lovers of Urdu poetry. My uncle keeps quoting Ghalib and other Urdu poets, so we have picked up some of the finer aspects of the language as well."

Rumi's maternal grandfather was a record keeper in the Indian Legislative Assembly, and the family shifted between Nainital and Delhi depending on where the government worked during winter and summer. After she was married, Rumi's mother lived in Calcutta as did her older sister, Lal bhai's mother. All of them, like other Muslims, opted to come to Pakistan at the time of the cleaving.

"Ammi, I did tell you that Rumi's cousin Lal bhai is one of the martyrs?"

"Yes! That is terrific," Ammi exclaimed. Realizing that she was applauding the death of a young man, she quickly added, "I don't mean that it's terrific he died but that he gave his life to such a great cause."

"Yes it is, Chachi."

"Beta, can I ask why do you call him Lal?"

"Lal was his *daknaam,* his pet name…"

"But why Lal? It means red?" Suri interrupted.

"No reason. Just like there is no link between my formal name Mansoor and my *daknaam* Rumi…"

"But there is a connection between Suraiya and Suri."

"It's a cultural thing," Rumi explained.

"You mean we have different cultures!"

"A little different, don't you think?"

"Now, don't argue," Ammi interceded. "We also have such customs like calling the youngest daughter Munni and the oldest Burhki."

"Ammi, can I go to Rumi's house?" Suri brazenly changed the subject.

"Yes, but only if Rumi's parents do not mind."

"No, they don't at all," Rumi said.

"Bring them over sometime," Ammi told him. "I'd love to meet them."

"I will, Chachi. You come too."

When Ammi left them alone in the drawing room, Rumi burst out laughing. "Asking your mother if you could come to my house was really too much, Suri. You are shameless…"

"Yes! And you love me for it!"

"I do. I do."

Each year the Martyr's Day commemorated the death of Lal bhai and five other young Bengali men killed by the police on the twenty-first day of February in 1952 while protesting the imposition of Urdu as the national language of Pakistan. When the day arrived for the first time after they met, Suri went with Rumi to the memorial in front of the Dacca Medical College. The memorial was covered with orange and yellow marigolds, and Suri was drawn into the moment. She derided herself for not having come before. When the early morning rituals at the memorial were over, Rumi asked Suri to come to his house in the evening to meet his cousins from Chittagong who had also come to pay their respects to Lal bhai. They were a lot of fun he said. Suri asked Ammi if she could go. Ammi said she could, but she must be back by nine. This was like the curfew hours in the dorm, but Suri did not protest. Dressed in her special white sari with green and gold paisley motifs and border, she left home early in the evening, her heart overflowing with joy. After greeting his mother, Suri followed Rumi to his room at the back where they had spent many hours together, especially when the classes on campus were postponed. They had taken rickshaws to come here and returned when it was time for the family car to pick her up. Suri knew this was sneaky thing to do, but she wanted to be with him all the time.

Rumi's cousins were there along with Lal bhai's son. The cousins were pop singers and played for a band called The Lightnings in Chittagong. Rumi's favorite music was the sound of the Beatles, the Shadows, and the Ventures. He loved Suri enough to lend her his records collection including his prized possession, Sergeant Pepper's Lonely Heart Band LP. He would strum Love, Love Me Do on his guitar and make Suri sing with him. She was an awful singer, tone deaf as Sadi would say, but Rumi thought she was good. Love is blind as they say and, as Suri always pointed out, in her case it was deaf as well. Rumi was so like Abbu who always said his Suri cooed like a koel.

All that evening they chatted, nibbled on salty white cheese, and drank tea. The cousins strummed their guitars and sang Simon and Garfunkel and Bob Dylan songs. Suri and Rumi joined in, to guitar accompaniment, of the cousins' rendition of popular *bhatiali* and *bhawaiya* folk songs like "*bogha kande rey*...the heron weeps in the middle of the pond." Why the heron would weep in the middle of the pond was not clear, but the lyrics sung by bullock-cart drivers as they plodded along in the night were really quite sad. As was the boatman's lament of "*aage jaanley tor bhanga naukae*...if I had known I would not have come on board your leaking boat."

That night Suri told the family at dinner about how Lal bhai's son did not speak to her. Ammi said maybe he was shy, but Abbu thought it was probably because she was Urdu speaking. On this day when his father's martyrdom for the Bengali language is being commemorated, he must have been emotional, Abbu said. He must think that because Urdu spoken by a minority was forcibly imposed on the majority who spoke Bengali, his father had been killed. It's hard to accept.

Still bothered by his nephew's behavior, Suri brought up the subject with Rumi the next day on campus.

"My nephew takes his legacy very seriously," Rumi explained.

"He must have been just a baby when his father was killed?"

"He was born three months after his father was killed and was taken to his father's grave for the first time when he was just a few weeks old."

"To the memorial?"

"No! He was brought to Azimpur graveyard where his father and three others were buried. The memorial was built later. In fact, his grandfather laid the foundation for the memorial, and perhaps, all this makes him so somber and serious."

"Why would he not talk to me?"

"I think it's because he is shy."

"Are you sure?"

"Yes, I am."

That year, life on the campus was tumultuous. The protests against the false Agartala conspiracy to cede from Pakistan imposed on Sheikh Mujib and other officers did not die down even after the Field Marshal gave up power to General Yahya. The student unions fully participated in the protest against the Martial Law that the General continued to adhere to. There were many clashes between rival student parties. Rumi and Moti supported the student arm of the League, as did Suri and Shelly, while others, purportedly more left leaning in their belief supported the National Awami Party, led by the firebrand Maulana Bhashani. Naveed, who was a Punjabi from Lahore generally stayed away from publicly discussing politics and union activities but privately sympathized with the League. Added to union clashes were unified protests against acts of the military government.

By 1970, the misgivings and complaints of domination over East Pakistan by West Pakistan became full-blown issues. To allay some of mistrust brought on by the conspiracy case as well as the fact that East Pakistan was left vulnerable to India's attack during the 1965 war, the General announced that elections for a civilian government would be held in December. Preparations for the elections began with student participation in huge numbers. Suri and Rumi attended many campaign meetings organized by the student arm of the League in support of their candidates.

Then on November 13, just a month before the elections, a catastrophic cyclone and tidal wave devastated the low-lying Ganges Delta. Three hundred thousand people were swept away by the thirty-foot storm surge and 115 mile per hour winds. A few days after the storm, Mannan, who still worked as cook for Suri's family, hurried off to his hometown, Patuakhali, that lay right at the mouth of the Bay. He came back, clung to Abbu, and howled and wept. His entire family including a seven-month-old son had been washed away. Only one brother and one brother-in-law out of his large extended family had survived. Abbu asked him to bring them over to Dacca, and he would help get jobs for them. But Mannan said it was better if they remained in Patuakhali and tried to rebuild their home.

No one was warned of the storm, and the people living in the area were taken by surprise. Even relief to the living was not properly handled. Ammi and Mrs. Ahmad and the rest of the Women's Association collected clothes and food, as did other private organizations, but it was not enough. The government's apathy at providing relief created even more resentment and misgiving against the government headed by the Army, who were preoccupied with their belief that during the relief operations Indian boats had brought in weapons to help a potential insurgency against the land of the pure. After the November cyclone, all student protests coalesced against the government of General Yahya.

Rumi was by now a regular visitor to Mirpur, and he ventured there even when the floods that followed the November tidal wave and cyclone cut off the area from the city. When he got off the boat and Suri met him at the edge of the water, she felt like the heroine of the Sohni-Mahiwal legend. Ammi's storytelling abilities had made legends like Shirin-Farhad, Laila-Majnu, Sassi-Punnu, the equivalents of Romeo and Juliet, come alive: Swimming across the River Chenab to meet her Mahiwal who was beaten up and injured by her relatives and could not come to her, Sohni had drowned in the raging waters. These folk tales of love always ended in tragedy.

The day Rumi came by boat to Mirpur his childhood friend Hiru, who was a captain in the Pakistan Army, was with him. He had been posted back home from Rawalpindi just before the devastating tidal wave and was to report to the regional headquarters in Comilla, a district in the southeast on the road between Dacca and Chittagong. The Cantonment there was close to the site of the Buddhist ruins of Mainamati and a World War II cemetery.

Hiru was dashing and full of adventure. They laughed and laughed when Rumi recalled the time that Hiru had come home from Rawalpindi the first time after his commission and taken Rumi to Pabna, his hometown in the north. Pabna was flanked by the Padma River, a main artery of the Ganges, and was connected to Kushtia by the Hardinge Bridge constructed by the British. The Jamuna River ran along its eastern side. Hiru was going there supposedly to see his uncle, but the real purpose of the visit was to meet his cousin Moyna whom he was deeply in love with.

"We reached the town in the evening, and after dinner, we lounged around with Hiru's uncle and cousins…"

"Moyna was not there?" Suri asked.

"I think the uncle is a bit religious, and there was segregation in the family…

Anyway! We were given the outer room to sleep in."

Late in the night, Hiru woke Rumi and told him that he was going to an inner room to meet Moyna. Rumi warned him that if his uncle found out he would kill him. Apparently Moyna had opened the door between the room they were in and the inner house so Hiru could go to her room undetected. Rumi went back to sleep, and the next thing he heard was a loud commotion and cries of "*chor…chor…*thief…thief…" and loud banging on the front door, and Hiru's urgent voice, "Rumi, quickly open the door! Open the damn door…"

Hiru was outside, quite frazzled. He told Rumi to keep the door open and ran back into the courtyard to join the group who had by now caught the thief. When he came back, he told Rumi the reason.

"You will never guess? Of all the damn things, while I was with Moyna, a thief sneaked in through the window. It was dark in the room, and I did not see him immediately. He actually sat next to the door and watched us…"

"What were you two up to…" Rumi laughed uncontrollably even as he narrated the episode.

"Never mind that…he ran when Moyna spotted him and cried out. I had to run after him…the others got up and ran after him… it was like a bloody chase…"

In all the confusion Hiru realized that he had not come out of the front door, and if it had remained locked, people would have guessed that Hiru was in an inner room, and it would not have taken them too long to realize which room he was in. That would not have been good for Hiru.

As the date of the elections came closer, it became clear that Peoples Party led by Zulfikar Bhutto would win handily in West Pakistan, while the Awami League led by Sheikh Mujib with the six-point demand for greater autonomy would hold East Pakistan in its sway. The Jamaat-e-Islami party was relegated to the background, but they were not entirely dormant. They supported the Army and wielded great power in suppressing dissent and acting as provocateurs.

When the elections were held in December, much to Abbu's chagrin, many in Mirpur cast their votes for the Jamaat-e-Islami. "This is not good, Mumtaz. It is a big mistake."

"I agree. The Jamaatis are pretty bad and vicious."

Abbu added, "My worry is that all of us Urdu-speaking people will be singled out as a group that does not support the main-stream League because some people from Mirpur have voted for the Jamaatis."

"But we have voted for the League!" Ammi exclaimed. "And so have many of our neighbors. And the League candidate has won from our constituency. In fact, the Jamaatis did not win a single seat from East Pakistan."

"Nobody is going to look at individuals," Abbu responded. "I am quite afraid of the backlash."

"Ji, what backlash? The League will form the government, and so why should it indulge in witch-hunting?" Ammi said. "Besides it's not like the Jamaati leaders are not Bengalis. They have a right to seek power. So why should the Urdu-speaking people, who support the Jamaat-e-Islami, be targeted? You are just being paranoid."

"You're right! I am being paranoid. Everyone has a right to vote as they wish."

After the elections the process of forming the government was launched. Zulfikar Bhutto saw his chance of becoming head of the Pakistan government literally washed away by the tidal wave of support for Sheikh Mujib. In contrast to the eighty seats won by Peoples Party, the League had won 160 seats to the National Assembly. Bhutto hemmed and hedged over sitting in the Assembly.

"Why does Bhutto not just come to the assembly and get on with it?" Ammi voiced her indignation at the delay.

"He is too ambitious and wants to be prime minister. He cannot conceive of not getting power," Abbu replied.

"But his Peoples Party did not win the majority! Why is the leader with lesser seats being given more importance by General Yahya than the party with the most seats?" Suri wanted to understand the dynamics of what would become a disaster.

"I know, but it's almost as if the army has assured him that he would be the next prime minister," Ammi responded. "It is so stupid of them!"

While the League did not win a single seat in West Pakistan, the Peoples Party failed completely in East Pakistan. The political chasm, centering on economic inequality and unequal say in the government, between the two parts of Pakistan was now deep and seemingly unbridgeable. There was much anger in East Pakistan at Zulfikar Bhutto for putting impossible conditions like having two prime ministers, one for each wing, and threatening to break the legs of anyone who attended the Assembly session in Dacca.

"This is all so ridiculous. He should stop trying to please the army to get power and behave like a representative of the people," Moti remarked when Naveed, Rumi, and Suri discussed the situation on campus.

"Look," Suri said, "Bhutto is from a feudal background and was nurtured as foreign minister by the Field Marshal himself. He probably thinks that Bengalis cannot rule the country."

"Nothing good will come out of this." Rumi was very worried.

Naveed did not say much except that Bhutto was a charismatic and intelligent man.

VIII

With the overwhelming December election victory in hand, student groups in Dacca began to plan the celebrations that were sure to ensue when Sheikh Mujib, their chosen leader and head of the League, was declared the Prime Minister of Pakistan. Through January and February 1971, the entire campus waited with baited breath for the outcome of the negotiations for the formation of the government. That February, Suri again went with Rumi to the martyr's memorial, and this time it seemed that Lal bhai's sacrifice had not been in vain. The people of East Pakistan would at last be able to have a say in their country. However, when the negotiations with General Yahya and the Peoples Party dragged on, some of the enthusiasm gave way to concern and even anger.

As 1971 led into March, the koel cooed as usual, and the scent of mango blossoms wafted in the air. The litchi trees covered with greenish yellow clusters of flowers ready to change to round red fruits, and the leaf canopy of the *jamun* trees interspersed with fragrant white flowers each promising to become a luscious purple berry gently swayed in the breeze. Life's renewal was signaled by the flooding of the rice fields for the sowing of the boro crop and the spawning of small tilapia fish in the ponds.

On the first day of the month, at around noon, Suri was attending classes when she felt a tremor run through the campus. There were excited whispers in the room, and some high-pitched voices could be heard coming from the direction of the canteen. The corridors filled up with students. Her professor became distracted, and when the commotion picked up in intensity, he dismissed the class.

Suri walked toward Rumi's department. Maybe he knew what was happening. She saw Rumi in the corridor heading her way.

"The damned general has postponed the opening session of the Assembly." He almost shouted. The General, unwilling to hand over power to Sheikh Mujib and his League, had decided to postpone the sitting of the newly elected Assembly to give Bhutto time to find a way to take over as Prime Minister.

"What?" Suri was aghast at this development.

Naveed joined them, and they stood in the corridor overlooking the grounds, watching the frenzy build. A large number of students gathered in front of the canteen shouting slogans against General Yahya and the Army. Then they marched out of the gate and turned right toward New Market, probably on their way to the Sheikh's house on the banks of Dhanmandi Lake.

Suri, Rumi, and Naveed waited for things to quiet down and then walked over to the British Council. Suri called Ammi on the public phone to tell her that the driver should pick her up at the Teacher Student Center before collecting Munni and Sami. They would have to take the longer route home through the Second Capital Complex since their usual route down the road in front of New Market was probably blocked with protestors.

Moti joined them in the Center. He had more information about what was going on with the protest.

"The teachers are getting ready for some big event." Moti's cousin was a Professor in the university.

"Like what?"

"My cousin thinks that the city will be placed under very strict martial law rules."

"Why doesn't the general just call the assembly session and let the leaders work it out?" Suri remarked.

"Do you think the army has brains enough to see that this is the best way?" Moti answered contemptuously.

"No, I don't..." Suri conceded.

"Besides they think we Bengalis are not capable of running the government."

"You do know what they say about the army…they shoot first and ask questions later."

Naveed reminded them of the time the soldiers did not shoot at the protestors.

"But that was Punjabi soldiers refusing to shoot at Punjabi protestors in Lahore. They will not hold their fire here. They think we are lesser beings…" The Pakistan Army consisted overwhelmingly of officers and soldiers from West Pakistan.

"Just wait and see how fast curfew is slapped on us," Moti told Naveed.

"We had all better get home as quickly as possible."

Two days later defying the curfew, some students and teachers raised a red, gold, and green flag in the campus declaring their intentions of forming a new state. This was a clear renunciation of Pakistan. The Pakistani flag was green and white. When she heard of this from Rumi, a chill went down Suri's spine.

"Does this mean that we in East Pakistan want a new country?"

"Can you blame us? If people are treated like dirt, this is what happens!"

"You're right. But maybe this is too extreme and too quick. We should leave room for talks."

"But they are the ones who say that if the people of East Pakistan do not budge from the six-point demand for autonomy, then there is no point in negotiating." Among the six points of demand were separate currencies and economic reform to remove the disparity between East and West Pakistan.

"Well! The League does say that this is what they will stick to at all costs. So both sides have to work it out."

"I agree, but the West Pakistani side has the might of the army and we do not. If they decide to let loose that force on us, what will we do?"

"Oh God, I hope things do not come to this. I am sure things will work out. After all, we did do the civilized thing and vote." Suri wanted to have faith in the system.

"I hope so too. But I am not so optimistic."

That night at dinner Ammi asked Suri about the design of the flag.

"Rumi says that a gold colored outline of East Pakistan is set within a red circle against a green background."

"Raising that flag is almost like declaring independence from Pakistan." Abbu was nervous about the unfolding events. "No window has been left open for compromise."

"It is just the students venting their frustration, Ji…"

"But Rumi says there were teachers there as well…" Suri told them.

"Now, that is not a good sign," Abbu said. "Politics should not be practiced by the teachers."

"But they cannot remain silent when things are so unfair, can they?" Suri protested.

"That is true. The people all over Pakistan have given their verdict in the first fair and free election held in the country," Abbu conceded. "And the League has won overwhelmingly, so it has made the rightful claim to govern."

"The bureaucrats will never let it happen. They always refer to the Bengalis as ungrateful, greedy, dark, and small. They refer to us as *bhookey Bengali* as if we are hungry and beg all the time. We only want what is ours."

"And that damned Bhutto has played along by agreeing to postpone the Assembly session. He is so ambitious and cannot concede that a majority of the people have not voted for him," Abbu finished her sentence.

The hoisting of the flag was followed by the launching of a noncooperation movement by the League, which ordered daily shutdowns of all businesses from seven in the morning to two in the afternoon. All across East Pakistan, everything ceased to function during those hours. Abbu came back from office every day more worried than before.

"Mumtaz, many of my colleagues from West Pakistan sensing danger are trying to leave. One of them said that young men carrying guns and knives stopped him and his family at a road block on airport road and looted their luggage."

As the political atmosphere heated up, bands of young men carrying guns calling themselves the "Liberation Front" were seen in the streets. Abbu worried that the General would surely see this as proof that Sheikh Mujib's intentions were untrustworthy and that he wanted an armed insurrection and maybe even secession of East Pakistan from the State of Pakistan. When Suri asked Rumi about these fighters, he told her that young men were being trained by a Colonel Usmani to face any potential Army violence perpetrated on the Bengalis.

"Is this Colonel from the Pakistan Army?"

"Yes! And I think they are using the weapons from the paramilitary East Pakistan Rifles stock."

"Weren't there rumors that Indian boats had brought in weapons for rebels under cover of relief operations after the tidal wave in November?" Without waiting for Rumi to answer, Suri added, "Abbu says that he has seen young men carrying weapons during the protest marches. Maybe we will not be able to just talk our way out of Yahya's stupidity of cancelling the assembly session."

"Let's see what happens! At least we are not taking anything they throw at us lying down." Rumi was elated at the prospect of defying the rulers at last, but he hoped it would be political defiance and not through violence.

On March 7, the Sheikh addressed a public meeting in the racecourse ground. Rumi and Moti were there, as were thousands of East Pakistani students and hundreds of thousands from all walks of life. Everyone carried the red, gold, and green flag. The Sheikh laid out the history of the deprivation imposed by West Pakistan on East Pakistan and the struggle for the Bengali language thus invoking Lal bhai's martyrdom. The milling crowds heard the impassioned pronouncement, "This time our struggle is for independence…"

Rumi called her as soon as the rally was over. "It was a rallying cry, Suri. It was as if a wave of energy shot through the crowd. The entire racecourse was drowned in the deluge of screams and shouts of victory…victory…*joi*…*joi*. But," he added, "Moti is disappointed that the Sheikh has not declared the independence of East Pakistan and instead called for a struggle toward it."

Abbu, however, was glad that the Sheikh had withheld the declaration of independence from Pakistan, and he expressed his relief at this at dinner that night.

"But the Army is pushing them toward it," Ammi responded.

"Yes, it is! At least for now, there is still some time to continue talking."

"But he did say that today was the first day of the struggle for independence and that each home should be turned into a fort," Suri reminded Abbu.

"He probably meant it in a metaphorical sense." Ammi still wanted to believe that there would be no violence.

"I hope so!"

"It is not right that the Army does not want the League to form the government. They have conducted the elections and should get out of the picture now," Suri asserted.

"They never have and never will take a backseat." Ammi never failed to show her disdain for the Army.

"And that Bhutto will never accept the six points. He says it preempts any attempt to reform the constitution of Pakistan that the Field Marshal formulated in 1962," Abbu said.

"And why will he not? It is a legitimate demand," Suri asked.

"Do you think they will give power to us in East Pakistan? That is impossible," Ammi responded.

Several days later Rumi's cousin, Tabu, called from Chittagong. "You heard of the troubles in Chittagong Port?"

"We did hear something. But what happened? Are all of you all right?" Rumi asked.

"We are. The trouble took place in the dock area. The workers refused to unload a cargo of ammunition that had been shipped from Karachi," Tabu told him.

Word had spread in Chittagong, and thousands gathered in the port to physically stop the deadly cargo from entering the city. They knew it would be used against them by the Army. The port authorities called in the East Pakistan Rifles to subdue the crowd.

"Was anyone hurt?" Rumi asked.

"No, the paramilitary refused to fire on the crowd…"

"Good!"

The General was livid and responded to this incident of defiance by the people of East Pakistan by sending for General Tikka, known as the Butcher for his expertise in brutally quelling disturbances. He was made the Army commander of East Pakistan, and then the General himself arrived in Dacca with Bhutto to conduct negotiations with the Sheikh.

While the talks continued, curfew was imposed in Joydebpur. This was done when an Army commander while returning after touring Joydebpur Cantonment, passed through the local bazaar and found his way blocked by a train carriage placed at the level crossing. A crowd gathered around the convoy and refused to move even when threatened. When the soldiers tried to remove the carriage, protesters fired on the soldiers, three of whom were seriously wounded. The soldiers returned fire, and two protesters were killed and several injured.

The Army commander managed to reach Dacca in the evening after removing several barricades. General Yahya and the Butcher were livid. The clash confirmed reports that local leaders had collected large quantities of arms and ammunition for use against the Army. This convinced the two that time had come for the large-scale use of force against Bengali rebels that they had been planning and providing for under cover of negotiations. The General had by now amassed a large Army of marauders in Dacca.

While negotiations continued in Dacca, the increasingly organized Liberation Front consisting of young Bengali men took over Kalurghat Radio Station near the Karnaphuli River and declared it to be the Radio of Free Bengal. They began to broadcast programs against the Army and their supporters. Tabu heard the broadcasts and worried that it would result in harm to his Urdu-speaking friends.

"They are calling for protests against the postponement of the Assembly session and for revenge on those who are not of this land Rumi. It's not good," Tabu told Rumi over the phone.

"What does it mean 'not of this land'?" Rumi asked.

"They mean all those who are from West Pakistan and…"

"And who else?" Rumi was apprehensive of Tabu might say.

"And those that have come here from India…"

"That is nonsense. We also came from there," Rumi responded angrily.

"True, but we are not Urdu speaking…that is how it is Rumi. I am afraid for all our friends who live in Chittagong! You know how the local boys hate the Ispahani boys." The descendents of the Ispahani families were originally from Isfahan, Iran. Their ancestors were scholars and historians in the Mughal Courts. Through court patronage they became successful businessmen. When Pakistan was formed Mr. Jinnah asked the Ispahanis to move their assets to East Pakistan. The Ispahani Jute Mill set up by them was the second largest such mill in Asia.

"I'm sure it is some mischief mongering." Rumi could scarcely hide his apprehension. He was worried about Suri and her family as well as Naveed.

"I hope so too."

As the port city of Chittagong descended into chaos, negotiations between Sheikh Mujib, General Yahya and Zulfikar Bhutto continued in Dacca. On March 23, a date that was celebrated as the day when the resolution for the creation of Pakistan was passed, the green and white Pakistani flag was flown on public buildings throughout the country. The Sheikh, however, decided not to do so. Instead he hoisted the red, gold, and green flag on the roof of his house in Dhanmandi. The car that he took to the President House on Bailey Road, where the talks were being held, was embellished with a similar flag. This flag fluttered over the rooftops of countless buildings across East Pakistan in a public declaration of secession from Pakistan.

Two days later, Rumi told Suri that there was an air of misgiving all around Dacca. The anxiety was palpable as if a storm was gathering and would strike at any time. "There were rumors all of last week that a forceful push will be made by the army to stop the protests. It has an ominous feel to it. Everyone is really worried," Rumi said.

"What is to happen?" Suri asked.

"Nothing good, I am sure."

"Please be careful. Stay indoors."

"Moti says that the students are sure to be the main targets because we are the most vocal and organized in our protests against what General Yahya is doing. This is horrible."

"Yes, Sadi's friend Tutul told him to vacate the hostel and stay at home," Suri said.

"Tutul is active in the Students Action Forum, so he must know something more than us," Rumi replied.

By evening the tension was so high that people came out into the streets.

At around ten that night, Sadi was sitting on the roof, of their house in Mirpur and he saw two flares light up the sky in the distance. He called out to everyone to quickly come and see what was happening. In the time it had taken them to run up the stairs, the sky in the distance had begun to glow in fiery shades of yellow and orange lined with cordite green.

"This looks like a full-fledged invasion of an enemy country. This is incredulous!" Abbu exclaimed.

"Why would the Army do this?" Suri was aghast at the sight.

"This is unbelievable! What an utterly unnecessary thing to do." Ammi was livid. "How many people that disagree with you can one kill? It will not end anything."

"All the flames seem to be from the direction of the university." Sadi hoped that Tutul had left before all this began.

As the orange flames leapt higher and higher, it was clear that General Yahya, the commander of the Pakistan Army, had given orders to use force and violence to deal with the demands of the Bengalis to form the government of Pakistan. The skies over East Pakistan were set on fire, and its streets became rivers of blood. Following his orders, and with the tacit approval of Bhutto, who is said to have watched the spectacle from his room in the Intercontinental Hotel and uttered the words 'Pakistan has been saved', Dacca was lit up with flames and explosions. Blood flowed freely in its streets.

Moti also saw the two flares shooting into the sky at ten in the night from his house in Hatkhola. The first flare seemed to have been fired from the area around Gulistan Cinema. The office of the Ittefaq newspaper sympathetic to the League was just opposite

Moti's house, and it was bombed that night. Moti saw the second flare rising from the area of the Police Lines in Shantinagar. Then he heard the sound of gunfire, and the tanks rolled in around midnight and took position at the roundabout about a hundred yards away from his house.

With the first mortar shell the press caught fire, and the flames quickly engulfed the entire building. Moti could feel the heat from the flames in his house. Many who worked in the press were able to get out through the back door, and some were trapped inside. The fires and shootings raged on for about two hours, and Moti and his parents huddled under the stairs until things quieted down. The next morning, in spite of his mother's pleas not to do so, Moti crossed the road and scooted over to the press.

Moti was distraught when he saw the horror the Army had perpetrated. There were bodies scattered all over the printing room, most of them burned beyond recognition. The room had been hit directly with mortar and the people inside probably died instantly. When he told his mother she became almost hysterical with fright. His parents immediately decided to send him to their hometown Tangail forty five miles from Dacca. He was their only son, and with the teacher cousin so involved in politics, the Army was sure to come around asking questions about his whereabouts.

The Army quickly took control of Dacca. The Sheikh was arrested and hauled off to an Army prison in Rawalpindi.

The next day, on 26 March 1971, Major Zia, a Bengali officer of the Pakistan Army, announced on the Radio of Free Bengal from Kalurghat in Chittagong that, on the direction of the Sheikh, he was declaring that the independent People's Republic of Bangladesh had been established. Major Zia also said that the Sheikh had instructed him to take command as temporary head of the Republic. In the broadcast, he called on all Bengalis to attack the Pakistan Army. He closed his announcement with "Victory will be ours by the grace of God." The range of the radio was not very large, but some ships in the Bay of Bengal picked up the sound waves. Eventually Radio Australia broadcast the message to the world, as did the BBC.

While the independence of East Pakistan was proclaimed, General Yahya broadcast his own message on Radio Pakistan. He viewed the noncooperation movement as an act of treason committed by the Awami League. The Sheikh and his party had defied the lawful authority for over three weeks; they had insulted the Pakistani flag and tried to run a parallel government. They had created turmoil, terror, and insecurity. The Armed Forces of Pakistan had been subjected to taunts and insults of all kinds. The General also complimented the Army on the tremendous restraint they had shown. He proclaimed that he was proud of them. He then gave all authority to General Tikka, the Butcher, to destroy the rebels who sought the dismemberment of Pakistan.

Thus Operation Searchlight was launched to rout out the rebels.

IX

As soon as Major Zia announced the sovereignty of Bangladesh, all hell broke loose in Chittagong. Thousands of rounds of ammunition were fired by the Liberation Front aligned to the League, and all that could be heard were explosions and gunshots. At this time the Pakistan Army in Chittagong was confined to the Cantonment. Rumi's cousin, Tabu, felt as though everything was being leveled to the ground. The Free Radio continued to broadcast inflammatory speeches against the Army and declared that all those who were not Bengalis were supporters of Pakistan and should be dealt with with force.

The same morning Razzak walked into the drawing room of Suri's friend Haseena's house in the Ispahani Jute Mill housing colony on the banks of the Karnaphuli River and, without as much as a greeting, made himself comfortable on the sofa. Haseena's father, who as senior manager in the mill, had dealt with Razzak, a labor union leader, over the past year was surprised by this unwelcome visit.

"Razzak, can we meet in my office? I do not do business in my home."

Razzak crossed his legs in an apparent show of making himself comfortable and in a defiant voice answered, "You have no manners, Hasan! Is this the way you treat your guests? First get me a glass of cold water."

Haseena's older brother, Ali, who was in the drawing room with his father, was aghast at his disrespectful manner. "Behave yourself!" he commanded. "You cannot talk to Daddy in this way."

"What will you do, eh?" Razzak shouted back, mocking him.

"We will get you fired!"

"I do not work for you or your father…so shut up, you son of a pig! Or else…"

The father took Ali aside and whispered in his ears that Razzak was now probably a part of the Liberation Front, so it was best to just do as he said. With the chaos in the city, it was better to swallow feelings of indignity and comply. Ali headed toward the dining room to get the water.

Razzak shouted at him, "Not you! I told him to get it," pointing at the father.

The father quickly ran to the fridge, poured out water in a glass, and handed it to Razzak. Instead of taking the glass he violently pushed it away.

"You have no manners! Don't you know you have to serve water to guests on a tray? "

"Sorry!" The father brought back the glass on a tray.

Haseena and her mother walked into the drawing room to see what the commotion was about. They stood silently watching.

"Now all of you listen. There are great plans for you."

"What plans?"

"All of you are to be sent upstairs." Razzak pointed upwards with his index finger.

"What do you mean?"

"Ha…ha, you will see. You will go upstairs." He seemed amused at the clever use of the word *upstairs* by which he meant dead with the soul rising to the sky.

"Why? What have we done?"

"You Pakistani sons of pigs took our money and our sweat and our blood. And all of you are going to pay for it. You bastard agents of Pakistan! You have sucked our blood dry for too long!"

"But we did not take anything from anyone, and we have always lived in East Pakistan…"

"Enough! We know who you are. All of you Biharis think we Bengalis are animals…"

"But…but we have lived here in Chittagong for twenty-five years ever since Pakistan was created. We have no connection with West Pakistan or Bihar…"

"*Chuup kor*…shut up…we are going to deal with you…just wait and see," and he unfolded his legs from the sofa and left.

The following morning Razzak was back with several men. He pounded on the front door with his fists and shouted that everyone inside had better come out. Haseena's family assembled in the front lawn of the house, where the radhachura tree had begun to bud its yellow blossoms, and the beds were dug up in readiness for planting the summer bounty of zinnias and sunflowers. Beyond the boundary wall, the river gently flowed by, and Kalurghat Bridge was visible in the distance One of Razzak's men pulled the father away and slapped him hard on the cheek. Haseena cowered behind her mother, who screamed at the men to behave. They all laughed. Then Ali was meted the same treatment. Another man tried to grab the younger brother Zaid, but he clung tightly to his mother's legs. After a few tugs, the man gave up. They pushed and shoved Haseena's father and brother toward the gate of the mill. Razzak remained in the garden until they had disappeared from view and ordered the three to go inside the house and wait.

Dazed and shaken, Haseena, her mother, Tehseen, and Zaid went back into the house, locked the door, shut the windows, and drew the curtains. Why were Hasan and Ali taken away in this manner? It was all some mistake, they assured themselves. Razzak was just trying to take revenge for some perceived indignity. As soon as the matter was cleared up, the two would be set free. Haseena kept vigil by the window peeking out from behind the curtains while her mother sat on the prayer mat all day reciting from the Quran, seeking solace in the words of the holy book.

In the evening, there was a knock on the door. Haseena's heart leaped with joy. Her father and brother had returned, but it was their neighbor, Mr. Azad, who stood at the door. After the customary greeting, Tehseen asked him if he knew where they had taken her husband and son.

"Bhabi, there is a lot of trouble in the city, and there might be trouble here…"

"What is happening? I know that the Kalurghat radio station has been taken over by the Liberation Front, but why have they taken away Hasan and Ali? Do you know anything about all this? Where are my husband and son?"

"Bhabi, I don't know, but please listen…"

"You have to know. Tell me please for the sake of our long association…" Haseena's mother pleaded.

"Bhabi, please listen to what I have to say. There is not much time. Do not stay alone in this house. Go and join the other women in the guesthouse." This was the same guesthouse that Haseena had arranged for Suri and the others to stay in when they made the school trip to Chittagong four years earlier.

"What women? Where are all the men…?"

"Just listen. Go to the guest apartment. It is not safe here all alone. Just go."

"Where is your wife?" she asked.

"I have sent my family to Chittagong city," Mr. Azad said. "I only came back to collect some clothes for them. Everyone has…"

"Then I should go to the city as well if it is safer there. Why should I go to the guesthouse?"

"You cannot leave this area. It is not safe in the city for all of you…" He did not offer any information on what specific danger they faced. Tehseen had also heard that there were frequent processions in the city, and slogans were raised against the General and against Pakistan.

"Why did you not tell us earlier about sending your family away, and why is the phone dead, and why is everything so still, and why is there no water in the taps?" Her questions came tumbling out.

All Mr. Azad said was, "I am doing you a favor by telling you this. Haseena is like my own daughter. Go to the apartment."

And he walked away.

News of the Army crackdown against the students and League supporters in Dacca had spread like wild fire in Chittagong. Tabu, who lived close to the main Chowk Bazaar in Chatteswari, could see Mr. Mukhtar's house from his window. Mr. Mukhtar was a businessman from Lahore who supplied engineering material to the railways. A few hours after Major Zia announced the creation of the Republic of Bangladesh, Tabu saw a mob armed with sticks and knives attack the house. Some from the mob scaled the boundary wall and opened the gate to the garden from the inside. Tabu narrated the events of the day to Suri and Rumi when he visited Dacca a couple of months later.

"I was watching and saw that a car approached the mob, and some people got down," Tabu said. "I could make out that this car belonged to some friends of ours as well as those of Mr. Mukhtar. They seemed to be arguing in loud voices with some people in the mob…"

"But how is it that a frenzied mob was listening to anyone?" Suri asked.

"The four men who came in the car were well known in the city," Tabu replied. "We all knew them, and they had one man with a gun—you know, the regular guns that we use in the rifle club. They were probably trying to persuade the mob to disperse, but without any success."

The mob was incensed with the stories of the acts of wanton killing of Bengalis that the Pakistan Army had carried out in Dacca and was not willing to listen to anyone. But the men in the car were able to take away Mr. Mukhtar's wife and daughter. When they left, the mob entered the house, and the two sons and Mr. Mukhtar were dragged out. There was mayhem and shouting. Tabu withdrew from the window not having the stomach to see what he knew was to transpire.

The following day when the sounds of shooting and explosions subsided, Tabu ventured out to take stock of the situation. As he went down the slope, he saw one of Mr. Mukhtar's sons lying face down on the side of the large open storm water drain that ran in front of the house. His body was badly beaten and mutilated. The father and the other son were nowhere to be seen.

"And no one has seen them since," Tabu concluded.

"What happened to the wife and daughter?" Rumi asked him.

"The family friends who had intervened kept them in their house and then handed them over to the Army when it gained control of the city a week or so later. I think they were sent off on one of the ships to Karachi."

"Do you think Mr. Mukhtar is alive and imprisoned somewhere?" Suri asked.

"Not likely Suri. No one could have escaped the fury of that mob. There were rumors that their bodies were dumped in the river."

In the mill under Kalurghat Bridge, Haseena, Zaid, and Tehseen took Mr. Azad's advice and walked over to the guesthouse apartment. Maybe there they could find out what was happening in the colony and the mill. There was no one moving anywhere, and the strange stillness in the air was terrifying. The diffused light, coming through the curtained windows of the guesthouse, was the only bright spot in the gathering darkness. A sick, cold feeling pervaded Haseena's body as she climbed the two steps with her mother and Zaid to the ground-floor corridor of the building.

The two apartments on the ground floor had padlocks on the front door. They walked up the stairs and knocked on the front door of the apartment from where light was visible. There was no answer, but voices could be heard inside as if someone was shushing people up.

Haseena's mother called out her name, "It's me, Tehseen, Mrs. Hasan. Please open the door."

The whisperings inside ceased, and they could hear the sound of a bolt being freed. A woman's face emerged through the half-open door. They did not recognize her. The woman told them to quickly come inside, and once they were in she locked the door. Haseena and her mother were shocked at the sight of so many women.

"Who are all of you?"

"We came here from the city," replied the woman who opened the door.

Tehseen had heard that some families had fled the city.

"But why did you need to leave Chittagong city and come to Kalurghat?"

"Everyone said it was safer here in the mill for us."

A couple of women emerged from one of the rooms. They were from the mill housing colony. "Tehseen Bhabi, where were you?" one of them asked. "We wondered what happened to you and Bhaisahib?"

"Khadija, Razzak and his men took away Hassan and Ali this morning," Tehseen told her. "Khadija, where are your husband and daughter?"

"From our window Mahmood and I saw Razzak drag away Hasan bhai. I told Mahmood to hide in the mill. I came here with my daughter," Khadija replied.

"Are all the women of the colony here?" Tehseen asked her.

"No, Bhabi, not everyone is here. Only the ones like us."

"What do you mean?"

"It seems that all of us are Urdu speaking," Khadija revealed.

"Where are the Bengali families?" Tehseen asked her.

"I think they all moved out to Chittagong city."

"Really! But why?"

"No idea. Now that I think of it, they all left rather furtively and hurriedly. In fact, when I saw Dalim leaving, I asked her where she was off to in such a hurry, and she said she was going to visit her mother," Khadija said.

"It is frightening to be alone, but I do not want to leave my house locked. What if Hasan and Ali come back? How will they get in?"

"I think it is better that we stay together until the men come back."

"But they will be back soon!"

"*Insha-allah...*God willing!" Khadija assured Tehseen.

While her mother was talking to Khadija, Haseena counted the number of women in the apartment. There were fifty-seven women and girls, and one boy, Zaid, distributed in the three bedrooms and one drawing-cum-dining room. Tehseen noticed two pitchers and a glass jug filled with water on the dining table.

"Is there water in the taps here? We do not have any in our house."

"No! Late last night some women went down to the tube well at the back and brought back some water," Khadija responded. Tubewells were deep borings in the earth to get to the aquifer. The water was brought to the surface with hand pumps. "They have been taking turns getting water. Whatever water was there in the overhead tank finished quickly with so many people here. There is no food either."

"I have some rice, lentils, and flour at home. You can use these…Maybe we can go and get food from the Utility Store as well." This well-stocked store was adjacent to the mill area, and everything of daily use was available there.

"Maybe we can! But don't go now. Wait for morning."

"Okay, just for tonight," Tehseen conceded, "I am sure everything will be settled and things will return to normal."

"God willing!"

Haseena, Tehseen, and Zaid found some space on the floor of one of the bedrooms. The one large bed in the room was occupied by two little girls and their mothers.

Several hours later the sound of someone pounding on the apartment door woke everyone up. Tehseen went into the hall and switched on the light. Maybe it was someone else seeking comfort in numbers. But no one got up to open the door. They signaled to Tehseen to keep quiet. Khadija, who followed her into the hall, whispered, "The others say they did the same thing last night. When they did not open the door, they left."

"What do they want?"

"God knows! But late in the night what do men want?"

"Oh, god no…Oh god! No…" Tehseen ran back to the bedroom and ordered Haseena to get under the bed and not come out until she was told to do so. Haseena was too sleepy to protest.

The pounding on the door persisted, and it seemed as though someone was trying to break it down. Whoever was outside kept throwing his weight against the door. The thrusts became more and more forceful. The bolt gave way, and the door was flung open. Several men entered the apartment. Tehseen recognized Razzak and challenged him.

"Why are you here? Can you not see we are only women here? What do you want?"

"What do we want? Ha, ha, ha…you whore! We want her and her…" He pointed at two younger women in the hall.

"You cannot take anyone away from here!"

"Who will stop us?" Razzak mocked her. "But do not worry. We will not take them away permanently, just for a couple of hours. They will be brought back. So tell them to come with us!"

The women who Razzak pointed out ran into the bedroom. Two men followed pushing through the throng of women in the small space of the apartment. The man with the pistol threatened to shoot anyone who got in the way.

The two young women screamed and struggled. Other women tried to pull them away. Some screamed and wailed, but the men were able to drag the two young women to the door and out of the apartment. It was dark and still outside, and inside there was absolute mayhem and panic. The men bolted the door from outside, so no one could follow them.

One of the women taken away was a young bride whose husband had recently begun working in the mill. The couple lived in the housing colony. The other was a stranger. She had probably come from the city to get away from the threat to Urdu-speaking Pakistanis.

One woman began to recite the *ayaatul kursi* in a loud voice, *allaho la illaha illahua, al haiyul qayyum, la takhida seenatum walain um*…Others joined in. As part of Sura Yaseen, it was the prayer of deliverance and protection from the enemy. The apartment echoed with incantations.

No one heard the sound of the bolts being drawn outside. The two young women were pushed in and the door bolted again. They were disheveled and dirty and pieces of grass and twigs stuck to their clothes and hair. The qameez of the woman from the city was stained with blood. Both lay still on the floor. Some women went up to them to help them up. The woman with the blood-stained qameez whimpered, "Leave me alone." Her eyes were glazed. The young bride got up and went into the bathroom not saying a word.

Haseena remained under the bed. Her mother let her be.

X

Three days after that March night massacre of Bengalis perpetrated by the Pakistan Army, Abbu was able to go to the office. He returned home in a very agitated state.

"There was a bloodbath in the campus hostels and the police lines," he said. "The East Pakistan Rifle regiment in Peelkhana has been decimated after the soldiers were disarmed by the Army. Some are saying that the guards at the President House were taken to Ramna Park and shot."

"Who told you all this?" Ammi asked him.

"Everyone in the office is talking about it. There is talk also of many students and leaders having crossed over to India, and the Prime Minister Indira Gandhi has announced her support for the refugees."

"But why should people run away from their own country?"

"What can they do when their own country turns against them and uses so much force against them?" Abbu responded. "The Army used tanks and machine guns and grenades. The entire shanty settlement at the back of the hostels was set on fire. Even today they say there are bodies smoldering. The Hindu enclave, Sakhari Patti, in the old town was also attacked."

"I hope Tutul left the campus." Sadi was worried about his friend. "But I am afraid that he is so dedicated that he might have decided to confront the Pakistan Army."

"Judging from all the fires we saw on the night of the twenty fifth if he was in the hostel, he could not have survived," Suri told him.

"Can I go to the campus?" Sadi asked Abbu.

"Not for a few days…"

"Do you think they are going to round up students from the city, Abbu?" Suri was afraid that Moti would be arrested because his cousin had taken part in the flag-raising ceremony on campus on the third of March.

"I hope not." Abbu then added in a worried tone, "It is going to take a while for things to settle after this horrible act. I hope there is no backlash!"

"Against whom and by whom?" Suri asked him.

"Against us, the Urdu-speaking people!"

"Why us?" Suri could not understand why the Urdu-speaking people would be targeted.

"The Liberation Front may think that we support the Pakistan Army and retaliate against us! We are soft targets, you know. "

"Why would they think that?" Ammi asked. "Our family does not support the Army at all."

"I know that," Abbu responded, "but in times of conflict, people are targeted for the most meaningless differences. Remember what happened when Suri joined the university? The authorities wanted to know if she was born in East Pakistan only because she had taken Urdu as the vernacular subject."

"But how will they know that we are different? It's not written on our foreheads, is it?" Ammi did not like such talk.

"I don't know. I hope the Army does not take the violence any further."

"They should not have done this in the first place," Ammi asserted.

"You're right. One does not solve political issues by the gun. They should have kept on negotiating until an agreement was reached."

"Abbu, when will the phone lines be restored?" Suri asked.

Sadi rolled his eyes. "Is that the only thing you care about?"

"No, but we need to make sure our friends are okay. Najma lives near the British Council, and you know how close it is to the campus. Thank god Shelly went back to Narayanganj."

"In a couple of days I think!" Abbu said. "The Army wants the phones to remain shut so that people cannot communicate and spread rumors. They are allowing essential services to move around. I have been given a letter of exemption from the curfew that the Army has imposed to suppress any response by the Liberation Front. But what has happened in these three days of Army action is a catastrophe."

"What did the army do? Did it save the land? The stupid arrogant…" Ammi stopped before an expletive escaped her lips.

Shelly had vacated her room in Rokeya Hall hostel soon after curfew was announced. Naveed moved in with Rumi. His father called him from Chittagong, and when Naveed wanted to go home, he said it was better for him to stay in Dacca for now. They were being harassed, but they would manage. It was some miscreants stirring trouble. Everything would calm down soon.

There was much anxiety before that March night, that the campus would be the main focus of attacks by the marauding Pakistan Army, especially since Iqbal Hall was the head office of the Student's Action Committee. Another hall reserved for Hindu students was also sure to be targeted because the Army considered them as supporters of India and hence instigators against Pakistan.

A week later the daytime curfew was lifted and enforced only from dawn to dusk. Sadi drove to the university to see if the classes were to resume and if he could return to the hostel. Suri was not allowed to go. Sadi came back with more bad news.

"Suri, you know the thatch huts behind my hostel. They fired directly into the shanty town." When the huts caught fire, the men, women, and children ran into the hostel buildings, and they were gunned down on the stairs and hallways. The bodies of three boys were discovered in the water tank on the roof. They had been shot in cold blood. "Many of our teachers are missing. The soldiers went to the teacher's colony and shot the teachers who were there," Sadi told her. Ever since the teachers and students raised the flag of Bangladesh on the university premises, they had become prime target for the Army. Several of Sadi's classmates were untraceable, as was Tutul. Sadi hoped they were not in the hostel when the mayhem took place and were probably in hiding or had crossed over to India.

Suri went to the campus a couple of weeks later. It was devastating. There were shell marks and bullet holes everywhere. Several of her and Rumi's classmates were missing. The person who ran Madhu's Canteen behind Rokeya Hall was shot dead, and the man who ran the bookshop died trying to save some people. The guard at Iqbal Hall lived on the other side of the pond behind the Hall so he was able to see everything that happened. According to him a student leader came and told the staff to leave quickly, as the Army was about to attack. The students had set up barricades on the road so it seemed that the leaders were aware that the attack was to take place. With all the tension in the air and rumors that the negotiations between the Sheikh representing East Pakistan and the General and Bhutto representing West Pakistan over power sharing were not going well, everyone realized something was about to happen. The guard said that the attack began around midnight. He saw tanks and jeeps enter from both the main and side gates of the university and shell the buildings. The Army fired flares straight in the middle of the shantytown to create panic. Hundreds of soldiers took position to shoot at anyone trying to escape. The entire area was burning, and the guard said that he could feel the heat across the pond. The smell was overpowering. No one would survive the continuous firing from the tanks. His own family was safe, but he said that another hall bearer locked himself in the provost's office and was burned alive. His son came to him and asked for help locating his father, and they went to the office where they found his charred remains.

Naveed received news that there were killings of Urdu-speaking people by the Liberation Front in Chittagong, and he wanted to go to his family there, but there were no trains or flights to the city. Rumi tried to ring up Tabu to see if he could find out anything about Naveed's family, but the phone lines were still down, and there were rumors of fighting in the streets. Rumi had no news of Hiru, who was still at the border check post near Comilla.

Shelly did not come back, and Suri was unable to contact her. She called her house in Narayanganj every single day, but no one answered. Shelly's father had won elections to the Assembly, and it was rumored that the Army had killed or arrested anyone elected on the League ticket that they could find. Suri asked Abbu if she could take the driver to Shelly's house to see if she was all right. He suggested that first he would ask Doctor Wahid, who still commuted to Narayanganj every day, to see if Shelly and her family were safe. The Doctor knew Shelly's father and promised to go to the house to see why they were not answering the phone. A couple of days later Dr. Wahid called to say that Shelly's family had fled when they heard rumors that her father was to be arrested. Suri guessed they had probably gone to their village a few miles from Khulna in the southwest. Shelly's village was part of a large delta and adjoined the largest mangrove forest in the world. She had promised Sadi that one day her uncle would take him down the river by boat through the complex network of tidal waterways and mud flats to see the Sunderban forest famous for its Bengal tigers.

Many of the inhabitants of the villages near Shelly's were Hindus. They were especially targeted by the Army, who considered them to be Indian agents. It was easy to cross the western border from there and take the train to Calcutta.

XI

Through the March night Haseena lay under the bed in the guesthouse of the Ispahani Jute Mill by the flat, lush green banks of the Karnaphuli River. Only a faint movement disturbed the almost still water. The moon cast its beams on the ripples and the gentle waves lapped in a soft whisper against moored empty boats. No one was on the banks. The bridge across the river was empty of traffic, as it had been for several days now, for no one was going to the beach even though the weather was perfect. The gate to the mill was open, but the doors of the Community Hall on the left were shut tight. The playground in front of it lay empty. The young woman with the stain on her qameez had remained on the floor in front of the door during the entire night. When the sun came in through the glass window, Haseena woke to the sound of the little girl on the bed whimpering.

"I am hungry. Give me something to eat."

"Go to sleep. I will get you something in the morning," an adult voice answered.

"It is morning, Mummy. I am hungry."

No food could be found in the apartment, and the front door was locked. But there was another exit through the kitchen opening on to a small balcony and winding stairs that led down to a grassy stretch adjoining the boundary wall along the river. The mother of the hungry girl went into the kitchen and opened the back door. Tehseen followed her to the balcony. Not a soul was stirring. It was as if the landscape had been wiped clear of humanity. The crows, however, were still around and as noisy as ever. A water bird skimmed over the surface of the river looking for fish, and boats bobbed gently on the water.

"Your daughter is hungry. Should we go to my house and get some food?" Tehseen asked.

"Everything is so empty. Where is everyone?"

"Perhaps it's too early and no one is up yet," Tehseen said. "Maybe I should see if Hasan and Ali have returned?"

"Maybe... But they took my husband the day before yesterday, and he is not back yet."

"What would they want with them?"

"I don't know."

"How long have you been here?" Tehseen asked her.

"It's been three days now," the woman answered. "We live in Chatteswari. After mob attacks there, we decided it would be safer here. We were given space in this guesthouse by the owners who are friends of my husband. The others came to this apartment a couple of days ago."

Khadija joined them on the balcony. "What should we do, Tehseen Bhabi?"

"First of all, let us go down and open the front door," Tehseen replied. She felt doing so would relieve the feeling of imprisonment.

Tehseen and Khadija descended the spiral stairs, walked to the front of the building, climbed up the main stairs and slid open the bolt. They stepped over the young woman who still lay across the door.

"Who is she, Khadija?"

"No one has seen her before. But she did say that she came to Chittagong to visit her cousins," Khadija replied.

"Who are her cousins?"

"I have no idea. I think she is related to the Ispahanis because she said they sent her here to stay in the mill's guesthouse until the city calmed down."

"Is she from West Pakistan?"

"I think so," Khadija responded.

Tehseen sat down beside the young woman and gently laid her hands on her shoulders.

"Let me help you to the room. We are sorry we could not prevent the violence against you. What could we do? Let us help you now, please."

"Leave me alone," the young woman whimpered.

"Please let us help you," Khadija told her.

"Leave me alone."

"What shall we do?" Tehseen sounded helpless.

The women gathered around had no answer.

"We cannot remain in this apartment. We have to look for our husbands," Tehseen said.

"Where would we look?" Khadija asked.

"Let's go to the Community Hall and see if someone is there," Tehseen suggested.

"But first we must get the children something to eat," said one of the women gathered at the door.

"Let's all go to my house. I have some provisions," Tehseen offered.

"Okay. But should we all go or just get the food here?" Khadija asked.

"It's just that my house is bigger, so maybe we will be more comfortable there while we wait."

The women agreed. They had to leave this apartment. The door could not be locked. But some were reluctant to leave. They were afraid someone might be lurking outside. Tehseen and Khadija told them that there was no one outside and everything was still. This was exactly what frightened them, so the two decided to go out and look around to see if the area was safe and then call the others. As they got ready to step out, Zaid came running to his mother.

"Mummy, Haseena Apa wants to know if it is safe for her to come out."

Tehseen had forgotten that her daughter was still under the bed. She ran into the bedroom. "I am sorry, sweetheart...you can come out now, but you are a good girl for waiting for me to tell you when it was safe."

Haseena was bathed in sweat as she slid out. Her body ached from lying in one cramped position all night.

"I am going with Khadija to see what we can find out. Look after Zaid. I won't be long. Then we can go home."

When they reached her house, Tehseen opened the front door with her keys and said, "I think we should ask the others to quickly come here."

The women and children left the apartment and walked over to Haseena's house. Some women carried bundles of possessions that they had brought with them from their homes, but most were empty-handed. The young woman lying across the door was helped up by two women and carried to the house. Once everyone was inside, the doors were locked. Tehseen lit the stove to boil water for tea, but there was no water in the taps. There were some bottles of water in the fridge and some at the bottom of the underground tank just outside the kitchen door. Khadija tied a small tumbler with a rope and was able to draw up some water. Tehseen took out a bag of flour from the pantry and gave it to the women who had volunteered to make parathas for the children and plain roti for the grownups. The supplies would last for a couple of days. The young raped woman drank some tea and threw up. Haseena helped her up and took her to her room. It was almost noon by the time everyone was fed breakfast. There was still no sign of any life outside.

Tehseen, Khadija, and two others decided to venture out towards the gate. As they approached the Community Hall, they saw some men sitting in a circle in the veranda playing cards and a couple of men lounging around. All the doors and windows of the Hall were shut. Tehseen felt a premonition of disaster, and her heart beat uncomfortably. There was a strange smell in the air. The others felt the fear as well and wanted to turn back. But Tehseen walked on, and the others followed. As they neared the Community Hall a man saw them and shouted at them to stop.

"Why are you all outside?"

"We are looking for our husbands. Do you know where they are?"

"You'll be joining them soon enough. Now go back."

One man shoved Tehseen. She tried to keep her voice calm. "We will not go unless you tell us where everyone is. And who are all of you?"

"Just shut up and go back home."

"Let's go back…" one woman suggested.

"Go back. Otherwise we will lock you up in the hall as well," the man threatened.

"Are my husband and son in there?" The calm in Tehseen's voice belied the thumping fear in her heart.

"Yes they are." The man laughed as he told them this. "What do you want to do about it? Eh!"

"Take me to them…" Khadija challenged him.

"Get going, you Bihari whore, or should I…"

"Mind your tongue," Khadija seemed to have found her inner strength.

"What will you do?"

Tehseen tried to calm down the situation. "Bhaisahib let us meet them. Did they get any food?"

"You cannot see them," the man said. "We are keeping them here for their own good."

"What are you protecting them from?" Tehseen asked.

"We just want to keep them here for a while. Now go away," the man said in an impatient voice.

"Please let us meet them," Tehseen pleaded.

"That is not possible." He turned sharply and went back to the Hall.

Strangely enough the women felt comforted. At least the men were on the premises. Nothing had happened to them. Everything would be all right. In the house, everyone clamored for information.

"All our men are in the Community Hall," Tehseen told them. "I think they are keeping them safe there so that the fighters do not get to them."

"But who are the men guarding them?" one woman asked.

"No idea," Khadija answered.

"What about what happened last night?" Another woman wanted to know.

"Please let's just calm down and plan for the next couple of days," Khadija said.

"We can go to the mill utility store. There must be foodstuff in the store."

"Yes, there is a warehouse for food and things at the back. We can look there."

"What will happen in the night?"

As they talked, a scream pierced the room. "All of you did nothing to help me....you selfish women...you betrayed me..." The young woman who had lain across the door was sobbing and screaming.

Tehseen ran up to her, but the young woman pushed her away. "Do not come near me...all of you did nothing..."

"What could we have done?" Tehseen's voice was tinged with agony.

"If it was your daughter, what would you have done?" the young woman wailed.

"Please do not say that..." Tehseen pleaded with her.

"She is right. We need to make sure nothing like that takes place tonight," Khadija said.

"What about me...?" the young woman cried out again.

"Please, beti, pray...it will bring you relief..."

"Pray to whom and for what..."

The young woman's plaintive voice rang through the room. Haseena hugged her and gently helped her to her room.

At dusk the women decided to cook some *khichri*. They put a mixture of rice and lentil to boil in a big pot, and when it was done, doled out small portions to everyone. The doors leading to the outside were locked and barricaded with sofas and chairs. The women distributed themselves in the rooms to prepare for night. Tehseen and Zaid went into Haseena's room to sleep. The room was small. The bed and a writing desk piled high with books took up most of the space. Calm descended over the house as the women and children slept.

The sound of footsteps outside woke Haseena. She could hear someone whispering and skirting the house. Then she heard someone running on the roof. Thank God the door leading down the stairs from the roof was locked. Tehseen signaled to Haseena to hide under the bed. There was a gentle knock on the front door and then the back door and then again on the front door, almost furtive knocks.

The young woman could not contain her terror. She began to scream and weep and flailed her arms. Haseena called out to her to lie with her under the bed. This calmed her down, but the screaming had woken up the women in the other rooms. The shadows outside moved about and then disappeared into the night and again reappeared. There was more knocking on the front door, and a soft voice filled with compassion filtered in. "We have come to take you to your husbands."

"If you open the door we will bring you to them," another added.

When she heard this offer, the young bride ran to the door and began to pull the sofa that was wedged against it. Others tried to stop her.

"Let me go. They say they will take me to my husband."

"They are lying…can't you see?"

"What more can they do to me? I want to go to my husband," she screamed.

She climbed over the sofa and unlocked the front door. Someone pushed the door from the outside with great force, moving the sofa away. The young bride was thrown off. One man edged himself through the opening between the door and the sofa. He pushed the sofa forward and entered the living room. Another man followed with a pistol in his hand. Two others came in behind him.

"Our leader sends this message. Anyone coming with us will be taken to the Community Hall where your husbands are staying as our guests. We will not let any harm come to you. You are like our mothers and sisters."

"What leader? Is your leader Razzak? What he and his men did last night is not what one does to mothers and sisters!" Tehseen challenged them.

"Come on…Who wants to meet with their husbands?"

"I will go with you," the young bride replied.

"I will come as well." The woman who had stood in the balcony with Tehseen got up to leave. "They have called us their sisters, so they will not harm us. These are not like the men last night."

Another woman from the city said she too would go to her husband with the men. Just then Zaid walked into the room rubbing his eyes. This infuriated the man with the pistol. "Why is he here?"

"He is my son…he is sick…" A cold feeling began to take hold of Tehseen.

"He cannot stay here…"

"Let him be with me. His father and brother cannot look after him."

"He will have to come with us. We will take him to his father."

"Mummy, let me go with him. I will be with Ali bhai and Daddy."

"Please let him remain with me." Tehseen was now begging, but Zaid was already out the door.

The men left with three women, one little girl, and one little boy.

Tehseen lost her strength and will to resist. Her baby was gone. It was no use locking and barricading the door. The men were able to enter anyway.

"Bhabi let us go to the hall and see if we can get Zaid back."

"I am afraid to go there, Khadija. Something terrible has taken place there, and I am afraid."

"Bhabi, nothing can happen. We have not done anyone any harm. So why would anyone harm us?"

"Then why have they separated us, and why is there no one around? Why are all the houses empty?"

No one had any answers to these questions.

Tehseen went to her daughter's room and sat on the bed. Haseena emerged from under the bed and saw her mother sobbing. "Mummy, what is the matter?"

"My baby is gone! My baby is gone…"

"Mummy, where is Zaid?"

"Your brother was taken by the men. They said they would take him to the Community Hall to be with your father."

"It's okay then?"

"I don't know."

"If they are taking him to Daddy, then it is all right, is it not?"

"I don't know!"

Then through the stillness of the night, they heard sounds of vehicles speeding over Kalurghat Bridge. There were other sounds of cars or jeeps passing by on the road, bypassing the houses to the mill area.

Throughout the next day the women waited and prayed. The night was quiet except for sounds of cars over the bridge. No one disturbed their uneasy sleep. Early next morning, on discovering that there was no more water in the underground tank, two women volunteered to go to the tubewell near the apartment buildings. By now they had started to feel that whatever danger lurked outside could just as easily strike them inside the house.

"Maybe some of us should go to the utility store and see if we can get any food from there," Khadija suggested to the women sitting around her in the living room.

"I don't think it is wise to go to the mill area," one woman said.

"You're right. But what will we do after today for food?" another responded.

"God willing we will not need..." Khadija said.

"What do you mean we will not need any food?"

"Let me finish. I mean maybe our men will be released. There are men coming and going, so something must have been resolved."

"God willing this will happen."

The women returned with the water and reported that there were cars and vans coming in the gate and heading toward the mill area.

Through the day more and more men crossed the bridge.

That same day Tabu saw troop movement near the Chittagong Medical College close to his house. When they came in view he realized that these were soldiers from the Pakistan Army. Their bedraggled state showed they had probably walked all the way from the Cantonment in Comilla, fifty miles to the northeast. Tabu could still hear rounds of firing in the distance. In spite of this, he walked over to see if his girlfriend and her family were okay. Her father, Mr. Arif, worked for the Isphanis, and his house was on the same hill as the mansion of the owners.

An old woman whose son worked in the mill was in the house when Tabu walked in. Her son was recently married and had shifted into an apartment in the mill's colony with his bride. She had not heard from him since the day of the declaration of sovereignty of Bangladesh by Major Zia and was worried. She pleaded with Mr. Arif to find out if he was all right. With all the trouble in the city, it was not safe to venture as far as the mill, but he assured her that he would check as soon as possible.

Then a Pakistan Army contingent moved into Chittagong. The Free Radio was bombed into silence by Pakistan air force jets. The Liberation Front put up a brave fight against the Pakistani soldiers. A dramatic gun battle ensued in the bazaar. Explosions ripped through the air. The nascent fighters battled a regular well-armed national Army. All day the fight between the two unequal sides continued. Things became quieter as night fell, but sharp sounds could still be heard at sporadic intervals. Some fires were visible in the night.

The next day there was a lull although there were still some pockets of resistance. The Pakistan Army had taken complete control of Chittagong. All the resistance by the Liberation Front was put down, and Army jeeps patrolled the streets.

Overrun by the Army, and the only escape route for the fighters of the Liberation Front was to the south over Kalurghat Bridge to Kaptai and then across the East Pakistan borders to the Indian state of Tripura. The Ispahani Jute Mill was on the route to the border.

XII

As darkness descended on Haseena's house, no one bothered to lock and barricade the door. It was useless to do so. In the middle of the night, the front door was violently thrust open, and three men barged in. Two carried machineguns and the third a pistol. They shouted at the women to gather in the living room. As soon as Haseena heard their voices, she slid under the bed. There was panic, but the women complied. When the room filled up, the men opened fire. Some women tried to run into the inner rooms. The three men followed stepping over fallen bodies continuing to fire. The lights were hit, and the room plunged into darkness. From under the bed, Haseena could hear the loud bursts, shots, screams, and shouts. She did not wait for her mother to call her and crawled out from under the bed and ran to the living room.

"Mummy, where are you?"

The sounds of rat-tat-tat drowned out her voice.

"Mummy…"

Someone fell against her and she slipped. She felt a searing pain in her throat.

Haseena woke up with a start as if from a nightmare. She did not know how many hours she had been asleep. The side of her neck throbbed. She touched it and winced. The room was totally dark. Her whole body was drenched. She called out to her mother. Someone called back asking if she could get up. A heavy weight lying on top of her made it difficult to move. She pushed and heaved and was able to emerge from under it. Her throat pulsated with pain. She peered in the dark, and when her eyes got used to the darkness, all she could make out were huddled heaps. A nauseous smell overpowered her.

Haseena called out to her mother again. Someone moaned in a barely audible voice in reply. It seemed to be coming from up ahead. She crawled toward the sound. Her hands slipped on a viscous fluid. The floor was dark. The moaning voice now called out for water. Haseena answered that she would get her some. She stood up and tried to walk in the direction of the dining room. She knew that on the sideboard lay a jug with some of the water from the tubewell. She slipped again and fell, but a soft body broke her fall. The strange smell was strong. No one else moved. She called out again to her mother, and someone moaned in reply. The voice did not belong to her mother.

Haseena began to crawl toward what looked like an open space in the dining area. Her hands were wet, and she felt cold. After what seemed like an eternity, she managed to reach the sideboard. She held on to the edge and stood up. Her throat throbbed and felt completely parched. She got hold of the jug and brought it to her lips to soothe her throat. A million pins pricked her tongue as the water entered her mouth. She spat out the water and glass shards. The mirror over the sideboard was shattered by the firing, and bits of glass had fallen into the jug of water.

Haseena was unbearably thirsty, but where could she find water? The will to live consumed her. She put the anchal of her dupatta over the glass and poured water through it. The water ran clear, but not entirely. It was tinged with red-brown, but she could not make out the color in the dark. She took a mouthful. It soothed her throat, but it tasted salty. She poured more water through her dupatta and called out, "I have water. Does anyone want water… Mummy, I have water…?"

There was one feeble reply, and Haseena walked toward it. She slipped and decided to crawl toward the sound. She called out again, and this time there was no reply. She did not know where to go. No one else moved or answered. She crawled to the nearest heap of bodies and shook them, but there was no response. She ran her hands over a prone figure until she reached her face. The face was cold and still. No one moved. Haseena sat near the mound of bodies. She was overwhelmed with fatigue.

As she slept, the rays of the sun lit up the room and revealed that the color on the floor was not black but a deep, deep red.

XIII

After taking control of Chittagong, the Army set up a picket in a compound on Chatteswari Road. Tabu and his father persuaded some neighbors to come with them to see if the officer in charge could help them get the water turned on and the shops open so they could buy food and even go back to work. All businesses had been shut for days. The people were fearful. Just the day before Tabu and the neighbors had seen Pakistani soldiers mercilessly beating Bengali men, although it was not certain whether they were fighters of the Liberation Front or not. The Army seemingly considered every Bengali young man to be involved with the rebellion against Pakistan. Nonetheless Tabu and his father felt there was no option but to do something to alleviate the discomfort of their neighbors and themselves.

When they entered the picket compound, the sentry on duty stopped them. Rumi's uncle asked in Urdu to see the captain. The tent that served as office of operational command was on the far side of the compound. An officer came out and in a reflex action picked up his rifle from outside the tent. The neighbors cowered behind Tabu as his father greeted the officer addressing him as captain. The officer tersely informed them that he was not a captain but a major. Everyone apologized for the error and requested if he could do something about food and provisions.

"I'll see what I can do, but there are no guarantees," the major answered. "These damned fighters from the so-called Liberation

Front are everywhere, and my task is to get rid of them. Just a few hours ago my soldiers shot one crossing the railway track."

After talking to the major, Tabu walked over to his girlfriend's house. The same woman whose son worked in the mill was there again, desperate for news. Tabu informed Mr. Arif about the meeting with the major and suggested that perhaps it would be a good idea to ask him about taking supplies for all those who were stuck in the mill. Mr. Arif asked the owners to request the major for transport and security. The major agreed, and two army jeeps with a lieutenant in charge accompanied by Mr. Arif and another officer from the mill entered the gate and drove toward the housing colony to see how the residents were doing.

The entire area was deserted. This was odd considering the number of families who lived there. They drove around without encountering a single soul. Mr. Arif asked the lieutenant to wait by the gate. Maybe people were afraid of the Army and were hiding in their houses. He and his colleague then headed toward the sheds in the other jeep. The utility store shutters were open, and there was nothing inside. It looked as though it had been hurriedly looted. The warehouse at the back was also almost empty. Someone had carried off all the food and supplies. The two men then went into the sheds. Nothing seemed to have been damaged.

As they walked into the fiber-spinning area, they heard someone calling out to them, "Arif sahib…Arif sahib…help."

The sound seemed to be coming from near the window on the other side of the hall. They ran toward it and saw an emaciated man sitting with his back to the wall.

"Mahmood bhai, what is the matter with you? Why are you here?"

"Help me…I have been hiding here for a week, for ten days…." whispered Khadija's husband, Mahmood.

"Hiding, why?"

"They were taking everyone away!"

"Who was taking who away? Where is everybody…?"

"I don't know…I saw them taking away Hasan sahib…"

"Who was taking him away and where?" Mr. Arif repeated his question.

"From my window I saw some men taking Hasan sahib away… Khadija told me to run away and hide in the mill."

"Where is your family?"

"They are at home," Mahmood stammered. "Khadija said I should hide…my daughter is with her at home…I saw the men beat Hasan sahib and his son and drag them toward the gate…I ran away…they beat Hasan sahib…I was afraid…"

Mahmood was increasingly incoherent. He smelled of sweat, and saliva dripped from the side of his dry, cracked lips. Mr. Arif helped him up and took him outside. Mahmood needed medical attention so they went back to the Community Hall.

The lieutenant, who had waited in the other jeep, parked alongside the blank wall of the Community Hall asked Mr. Arif about the situation. It seemed there was no one anywhere except Mahmood.

"It does not look good." Then turning around, Mr. Arif asked, "And what is this smell?"

"I have been wondering myself…it is sort of like metal?" the lieutenant answered.

"I cannot recall where I have encountered such a smell…"

"Also, Mr. Arif, I have been waiting here watching that dog going around the playground sniffing and trying to dig up the loose earth. Why would the playground be dug up in such a haphazard manner?" He pointed to the ginger pye-dog roaming around poking his nose in the dug up playground.

"I don't know. But let us check out what is inside the hall," Mr. Arif suggested. "The smell seems to be coming from there."

"I have parked on this side of the building away from the windows to safeguard against any incident. There may be armed men hiding in there, and we should be under cover."

"Maybe we should be…but I doubt it…"

The lieutenant instructed the soldiers to be ready to shoot at the slightest hint of movement at the windows or doors. Mr. Arif and one soldier walked up to the main door of the Hall. It was not locked. As they opened it, a strong metallic odor assailed them. "I know what it is…it is the smell of a *zabakhana*…an abbatoir…Oh God! I hope I am wrong…it cannot be…"

Mr. Arif's feet trembled, and with great difficulty, he stepped inside. He was hit by an oppressive damp odor of a mixture of urine and blood. In the stream of light through the open door, large dark brown blobs of blood were visible. Just inside the door, Mr. Arif stepped on a pool of congealed blood. The soles of his shoes were wet with the red-brown gelled liquid.

"Oh my God! Oh my God! This is a killing field." He reeled out, vomit rising in his throat.

"What is it?" the lieutenant asked nervously. "What is in there?"

"I do not know…there was a slaughter in there…"

The lieutenant braced himself expecting the worst. He ordered a soldier to open the windows. There were no bodies around, only trails of blood on the wall and puddles on the floor. It seemed as though bullets were not used on those whose blood stained the floor and the walls. The blood spurts on the walls indicated that the victims' throats had been slit. In places, the floor was thick with blood. Then he heard knocking and cries for help from an adjoining room. Two soldiers broke down the connecting door. Inside were three women and a little girl, disheveled and stricken with horror. They ran out and clung to the lieutenant.

"Oh God save us…Take us away from here…"

"Who are you? Where are the others? Where is everyone else? Who was here?"

"Oh God! Oh God!"

"Tell us who was here?"

"They told us they were taking us to our husbands!"

"Where are they?"

"We don't know. Oh God, we heard screams and pleas for mercy from men in the hall."

"Why are only you three here? Where are the others?"

"We were told that they were bringing us to our husbands…"

"Who were they?"

"Razzak's men…Men with knives…"

"Did they hurt you?"

"Please help us….my child is so small. They did not even spare her. Take us away please…please!"

These three were too terrified to give them any information.

Mr. Arif in the meantime walked to the playground and shooed the dog away. A feeling that something was amiss made him remove the earth from one seemingly freshly dug up area. He had not dug beyond a few inches of dirt when a human body became visible. It was the body of a little boy. Mr. Arif recognized him. It was Zaid's body. Two soldiers removed earth from the remaining dug up areas and each revealed a body. They were not decomposed. It was clear the men's bodies had been put in the earth recently and hurriedly for the graves were shallow.

The young bride who had been escorted to the jeep from the Community Hall jumped off and ran to one grave site. Her husband's body was visible with his throat slit so deep his head lay askew. She sat down beside him and cradled the lifeless head in her lap.

The lieutenant radioed his command post and asked them to send more troops. The major wanted to know if he had encountered resistance and needed back up.

"No, I need men to search the houses here...we have found many bodies buried in the playground. I think there may be more in the colony. I need help with the search."

The major called up the Ispahanis, the owners of the jute mill, to inform them of the discovery and asked them to accompany the reinforcements. At the mill, they identified the bodies. Most of them were their employees, and one of them was the friend whom they had brought to the mill to take refuge in during the trouble in the city.

"Why were these people slaughtered?" The lieutenant was confused. "They were employees of the mill and do not seem to be armed or anything."

"I don't know...these people were not involved with any politics!" Mr. Arif pointed out that all of these dead bodies belonged to Urdu-speaking people.

"How can you tell?"

"I know them personally. They have worked here for years."

"Where are their families?"

"They must be in their houses here, but I did not see anyone when I drove around the colony," Mr. Arif answered.

The lieutenant went into the residential area to search the apartments and houses. He too did not see any sign of life there. His soldiers went up and down every single block of flats without sighting a single soul. Most of the apartments were locked. The door of the guesthouse apartment was open, and there were signs that someone had stayed there recently. Everything inside was in disarray.

The jeep moved toward the manager's bungalow. The door was bolted from the outside. There was an eerie aura around it but no sound. The soldiers disembarked to check. One of them drew the bolt and stepped inside. His rifle fell from his hand with a thud. Haseena heard this and looked up. She heard someone crying.

"The monsters! These bastard Bengalis have killed everyone!"

"There are only women here! Oh God, what have they done?" Another voice joined in.

"We will get you for this, you bastards."

"I am here," Haseena called out.

"There is one alive! There is one alive."

Haseena saw one man in a khaki uniform walk slowly along the walls of the room and come toward her. She could not focus. Then she felt as though someone had picked her up. The man was weeping uncontrollably.

"Where is my mother?" she asked him.

"We will come back for her. We need to get you to a hospital."

"My father is in the hall. Please tell him I am okay, and we will come back for Mummy."

"Quickly, take her to the hospital. A bullet seems to have grazed her neck. We may be able to save her."

Then news of the massacre of Urdu-speaking people conducted by the Bengali Liberation Front broke in Chittagong. People in the city were overcome with the horror of what had happened. Relatives and friends flocked to the site, but no one was found alive. There were many not accounted for. Mr. Arif identified Zaid and Tehseen's bodies, but Haseena's father and older brother were not seen anywhere.

Perhaps, they were dumped in the river and ended up in the bay eaten by whatever lurked beneath the water.

Or they had been taken to the government's Station Rest House close to the railway station.

The next day, wives and other relatives of the Urdu-speaking men who were taken away by the Liberation Front from various locations in Chittagong went to the Army picket on Chatteswari Road. They informed the major that they had heard of strange activities going on in the Station Rest House since the troubles began two weeks back. It was reported that many men, including some Pathans who worked as guards in the banks and the Punjabi head of the port authority as well as ex-army officers who ran security businesses in the city were taken to the Station Rest House and imprisoned there. Could the major get them released? The major agreed to go there and take a look.

The rest house was a simple U-shaped building, with rooms in a row, located on the Station Road with the Savoy bakery just ahead and the Fresco restaurant opposite it. The large station yard at the back of the rest house was an old pothole-filled dump littered with old railway equipment, scrap, old tracks, and wheels.

Two soldiers walked up to the door with their weapons ready to fire at any movement from inside. They were not sure if fighters of the Liberation Front were hiding inside. But nothing moved. The soldiers opened the door and walked in slowly. A few minutes later one of them rushed out and stuttered, "Sir, we are too late. We are too late!"

"What is inside?" the major asked.

"Sir, take a look yourself. I cannot explain."

"Is anyone inside?"

"Sir, I saw just one person."

"Is he dead or alive?"

"I don't know."

While they were talking, the second soldier walked out. "Sir, please come inside. Maybe we can save some of these men!"

The major went in followed by some others. The smell of fresh blood was overpowering. A man was slumped over a chair. He seemed lifeless, but his body felt warm. Next to the chair was a pail filled with dark blood. A skin had formed over the surface of the liquid. The lifeless man had a needle stuck in his arm with a small tube attached to it. The blood had been drained out of him. There were other bodies lying around. Some were heaped along a wall. The man barely alive when discovered died on the way to the hospital.

Perhaps it was for all those found bloodless in the Station Rest House that Joan Baez had sung: *And from their bodies every drop of blood was drained No time to comprehend and there was little pain…* For as their life slowly ebbed away, at first an all-consuming tiredness set in, and then as the muscles drew on other systems in the body for oxygen, the acid bye product damaged the tissues and finally their hearts were unable to pump any more.

Naveed identified his father's pale bloodless body in the morgue. He had returned to his family in Chittagong a day after the bodies were found in the Station Rest House. Rumi was unable to get in touch with him. Tabu called to say that he had gone with Naveed to the hospital.

"Naveed went berserk. He got hold of an officer's revolver and rushed out of the morgue screaming and howling," Tabu told Rumi.

"Why did you not stop him?"

"He had a gun and was willing to use it. Even the soldiers did not try to do anything." Naveed rushed out and randomly shot three workers in the hospital. Then he shot himself.

"Where are his mother and sister?" Rumi asked Tabu.

"The port authorities put them on the ship for Karachi."

"What about Naveed's body?"

"The army took it away, and we do not know what happened to it."

XIV

A couple of weeks after that March night when Dacca was engulfed in blood and fire, Hiru's mother sent a message to Rumi that he should come and see her. Rumi rushed to Hiru's house in Shantinagar. Hiru's mother told him that there had been a skirmish between the West Pakistani and Bengali officers of the Pakistan Army at the Comilla border post where Hiru was serving.

"It was a brave act of mutiny," she said.

Several soldiers on both sides were killed. Bengali officers of the Pakistan Army, loyal to Sheikh Mujib and those in the paramilitary East Pakistan Rifles were deprived of their rank and arms, and some had even been executed. Others had managed to escape across the borders to India.

"They gave Moyna Hiru's…"

Before Hiru's mother could finish her sentence, Rumi cried out, "Oh my God! What are you saying?"

"Calm down, son, calm down."

Hiru's mother recounted that when Moyna saw the body purported to be that of her husband she did not recognize it. It was not Hiru, but she kept quiet letting others believe that it really was him. Knowing how daring Hiru was, she immediately guessed that Hiru had managed to escape by feigning death and exchanging his clothes with the body of a dead soldier. He had left his identification tag on the dead body. She hoped he had taken off across the border. He was close enough to have done that. All he needed to do was walk over the border and Agartala was five miles away. Moyna had heard that Bengali refugees were being welcomed there and provided security by the Tripura state government. The local Pakistani Army officers thought Hiru was dead, so his ploy worked. Hiru's mother had called Rumi to tell him of the matter before he heard from other sources that his best friend was dead.

"Is Moyna bhabi okay?"

"She is with her father in Pabna."

"But it is safer in Dacca. You should get her back here. I can go get her."

"Baba, she is okay for now. If we feel she should come back, I will send you. Who else can I trust?"

Suri hoped Rumi would not have to go to Pabna. After that March night, with the city under control, the Pakistan Army had extended its marauding and killing to the towns and villages outside Dacca.

Mrs. Akhtar Jahan, who now headed the Women's Association that Ammi was so proud to belong to, called to say that she had some really bad news to convey and if Ammi could come to see her as soon as she could. Akhtar Jahan lived in Dhanmandi and had come to Dacca from Karachi twenty years ago. Ammi returned from the meeting distressed and bereft.

"You know all those rumors that we heard of the killing of Urdu-speaking people all over East Pakistan are true."

"Does anyone know who killed them?" Abbu asked her.

"Apparently scores of families were set upon by Bengali men calling themselves the Liberation Front," Ammi said. "Did you get word from your brother yet?"

"Yes, I did. They are okay. He did not give any details except to say that they are with his daughter's fiancé. He has helped them a lot. But Bhaisahib was evasive when I asked him about his son. He said he was away."

"What do you mean?"

"I think he crossed over to India, and Bhaisahib does not want to talk about it."

"Akhtar Jahan says that the army has rescued many Urdu-speaking women and children and is now bringing them here," Ammi told Abbu. "They have asked her as head of the Women's Association to help set up relief camps in the schools of Mirpur."

Scores of wounded were transported by the Army to Dacca. All of the survivors were those whose husbands or fathers had come here after the cleaving, and worked for the railways in Dinajpur, Bogra, Rangpur, Saidpur, and other towns and cities across East Pakistan. Ammi was deputed to provide relief to the women and children in the school closest to where she lived. Every day she came back with horrific stories.

"One Urdu-speaking woman from Khulna says that during the early days of the noncooperation strikes, nineteen people of her family were killed by Bengali men in the Star and Crescent Jute Mills. The women have horrible wounds from *daos* and *baithis* and knives. Some children in the camp cry all the time while others do not utter a single word and just stare in the distance."

Akhtar Jahan had asked an Army captain about the killings in Khulna and he said that the League supporters in the southwestern city of Khulna killed four thousand Urdu speakers around the Star and Crescent Jute Mills.

"Why did the soldiers not intervene and stop this?" Ammi asked Akhtar Jahan.

"I think they concentrated on Dacca, and by the time they arrived in Khulna and Chittagong, the acts of vengeance on the Urdu-speaking people who were supposed to be supporters of Pakistan had been perpetrated." In Jessore, north of Khulna, thirteen Pakistani soldiers were murdered on the first day of April. The severed head of an Army officer was displayed at a border outpost en route by road and train to Calcutta.

The Women's Association collected as much food, clothing, and utensils as it could for those who were brought to Dacca as they had come here with nothing except the clothes on their backs. The Army helped with the effort, and some of the survivors were taken to Karachi in Army planes. Members of the Association, like Ammi's friend Mrs. Ahmad, who still lived in the Azimpur Colony, did not volunteer to help these hapless souls.

"I called her many times to come to help, and each time she said she was too busy. This has never happened before." Ammi could not understand her friend's reticence.

"Maybe she is busy and cannot give time?" Abbu tried to explain to her.

"Maybe, but this is not like her. She is so full of energy. But now she does not even want to discuss the plight of these women in the camps."

This response to the wounded and helpless troubled Ammi, but she rationalized that after the brutality unleashed that March night by the Army, people were too preoccupied with their own safety and security.

Slowly tales of what the Liberation Front had done to those they considered not of the land of the Bengalis, collectively calling them 'Biharis', trickled into Dacca from Chittagong: of bodies uncovered in the mill by the Karnaphuli River, bloodless bodies discovered in the Station Rest House, Pathans and Punjabis killed in random acts of violence. All the survivors from Chittagong were taken to Karachi in the two ships usually used for the Haj pilgrimage trips to Mecca. Mr. Mukhtar's wife and daughter and Naveed's mother and sisters were among those who returned to Lahore.

Sekina's family moved from Chittagong to Mirpur next to Suri's house in April. Ghazala's father went to Chittagong to look for his brother's family. He found Haseena in a hospital and arranged for proper burial of Tehseen's and Zaid's body. His brother and nephew could not be found.

When the newspapers in West Pakistan reported stories of the survivors, a huge outcry broke out against the Bengali Liberation Front. The Army felt even more justified in the massacre they had unleashed that March night. Families who had relatives or friends in West Pakistan sold off their homes and goods at whatever price they could get and took off to stay with them.

Lal bhai's younger brother, a doctor, also left for Karachi. His wife was Urdu speaking, and her family had come to Dacca from Bihar. Soon after that March night they moved to Karachi and he went with them. Lal bhai's son considered this to be an act of treason against the Bengalis. His uncle had betrayed his father's sacrifice. When challenged before he left, his uncle told him that he was only going to another part of his country, Pakistan. It was all very confusing. Both the uncle and nephew were taking legitimate positions. One believed that Pakistan consisted of both the eastern and western parts, and the other that East Pakistan had seceded and was now Bangladesh.

Ghazala's father also decided to leave for Karachi and start life from scratch. Suri went to see them a couple of times before they left. Haseena did not talk much except to say that her father and brothers were waiting for her in the Community Hall. Ghazala was able to piece together Haseena's ordeal when she spoke of it, off and on, when not in a sedated stupor. In a halting voice, Haseena would say, "It was morning when I got out from under the bed... Mummy, it's hot and dark in here and I will die of suffocation...Do not come out even if you do...I must get the water to Mummy... she is calling...the glass...I must strain the water...What is this smell...Daddy is in the hall...please get him..."

There was distress everywhere. Rumors and calls for revenge, the Bengalis against Pakistanis and the Urdu-speaking people against Bengali Liberation Front, permeated through East Pakistan. "Who drew first blood?" was a question asked by many Urdu-speaking young men. They became a ripe source for the Army's recruitment of *Razakar* volunteers.

In Dacca the campus quickly returned to normal. Almost all the students in Suri's class returned, but there was no news of Moti or Shelly. None of the Hindu students returned, nor did teachers of that faith.

The Army interfered in the day-to-day running of the government departments and asked Urdu-speaking officers to be their eyes and ears and report any Bengali officer who acted against Pakistan. Those who agreed to do so were promoted and put in posts beyond their level of competency. Abbu was worried about being called on to play the role of spy and worse, traitor to his colleagues. The Army brought in officers from West Pakistan to all the government departments to replace those it suspected of not being totally loyal to Pakistan. Most Bengali officers lay low, hoping to survive the misfortune that had befallen them. Some were arrested on trumped-up charges. Abbu's colleague Mr. Rahman was arrested from Azimpur Colony. Abbu and Ammi went to his house to inquire after the family. They were bearing up as best as they could.

With the Army in full control of East Pakistan, it was a terrifying time to be a Bengali. But some Bengalis openly supported the action of the Army, and were rewarded for their loyalty by being given positions of authority.

Abbu was determined to remain in Dacca, as were many others like him. They had come here when Pakistan was created in the name of their Islamic faith and they were not going to leave. The Army had done great damage. It was almost as if they did not consider East Pakistan as part of their country but one they had conquered. The Army would have to relent sooner or later.

Moti hid in his house in Tangail for two weeks before heading out and establishing contact with fighter commanders, all of them Bengali officers of the Pakistan Army who sided with their people once the marauding began. A few weeks later he came back to Dacca with some friends and sent a message to Rumi to come and see him.

"Moti was so energized and filled with optimism about the struggle." Rumi's face glowed as he told Suri of the meeting. "He said soon we will be living in a new country, in Bangladesh, and that he was going to make it happen."

"How long was he here? It's not safe with all these soldiers milling around."

"He went back within a few days," Rumi replied. "He realized that he could do little in Dacca, so he decided to go up north and try to cross the border."

After two weeks on the road, Moti managed to reach Agartala. From there, he went to the training camp set up for the Bengali Liberation Front thirty miles to the south where the nearest city on the East Pakistani side of the border was Comilla. Once in the camp, many like him took crash courses in the use of small arms and explosives from officers, like Hiru, who had trained in the Pakistan Army. These batches of young Bengali men became trained guerillas and began to carry out sabotage operations against the Pakistan Army across the border in Comilla and the surrounding areas.

There was much information floating around, especially among the students about these brave fighters for freedom. All aspired to take part in getting rid of the Pakistani usurpers of their land. Rumi wanted desperately to join them but was persuaded by his father to complete his law studies. The country needed professional men as much as they needed fighters. Besides there was much he could do in the city to rid their land of the occupying Pakistan Army. Rumi felt that he was failing Hiru and Moti, who were confronting the enemy head on.

By mid-April, news of punitive action by the Army spread throughout Dacca. The Free Radio reported these wanton acts of the Army against villagers. After the bombing of the radio station and the Army control of Chittagong, the Free Radio was shifted to a center in the forest of Bagapha across the border near Agartala. The most popular broadcasts *Jallader Darbar*—"The Court of the Executioners" by Mitra and *Chorompotro* by Mukul ridiculed the Army. The broadcasts were listened to avidly all across East Pakistan. The Prime Minister of India, Indira Gandhi, supported the broadcast ridicule and exhortations.

A number of prominent elected League members who managed to escape that March night met at Baidyanathtala, which was mainly a mango grove in Meherpur near Kushtia and on April 17 declared the independence of East Pakistan. They also inaugurated the national anthem of Bangladesh, '*amar shonaar Bangla*', 'My Golden Bengal,' written and composed by Tagore in 1905. They renamed Meherpur as Mujibnagar.

BBC reported this historic event and said that the elected League representatives had formed a government in exile, and a cabinet had taken responsibility for the day-to-day running of the freedom struggle. A close confidante of the Sheikh was named prime minister and given the authority to lead the effort. He declared that his land was at war. It had no choice but to secure its right of self-determination through what he termed a "National Liberation Struggle" against the colonial oppression of Pakistan.

This government in exile also established bases in Calcutta and New Delhi to coordinate with Indira Gandhi. The Marwaris in Calcutta, many of whom had been forced to leave East Pakistan by Field Marshal Ayub Khan when he declared Martial Law in 1958, began to pour massive funds into the coffers of the Bangladesh government in exile.

In Dacca, the Army began to contact Urdu-speaking students to obtain names and details of activists and leaders. It was an insidious way of seeking information. Sadi came home one day in a very agitated state. A Major Mustafa had come to the campus and introduced himself as Abbu's friend and asked him about his class fellows, especially about Tutul. Sadi told the major that he did not believe in politics and did not know anyone who was a part of the student union.

"Why did you tell him about me?" Sadi asked Abbu. "He said he knew you."

"I did not! But these people have a way of finding out everything."

"This is absurd." Sadi was quite upset. "He put me in danger. What will my friends think? That maybe I am an informer or something."

"Ji, can't you tell someone to stop him from doing this?" Ammi said. "It exposes our children to much danger."

"These people do not listen to anyone. They think they are *aqle-qul.*" Abbu was calling them all knowing.

"This Major Mustafa is getting out of hand," Ammi replied. "Look at the way he forced himself into our home."

One day Major Mustafa asked Abbu to take him to his quarters in the Shamoli Housing Complex on Mirpur road. The Army had commandeered this krishnachura tree filled compound of red tiled roof houses for accommodating its officers. Major Mustafa insisted that he would drop Abbu first as he wanted to see what the Mirpur settlement looked like. On reaching Mirpur, the major followed Abbu into the house and literally forced an invitation to lunch. Ammi was not happy about this, but she could not ask him to leave. He sat with them through the meal asking subtle questions about their background and about their friends. He asked Suri if she would like to go to Lahore to study. Suri told him that he should know that the standard of education in East Pakistan was far superior to that in West Pakistan.

"How do you know?" the major asked.

"We can see the syllabus, and we have had students from there who come to study here and who do quite badly," Suri explained. "On the other hand our students do very well in schools and colleges in West Pakistan."

He asked if there were any students from West Pakistan in her department.

"Not in mine," Suri said. "There was one in Rumi's department!" She was referring to Naveed but checked herself before she gave any details.

"Who is Rumi?"

"He is a family friend's son," Ammi chimed in.

"Is he from here?"

"What do you mean? Of course he is from here, just as we are!" Ammi's voice barely hid her disdain for the question.

What Major Mustafa wanted to know is whether Rumi was Bengali or Urdu speaking. Ammi was having none of it. She told him he spoke both and English as well, just like her family. The major was unfazed.

"Can I meet him some time?"

No one answered. Suri was by now cursing herself for having uttered Rumi's name.

The major left after lunch promising to visit them again for he had had such a pleasant time and the food was delicious. No one told him that he was welcome. Major Mustafa probably worked for the dreaded General Rao, who was chief intelligence officer of the Army and had become advisor to the governor. Suri felt sick when she realized that the Rao was their Convent College friend Maheen's father. They had the same surname.

"This Rao suffers from a strange complex. He does not consider us to be true believers of Islam." Abbu had met him once on official duty.

"Maheen was not like that at all. In fact, she kept in touch with us through letters for months after leaving and promised to visit soon."

But the March night had taken place, and no one from West Pakistan was coming here for visiting purposes. It was a good thing that Suri had not blurted out that she knew Rao's daughter in front of Major Mustafa. God knows what he would surmise from that information.

The Army had not reckoned that they would be fighting a rebellion against its brutal action in East Pakistan. General Yahya was sure that if he killed three million of these Bengali sons of bitches, the rest would soon obey him. With the resistance to his brutal actions increasingly evident, in a bid to restore order, General Yahya replaced the Butcher with the Tiger. General Niazi had fought in World War II and earned the title of Tiger from the commander of the British army for his bravery against the Japanese. The Butcher, however, did not leave and remained as governor of East Pakistan. Rao became his advisor.

Around the beginning of May, Shelly came back to the hostel. She had lost a lot of weight. When Suri went to see her in Rokeya Hall they hugged and wept.

"Suri, it was horrible. Ma and Baba were so upset, and we did not know what lay ahead when we left home after hearing of the Army's crackdown on political activists in Dacca."

"Shelly, please don't cry. Everything will be okay. Tell me are your parents okay?"

"Yes, for now at least they are."

"What do you mean for now?" Suri asked.

"You never know what might happen next."

"Listen, everything will be okay. There is a push back by the world powers, so this horrible treatment by the Army cannot last long."

"I know," Shelly said. "But who will be the next victim frightens me. I know we will win in the end. If anything happens to Baba, we will be destroyed. Ma cries all the time."

"These are bad times, but things will be okay I am sure," Suri consoled her. "Listen, I want you to come and stay with me. This room is so depressing."

"I need to stay here to keep in touch with Ma."

"Can you not do so through our phone?'

"I think it is better that you are not dragged into our situation," Shelly replied.

"What do you mean?"

"If the Army comes to know that you have the daughter of a hated League member in your house, they might…" Shelly did not complete her sentence.

"I don't care…you just come with me…"

"Then there is another thing we have to bear in mind."

"What?"

"They might not like it that I am staying with…"

"Who are they?" Suri asked.

"You know! Those who are fighting for our freedom…"

Suri guessed that Shelley meant that she could be marked as consorting with the enemy.

"It's so absurd," Suri told her. "All this talk of enemy and friends is just talk…"

"It is not just talk!"

"Who is whose enemy?" Suri asked her. "Do you know what happened with Ghazala's cousin Haseena and with our friend Naveed?"

"I heard that Ghazala left Dacca to go to Karachi. What about Naveed?"

Suri told her the details of Haseena's ordeal and Naveed's death.

"Oh God," Shelly was aghast. "I did not hear of this…who was responsible…"

"Naveed is dead, and his father had the blood sucked from his veins. Haseena's family was massacred in Kalurghat…who would you blame for all that? The Liberation Front is supposed to have perpetrated the massacre."

"I don't believe this…they were our friends!"

"Everyone has gone mad. But we cannot take sides."

"I don't know what to say…"

"Don't say anything. We will get out of this madness soon."

Shelly agreed to visit Suri in her home some weekends. Suri wanted to talk to her mother, but Shelly thought it would not be too wise to do so at this time.

During the next couple of days, Shelly recounted to Suri what had transpired from the time they left their home in Narayanganj. It was awful running away as they did, but there was no other recourse. That night they crossed the Sitalakhya River in a small boat and hid in their uncle's house in Sonargaon for a few days. Then her father took off alone to join up with his League colleagues who were gathering near Kushtia. After things quieted down, Shelly, her mother, and sisters took a steamer to Khulna and then a bus to their village. They remained for a few weeks until the father was able to send them word that he was fine and in the company of other representatives of the assembly in Mujibnagar.

"We spent each day in the village dreading the passing of Army trucks or jeeps," Shelly recalled. "Even the slightest suspicion set them off."

"What kind of suspicion?"

"Sometimes it was betrayal by someone from the village, and at others suspicion that members of the Liberation Front were hiding inside," Shelly explained. "Sometimes they would come and ask if everyone believed in the Prophet."

"What happened in neighboring villages?" Suri asked. "There are many reports of abandoned villages, burned up villages, and villages where everyone was massacred by the Army."

"Most Hindu villagers ran away across the border. Some were shot. A village right next to ours is completely empty. They must have gone before the Army took control and closed down the border opening at Benapole."

"But these people have lived here for generations. It is their land," Suri said.

"They don't care!" Shelly explained. "The soldiers were told to consider everyone as godless and non-Muslims and Hindus. It is horrible…"

"Did they come to your village as well?"

"Luckily nothing happened in our village."

"Thank God!" Suri said. "But how were you spared?"

"Ironically enough a couple of thugs who lived in the city and were, perhaps, some kind of labor leaders or something came back and proclaimed themselves to be our savior," Shelly revealed. "They had contacts with the Army. These two men demanded that each villager give them a certain amount of money to keep them safe. Everyone complied out of fear. At least these two were our own thugs…"

For Shelly, the few weeks of living in the village were really hard. "You know, Suri, the reason I did not visit my relatives too often was because they do not have bathrooms. Everyone uses the field, and the women do their thing in the morning. It was very difficult to get used to this. But there was no other place we could hide."

Shelly's sisters and mother remained with their uncle across the river even as she came back to the hostel. They were too afraid to go back to their own house.

That same month, Gholam Azam, the Bengali head of the East Pakistan Jamaat-i-Islami party met the Butcher and offered to help him quell the opposition to the Army. He suggested forming a paramilitary brigade with the members his party spearheading it. The Butcher gave his blessings to the suggestion. Two brigades were formed, Alshams, the Brigade of the Sun, and Albadr, the Brigade of the Moon. These Brigades soon became a vital part of the Army's operations, serving as informers, killers, and even carrying out despicable acts like providing women for the pleasure of Pakistani soldiers. There were many reports of women being kept imprisoned in Army quarters all over East Pakistan. To ensure that they did not run away, they were made to spend their days and nights in a naked state.

The Army also formed its own volunteer brigade to counter the Liberation Front. Many Urdu-speaking young men joined this Razakar Force, some for revenge for the killings of their people in March and some for a genuine feeling that the Liberation Front was committing treason against Pakistan by their insurrection against the state in cohort with their arch enemy India. That the Liberation Front had established training bases all along the border between East Pakistan and India, supported by Indira Gandhi, was widely known.

As the days went by, the streets of Dacca were overrun with thousands of militiamen. The Army had flown them in from the rugged mountainous North West Frontier Province in West Pakistan to take over the law and order in the city. These Pathan men were tall and big, and in their dark grey shalwar-qameez uniforms, they struck terror in the hearts of city dwellers. It was terrifying to encounter them, especially in the night, as even an imagined provocation would set off shooting sprees. Being of Pashtun origin they did not understand or speak Bengali and even their Urdu was rudimentary. They were in charge of checking people's identities and questioning their movements. There was no doubt they had been told that all these skinny dark Bengali people were godless or at least they supported the godless ones, and thus the encounters were made out to be the fight between the pious and the impious. These militiamen were also tasked with rounding up men to work on construction sites.

Dacca slowly became a silent city as if it had died. Nobody went out after dusk unless they had to. The Army officers were smug and filled with zeal to secure the Muslim character of Pakistan, and make it truly the land of the pure. Shops and businesses bearing Hindu names were almost always raided and even burned down. Any hint of resistance, however insignificant, was dealt with harshly by burning the entire village and killing all the men. The officers took pride in the number of heads of the "godless" ones they had shot. Women were generally spared death, but thousands of cases of rape were reported. Some villages literally became communities of widows.

Soon resistance to the Army's senseless acts of violence began to be visible throughout East Pakistan: the damaged bridge over Teesta River in Rangpur, blown up portions of the two-hundred-mile Sylhet-Dacca rail link, boatloads of jute sunk near Khulna, and pamphlets distributed urging resistance. Each act was brutally dealt with by the Army by killing and burning nearby villages and settlements. Exploits like the hijacking of the Rocket River Steamer by the Liberation Front became the stuff of legends. Disruption of roads and railways made communication impossible. These acts led to food shortages in some areas, and there was fear that famine might occur unless the Army could restore the transport system and distribute available food. But there was no work force to carry out the repairs. The Army did not want to admit that it had not been able to protect the train and land routes. It tried bringing in people from West Pakistan to work on repairs, but it was not possible to transfer the large numbers required. So it began to randomly arrest people and force them to work in chain gangs. The sight of truckloads of prisoners with shaved heads, arms and legs in fetters wearing only shorts, so that they could not escape, further fueled the feeling of humiliation, and the resistance became stronger.

By June, the sight of army trucks rolling through the half-deserted streets of Dacca was commonplace. Every day planes brought in troops into the city. The names of the streets were changed to remove all Hindu names as well as names of Bengali nationalist leaders. This was an open attempt to stamp out the culture of East Pakistan. The soldiers would disdainfully tell those they searched that Bengali was not really a civilized tongue and that they should start teaching their children Urdu if they wanted to be called Muslims.

The classes in the campus continued unhindered. The final examinations were held just before the monsoons and the campus closed down for the summer. Rumi came to Mirpur at least once a week. Occasionally Suri went into the city and of course she went straight to Rumi's house; these were the days she lived for. Shelly went back to her uncle's house and Suri did not hear from her till she came back to the campus after the holidays.

Sadi left the hostel. He had begun to feel a bit unwelcome there. Ammi suggested that maybe he should go to Karachi and live with her brother. Sadi was not sure he wanted to do this. Abbu was upset with Ammi for making the suggestion. Things will get back to normal sooner or later, he said. Sadi was confused. Tutul had also advised him to go to Karachi for, according to him, a prolonged liberation struggle would take place. He did not want his friend to become the victim of any violence. On the other hand his Ismaili friend, Pippi, who had left school to look after the family business, assured Sadi that things would be all right. Sadi often went to his electrical goods shop in the Dacca Stadium market to while away the summer. He even took a trip with Pippi to

Khulna to visit his married sister who lived there in a large Ismaili settlement.

As the monsoons approached, it became easier for the Liberation Front to conduct harassing actions against Army units bogged down by the rain and slush. They disrupted river traffic and prevented the harvested jute from reaching the factories. Barges carrying the fiber to the Crescent and Star jute mills in Khulna were sunk. The tea industry in Sylhet was badly crippled, and the government had to import tea from abroad for the tea drinkers of West Pakistan. Rice fields remained untended and choked with weeds.

Through radio broadcasts and speeches, the Indian Prime Minister consistently hammered the fact that ten million Bengalis had fled from East Pakistan to her side of the border. The Army insisted that most of these refugees were of the Hindu faith and therefore more loyal to India than Pakistan. The refugees were said to be living in utterly inhuman conditions in over eight hundred camps along the border.

The plight of the refugees turned into a cause celebre when George Harrison, of the erstwhile Beatles fame, in two concerts held in the Madison Square Garden and Central Park, New York offered salvation. When asked by reporters why he had chosen to raise funds for the refugees from East Pakistan, he said, "Because I was asked by a friend if I would help, you know, that's all." He was referring to Ravi Shankar the Indian sitar maestro who was born in Jessore. The city was famous for its eleven temple complex dedicated to the god Shiv. Rumi was excited about the song specifically written for Bangladesh but Suri was not so impressed. Why did the Beatle say 'although I couldn't feel the pain'? in the song '*My friend came to me, with sadness in his eyes/ He told me that he wanted help, before his country dies/ Although I couldn't feel the pain, I had to try/ Now I am asking all of you, help us save some lives.*' It sounded rather callous to her and hypocritical. Besides his friend's country was India, so who was he asking George to save it from!

"Of course he is asking for his place of birth to be saved." Rumi was exasperated at Suri's skepticism.

The concert raised a large sum of money for the refugees and put Bangladesh squarely into people's consciousness all over the world.

Then Indira Gandhi herself undertook tours across Europe and America to appeal for help in returning the refugees back to their homes. She was successful in getting England to support her on the refugee issue. Her greatest achievement, however, was the signing of a twenty-year treaty of friendship and cooperation with the Soviet Union in August 1971. This greatly shocked the President of the United States, Richard Nixon, and his Secretary of State Henry Kissinger. Both were strong supporters of Pakistan.

Soon after, General Yahya sent General Tikka a.k.a the Butcher, packing and appointed Abdul Malek, an East Pakistani bureaucrat who had professed loyalty to the Army, as governor. This was an effort to show that he was lifting the draconian martial law in East Pakistan. General Rao remained as advisor to this governor, thus making sure that he had a say in everything that went on.

Then Moti was killed in an encounter with the Army. Rumi was shattered. But his friend was a martyr to their golden land, and Rumi was proud of him. When he went to Moti's house for condolences, Suri went with him. The pride that Moti's parents felt mixed with their heartbreak was palpable.

"We saw him last in October," his mother told the ladies offering their condolences.

"How did he come back to the city in October? There are so many check posts all over with the awful militia everywhere?" Suri asked Rumi when they left Moti's house.

"He came disguised as a beggar and only stayed for a very short time. He wanted to see his parents before what he said was the final assault."

"Did you meet him as well?"

"I did very briefly…" Rumi told her.

"You did not tell me?" Suri said.

"I did not want to burden you with the information."

"Did you not trust me?"

"It's not that!"

"Then what is it?"

"Nothing…just let it go…" Rumi sounded irritated.

This was the first serious disagreement they had over the event of the time.

Moti was trained as an officer in an Indian camp and had taken the risk to come and see his parents before going to Jalpaigurhi, a town whose name literally meant the "place of olives" from where he was to conduct major missions against the Pakistan Army inside the northeastern border of East Pakistan.

"How do you know these details, Rumi?" Suri asked.

"When we went to the house to pay our respect, Moti's personal aide was there, and he told us in detail of the day he was killed." The women and men, as was customary, had separately offered condolences to the mother and father.

The Army had set up a strategic stronghold near the border, and Moti's mission was to rout the Pakistani soldiers from this bastion so that they would be pushed inward. The Army had placed machine guns and other high-power firearms over the bridge across the river as well as in several buildings near it. The Liberation Front and Indian troops, who together made up the Mitro Bahini or Brigade of Friends, decided to launch an attack against the Pakistan Army on the bridge. The fighters of the Liberation Front were under Moti's command. They were to advance in the dark of night, dig in their positions on the bank of the river, and take on the enemy. The aide narrated the details of the maneuver. "The advance was smooth, but when we began to dig in, a mine exploded nearby. The Pakistan Army opened fire. It was deafening, and everything went berserk. All our planning was thrown out the window."

According to the aide, Moti was in one flank, and he ordered his fighters to take cover.

"Captain Moti told me to leave my wireless set with him and take cover. I did not want to leave, but he forced me to."

The fighters of the Liberation Front as well as the Indian troops found it difficult even to find places to protect themselves.

"I did not expect the firing from the Pakistan Army to be so intense. Sir fired back to give us cover…"

The Army immediately concentrated all its fire on Moti. This lasted for twenty minutes, by which time the fighters of the Liberation Front and the Indian troops reached safety.

"The firing stopped, and I ran over to see if Sir was okay." The aide began to weep. "Sir…was dead. His shirt and neck were covered in blood. I turned him over. A part of his head was smashed."

The Brigade of Friends finally overran the Army's position. Moti was buried in the courtyard of a mosque nearby and was honored with a twenty-seven-gun salute. His parents were informed, and they were devastated. But the family was supportive of the struggle against the actions of the Army, and soon their heartache turned to pride on being the parents of a martyr.

"The aide is not more than sixteen or seventeen," Rumi told Suri, "and he said he had to go back to the camp the next day."

The freedom struggle could not afford to let anyone have any respite.

XV

By November Dacca throbbed with news that something big was to happen. Radio reports from BBC talked about "a massive military buildup" and that another round of war was sure to break out between two traditional enemies, India and Pakistan. They had already fought two wars over Kashmir, one right after the cleaving in 1948 and another in 1965. Indira Gandhi added to the urgency of the situation by vociferously claiming that the refugees were a big burden on India, and they would have to go back to Pakistan. However, she added, they could not do so unless there were guarantees given that they would be safe and secure from religious persecution, for a large percentage of the refugees were of her faith. No such guarantees were forthcoming.

General Yahya, in turn, blamed Indira Gandhi for supporting the insurgency against Pakistan. He accused her of providing arms and training to the Liberation Front and even sending her regular army troops to carry out sabotage inside his territory. The help provided by the Brigade of Friends meant that India was continuously trespassing into the territory of Pakistan. Doing so was an act of war. Both sides continued to blame each other with ever-increasing intensity.

In the third week of November, on the day after Eid-ul-Azha, the day of sacrifice, the clash on the Boyra Salient erupted. This thin sliver of Indian land points sharply into East Pakistan in the south, twenty miles west of Jessore. It was considered vital territory because it included the highway to Calcutta. General Yahya announced that India had launched an all-out offensive, without a formal declaration of war, and that Indian troops supported by tanks had moved into East Pakistan. He launched a counteroffensive that failed to stop the advance. Jet fighters moved in to assist the soldiers on the ground, but were all shot down. The pilots who ejected were captured by the Liberation Front and handed over to India as prisoners of war.

The Free Radio gloated over this event, and Indira Gandhi acknowledged publicly that her troops had indeed crossed the border, but she added that it was "to repulse...enemy attack." She announced that from now on her troops would be allowed to enter East Pakistan "in self-defense." The Indian Prime Minister had invested too much in the nine months after March to forego the last push. General Yahya, on the other hand, was not going to give in to his enemy without a fight.

Hiru's group was part of the Brigade of Friends that joined the Indian advance to secure the northern city of Bogra, which if controlled would make Indian access to Dacca from the north much easier. The Brigade approached Bogra from the northwestern border area of Dinajpur. The Pakistan Army in turn also realized the importance of Bogra due to its strategic location in the northern part of East Pakistan and prepared to defend it vigorously. Here too, just as at the Salient, the attacks began the day after the Eid of sacrifice.

That year on both the Eids, no celebrations were held in East Pakistan. There was too much sadness and anxiety. Only the minimum required community prayers were offered. Abbu, Sami, and Sadi said their prayers in the Mirpur *eidgah* just across the main road within sight of their home. Rumi, his father, and little brother went to the large square Baitul Mukarram mosque, next to the stadium and opposite the General Post Office. No one made new clothes or even cooked the celebration sweets or visited one another. Only Sadi went to offer Eid greetings to Tutul's mother, and when he came back, he told Ammi that he had met Ferdousi Begum, her favorite folk singer. She was Tutul's next-door neighbor.

The day after the Eid of sacrifice, General Yahya declared a state of emergency and asked the people of Pakistan to prepare for war once again. The war between the two enemies was in full swing. Unlike the last two wars between India and Pakistan, which were fought in West Pakistan, this war was being fought in East Pakistan. Life on the ground came almost to a standstill, but the battle heated up in the skies.

On the third of December, Indian radio reported that Pakistani air force jets had flown deep into its territory and attacked a training camp. This was a declaration of war and a swift counterattack ensued. Even though it was expected, people were startled when the first roar of a fighter jet cut through the winter sky in Dacca. The sound was deafening, and the earth shook. The jets dodged and dipped and sometimes came so low that it seemed that they would surely crash into buildings. They swooped and swerved, and it was difficult to tell which jet belonged to whom. One jet was downed and then two and then seven. Who was shooting whom out of the skies and how was totally confusing. There was the akakakak sound from the ground, planes catching fire and careening downward. This was what war looked like. Radio broadcasts reported every move and declared the success of their side, depending on which station was being listened to.

After two days of high drama in the skies over Dacca, things quieted down. Dacca Airport runway was bombed. A huge crater made it impossible for the fighter planes to take off, ending any aerial warfare from there. Rumi actually saw a pilot bail out from his roof. Suri did not think it was a good idea to be out in the open when there were bombers in the sky, but for Rumi, it was the most exciting thing he had ever seen. He heard that an Indian jet had crashed in Kurmitola near the airport and was planning on going to see it. Everyone was going he said. Not a good idea was Suri's retort. Nevertheless, when she told Sadi about the jet, he too was eager to see the downed plane. Suri could not understand the excitement over the wreckage of a killing machine. It was all so meaningless!

Abbu was told to be on call twenty-four hours because many officers were not cooperating with the Army. Not wanting to be part of whatever the Army was planning to do, Abbu applied for leave which was not granted.

Abbu and Ammi were clear about whom they were supporting. They had made a choice to leave India and come to East Pakistan twenty-five years earlier, and here they were staying. According to them, in her attempt to dismember Pakistan, Indira Gandhi was using the political discontent of the people of East Pakistan and the terrible way they were treated by their own Army. She had invested nine months into this effort and saw the war as the final blow and was convinced that thousands of fighters of the Liberation Front, trained in the camps all along the Indian side of the border with East Pakistan, were ready to help and would do their utmost to defeat the Army from within. The Indian Prime Minister knew that the Army had bred much discontent and anger with its wanton killing and humiliation since that March night and people were willing to die to rid themselves of their oppressor. Abbu was clear that they all had to help in the fight against injustice. If East Pakistan chose to change names and be another country, so be it. Borders were redrawn all the time in history. Did Abbu and Ammi not leave India, the land of their birth, to come to Pakistan when boundaries were laid down for Muslims, the people of their faith? They had made that trek across the borders, and that was it.

The Free Radio reported that a train carrying a contingent of Pakistani soldiers was bombed in the railway headquarters town near Jalpaigurhi causing many deaths. The Indian troops still fighting to get control of Bogra were able to a capture a railway station after a hard-fought battle. A simultaneous assault by another group led to the capture of a major town in the southwest. The people there gave the Indian troops a rousing welcome. Indira Gandhi, pleased with her overall success, declared she was recognizing the People's Republic of Bangladesh as an independent nation. General Yahya reacted by cutting off all diplomatic relations with India. This had never happened not even after the 1965 war.

Things began to change swiftly.

Every day brought news of greater success for the Indian troops. Jessore, a strategically important city due to its proximity to Calcutta, was captured without much resistance. When the Indian troops marched in, they were greeted with much joy and jubilation and cheered and garlanded and adulated. Jessore was the first to be liberated as the Army fell back to Khulna. They had evacuated the city in such haste that many maps and documents fell into the hands of the Liberation Front fighters accompanying the Indian troops.

In the meantime, in the north where Hiru was operating, Indian troops won control of Bogra. The same day, more troops were moved in by helicopters to a position just outside Sylhet. The ring around Dacca kept getting smaller, and it was apparent that the Indian troops had an upper hand with the help they were getting from the Liberation Front as well as ordinary people all across East Pakistan. Everywhere the Indian troops turned up they were hailed as heroes.

On December 7 Indian helicopters brought in troops to Sylhet on the banks of the Surma River. The same day the General Assembly of the United Nations voted overwhelmingly asking Indira Gandhi to immediately cease fire. She refused to do so.

All this time the battle for the seas raged in Chittagong. It began with the sinking of *Ghazi*, the warrior submarine given to Pakistan by the United States to defend Karachi in the 1965 war. It set sail to defend the sea front of Chittagong just after the fighting erupted in the Salient. On the first day of the war when the skies over Dacca were reverberating with the dogfights, the submarine was sunk by the Indian navy. The heavily defended port was attacked by the Indian navy with great ferocity and rendered useless within days. Then the nuclear-powered aircraft carrier the *USS Enterprise* arrived in the Bay of Bengal in support of General Yahya. The carrier's appearance was a signal from President Nixon and Secretary Kissinger to Indira Gandhi that they were going to prevent her from dismembering Pakistan. This move sent a glimmer of hope that perhaps now the war would end. In Mirpur from his patio, the neighbor on the other side of Sekina's house declared, "Now that the mighty fleet is here no one can harm us!"

From his patio Abbu argued, "How can they help?"

"They are going to allow our planes to fly from their decks, and the planes will strike at the enemy..."

"But how can they help when our own people are against the army?" Abbu asked. The neighbor angrily informed Abbu that if he could not see that these fighters were being used by the Hindus who had never accepted Pakistan and wanted to see that the East and West parts fail to hold on as one nation, then surely he was a traitor.

"What if the army had turned over power to the League since it had won the elections," Abbu responded. "Would there have been a war? After all, the entire rebellion began when Yahya refused to name Sheikh Mujib the Prime Minister of Pakistan."

"No, it will not...these Indians are bent on destroying us!" the neighbor insisted. "They cannot accept that we have defeated them in the 1965 war. India has never accepted the existence of Pakistan."

"But we gave India a reason to invade us by killing our own people. Why were our people forced to seek refuge across the border...?"

"What reason? They are all traitors! Why would they seek India's help against our country? Don't they know India is our enemy?"

"Are ten million people traitors?" Abbu asked.

"Yes! Don't you see that 80 percent all of those ten million that you are talking about worship idols? They are Hindus. They were never our people."

"That is ridiculous," Abbu said. "When our country was made, the first thing Mr. Jinnah told us was that people were free to worship in mosques, in temples, and in churches..."

"That was then...this is now. These people forced violence on us. You had better fix your views, Haq sahib, or..." the neighbor threatened.

"Or what will you do?"

"Or you will be called a collaborator, helping our enemy..."

"I don't think you will ever understand that there is such a thing as desire for freedom..."

"We got our freedom from the idol worshippers in 1947, and these people want to go back to the same situation."

"No, they want to be free from the tyranny of West Pakistan, which does not want to treat the Bengalis in East Pakistan as equals politically and economically. Why did Yahya not hand over power to Sheikh Mujib?"

"Haq sahib, you are siding with our sworn enemy India. They have always wanted to dismember our country. Be careful. And those calling themselves the Liberation Front are helping India against Pakistan."

"But the Bengali fighters are our own Pakistani people."

"No, they are not our people. They killed our people…and you are saying they are our people. Haq sahib, only when you lose your loved ones will you learn who is your own and who is not…"

Ammi heard the argument and asked Abbu to come inside.

"Ji, why do you get into arguments? You cannot convince people whose relatives have been killed in March that they are not thinking of the bigger picture. They cannot think straight."

"You are right," Abbu conceded.

Abbu apologized to the neighbor for his loss and withdrew into the house. This neighbor's brother, who was an assistant manager in Khulna's Crescent Jute Mill, was killed by the Liberation Front in the first week of April. His sister-in-law and her children lived with him now. His brother's son had a knife wound on his left shoulder that rendered his arm useless. Revenge was what he wanted.

It turned out that sending the American aircraft carrier was a useless attempt to support the Army. No sooner had it entered the Bay of Bengal, the Soviet Union, in compliance with the defense treaty with India, sent in naval ships to counter this obvious American intervention. Fearful of the conflict spilling out of the Bay of Bengal into a world war, the carrier left. All resistance to Indian troops vanished from then on.

While the war was underway, the civil defense department in Dacca informed the public, through leaflets and announcements, how to respond if attacked by air and on the ground. No one believed that there would be bombing, especially after the first two days. Why would Indira Gandhi target the people she was helping to liberate? The Army strictly enforced the blackout, so it was difficult to do anything after dark. The windows were sealed with dark heavy fabric, and no lights were switched on in the night. The suffused lights of kerosene lamps were used to light up the rooms instead. The smell of the kerosene lamps was a reminder of the nights spent after the cyclones knocked down electric poles and the streets of Narayanganj were littered with dead crows.

After the two days of the Indian and Pakistani jets screaming through the skies, the only sounds in Dacca were those of occasional gunshots and booms in the night. In the day, things were as normal as could be except that schools and colleges were shut down. Rumi and his nephew could not resist observing the remains of the jet plane that had crashed in Kurmitola. They came over to Mirpur afterward. When Sadi heard they had seen the downed jet, he was excited and asked for details. Rumi and Sadi seemed to bond for the first time. Suri wanted to know how things were in the city. Everything was quiet like the proverbial calm before the storm. Since every day brought news of victory for the Indian troops, it seemed the war would soon be over.

"What then?" Suri and Sadi were in the drawing room with Rumi and his nephew.

"It's not clear…" Rumi began to explain.

"It is clear. We will be free…" the nephew interjected.

It was not so clear to Suri. If Indira Gandhi was fighting this war with her troops and her soldiers were getting killed, she was sacrificing her people, so what would she seek in return? "Why would she just hand over the land she captures to us?" Suri asked.

"It's not as simple as it looks…" Rumi tried to explain once again.

"Look, Suri, maybe you are not fully convinced about the struggle…" Rumi's nephew blurted out.

"Stop it," Rumi retorted angrily before his nephew said that Suri was Urdu speaking and thus not a true supporter of the liberation struggle for Bangladesh. "You know where she stands, so don't say something stupid…"

"I don't mean it like that, Rumi bhai. But this war is being fought with the help of our fighters as well."

"Of course it is!" Suri said. "But they are only helping in the war. They are not fighting it. It is still a war between two countries that have been at daggers since they were created in 1947…"

The nephew was sure that Indira Gandhi's motives were pure. "She is doing it for our freedom."

"Granted that her intentions are pure, would she not have to answer to her own people of the sacrifice of her soldiers?" Suri was not sure as to why Indira Gandhi would give up her victory to others.

Sadi did not utter a word during this debate. After they left, he berated Suri. She was foolish to talk so openly about her misgivings. Did she want to be called a collaborator?

"I can talk to Rumi about anything," she said.

"What about his nephew?" Sadi asked. "Can you be sure of him?"

"I did not say anything against the struggle. I want to understand the situation. If the Indians win the war, then why would they not just take this part of the land and make it one of their own states?"

"I don't understand myself," Sadi responded, "but they are all very sure that we will get freedom in this manner. But you should be a bit more careful with Rumi around!"

His concern was touching, but Suri was adamant. "Not really, why should we not be able to discuss the issue? Maybe his nephew's opinion differs from mine, so what?"

As the war progressed, the sound of gunfire and explosions began to come closer and closer. Sometimes when the phosphorescent glow of tracer lights lit up the skies, Sekina's pet rooster would begin to crow. It all added to the general feeling of unreality.

Then news came that thousands of Indian paratroopers had landed about fifty miles from Dacca near Moti's hometown, Tangail, right in the center of East Pakistan, on the banks of the river of the goddess Dhaleshwari. Bogra had already been captured by the troops with considerable help from Hiru's group. Dacca was thus besieged from the north. The Army began to retreat toward Dacca. The Indian paratroopers, helped by a Liberation Front unit, took Pungli Bridge, a major structure over the Jamuna River and cut off the retreating soldiers on the Tongi-Dacca road.

Then Suri's birthplace, Kushtia, in the northwest was taken over by Indian troops. The Army retreated over Hardinge Bridge across the Padma River, and as they left, they were able to destroy one of the spans. The Indians were air lifted by helicopters over the river, and some crossed on motorboats. Meanwhile Indira Gandhi sent in some more of her helicopters to flank Dacca from the northeast. The south had already been secured with the fall of Jessore. This cleared the entire region for the Indian troops to take over East Pakistan. Now Dacca could only be defended by soldiers in the city itself. With the ring tightening General "Tiger" Niazi declared that Dacca would fall over his dead body.

The next day supersonic jets streamed over the city and bombed the Governor House. Governor Malek, who was inside in a meeting with members of his cabinet, was shocked at the accuracy of the attack. It was apparent that someone had provided information of this high-level meeting, and the Indians were able to strike deep into the heart of East Pakistan. The defense of the city collapsed almost without any resistance. The governor resigned and sought refuge in the Intercontinental Hotel. Indira Gandhi further shattered the Pakistan Army's nerves by dropping pamphlets from an aircraft asking them to surrender.

When the first mortar shells landed in Dacca, Indira Gandhi sent a message to General Rao who, following the resignation of Governor Malek, was now the head of the government, that if he did not surrender, his garrison would be reduced to rubble.

A Liberation Front unit joined the paratroopers and advanced along Joydebpur road.

The choice for the Pakistan Army was to fight and lose lives or surrender and save lives.

Then Dacca was hit with a high-intensity explosion. News of the kidnapping of Bengali teachers, doctors, journalists, lawyers, and even a film producer ran through the city like shock waves. The Alshams and Albadr Brigades of the Jamaat-i-Islami, aligned with the Army, had kidnapped intellectuals and shot and killed them. This was an attempt to destroy the morale of the people of the city, who were now expecting the Indian troops and the Liberation Front to make a triumphant entry at any time. It was the most brutal, savage thing to do. This was the scorched earth policy conducted by the Pakistan Army to leave behind a wasteland and tarnish the triumph of the victorious side and it decisively sealed the severance of East and West Pakistan. The two parts of Pakistan could not possibly live together after this act of butchery.

The Indian troops continued to advance on Dacca from the north. On this road also lay the bridge near Mirpur over the Turag tributary of the Buriganga River. The exchange of fire between the Army and the Indian troops could be heard all through the night. The Army seemed to want to defend the bridge. No one in Mirpur slept that night; Ammi prayed and Abbu listened to the radio.

Then the Tiger, the commander of the Pakistan Army, surrendered.

Abbu heaved a sigh of relief. It was over. The Army was not going to fight and thank God for that he said. Mercifully Dacca was spared the ordeal of again seeing dead bodies on its streets. The Pakistani commander of Dacca met the victorious Indian general at the bridge over the Turag to welcome him to the city. The Indian troops entered Dacca raising slogans of long life to their country and to their leader, Indira Gandhi. The people garlanded them as they marched in. The surrender document was readied, and a ceremony was held in the racecourse ground in the evening under the gaze of a mammoth jubilant crowd.

The televised surrender ritual in Dacca was the first ever in history to be held in public. Apparently General Jacob, a Jewish general in the Indian Army who had masterminded the entire campaign, insisted that it be so. The protagonists, Pakistan and India, were two traditional enemies. No one from Bangladesh was party to the surrender document. The Tiger signed the surrender paper and handed over his pistol to General Aurora, who had arrived from Calcutta that afternoon. The surrender ceremony was repeated all across East Pakistan. The Tiger, together with all the soldiers, the officers, the civilian staff, the government officers, businessmen from West Pakistan, and their families, ninety thousand in all, were confined in the Dacca Cantonment and then transported to several prisoners of war camps in India. With this victory Indira Gandhi had succeeded in dismembering Pakistan and creating Bangladesh.

XVI

The celebrations began immediately, and Dacca resounded with slogans of Victory...Victory...to Bangladesh." But the circle of revenge and counter revenge was yet incomplete. For those who did not speak the tongue of this now the golden land their time in the cycle was upon them. Going back the number of months it takes a human fetus to gestate in the womb, the blood of those who did not speak Bengali had been let by those that do; then the marauding army marauded those who spoke Bengali; in the continuum of bending this straight line to a circle it was time for the blood of those who did not speak Bengali to be let; and once again the streets of Dacca became rivers of blood.

Rumi called Suri two or three times a day with news of the city. According to him, things were slowly returning to normal, but it was still not too safe to go around. The victorious Liberation Front and their supporters were roaming the city with weapons. But Rumi said that as soon Sheikh Mujib was set free and he returned to Dacca, he would bring everyone under control.

"I will come and see you soon," Rumi promised. "Maybe you can even come to the campus."

"But," Suri asked him, "What about all the news we hear of killings in the city? Is it safe?"

"There are some bent on taking revenge," Rumi said. "There are a lot of weapons being openly flaunted in Dacca."

"Then all the rumors of reprisals against the Urdu-speaking people are true?"

"Some are, some are not...!"

"What about the public execution we heard of?" Suri asked.

"Unfortunately that did happen...I think..." Rumi was being vague.

"Is there anyone you know who went to it?" Suri did not want to believe that such a public execution had taken place.

"It's shameful. I would not even want to be near a person who would go to such an event." Rumi replied. Then he added, "But listen, they found some bodies in your area...of the teachers and others who were kidnapped..."

"This means they will think people from Mirpur did it..."

"No! Everyone knows they were kidnapped by the Alshams-Albadr bastards!"

"Who could have thought of this horrible plan?"

"Who else could be as evil as that General Rao?" Rumi said.

"What does Hiru say of the situation?" Suri asked. Hiru had returned to Dacca and proclaimed a hero for his role in the capture of Bogra.

"Hiru is sure that when the Sheikh returns everyone will be brought under control. He holds great sway over the people, and he would immediately order everyone back to work. Hiru thinks that all the hotheads will be reined in soon."

"What do you think, Rumi?"

"Maybe so...I hope so...Suri. Things have to settle."

Contrary to what Rumi had said the Liberation Front unit that entered Dacca with the Indian paratroopers, together with their supporters in the city, almost immediately set out on a rampage of vengeance against all those who were Urdu speaking. The leader of the unit celebrated victory in a public meeting in the stadium a few days after the surrender ceremony with five thousand cheering men, women, and children. During the event, he presented four bound and trussed Urdu-speaking men all of whom he said were 'Bihari' collaborators. He promised the crowd that he would seek justice for these men by giving them a proper trial. However, as soon as his speech was over, he signaled his fellow fighters to finish off the four men. The execution began with lighted cigarettes poking out their eyes, then they were bludgeoned and bayoneted, and with each thrust, the crowd roared, "Joi...joi...victory...victory!" After the bodies were reduced to crushed meat, the public dispersed but not before taking a closer look at what was left of the collaborators. It was reported by NBC America that while the crowd was going past the dead men, one body twitched and a fighter standing close by rammed his boot into the skull making sure that death was certain. This public execution was also reported by several newspapers abroad. There was even some footage of the spectacle filmed covertly by the NBC television crew.

Ammi heard of the event through Mannan. It was talked about in the bazaar and he reported it to her. She was horror struck. There was no way this was true. She cautioned him from talking about it to others because this would mean that he was spreading falsehoods. Soon afterwards Mannan asked Ammi for leave to go back to his hometown of Patuakhali.

Zulfikar Bhutto, who Naveed had characterized as charismatic, and who had created some drama in the UN by tearing up his notes and walking out in protest from the Security Council, took over as President of what was left of Pakistan from General Yahya. Sheikh Mujib was released from prison in Rawalpindi. On his way back to his liberated Bangladesh, he stopped in Delhi to thank Indira Gandhi for all her help and hospitality. He arrived in Dacca on January 10, 1972, to a tumultuous welcome.

A couple of days later three boys walking past Suri's house looked over the black metal gate and saw the deep orange-yellow marigolds spilling over clay pots in gay abandon. That year these flowers had blossomed in such profusion that the veranda was covered in an orange hue. The road to Mirpur was nearly empty since the return of the Sheikh. Everyone was waiting to hear what instructions he would give about the 'Biharis.' The quarrelsome shalik-myna couple berated each other perched on the branches of the lime green leaf laden branches of the krishnachura. One boy took hold of the long horizontal latch and banged it against the square metal plate while another clutched the gate and shook it shouting that it should be opened immediately. The birds were nonplussed at this din and took a break from their domestic falling out to see what was going on.

Abbu was in the living room reading Bertrand Russell's *In Praise of Idleness* now that for the first time in his life he remained at home during working days. He went to see what the commotion was about. Nuru with the one opaque eye raced in from the kitchen as fast as he could on his bowlegs, through the corridor between the boundary wall and the side of the house to the gate and, before Abbu could stop him, threw it wide open. Suri went out on the patio outside her bedroom on the first floor and leaned over the railing to see who had come. Maybe it was Rumi, although he never came without notice.

It was not Rumi, but three skinny boys in pants and untucked shirts who brushed past the delicate branches of the light green queen-of-the-night shrub, on to the concrete space in front of the boundary wall. Without uttering a word, the three boys picked up the pots of marigolds and walked out the gate to the barely green patch in front of the white boundary wall, where the grass competed for sunlight with the krishnachura tree.

More than five weeks still remained before these marigolds were to be offered to Lal bhai and the five other martyrs to the mother tongue. This year the celebrations would surely be the best ever, for it would be in freedom. But why were the boys collecting the marigolds now? Suri wondered.

The three boys came back to get the remaining pots. They were taking away Ammi's flowers, and Abbu was not stopping them, so Suri ran downstairs and out into the veranda, barefoot as usual.

"Where are you taking the flowers?" she challenged them.

"Do not interfere," one of the boys growled, "and do not talk to us."

"But hey! Tell her!" another added, "Maybe she should know! These marigolds are ours. They are growing on the soil of Bangladesh."

"But this is my house!" Abbu spoke at last.

"And these marigolds are mine," Suri emphasized.

"Nothing here is yours. We own it now."

"But all this is ours...?"

"We have taken over now, and everything is ours, so just shut up."

"You are stealing our plants," she put on her most threatening tone, "and I will call the police…"

"Police, you will call the police? Go ahead…Ha…hah." The three boys simultaneously doubled over with laughter. "Police? Whose police? What police…the police are ours as well."

"What do you mean yours? The police are for everyone," Suri said.

"They are for everyone of this land. Everything is ours now… we Bengalis liberated this land, and we do not have to explain anything to you…"

"Tell these two where we are taking these flowers," another piped in and laughed with much glee.

"We are taking it to decorate the dais for the reception for the Indian general who helped us in the liberation war against you bastards from West Pakistan."

"But we are not from there…" Abbu interjected.

"Shut up! Don't lie. We know where you are from. Now this is our country, and when the general leaves, you had better watch out."

"What will you do?"

"You'll see! All of you collaborators!"

After spitting out the word, the boys picked up the remaining marigold pots and left. Nuru quickly shut the gate and ran back in as fast as he could.

"Abbu, they called us collaborators!" Suri was stunned.

"Don't worry, Suri. It's just a term they use for those they think supported the Army in perpetrating the mayhem of the past nine months."

"But this is so dangerous…"

"These boys know nothing about the situation," Abbu explained. "When we spoke to the Indian major…"

"The boys said there was a general here," Suri said.

"No, he is a major, and he has been put in charge here by the Indian army command to see that the Urdu-speaking people are protected especially after what happened to them in the aftermath of the March crackdown. They are to be offered a choice to stay or leave."

Indira Gandhi had instructed her troops to guard settlements like Mirpur where the large majority of residents were not Bengalis. This was not so much out of the goodness of her heart, but because after the killings of Urdu-speaking people in March, the UN in its resolution had expressed concern that there would be reprisals against people who supported Pakistan. The resolution emphasized that it was the duty of the victorious Indians to make sure that the innocent were protected under the Geneva Convention of 1949 until their safety could be arranged.

"So everything would be like it was when you and Ammi came here?" Suri sought assurance from Abbu.

"Yes and one migration was enough for me and your mother. We came here from India in 1947. We made our choice to come to this land at that time. And by whatever name it is called, it is ours!"

Suri wondered why Abbu repeated this refrain whenever he got a chance. Maybe to convince himself! It comforted her nonetheless, and Rumi had said that Sheikh Mujib had announced in his speech on returning home that there would be no reprisals against anyone. All were from Bangladesh now. But Abbu was not called back to work. He was told that his status as a citizen of Bangladesh was yet to be determined. Rumi did not think it was safe for Suri to return to campus and did not want to discuss why.

Then February arrived spreading the melancholy shefali-laden fragrance. On the first day of the month at around ten in the morning, Suri saw the skinny men, it was always skinny men, speed by in a jeep on the road in front of her house. They brandished weapons and shouted out, "*Pakistanzindabad...*" This is so stupid, she had thought. Suri went downstairs to tell the others of what she had seen.

"These Jamaat-i-Islami goons from Albadr-Alshams are up to no good. Why did they have to do it here? Why did the major not stop them?" Abbu was furious.

"God, I hope Sadi is okay!" Ammi sounded worried. "But he left early, so he must be with his friend Pippi now." Pippi lived in

Scout Colony, a housing complex for Ismailis, behind the main Shantinagar Bazaar.

The sound of firing and slogans of *Pakistanzindabad* jolted Mirpur. Abbu along with some neighbors walked over to the police station to find out from the Indian major what was going on and why they had not stopped these Alshams and Albadr thugs. There they found that Indian troops had been withdrawn and Bangladeshi soldiers were in charge. It became clear why the Albadr and Alshams men went around in a show of defiance. They thought that now that the Indian army had withdrawn they could easily assert themselves over the Liberation Front with bullets and no one would retaliate.

Abbu railed, "They are so delusional. Can't they accept that they have lost? These idiots are so stupid!"

"Why did their leaders not rein them in?" Ammi responded. "They should go and make peace with the Sheikh. Not that he should forgive them for what they have done. But the Jamaatis are Bengalis, so that counts for something."

After the morning uproar a dull silence gripped the neighborhood. The next day passed by in dread and anticipation of some disaster. How would the government of Bangladesh react to this stupid provocation by the Jamaat-i-Islami goons was on everyone's minds? No one knew what to do.

Then the telephones went dead. This was the first sign of how things were to be.

Ammi fretted and prayed by turns. Abbu tuned in to all the stations that he could find to hear some news. Nuru's mother cooked some rice and lentils for lunch, but no one wanted to eat. At night they dragged the mattresses into the living room. Although the war between India and Pakistan was over, they had not gone back to sleeping in their separate rooms.

On the second night loud knocks and shouts of, "Open up, Open up! Or we will break down this door," woke everyone up. Someone had forgotten to lock the gate. Abbu rushed to the door.

"Who is it?"

"We are from the Bangladesh army. Open up. We want to check for weapons!"

"We do not have any weapons! Why would we have any weapons?"

"All of you are armed! Let us in before we break open the door!"

Abbu opened the front door, and four soldiers pushed him to one side and entered the room.

"We have to search the house."

"Okay, we will wait outside, and you can go through the house." Abbu gestured to everyone to follow him. Ammi grabbed Suri and Munni by their hands and pulled them toward the front door. In their half-asleep state, they were unsteady on their feet, and Munni stumbled over the edge of the mattress. A pillow broke her fall. Ammi pulled her up. The soldiers blocked her way. "Not so fast…"

"We will wait outside…"

"You and these two stay here," the soldier gestured toward Ammi, Suri, and Munni, "and show us where the rifles are hidden."

"Please, we do not have any rifles or anything. We will go out, and you can search the entire house freely…" Abbu pleaded, but his words were interrupted when a soldier kicked him with his heavy booted leg and pushed him out the door. Another soldier shoved Sami out.

Ammi again tried to leave, but a soldier barring the front door drew the bolt locking them in.

"Okay, you Bihari whore! Where is all the money and jewelry?"

"We don't have much money in the house. But take what jewelry we have!"

Ammi quickly took off the six gold bangles, gold ring, and the garnet encrusted round earrings she was wearing. Suri's hands shook uncontrollably as she tried to take off her small gold hoop earrings. The soldier with the thick black moustache was impatient and forcibly snatched it tearing her left earlobe, mercifully not all the way through as the hoop slid off. Blood trickled down Suri's neck, spread to the neckline of her qameez, and mingled with the red flowers printed on white. There was another scream from outside. The soldier had hit Abbu again. Munni was able to remove her earrings quickly. The soldier saw the watch Suri was wearing and pried it off her wrist. Abbu had given it to her when she was placed in the honors list in the Intermediate examinations.

"Okay! So where is the rest?" the soldier asked.

"You can look," Ammi answered. "We do not have anything in the house, and there is some money in the cupboard upstairs. Here is the key. Take everything but let us go out."

"Oh no! Not yet! You whores."

One soldier forced Ammi up the stairs, and one stood guard over the two of them. The third went around the house looking under the sofas, in the toilets, in the flush tanks, even in the overhead ventilator. "You know these people think they are so clever," he muttered aloud. "In the other house they wrapped jewelry in plastic and hid it in the flush tank...Remember the house where they hid it in sacks of rice...they think they can fool us...There is nothing here...I'll go and look in the kitchen."

He opened the back door and went out. Within minutes he returned with a scowl on his face. Nuru and his mother slept in the quarters next to the kitchen. They must have told him that these people had not hidden anything anywhere.

Munni had her arms around Suri's waist and held on tight as Suri pressed her wounded earlobe between the forefinger and thumb to stem the flow of blood. The soldier leered at them. The odor of this man was overwhelming. A mixture of unwashed body and mustard-oiled hair pervaded the entire room. He brought his face close to Suri's. She could smell stale *bidhi* tobacco in his breath. He laid one hand on her thighs and pressed the flesh. Then his hands went up to the crotch, and he edged closer to her pressing his body to hers. Suri began to shake with fear, and her legs gave way. The man held her tight pushing her down. Munni pummeled him with her fist, but he thrust her away. He had her on the floor now. Suri felt a heavy weight descend on her, and then darkness enveloped her mind.

Suri heard Ammi screaming, "Let her go, Let my baby go..."

"Get away you whore. I am only taking what is mine..."

"Please take me...leave my innocent child..."

The soldier relaxed his hold on Suri and leered at Ammi.

Then the sound of someone pounding on the door echoed in the room.

"What is it?" the soldier answered.

"Come on! The captain is on his way. We'd better not be seen inside the house!"

"The bastard…Why are we not allowed to take what is our due?"

"Come out…quick."

Ammi ran and got down on her knees next to Suri who was still lying on the floor. The blood at the neck had made a large splotch on her shirt.

"Suri…my sweet…my baby? Everything is all right" Ammi's voice trembled. God, oh God…nothing happened…nothing happened…get up…get up…God be praised nothing happened."

Ammi caressed Suri's face and helped her up. Abbu, clutching his chest, rushed in. Sami's shoulders heaved in a vain attempt to not cry. The soldier had hit Abbu repeatedly to make him reveal where all the cash and jewelry were hidden. Sami's cheek was marked with welts from the hard slap that the soldier whipped across it.

Abbu began to weep uncontrollably. Through the night, they sat huddled together. Everything would be all right in the morning. Did not the soldier say that the captain had better not find them inside! So in the morning, they would complain to the captain that four of his soldiers had abused them and hit Abbu and taken their money.

XVII

The next day was the fourth day of February 1972 and at the end of that day when the gathering dusk over the trees gave way to darkness in Mirpur, the coldness of the floor of the unfinished house, where Suri and the others had sought refuge, was replaced by the heat and sweat of live beings. Here they waited for the night to end.

There was no space for even a footfall in the room.

Munni wanted to sleep on Ammi's lap and tried to wiggle some space, but there was none, and she had to be content laying her head on her shoulders. Ammi looked like she was carved in stone. Only her lips moved silently in prayer. Sekina was in the room with them sitting beneath the window opening. She had carried the baby in her arms all day long, and now he slept peacefully hidden under the anchal of her sari. Naima who had held on to her sister-in-law's hands, afraid of being carried away by the crush of women in the lanes was now sitting next to her.

Ghousia fanned her pregnant sister Saleha with her dupatta. Saleha leaned against the wall with her legs spread out in front moaning continually. The women had made room for her on the dusty floor. Her eyes were closed. Ghousia comforted her with the refrain, "In the morning, we will go home." Saleha shook her head, not believing what was being said. Her qameez was wet under the arms and in the *V* of her heavy breasts. Sweat plastered her curly hair to her scalp. Her hands lay sometimes on her swollen belly and at others on the floor. The dust on the floor made a dirty brown splotch on the front of her qameez.

In the darkness of the damp night as soon as Suri nodded off, Abbu and Sami sat beside her. Then Rumi leaned over and kissed her lightly on the lips. How could he in front of Abbu? Then he brazenly kissed her closed eyelids, which fluttered at his gentle touch. A sharp ray of yellow light pierced the darkness and fell on her face. Rumi began to walk away from the light, and Abbu and Sami followed him. Suri called out to them to wait for her, but no sound came from her dry throat. She could not move. Her feet were cast in lead. A snake entwined around her legs stared at her with its unblinking eyes, and the forked tongue darting in and out touched her lips. Suri shuddered and raised her head from Ammi's shoulders. The light passed by and then came back to her face. She raised her hands to shield her eyes.

This first ray of light to reach them was not from the rising sun but from beams of flashlights careening over the women looking them over.

Ammi whispered, "Do not look up!" Suri turned away and faced the wall as a man's voice came through the void.

"Aaha, they were right! There are so many here. Let us call the others." Another voice joined in.

"There are enough here for all of us."

The sharp light veered down the stairs, and footsteps followed the light. Silent with fear the women shivered.

A woman whispered, "Were they soldiers?"

Another answered, "They were not wearing uniforms."

"Do you think they will be back?"

"He said they should tell the others."

"Why have they gone to call the others?"

"Are we to be taken out into the fields again?"

"Maybe this house belongs to someone they know and they want us to leave?"

"This time we will go into the mosque."

Saleha whimpered in deep agony, "Ghousia I want to die. I cannot bear this."

"Please Apa try to be calm. Everything will be all right in the morning."

"Nothing will be all right. I will die here."

"Please, Apa..."

Before Ghousia could finish her sentence, the sound of foot-steps echoed on the stairs, and everyone fell silent. Several men walked into the corridor and in the cold hard beams of flashlights looked the women over. A ray of light fell on Naima. She looked up defiantly. One man joyfully exclaimed,

"*Eta aamar*...She's mine...She's mine...I want her." He waded in through the bodies in the room but could not get beyond a few steps. There was no place on the floor to put even one foot. The women in the room shuffled closer together and denied the men space to walk. One man went round the corridor to the window to get a better view of the mass of women.

"Let us line them up in the corridor." The man who wanted Naima suggested.

"Good idea!"

"All of you come out. We need to count you."

No one got up.

"Get up and come out..."

Again no one moved.

"We need to force them out of the room?" an angry man's voice called out.

"How?" another asked.

Just then Sekina's baby began to wail. He was hungry again. The man by the window leaned over the edge and grabbed the baby. Sekina stood up, took hold of the man's arm, and shook it to make him loosen his grip, but the man pulled the baby out the window and laughed.

"Okay, you Bihari whore, you better come out now or I will toss this Bihari son of a bitch out."

Sekina scrambled over the window ledge to get to her baby. The upper part of her sari unraveled. The women near the window helped her heave herself out into the corridor. Part of her sari still remained in the room.

"Give him back to me. I will go with you. I will do whatever you want me to do…"

"Let's take her first," the man with the baby gleefully announced.

"But I want that one. This one is not young, and she is not a virgin!"

"Do not be so greedy."

"Okay, come downstairs with me if you want your baby back."

Sekina tugged at the end of her sari, extricated it from the room, flipped it across her bosom, and ran after the man and her baby. Suri buried her face in Ammi's lap as she made a personal appeal to God.

"Please forgive them," Ammi called out to God, "they know not what they are doing. Please forgive them…they know not what they are doing. Forgive them…"

The men in the corridor tried to pull out the woman nearest the door. Others held onto her, and the men had to let go. There was great deal of strength in numbers. There were not as many men outside as the women in the room, and like the women, they were unarmed.

"These whores are not going to let us have any fun."

"Why bother? Let's go to the other house."

"No, this will be our defeat. Let us get a rifle and see how these women listen to us then."

A voice called out below, "Does anyone else want this woman? I am done."

No one took him up on the offer. Sekina came back with the howling baby in her arms. Her sari was crumpled as though it had been bunched up at the waist. As she walked into the room, tears flowed down her face.

"I did it to save my baby. They would have killed my baby… Harris, forgive me…forgive me?" she whispered as if she was pleading with her husband.

The men clapped. "Look, we did not do anything to her. All of you cooperate, and everyone will have a good time. We even have food for all of you."

The women in the room bunched closer together. A sharp shot nearby rang through the silence. The women huddled even closer together. A man emerged out of the dark holding a pistol. The men clapped with joy. At last they would get their pleasure.

"If you do not line up in the corridor, I will shoot into the room."

"Just give us a couple of girls, and we will leave you alone," another offered magnanimously.

A wave of panic swept the room. A spontaneous lament rose pleading to God for help, but there was no one to listen to their pleas. A thunder clap like sound of a gunshot filled the room, and a woman screamed, "Stop, we will come out."

The woman nearest the door rose and headed out into the corridor. Another followed and then another. Ghousia cowered in the corner. Suri did not raise her head. Naima hid behind her sister-in-law. The men had now found floor space and walked into the room. The man with the pistol brandished his firearm. The glow of the flashlight made it glint.

As Naima was dragged out, she screamed and thrashed about, but they managed to take her into the corridor. The men laughed and smiled at the sight of her defiant struggle as though the prize was well worth it. Then the beam of light revealed Ghousia and her sister. One man grabbed Ghousia's arms, and another kicked Saleha's stomach. She groaned and slumped over. Ghousia was pulled out into the corridor. Suri buried herself in Ammi's lap. The light flashed nearby. A loud commotion distracted the two men who were still in the room. Naima had wrested herself away from the men taking her downstairs and run back into the room. The men followed. One of them grabbed her hair, and another held her by the waist. She struggled and screamed but was unable to free herself and was again dragged down the stairs. Suri saw feet shuffling near her head as Naima vanished from her line vision.

XVIII

Throughout the remainder of that February night, Saleha groaned at regular intervals as waves of immense pain swept over her. The shefali flowers blossomed, delivering the promise of sorrow to the women in the dark, unfinished room in Mirpur. The scent of *raat-ki-rani* attracted snakes and spirits of pregnant women who had died at childbirth. The spirits hovered around Saleha sensing, perhaps, that she too would join them before the night was over and the snake lay entwined around Suri's heart.

The sun rose at last and with Sekina's refrain, 'my life is finished, where is Naima? I did it to protect my baby. Harris will not forgive me,' echoing through their lives, the women headed to their homes.

Ammi took hold of Saleha under the arms and urged her to get up. But she pleaded, "I cannot...I cannot. Where is Ghousia... where is she?"

Sekina whimpered, "What will I tell Harris? Everything is destroyed! He will never forgive me. Our life is finished! Where is Naima...where did they take her?"

No one answered her. Afraid of being left behind, Sekina followed Ammi as she forced Saleha to walk slowly down the stairs. There was no one in sight. The women began to walk toward their homes on the other side of the open *eidgah*. Along the way, they were joined by others who had spent the night in other rooms in other houses. They looked just as bedraggled. Together they reversed the route they had taken in the night.

Beyond the *eidgah*, six green and white buses parked on the side came into view. Abbu and Sami were back. Suri's heart soared. Everything would be all right now. But a military truck with Bangladeshi soldiers blocked the road to their house. The appearance of the soldiers caused Suri's heart to plummet. Why were the soldiers here again? The women stopped. What was this new thing happening to them?

"Come forward all of you…come on." The soldiers ran up to the lanes and began directing the women toward the buses.

Some women ran back into the lanes. The soldiers chased them and herded them back. From the crossroad, Suri could see her forlorn and empty house. Abbu was not waiting at the gate for them. Neither was Sami or even Tonto. Did the buses not bring them back?

"Climb on…climb on," the soldiers shouted.

"Why should we?" a woman challenged them.

"Where will you take us?" another asked.

"We will take you to your men…you whores. And stop asking questions…these Bihari women argue so much! Get on the bus… get on."

"Ammi, what should we do?" Suri asked.

"They say we are to join the men. We are being taken to Abbu and Sami. So get on the bus. I'll join you," Ammi replied.

"Maybe we are to sign the papers as well. The reason they did not take us yesterday was that there were not enough buses," Suri reasoned.

Saleha could not walk any more and sat on the damp earth between the green field and the grey road. Ammi kept urging her to get on the bus. Saleha moaned and leaned on her hands trying to keep upright. But she could not and lay down on the ground.

"I am dying…help me…" Saleha murmured.

"Come on, beti," Ammi urged her. "Get up…have faith…come on."

Saleha's helplessness was palpable.

"I cannot…I cannot…"

"Ammi, let us go," Munni cried out.

"Go to the bus with Suri," Ammi told her. "I will join you. Go…"

"Hold on to my hands, Munni. We are going to Abbu," Suri said.

They boarded the first bus and walked to the back. Other women climbed on and the bus filled up quickly.

"Ammi, please come…" Munni leaned out of the window and shouted at her.

Saleha was now writhing on the ground. Her body tensed, and she screamed. Ammi looked utterly bewildered.

"Please, tell me, where is Naima? Please…" Sekina pleaded with the soldiers.

"Who is Naima?"

"My sister-in-law, she was taken away by the men in the night."

"Your sister-in-law…my sister-in-law…same thing…was she young…hahaha!"

"Please, tell me where she is?"

"Just get on the bus, you stupid woman."

"Please help me…"

"Amma, I am hungry," Gurhiya cried out.

"Oh God! What am I to do?" Sekina moaned as she boarded the bus with her children.

A soldier ordered Ammi to get up and get on the bus. "What about this poor girl?" Ammi pleaded. "She is in labor…can't you see?"

"Get on the bus. There is no time."

"Please help her," Ammi implored. "She will die…"

"So?" one soldier yelled, "That's not our business…get on the bus!"

The soldier was joined by others. One pointed to Saleha's crotch. It was wet, and blood had begun to spread on her pink qameez. A soldier hit Ammi on the shoulders and ordered her to get going.

"Ammi, come here to this bus!" Munni screamed.

"Let me go to my daughters…" Ammi forced her way out of the line the soldier was herding and boarded the bus Suri and Munni were on.

"Ammi, do not worry we are going to Abbu." Munni joyfully hugged Suri and Ammi.

"Yes…yes…" Ammi looked out the window and mumbled, "Will God intervene, or will she die bringing forth life? Rajabi also died bringing forth life. No, no, she died and the baby died too, so it was death she brought forth!"

Ammi's face darkened, and she closed her eyes. Suri saw the soldiers standing around laughing at Saleha. The protrusion on her crotch had become bigger. Blood covered her thighs, but she no longer groaned.

The bus began to move on the road toward Dacca city and left Saleha behind. After half a mile or so, the bus slowed down so that it could pass around a massive bulldozer placed at an angle on the road.

"So this is why there was no traffic on our road for the past three days," Suri told Ammi.

"I hope Sadi got through before they shut us out." Ammi said.

"But Sadi left before those stupid Alshams and Albadr men rode around with their weapons so he must be with his friend now." Suri reassured Ammi.

The bus continued on the road past the krishnachura laden compound taken over for Pakistani Army officers during the nine months of gestation of the golden land. It then took a left turn toward the Second Capital Complex.

"Well, well, so this is where Abbu and Sami are waiting for us." Suri felt elated. "Why did I not think of this? The government offices are all here. But then why did it take all day for the buses to come back for us?"

The last thought caused Suri's heart to plummet. The bus did not swing into the gate of this complex of square buildings and long waterways. It moved in a straight line away from the buildings toward the junction with Mymensingh Road that led to the airport on the left and to the rows of krishnachura trees on the right. Perhaps we are to be put on planes to Karachi, Suri reflected. Would Mamoo pick us up and take us to the banks of the Indus? No, no that cannot be, Abbu had said again and again that he would not leave the land he had chosen to be their home.

The bus turned toward the krishnachura trees and went past the Intercontinental Hotel on the left, the Shahbagh Hotel on the right, the racecourse on the left, the Arts Council on the right, the Student's Center and Rokeya Hall on the right, and the road leading to Lal bhai's memorial running alongside these places.

Perhaps everything was part of a collective nightmare. What in the world was she doing on a bus so early in the morning? This road was the one she had taken to get to her school, but since yesterday everything was rendered strange what with men dressed as women and women bringing forth life that did not cut away from the mother's belly and remained attached drawing death from her and dark nights in unfinished buildings and the bearing down on virginal thighs on the cold floor and now the ride in this bus!

Suri shivered in the early morning damp, and her legs began to ache. She should have worn socks when they left the house, but that was a silly thought, especially when she had not even worn shoes. "Serves me right for walking around barefoot all the time in the house," Suri chided herself.

Abbu had wept that no one had alerted him in the interregnum between that March night of fire-lit skies and the December day of the dogfight in the skies. "But Abbu," Suri heard herself saying, "even if someone had, you would not have listened! You had made one journey, and that was it. You had repeated over and over and over again everything would be worked out for all those who had opted to come to this place, now the golden land of Bangladesh."

"But why was I not alerted?" Suri wondered. "Even when the marigolds blossomed in such profusion I had not been alerted."

How in the world were marigolds blossoming in profusion the harbinger of bad news? But the summer that she left Narayanganj her guava tree had burst forth in such abundance and borne thousands of small stiff yellowish white flowers, just like the painting of a blossoming almond tree that Sister Marian had hung in the common room proclaiming from Kazantzakis, her favorite Greek writer, "I said to the almond tree speak to me of God and the almond tree blossomed." Her guava tree had blossomed and, like the marigolds, carried away to fete Indira Gandhi, the Mother

Goddess herself, it was not a moment of communion with God but one of moving on. Like the brightening of the sky before the sun finally sets, all the flowers in her guava tree had turned to fruit, and each bunch of three guavas was perfect. The fresh earthy aroma of crushed leaves and the light green tender shoots carried the heavy burden of understanding that this was a miracle wrought solely for her because she loved that tree and the tree was offering her a parting gift, just like the marigolds. Suri shrugged these silly random thoughts away. She was being taken on this bus to wherever her father and brother waited for her, and once they met, everything would be sorted out.

Rumi…Rumi…how will you feel when I tell you everything? Where was he? Did he know what his Suri was going through?

When the city was left behind, the bus moved forward on a road with rice fields and *paan* fields and brick-making yards on either side. An hour or so later, a graveyard came into view on the left. Wait a minute! Suri sat upright. This was the same one in which her little sister was buried in the tiny grave with the black cage over it. Ammi had instructed them that each time they passed it, they must pray so that the little soul finds a place in heaven, although she was sure to do so anyway considering that she was just a few months old when she died. But the black cage was not visible. Perhaps, another person was buried in the same grave, for was it not ordained that on the Day of Judgment each grave would reveal three hundred souls. Just like from the mass graves found after the world wars!

You are not of the earth when you are born on it but of the earth when you are buried in it. Now where did I read that? Suri wondered.

There was the lane leading to the house Shelly lived in. The bus passed her school. The building looked so small. Then a thought made Suri's heart leap with joy; she was going back to the red brick house, going back to her beginnings. The bus swung to the left at the large white building, passed under the banyan tree, and since it was still February, the mango tree had not yet flowered, so the female evil spirit still resided on it. But there was no need to cover her head and run, for, as she passed under the canopy of leaves, the roof of the bus protected her from the white messy goo. So there was no chance that they would be blessed with good luck.

When the bus took a right turn toward the boys' school and her red brick house, Suri shut her eyes in anticipation of the wonders she would see when they finally reached the green gate: the guava tree offering its fruits under the crisp green leaves, the jasmine bush its fragrance, the pond its field of mauve hyacinths. The djin on the roof of the police barracks must already know she was coming back to Narayanganj.

Then the smell of the silty water assailed her, and like certain smells do, it brought forth what lay hidden in the deep recesses of the mind, of days gone by: her entire school had lined up on either side of the path away from the jetty and waved the green and white flag of their country carried in one hand and the red, blue, and white Union Jack in the other when Queen Elizabeth came down the Sitalakhya River after visiting Adamjee Jute Mill. She had come with her prince consort, everyone said that he was not the king and she alone was queen. The queen in her pink hat and dress waved back at the children. The entire city was festooned with garlands of light. Abbu told her that the city was celebrating her birthday, and she had felt like a real princess. Sadi, of course, had injected himself in the situation. He told Suri, "Just because it is March, it does not mean the lights are for you. They are for the queen, so stop with all the princessy stuff."

When Suri finally felt that the bus had braked to a stop, she opened her eyes. She saw the Sitalakhya River. Each year its waters received the clay statues of Mother Durga and the wood and bamboo replicas of the mausoleums of the martyrs of the Levant. Was the river waiting to receive them? A large black hulled steamer was moored along the jetty. Some official-looking men were waiting for the buses. One man climbed on to the bus.

"Come down…we do not have all day. We need to send the bus back."

For Naima and Ghousia!

Suri was the last one down the two steps on to the hard road. First to get in, last to get out! The women disembarking from the buses were being driven like cattle on to the steamer. On the flat surface of the wooden jetty, Suri saw two white men with cameras and notebooks watching the women being loaded on the steamer. As she passed them, a feeling that she had to do something overwhelmed her. She pried her hands away from Ammi's, broke away from the throng of women heading toward the steamer, and ran toward the two men.

"Please help us. We do not know what is to happen to us. We have been brought here from Dacca. Please help us," Suri called out to them in English.

Her voice was not cooing like a koel, nor was it as shrill as Sadi would have it. It was reduced to a rasp for she had not drunk any water since the night the soldiers barged into their house.

"What are you saying? I cannot hear you," one of the men replied.

But before Suri could repeat what she had told them, the third man, who was showing them around, turned to face Suri and shouted at her, "Get going!"

"Where are they taking us?" Suri asked him.

"Go on...go on...get on the steamer before I..."

He was unable to complete the threat because one of the white men stepped in between her and the third man.

"Who is she?"

"Sir, she is from the village..."

"But I think I heard her say she is from Dacca and she was asking for help," and turning to Suri he said, "Will you repeat what you were saying?"

Before Suri could answer, the third man intervened. "I can explain...you see the Pakistan army burnt down villages and violated our women, and we are taking these poor women to a refuge down the river..."

"No...no, we are not..."

Ammi gripped her hand and pulled her away.

So he was telling them that she was one of those who were plundered and ravished after their men were killed in the villages by the Pakistan Army. But she was from the city, and the soldiers who searched their house and made sure she was not a man were from this golden Bangladesh and not Pakistan. It was Bangladeshis who took away Abbu and Sami, who dragged out Naima and Ghousia, and who laughed at Saleha lying by the wayside writhing in pain with the mass of slime and blood, and pointed to the protrusion in the crotch.

Ammi did not give her enough time to tell them that she was driven to the dew-drenched field yesterday, and her father and brother had been put on buses and taken to God knows where, and her feet were aching from the damp, and her heart was frozen from the night before.

Ammi pulled Suri and Munni along the jetty toward the steamer. Suri could see the water through the slat lines in between the black drums keeping the jetty afloat. The water was still silty, and the waves still gently rippled the surface. Nothing else had changed except her condition. They walked over the planks holding on to the rope support on both sides. Some men leaning against the steamer railings directed them to the upper deck. They climbed up the steel ladder to the upper deck and sat down on the wooden floor among others who had gone ahead.

To sit and wait, that was their destiny now. To sit wherever and whenever they were told to do so!

Some commotion on the jetty drew her attention. Suri saw the two white men arguing with the third man. Then one of them walked across the jetty and came on board the steamer. Ammi had also noticed the argument on the jetty and she cautioned Suri, "You better not say anything anymore."

"But they are telling those reporters a blatant lie. We are not women from the villages."

"Listen to me," Ammi said. "They have total control over us. Do not do anything to make them angry!"

"Why? What can they do to us? We have not done anything to them."

"Suri, please do not argue. They have your father and Sami. If you make these people angry, we may never see them again."

"But where are they taking us?" Suri asked.

"To the same place they have taken your father…I think…I am sure. Where else could they be taking us?" Ammi replied.

While Suri and Ammi whispered amongst themselves, one of the white men climbed up the steel ladder to the upper deck. Not wanting to annoy Ammi by confronting the man, Suri drew the dupatta over her head and sat with her face resting on her knees until the white man left.

Now the world will, perhaps, never know who we are. Suri said to herself. Rumi will never know. No one will know.

All this melodrama was so stupid, Suri reproached herself. Of course, as soon as they met up with Abbu and he had by now opted to stay in Bangladesh, then everything would be sorted out and they will go home, and she will call up Rumi and tell him that maybe it was not a good idea to get married so soon. They should finish their studies first!

XIX

Late in the afternoon, the steamer began to move. The women no longer talked to one another. Nor did they mumble prayers under their breath. All these avenues of solace had been exhausted. On this steamer on a river, which received Mother Durga and mausoleums of the martyrs of the Levant, everyone was silent. It was no use asking each other anything. No one knew what was to happen. The jetty was empty except for those supervising the loading of the human cargo. Not much business was being conducted in the river port that day. The boats tied up along the shore bobbed up and down when the waves hit the sides. The trees along the banks stood still and desolate.

The churning of the water as the steamer moved forward caused the moored boats to collide with one another. The jetty began to recede. Everyone huddled on the floors of the decks. The wheels churned through the brown water, and on the high embankment Suri saw some boatmen hauling a barge full of goods. So if the boatmen were hauling goods in the opposite direction to the steamer's journey, then perhaps the steamer was going downstream. Why on earth was it necessary to haul the barges? Why not just take the road? But in Bangladesh, the forty-four main rivers that crisscrossed the land were the roads. Suri thought of the Volga boatmen she had read about during the time everyone was studying Russian literature. The Volga Burlak's sang, "As the barges float along, to the sun we sing our song, Ay-da, da, ay-da!

To the sun we sing our song, hey hey let's heave along the way, to the sun we sing our song," and perhaps the sun god helped them on their journey. What about this journey? Does the sun god only help those going upstream? Stop it! Suri again rebuked herself.

But really, Suri reflected, since the day they left their homes, the women on board the bus had, perhaps, become the meaningless ciphers that Sister Marian so avidly discussed with them. No one had eaten or drunk anything for two days. No one seemed to be hungry, or thirsty, or upset or anxious or anything, in spite of the unreal situation they found themselves, first in the field, then in the dark room, then on the bus and Saleha writhing on the ground and her crotch turning red, and the man wearing the red sari and his mother wiping the blood from his temples, and Sami and Abbu not returning even after one day and one night had passed, and Nuru's father on the patio and men with flashlights dragging girls out of the rooms of unfinished houses. All feelings and emotions were shut down. Had they become meaningless ciphers? Suri repeated to herself. Shut up, Suri! She scolded herself.

The trees were outlined in black as the steamer edged closer to the banks of the river. Quiet descended as the engines were switched off and the wheels stopped churning the water. A man came up on the upper deck and called out, "All of you, everyone, get up and go down!" Everyone on the deck stood up promptly, as if they had rehearsed for just this one command all their lives, and got into line. They shuffled along and one by one walked along the narrow plank between the steamer and the clay banks. When Suri's eyes adjusted to the dark, the outline of a large building with white arches became visible on the right. As they walked toward it, some men carrying kerosene lanterns directed them to sit in the field in front of it.

And then it began to drizzle. It rarely rained in February in Bangladesh. Maybe the skies were weeping. Now this was cliché straight from Urdu poetry and as unreal as the thought that the sky cared at all. It was raining not in sheets but a sprinkle of drops, the kind that mists up the land. It became cold, and as usual, Suri's legs began to ache from the damp. Ammi's eyes searched in the dark for Abbu and Sami. Suri reasoned they had not come bounding out of the dark mansion because they could not see them sitting in the dark mist along with all the others. That was it! It had to be.

The steamer left and the river went back to softly lapping the shore. The women sat on the riverbank so thirsty that their throats felt like a million shards of glass had been embedded in them. Some men appeared from the shadows with flashlights and kerosene lanterns and ordered the women to go inside. The women seated on the fringes stood up and walked toward the mansion like building. Others joined them, in a sort of single file, urged on by the men. They climbed the two steps to the veranda and across what seemed to be a hall and then emerged on a corridor at the back. Pushed along by those behind and kept moving by the men the women turned left, at the end of the veranda ascended a flight of stairs, crossed another corridor, and finally through a door into a large room.

Suri recalled what Haseena had said in her medicated stupor: "There were fifty-seven women and one little boy in the room in my house. I heard the sound of shooting...Mummy, where are you? I have water for you..." Suri did not count the number of women with whom she had spent the night before or was to spend that night. And there was no bed to slide under. Just many warm bodies. But she felt her father was here, and she would find him in the light of the morning. This last thought comforted Suri, and she at last felt pangs of hunger. The children were all quiet, and only some babies lying in the laps of their mothers cried out.

On the wall opposite the door were a series of wide shuttered windows. It was stifling inside, so Ammi tried to get to the window. But she could not pass through the thick layer of human beings and gave up. All they could do was once again sit on the floor and wait for the sun to rise and the night to pass.

Long into the night, Suri thought she glimpsed stars in the sky through the chinks in the window shutters, heard the lapping of the waves on the shore, a dog barking in the distance, a snake slithering across the room. The room was still, for everyone was lost in the disbelief of what had happened. But they found solace in the belief that their fathers and sons and husbands were in the same building. Other than this hope there were only aching bones and a vast void where the heart was supposed to be.

"And then the loud rat-tat-tat of machineguns split the air," Haseena had said of the massacre of Urdu-speaking women in Chittagong in March 1971. Was this to happen to them as well? Rumi...Rumi...Rumi...Do you know where I am? Will you look for me?

Suri managed to get enough space to stretch out in a fetal position on the floor. Munni was nestled in the arc of her body, and Ammi sat looking into the distance, perhaps, contemplating the speed with which they had been made destitute.

The sun began to seep into the room but was unable to break through the February fog. Suri sat up and looked around. There were women and more women and girls and babies, and she was still in her nightmare. As the light grew brighter, she could see a door on the far side of the room. Suri walked over the still sleeping bodies, opened the door, and saw a long covered corridor with arched windows and shutters. The now brighter sun made semicircular fanlike patterns on the opposite walls as it filtered through the glass portion on the top of the arches. Some of the glass windows were broken and others were cracked. The latches on the shutters were drawn, but there were no locks on them.

Suri slid open one top shutter. The river still flowed gently, but no one was in the field below. Resting one hand on the smooth wooden balustrade, she pulled open the lower portion to reveal waist-high rusted railings. Perhaps this was to prevent anyone from falling or jumping out of the window. The peeling paint on the walls and patches of green mildew made it obvious that this large building had not been lived in for a long time. Suri stepped on the narrow inside ledge and, with both hands holding the wooden balustrade, bent half her body forward and outward to see the far side of the mansion. The outside wall was made of red brick.

Perhaps, her dreams and her nightmares would both be in houses made of red bricks. How ironic? Maybe these bricks came from the kilns she had seen yesterday from the bus as she was taken from Dacca and dumped by the river. This building was really old and perhaps had been made by the same people who had made her red brick house in Narayanganj. Where had she seen a mansion like this before? A mansion by the river was depicted in the film by Satyajit Ray from Calcutta whose Bengali title meant *The Music Room*. It stood on the clay banks of a river much like this one. One stormy night the owner's wife and child drowned in the river while he hosted a music concert in his house. Uff...this was so stupid. That was then and this is now, and that was there and this is here. Why was she even thinking of this tragic moment? There was no storm in the river. It flowed by so peacefully and played no part in any of the misery.

Suri called out to Munni to come to her so they could look for Abbu and Sami in the other rooms. Sekina, with the baby, joined them, leaving Gurhiya with Ammi. She wanted to look for Naima as well as her husband. The grey wooden door that led to the room next to theirs was not locked, and it opened easily. An overpowering smell of urine mixed with the smell of vomit overcame them. When they regained their composure, they saw the room was filled with women. Sekina went in and called out for Naima.

"My name is Naima," an elderly woman answered.

"But you are not who I am looking for."

"Who is your Naima?"

"My sister-in-law, she is very young, and she is missing since last night."

"We have been here since the day before. Maybe she is in one of the other rooms."

"Where are the men?" Suri asked.

"I don't know."

"Do you know if they are here in this building?"

"I don't know...I have not gone downstairs, but the others have. Ask them."

Ammi appeared in the corridor and shouted out to them to come back immediately. She had heard some men talking outside the door. They ran back into the room. The voices became louder, and then the door through which they had entered the room the previous night was flung open. Haseena had said that the ratrattat of machineguns had filled the room. But that was late in the night, and this was early in the morning.

Three men wearing lungis and vests stood at the door. They were not carrying guns or sticks, but a big pot balanced on two long bamboo poles. One man had a heap of enameled tin plates in his hands. The men set the pot down and shouted to the women to make a line and file past. Everyone quickly queued up. Some women carried babies in their arms, and others had small children on their hips and held on to others by the hand. Each family was handed one plate with a gooey yellowish blob plopped on it with a long metal spoon. Ammi began to weep as a plate was handed to her.

"Have we become beggars?" she whispered.

The plate was chipped and its base marked by a complex net of thin cracks was barely covered by the food. Munni reached out, took the plate, and said, "Hush, Ammi, let's go back and sit in our place."

"Oh God, what is this?"

"Please, Ammi," Suri said. "Let us eat and then we will see what is to be done."

"We will never leave this hell," Ammi continued to wail. "Where will we go?"

"Ammi, everything will be okay. Just wait until Abbu finds us," Suri consoled her mother.

"Sadi bhai will also look for us," Munni added. "You wait and see."

What if Sadi too has been taken away, along with Pippi and his Ismaili community who had migrated to East Pakistan from Bombay and Gujrat at the time of the cleaving, and were not Bengalis? But they were influential people and had their imam to protect them. Maybe Rumi will find us here and take us home. Suri's heart filled with the possibility that since Rumi was Lal bhai's cousin that surely counted for something with the authorities. Hiru, Rumi's childhood friend, had captured Bogra, and that made him a hero. The minute he finds out what has happened to his best friend Rumi's...what...Rumi's, what was she to Rumi? In any case as soon as he finds out he will come and get us. Maybe! But suppose Rumi does not care enough to risk helping them. He had not told her everything about Moti and maybe other things during the nine months. Did he not trust her? A tiny whisper of doubt managed to pass by Suri's ears.

With the plates in their hands, everyone returned to exactly where they were sitting since that night, as if these spaces were reserved for them like the tables in a wedding buffet. Perhaps, there was some comfort and safety in what was familiar even if one came by it just one night ago. Suri was ravenous and dipped her finger in the gooey yellowish blob and put it in her mouth. It tasted like the smoky rice and lentils *khichri* made over wood fire on the tenth day of martyrdom, the day of Ashura. Ammi did not touch the food and continued to weep silently. Munni ate a little. Ammi gave what remained on the plate to Sekina, for by the time her turn came to get food, the pot was empty. The men announced there was a tubewell downstairs where they could get water, or they could go down to the river. The men also added that the plates must be clean when they returned the next day.

Ammi felt faint with the constant weeping, so Suri decided that first she would go down to the tubewell and get some water for her and then look for Abbu. With Munni and Gurhiya in tow, she walked along the back corridor. Some of the rooms had large padlocks on the doors while others were ajar. Peeking inside the open rooms, Suri saw only women inside. Maybe the men were in the rooms downstairs or in the locked rooms. All the doors of the Community Hall by the mill were locked! No, no, that cannot be. These rooms were definitely empty! There was no strange smell coming from inside so even if the men were inside everyone was okay!

They went down the stairs and stepped into the field. Munni held on to the plate. Gurhiya wanted to go to the bathroom. Maybe they could find one, or at least find a place under the trees or behind the bushes or something.

"Where is the tubewell?" Suri asked a woman passing by.

"At the back," she answered.

"Is it safe to go at the back?" Suri asked.

"What can happen?" the woman replied.

A large crowd of women was milling around the tubewell. There was not a single man among them. Most women were forming cups with their hands to drink water. Suri stood on the fringes and watched the activity. Munni led Gurhiya behind the nearby bushes. Suri asked a woman waiting to take her turn at the tubewell.

"Where are you from?"

"From Muhammadpur," she said. Muhammadpur was a settlement in Dacca down the road from New Market adjoining Dhanmandi. It was similar to Mirpur since many who lived there served in various government departments or were skilled artisans who had brought their crafts of weaving and embroidering textiles with them from all over India at the time of the cleaving.

"Are you alone here? What about your father or husband?" Suri asked her.

"My father was killed in March in Khulna," the woman replied. "I had shifted to Dacca after my marriage early last year. My husband and his brothers were taken away by bus, and we were brought here day before yesterday."

"Are they not here?"

"No!"

"Have you looked?" Suri persisted in her questions.

"Yes."

Another woman who was listening to the conversation said that she had come here from Narayanganj. "We were surrounded for days in the Adamjee Jute Mill area, after the Sheikh came back."

"Were there many of you there?" Suri asked.

"Hundreds of us worked in the mill…"

"Are there only women here? Where are the men?"

"God knows," the woman replied.

"No one tells us anything. Every day they bring this food, and that is it," the woman from Muhammadpur answered.

Suri's earlobe began to throb with pain and her toes, both injured by Bangladeshi soldiers, began to ache. She ran back into the building.

"Apa, wait for us," Munni called out.

When she reached the room, Suri flung herself on Ammi's lap and cried out, "Ammi, they are not here!"

"What are you saying?" Ammi asked.

"Abbu and Sami are not here."

"Oh God!" Ammi cried out. "What is this place? Where are they?"

"I do not know," Suri replied, "and there is no one here that can tell us anything. We have been abandoned. There is not a single woman here who seems to know anything."

Ammi was sobbing loudly now. "This is the end….we will all die here…"

"But why would anyone do this to us? They did give us food in the morning, which means there is some kind of arrangement," Suri tried to reason with herself.

"This is a refugee camp now, and we are refugees," Ammi wailed.

"Ammi, don't be so dramatic," Suri admonished her mother. "We are in our own country. So how can we be refugees?"

"We are not in our homes, and this makes us refugees."

"I don't accept this. I will go down and see if I can find out anything."

Suri headed out again. Munni followed still carrying the plate. She clung to it as the only possession. Downstairs the women still milled around the tubewell. Suri asked one woman and then another and another, but no one knew what this place was. Munni and Gurhiya headed toward the river. There were women everywhere. Suri followed Munni and saw her washing the plate in her usual meticulous manner, rubbing it with her hands and splashing water on it.

"Munni, please stop."

"Apa, I'm just cleaning the plate," Munni answered. "Otherwise we will not get any more food."

Suri put her hands around Munni's shoulders and began to weep. What else could she do?

"Apa, why are you crying?"

"Abbu and Sami are not here. What are we to do?" Suri said.

"Maybe they went back home and will come for us when they find that we are not there," Munni answered.

"That is not going to happen."

"It will!" Munni said emphatically.

They heard Ammi calling for them. Suri and Munni turned around shading their eyes from the sun that now shone brightly having dispersed the mist of the night.

"Come inside," Ammi said.

"What will we do inside?"

"Nothing, at least it is four walls…"

"Ammi, I am waiting for the steamer to come back," Munni chimed in.

Suri sobbed aloud now. They had been abandoned here to die slowly of grief and isolation.

"Apa, do not cry," Munni said. "Let us go and see what lies further along the river bank."

Where did this little girl get the strength? Suri was ashamed that she had given up so easily.

"Okay, but what if there are soldiers there?" Suri asked.

"What can they do to us now?" There was defiance in Munni's voice.

Sekina joined them, and with Munni leading the way, they walked along the banks of the river. There was a determination in Munni's walk as if she was sure that this could not be the end. Some women saw them heading out and came along as well. After walking for about half an hour, the ragged group of women saw a cluster of huts surrounded by date palms. Could they be in Chandpur? Suri thought. Abbu had taken them there one winter by steamer. In the cold early morning mist, they had gone out into the fields to see the juice from the date palm being collected and placed in large vats over wood fire and stirred until it solidified into jaggery. Abbu said all this had to be done quickly; otherwise the juice fermented and turned to a cheap toddy. Nuru always said his father drank *tarhi*, and it made him cruel. But Chandpur was on the other side of the Sitalakhya, and they had not crossed the river. So this was not that place.

A couple of men were sitting on a narrow wooden platform that jutted into the river. Suri suggested that maybe they should turn back. But Munni was undeterred and walked toward the men. A pye-dog stopped sniffing the ground and watched the approaching group with interest. The two men stood up and looked surprised at the presence of the rag tag group.

Suri gathered enough courage to speak to them. "Can you tell us where we are?"

"Have you come from the *kuthi*...the mansion?" one of the men sitting on the platform asked.

"Yes, we came here last night on a steamer," Suri answered.

"They said you are to stay here in Murapara for a few days..."

"So this place is called Murapara!" Sekina exclaimed. "Who told you about us?"

"The men from the city," the man answered. "They said you all needed to rest and will be looked after."

"Rest from what?" a woman in the group asked.

The realization set in. These men had been told that the women in the mansion had been raped and plundered by the Pakistani Army.

"Oh my God, what lies!" one woman exclaimed loudly.

"Sister, don't make such remarks. Think of what we must do now?" another admonished her.

"Can you tell us if they brought any men here?" Suri asked.

"No! They said you do not have any men."

"Forget what they told you. We are not those women..." the impatient woman began to tell them and was stopped by another.

"What is the use of arguing with these people? They have nothing to do with what has taken place..."

"Are you not the women the Pakistan Army defiled?" the man asked, sensing that there was something amiss.

The women thought it prudent not to answer. Instead they asked if there was any food that they could give them.

"We are poor people and depend on what little we can grow and sell," the man told them. "However, if you have money, then we can walk into the *haat* bazaar a couple of miles away and get some rice and vegetables for you." *Haats* were farmer's markets.

No one had any money. By now a group of women and children from the hut area had gathered to look at them. Everyone expressed sympathy tut tutting at the atrocities they had endured at the hands of the Pakistani beasts.

"Let us ask them if there is any way we can get to the bazaar that they are talking about," one woman whispered to Suri. "Maybe it is really a town. From there we can contact someone."

"Can we get to the bazaar?" Suri asked the man.

"The *haat* takes place once a week," the man responded. "Yesterday, we went to this week's bazaar. It is one hour on foot."

"Let us go there," Sekina suggested. "There must be something there to take us back home."

"Home, where is your home now?" one woman reminded them bitterly.

"We cannot just be left here," Sekina said.

"We have been left here!" the woman answered.

"Surely," Sekina responded, "if they have told everyone we were violated by the army then they must at least pretend to look after us?"

"You're right!" Suri said. "They will probably come back if there are questions raised as to how an entire settlement was emptied."

"But who will ask the question?" one woman asked.

"Someone will!" Suri answered. Suri was sure after her encounter with the two white men on the jetty she had at least made them question the veracity of the claims made by the officials of Bangladesh that they were indeed those women violated by the Pakistan Army. But why would reporters care? Women raped by marauding armies made better stories anyway!

"Who does the mansion belong to?" Sekina asked the men.

"A Hindu landowner lived here. They say he went away to Calcutta when Pakistan was created. The mansion was then used to keep children who had committed crimes."

"This is a juvenile home?" one woman exclaimed.

"Yes," the villager answered. "And we got some work in the kitchen. But it has been empty for some years now. We heard they were bringing you poor women here, and they would look after you."

Sensing that there was not much the villagers could do, the women with Suri decided to return to the mansion. As they turned to head back, a woman called out to them, "Wait, I have something for you." The woman ran into her hut and came out with a small bundle in her hands. "Here, take this." She handed the bundle to Gurhiya.

The bundle contained puffed rice. Puffed rice with date palm jaggery was the perfect soul food. Probably without meaning to, Munni blurted out, "Do you have any *patali gur*?"

"No!"

"Don't be stupid, Munni."

"But I was just asking!"

"Come back in four or five days, and we will get you food from the market," one of the men offered.

Four or five days...four or five days, will we still be here? No, no, not possible. Already it seemed like eternity, thought Suri.

The women went back to the mansion. It sounded so grand. In reality, it was an abandoned building used as a borstal before being turned into an internment camp for Urdu-speaking Pakistani women brought here by steamer.

"Did you all find out anything?" the women in the camp asked when they returned.

They were told of what had transpired.

"When are we going back?" one woman asked.

"Stop asking stupid questions. No one knows anything," responded a woman who had accompanied Suri and Munni to the village.

"I have to go back...I left my husband who is sick and was beaten by the soldiers. I left him on a cot by the road..." Suri's Nepalese neighbor from Mirpur whimpered.

"I left Naima behind," and then almost on cue, Sekina added, "What could I do? Harris will never forgive me!"

"Will we have to go behind the bushes again to pee?" Munni cut through the chatter.

"Does this building not have bathrooms?" Suri asked the assembled women.

"It does have three...we checked, but the doors are locked."

"We will break open the door…we cannot go in the open," Suri said.

"But I am sure someone will come to get us out?" one woman said.

"Not unless they release the men," Sekina answered.

"Where could they be?"

Most women hovered around outside. They sat by the river, on the steps of the mansion or out in the open. The rooms had become oppressive. The smell of urine and feces from the babies was overpowering. There was nothing they could do but wait for something to change. The only sustenance was the water from the tubewell, and a crowd constantly milled around it. There was enough water beneath the surface of the earth for all of them, and there was water in the river. But water alone could not sustain life.

Munni held onto the plate while she dozed off on the grass. Suri did not want to close her eyes. She wanted to see everything and bear witness. She was going to tell the world of everything that had taken place; but then, bear witness for whom and for what? Did not God, who Ammi prayed to with such faith, already know everything? And what had the devout hermit said to Kazantzakis? "From the full stomach to hunger, from the slaked throat to thirst, from joy to suffering, God sits at the summit of hunger, thirst, and suffering."

XX

The sun was overhead when a truck came up the road behind the mansion. The back of the truck was covered with tarpaulin. When the two men sitting next to the driver jumped down, a wave of panic ran through the field. But they did not approach the women and instead walked to the back of the truck and lowered the flap. A couple of men got down from the back, but no one was in uniform and no one carried any weapons. The women relaxed. The men began to unload sacks and some bundles tied in old graying sheets from the back of the truck. After everything was unloaded, two men came up to the women and ordered them to line up. There was some movement among the women, but no line was formed.

"Come here now…We don't have all day!" a man bellowed.

No one complied.

"Okay, do what you want," the man said impatiently. "We have brought rice and *daal* and salt and some pots for you. We have already given you plates. There are some sheets and saris as well. We will leave these here for you."

"Who are you?" one woman shouted at him.

"Never mind who we are…"

"Who are you, and why are we here?" another woman asked.

"I said do not ask questions," the man said. "Be grateful we are not letting you starve."

"What is this? We demand to know…"

"Shut up! We will come every alternate day with food for you."

"Who are you, and why are we in this place?"

"Do not ask so many questions." The man sounded annoyed. "Stay here and we will look after all of you."

"Is this what you mean by looking after us?" a woman responded. "Are we beggars or destitutes?"

The man did not answer.

After the truck left a couple of women inspected the pile on the ground. Then there was a rush to get at the things that had been unloaded. Women grabbed at the sheets, the saris, and the pots.

"They have children to feed," Suri whispered to Munni.

After a while the frenzy died down.

"Ammi, should we also go and get some things for ourselves?" Munni asked.

Ammi's face was clouded with dismay when she answered, "What will we do with those things? How long will we be here? God have mercy on us?"

A couple of older women who were unencumbered by babies or daughters walked up to the women trying to gather rice and lentils in the anchals of their dupattas and saris.

"Sisters, what will you do with this? How will you cook the grains?" one of the older woman appealed to the crowd. "We have to tackle the situation in a calm manner."

"Let us see how everyone can get a share," the other older woman suggested.

"Okay, what do you propose we do?" someone from the crowd asked.

"Let us form groups and portion out the rice and *daal* and the pots and see how it can be cooked."

"There is no kitchen here, so what should we do?" another woman from the crowd said.

Suri remembered that when the family went on picnics to the forts and parks, tea was boiled in kettles placed on makeshift stoves made of three bricks placed to form a U. We can do the same here and pretend we are on a picnic! Suri did not think it wise to offer such advice lest they think it frivolous.

The shed like room at the back was locked. One woman pounded at the rusted latch and lock with a stone, and it gave way. It was dark and gloomy inside. The four clay stoves were full of soot, ash, and pieces of coal. Suri ran back to tell Ammi the good news but did not elicit any response.

"Ammi let us help the women cook." Suri wanted Ammi to get up and participate, but she did not move.

"How are they going to light the fire Apa?" Munni had to ask the most practical question.

"Let's check and see if we can help."

The women had put rice and lentil in three pots, filled them with water from the tubewell, and set it on the stoves. Some women looked for wood and twigs.

"Do you have matches to light the fire?" Suri asked one of the two older women who had taken charge.

"No, we don't. I will go around among the women to ask if anyone has matches."

"We can go down to the village and get you some," Munni offered.

"Good idea. Take a couple of the others with you."

Munni, Suri, and Sekina walked along the banks of the river toward the cluster of houses. The same two men were sitting on the rickety wooden platform, and to their delight, one of them was smoking a *bidhi*. Munni went up to him and asked for some matches. He said that he only had one matchbox and could not give it to them.

"But we need it to cook our food."

"Okay, I will light this *paater roshi* for you, and you can use it to light some twigs."

Munni took the burning jute cord and ran as fast as she could back to the camp and handed it to the two older women. They quickly gathered some dry branches and, with the glowing end of the cord, touching the twigs blew gently over the small heap. Soon there was smoke and finally the twigs caught fire. The women clapped with joy. The pots were set to boil, and the women in the field outside the mansion waited for the rice and lentil to soften. Those women able to get the rough grey sheets of cloth spread them on the ground and sat on them, perhaps, feeling a bit more privileged than the women who did not have any. When the food was ready, Munni queued up with the plate she had washed in the river. She came back with the food and sat down with Gurhiya and Sekina. After they had eaten, she ran back to get food for Suri and Ammi.

When they had finished eating, all the excitement abated, and a feeling of gloom descended on the gathering of Urdu-speaking Pakistani women in Murapara internment camp. It was also time for the sun to set and the sky to glow, a reminder that they had spent an entire day out in the wilderness. And to survive they had eaten what was handed to them as if they were refugees or, worse, beggars. Would the Bengali men in the trucks come every day with rice and sheets of cloth and dole them out, and for how long? Nine months? Is that how long the desire for revenge lasts? Now Suri had no illusions that this indeed was revenge for what the soldiers of the Pakistan Army had done to the Bengalis of East Pakistan.

But now what was the difference between those who were Bengalis and those who weren't? Both were capable of atrocities when circumstances permitted.

When the moon came up, some women went into the rooms to sleep. Suri, Ammi, Munni with many others decided to remain outdoors. The feeling of imprisonment inside the mansion was unbearable. Out in the field, they lay down close to each other, some facing the stars, others with their cheeks against the grass. As the moon traversed the sky, it was feeding time for the mosquitoes. The sky shed some of its moisture, so Ammi covered Munni's face with the anchal of her sari. Suri spread her dupatta over her body.

The river flowed gently by the uneasy souls tossing and turning on its grassy shore. The chirping of crickets cut through the silence. Mosquitoes zinged around the ears. A dog barked in the distance. Poor Tonto! Suri thought. He was such a cute little puppy. Rather scrawny when Munni brought him home from school. She had rescued him from the cruel dogcatchers who used long steel tongs to get hold of stray dogs. Sami laid claim to him instantly naming him Tonto. He was into *Lone Ranger* comics those days. Who will look after Tonto in his old age? Nuru's mother did not like him.

She said he was impure, and his saliva was the devil's potion rendering everything it touched unfit for human touch. So she would not let him stay inside the house. Where would he go?

A baby wailed. Someone sobbed aloud, and the moon made its journey across the sky. When it reached the end of its travel, the sky began to brighten. The chirpings ceased, and the gorged mosquitoes completed their cycle of life. Suri's stomach grumbled and the sky shivered as the stars faded one by one.

XXI

Suri sat on the edge of the river with her feet in the cool water. The long-legged midge fly walked over the water, and the almost transparent guppies with orange and white bellies darted among the submerged plants. A bubble formed here and another there.

Would the river take her back to the red brick house on the banks of the Sitalakhya or join with the Buriganga River, the old Ganges, and bring her to Dacca or join with the Brahmaputra and take her to Mymensingh, city of the rebel poet...and when the rebel poet returned to the land of his birth he was showered with flower petals, and with all the flowers around, perhaps, in his mind he had hummed...why is it that in this festival of flowers the poet is so sad...and he had felt the melancholy...but why would he? He was coming home, and she was here away from home on the banks of this river. Would she be condemned to live on its banks forever? The river had been the final resting place for many. The water rises and enters the lungs and death comes quickly. The river takes what is in its bosom to the sea as it did Haseena's father and brother!

"Suri, come here." Ammi's voice brought her back to the banks of the river again.

The others moved around aimlessly.

"Come and sit by my side."

"Ammi let me be!"

"Come here. I want to talk to you."

Suri walked over to where Ammi still lay on the ground and sat down beside her.

"Suri, we have been left here on our own. I want to die. I cannot bear this…without all my children…your father…"

"What about us?" Suri felt anger rise within her. "And how do you propose to die?"

You hypocrite…a voice on her shoulder told her…why was she telling Ammi about living when she was thinking of dying… shame!

"I don't know…please, I love you and Munni but I also cannot live without your father and my sons…"

"Listen, we are with you," Suri said more gently this time. "And we will find Abbu and Sami wherever they are. Besides, Sadi is probably looking for us at this very moment."

"What makes you think that Sadi can find us?" Ammi asked. "Who can find us here? It is so far away from anywhere!"

"But," Suri responded, "There is contact with the men bringing the rice and all. Someone is organizing all this…"

"But they have led everyone to believe we are the women who were ravished by the army during the fight for freedom."

"Okay, Ammi, we will all die together," Suri shouted. "I will not let you die alone! Let us go and drown ourselves in the river… let us all do that…if you have no hope then let us do it now…Oh God! Oh God!"

Suri ran back to the river. Munni followed her, imploring, "Apa, please do not cry…we will find a way out."

"And go where…and to whom? This is the end…" Suri cried.

"Apa, what are you going to do?" Munni asked.

"Leave me alone. I am not going to kill myself…not today."

Suri tried to blank out her mind.

Even her Rumi had forsaken her, and he had said he wanted to marry her—liar!

On the far side of the field, the truck bringing in supplies appeared. Sometimes they forgot to come. How many days had passed by?

She heard the sound of another vehicle drive up the road. So this time they had come in two trucks. She continued to sit by the river.

"*Borho Apa*…She is there. I can see her."

The voice was familiar. It sounded just like Nuru. He called her *borho Apa*, his older sister, and Munni *chotto Apa*. But how could he possibly come here?

"Suri!"

The voice sounded eerily like Rumi's. Had things come to this? Had she begun to dream even when awake?

The voice called out again. "Suri, it's me, Rumi. I have come to take you back."

These dreams sure were funny! Take her where?

"Suri, look at me!"

She heard Munni ask, "Nuru, how did you get here?"

"*Chotto Apa*, I came in the jeep with Rumi bhai and his friend."

"Apa, look, it is Rumi bhai," Suri heard Munni say. "He has come to get us!"

Munni laid her hands on Suri's shoulders and shook them. "Apa…look up."

It really was Rumi.

"I have come with Hiru. We must hurry."

This was exactly how she had thought it would be, sitting by the river with Rumi holding his hands out to her.

"Rumi ! You came. I knew it."

She took hold of Rumi's arms and wanted to hug him but held herself back with great effort. Not in public. She brought him to where Ammi still lay on the grass.

"Chachi, please get up quickly and let us go," Rumi said, his voice urgent.

"Beta, do you know where Sami and Suri's father are?" Ammi asked him.

"I don't know. But we will look for them once I take you home," Rumi replied.

"Are you taking us back to our house? Is Sami there?"

"Chachi, I went to your house to look for all of you. Hiru told me where they had taken all the people from your area…"

"Where is Sadi?"

"I don't know," Rumi answered. "But please, Chachi, for now, please just come with me. I came with Hiru in his jeep. He will take us to my house. Then we will look for the others."

"Ammi, let's go!" Munni was already walking toward the jeep parked behind the truck. A group of women gathered around them. Sekina ran back from the bushes where she had taken Gurhiya to pee. She wanted to see who had come in the jeep.

"Do you know how long we will be kept here?" one woman asked Rumi.

"I do not know anything. I just came here to get my aunt and her daughters."

"What has happened to the men?" another asked.

Rumi was unable to answer.

"Chachi, Suri, let us go now."

"Do not leave me…" Sekina cried out.

"We cannot take anyone else from here. Hiru got permission for just the three of you."

"Permission? From whom?" Suri asked.

"I will tell you everything later," Rumi told her. "For now let us just go."

"How can we leave everyone else here?"

"Suri, if you come away, we can help everyone. I promise. Let us go."

He took hold of her arms and, with the other, gripped Ammi's shoulders and pushed them toward the jeep. A group of women followed them.

"Take us with you," they cried out. Each time Suri hesitated, Rumi urged her on.

"Suri, I promise we will do something for the rest. But now just come away…do not stop. It will take us three hours to get back home. Come now."

Hiru had not stepped out of the jeep. He was wearing his army uniform. They climbed in the back. Rumi and Nuru sat in front with Hiru driving. He gestured to them to remain silent. As they pulled away, Rumi whispered to Suri in English that they were taking them at great risk to Hiru and pointed to the men unloading the truck. They must not suspect anything, Rumi warned. Anyone of them could have been a fighter in the Liberation Front. They have been told that a mistake had been made and they were actually Bengalis, and Hiru had vouched for this claim.

Suri sat in silence until the jeep entered the open road with paddy fields on both sides. "Why was this done to us?" She could not keep silent any longer.

"Hush…Suri, we can discuss all this later," Rumi reprimanded her.

"No, I want to know right now why this was done to us. We have been made destitute…Why?"

"Some of your people brought this upon you," Hiru replied.

"Who are my people? The Jamaat-e-Islami thugs?" Suri asked.

Hiru, now a major in the Bangladesh army, told her that those who migrated from India to East Pakistan, now Bangladesh, sided with Pakistan and had joined the Alshams and Albadr Brigades who with the Pakistan Army brutalized the Bengali people. All such people had been removed to camps to control them. Suri reminded him that the brigades were organized and led by Bengali Jamaati leaders, and while it was true that some who were migrants from India had joined them, how can it be their responsibility alone? Have they done the same to all supporters of Pakistan? So many Bengalis supported Pakistan as well!

"We will get all such Bengali traitors," Hiru said.

"Then you should catch those who are in the Brigades, not us," Suri responded angrily. "My father and brother are not with anyone but the struggle against the injustices of the Pakistan Army. Also tell me why were Haseena's people killed in Chittagong in March? The struggle for liberation had not begun then."

Hiru did not answer her question. All he said was that he was a soldier and would defend Bangladesh.

"But," Suri countered, "You did not defend the country in whose army you were trained and nurtured."

"Now this is my country, and for the sake of my friend, Rumi, I have come to get you."

"For Rumi's sake and not for the truth?"

Rumi was distressed at Suri's outburst. "Suri, we will discuss all this once we are home. Please for now keep quiet."

Suri did not want to stop the questions. The storm gathering within her was about to explode, but when she saw Ammi and Munni beseeching her to be quiet, Suri managed to control herself. Rumi was taking them back home, and she should be grateful.

The jeep entered Dacca and, after passing the level crossing, went down Jinnah Avenue in front of Gulistan Cinema Complex and turned off toward Rumi's house in Maghbazaar. As they entered the lane to his home, Suri asked him, "Can we not go back to our house?"

"For now, you will stay with me in my house…"

"Why? You went to Mirpur and got Nuru."

At the mention of his name, Nuru looked back. "*Borho Apa,* there is nothing in the house."

"What do you mean?"

"Everything is gone."

Rumi added that the house had been completely stripped. Apparently Nuru's father and his friends took everything away. When Rumi went to the house, all he found was heaps of books lying on the floor, photographs strewn everywhere, and pieces of smashed gramophone records. All the houses in Mirpur now lay empty.

"Where is Tonto?" Munni asked Nuru.

"*Chotto Apa,* Tonto came back, but my father did not want him in the house and chased him away. I do not know where he is."

"Why did you make Rumi bring you with him? Why did you not stay with your father?" Suri asked him.

"*Borho Apa,* I want to live with you. Please do not send me away."

By now, the jeep had entered the driveway in Rumi's house. He closed the gate and then helped Ammi step out of the jeep. Hiru left as soon as they had descended. Rumi's mother was waiting at the door, and she embraced Ammi. "Thank God you are okay. We were very worried."

"Where are my sons and their father?" was the first thing Ammi asked her. "Do you know anything about them?"

"*Inshallah*, God willing they too are safe. You will find them," Rumi's mother said.

Suri and Munni entered the front room and were greeted by Rumi's younger sister, "What happened to the two of you? You look terrible."

"Take them to my room." Rumi was irritated by his sister's nonchalance. "We can talk after they have bathed and eaten something."

When Suri saw herself in the bathroom mirror, she was stunned. She looked like Rajabi. Her face was greasy with dirt, and her teeth were coated a dirty brown. Her hair was matted, and pieces of grass clung to her scalp. Her feet were mud encrusted and her clothes smelled. As she sat on the little wooden stool and poured water over herself, the salt of her tears flowed out the drain. Rumi's mother had given all three of them clothes, a sari for Ammi and qameez and shalwars belonging to Rumi's sisters for Suri and Munni.

There was a feast laid out for them in the dining room. Rice, lentil, chicken curry, and potato *bhaji*, all freshly cooked. The three tried to eat but were unable to swallow more than a few mouthfuls. After the meal, Rumi's mother told them to rest. But Suri said she could not rest.

"Please Rumi, can we go and see if we can find out anything about Abbu and Sami? Who do you think will know where they have been taken? Maybe Hiru can tell us?"

"I asked Hiru and he thinks that perhaps the buses with the men were taken to some jail." The Mirpur operation to cleanse it of the Urdu-speaking residents had been carried out under the direct command of the Bangladesh army. Their orders were not a single family would be allowed to remain in their homes.

Rumi said he would make inquiries about Abbu and Sami's whereabouts but had to be discreet. With emotions running so high and guns in the streets, it was not something he could do openly. Also it would be wiser for the three of them to only speak in Bengali. No one must hear Urdu being spoken. There have been cases of reprisals against anyone suspected of harboring Biharis.

"So now you are also calling all Urdu speaking people Biharis? We are not from Bihar but from East Pakistan and now Bangladesh!" Suri was upset.

Rumi's face fell. "I don't mean anything by it. It is no more than a term that is now commonly being used to refer to all Urdu-speaking people. So don't make an issue of it."

"I'm sorry, Rumi. Please forgive me. I am so confused. I did not mean to accuse you of anything."

"I understand, Suri, but, I cannot emphasize enough that if anyone suspected that a Bihari was hiding in our house, it could give some mischief-monger a chance to demand that you all be handed over to them. There have been cases of torture and murder of Biharis and arrest of those found hiding them."

"How can we find out about Sadi?" Suri asked. "He left before we were thrown out of Mirpur."

"Do you know where he went?"

"He went to stay with his friend Pippi. He lives in Scout Colony behind a bazaar."

"I know where it is," Rumi responded. "It's near Hiru's house in Shantinagar."

"But this is confusing," Suri said. "If the operation was against everyone who was Urdu speaking, then those in Scout Colony were also removed. Maybe that colony is empty as well."

"The Ismailis were not touched!"

"Why? Most of them are from Bombay! Why is it that they were not herded into the camps like we were?"

"I think it's because they are all businessmen and their imam has intervened on their behalf. Apparently Sheikh Mujib does not want them to remove their investments from Bangladesh." Ismailis, the followers of Agha Khan, were a large business community with much capital invested in East Pakistan, now Bangladesh. They were active in key industries including jute, banking, hotels, insurance, and construction. The community was spread in Chittagong, Dacca, Khulna, and Narayanganj.

"Really?" Suri exclaimed.

"I think their imam negotiated with our government to keep them safe."

Suri was taken aback at the revelation. This meant that the Sheikh gave direct orders as to who was to be taken to the refugee camps and who was not.

"We would have talked to him," Suri said. "No one gave us a chance."

"Look, let's now concentrate on finding the rest of your family. We can discuss what is right and what is wrong later. I'll go and look."

"You also promised you would help the others. We left Gurhiya and her mother and all the others…"

"Rest now!" Rumi replied. "We will talk of this later."

That night as Suri slept, she saw the snake that had hung on the shefali tree now wrapped around her bosom, and then it slipped and slithered away. Sadi was in its way, so it climbed up Sadi's legs. Why did Sadi not run? When a snake chases, you do not run in a straight line, you zig and zag. You must confuse the snake!

XXII

"Is Sadi with him?" Suri asked Rumi the next morning. He had gone to make inquiries during the night while Suri slept.

"I did not meet him."

"Did Pippi say where he was?" Suri asked.

"I did not meet Pippi either," Rumi replied. "His mother was suspicious of my questions."

"Why was she suspicious of you?"

"No one trusts anyone these days."

"Do you think anyone knows about our dispossession?"

"I did not see any newspaper reports or anything. I myself only found out when I asked Hiru if he knew anything about the phone lines to Mirpur being cut."

Suri told Rumi of her encounter with the two white reporters on the jetty just before boarding the steamer and how they had come on board probably looking for her.

"So members of the foreign press know that something is up. That is good," Rumi said.

"I don't know if they understood," Suri told him. "It all happened so quickly. I overheard a man telling them that we were the women raped by the Pakistan Army."

"They will investigate if they are suspicious that the transfer of entire settlements has taken place."

"Maybe! But we have to let them know what has happened to my people."

Suri was surprised at herself. She too had begun to talk of my people and your people and his people!

"Please, let us concentrate on just your family," Rumi suggested.

"But you promised we would do something for those left behind," Suri reminded Rumi.

"I do not want to expose anyone to any danger."

"Look, Rumi, I speak Bengali as fluently as you do. Who will know that I am not of your people?"

"That's true. But why are you calling them my people and others your people?"

"That is the reason why we were removed from our homes and taken to that refugee camp, is it not?"

"Yes! But it's not what I support..."

"I'm sorry, Rumi. I don't know what to think anymore."

"I understand! But you must not for even think for one minute that I support this division based on the mother tongue, although my own cousin is a martyr to the cause of precisely that."

"I know, Rumi."

"What we must do now, Suri, is to find out where the reporters are staying and try to meet them."

"You're right," Suri agreed. "We should also talk to the Red Cross people to get aid to the camp."

"This sounds like a better idea. I think most of the people from the foreign press and relief organizations are staying in the Intercontinental Hotel."

"Yes, yes," Suri exclaimed. "If news goes around the world about what has happened to the Urdu-speaking people from Mirpur someone will do something about it." Nothing about last year's killing and maiming of the Urdu-speaking people was reported. No one wrote or spoke of what happened to Haseena and Mr. Mukhtar and those others in Chittagong, Khulna, Saidpur, Rangpur, Narayanganj, and all across the golden land. It was as if blood flowed on one side only. Sheikh Mujib had used the word genocide again and again to describe the cruel and unjustified killing of Bengalis by the Pakistan Army during the nine months of their freedom struggle for Bangladesh. He had not mentioned even once of the killings of the non-Bengalis carried out by his

Bengali Liberation Front in Chittagong, Khulna, and of Naveed's father and others found in the Station Rest House. He did not admonish his followers for the rape and killing of the women in Ispahani Jute Mill or about Zaid and others in the shallow graves. All was justified by saying that they were collaborators against the golden land and assuming they had joined the Jamaat-e-Islami sponsored Alshams and Al Badr brigades to kill Bengalis in East Pakistan.

"Let me first see what we can find out about your father," Rumi said. "Then we can do other things."

"But if the world knows of what has taken place, will it not be easier to find them?"

"Or maybe it will be harder if misdeeds are covered up!"

"Oh God! Do you think there has been some horrible misdeed..."

"I don't know."

"*Salamalaikum,*" Rumi's father greeted Suri as he entered the room.

"*Salam,*" Suri answered.

"Are you rested, beti?" Rumi's father asked Suri.

"Yes! Thank you."

"You and your mother and sister are welcome to stay here for as long as it takes to find your father."

"Thank you. Can you help us find out of their whereabouts?"

"I will do all I can," Rumi's father said, "but the fact is that no one seems to know. But I'll keep asking around." He turned to Rumi. "Are you going to the university?"

"Yes, I am, Baba," Rumi answered.

Rumi left for the campus. Ammi helped Rumi's mother with the cooking.

"What if Sadi bhai does not remember where Rumi bhai's house is?" Munni asked Suri as they sat on the patio.

"Do you think we should go to Scout Colony?" Suri asked.

"I think we should. But how? Rumi bhai told us that it is better if we do not go out alone. Besides how will we get there? It is too far to walk is it not?"

"We will take a rickshaw."

"We do not have any money."

Tears welled up in Suri's eyes. They did not even have their own clothes. She could always borrow clothes from Shelly and Najma. They exchanged clothes all the time. She would call them up and tell them of what had befallen her, of her dispossession. But Suri could not remember their phone numbers. She had not talked to them since the days of the December War.

Around noon Rumi returned. "Did Pippi call?" he asked Suri. "Not yet."

"I don't know why?" Rumi was surprised. "And if Sadi knows that you are here, why has he not come?"

"Maybe he does not know the house? Or is afraid to come? Did you tell Pippi's mother that we were safe with you?"

"I did, and I hope she believed me."

"I don't know why he has not called," Suri said, "but at least we know Sadi is okay? Should we go and see Hiru? Maybe he has found out something about Abbu."

Rumi thought it better to go alone.

Hiru did not know for sure, but he believed that the busloads of Bihari men from Mirpur were taken to the city jail. So maybe Abbu and Sami were there.

"How do we check out who is in the Dacca City Jail?" Suri asked Rumi when he came back.

"Let Baba come back," Rumi replied. "I am sure he knows some higher up who can give us a list."

"Okay…if Abbu was taken to the jail, then he has to be tried right?"

"I guess…" Rumi did not sound sure.

"Then your father can defend him and get him out. Right!"

"Let us first see if he is there."

"Look, Rumi, I cannot sit and let all this happen to my people," Suri said. "I have to do something. Can you give me money to go and look for Sadi and then go to the hotel and give the Red Cross or someone information about where the camp is located?"

"I will not let you go alone," Rumi said. "I will go with you. But let us wait for Baba to come back first. If they are in the City

Jail, then he will probably be able to talk to the city magistrate to find out. "

Rumi's father readily agreed to talk to the magistrate at his office the following day.

"Could you not call right now?" Suri insisted.

"It is better to talk of this person to person," Rumi's father said. "But surely…"

Rumi told her that she should leave it to his father's judgment.

"Beti," Rumi's father's explained, "I know how worried you are. But we have to be careful. But I don't think there is any harm in going to the Intercontinental Hotel to get word to the Red Cross about those in the camp." Rumi's father was unhappy about what Suri's family was enduring. This was not how a new nation starts off. Everyone was to be given the option to stay or leave Bangladesh, and it was up to the government to reign in any mischief-makers.

The last time Rumi and Suri had come to the Intercontinental Hotel was for Nargis's wedding reception.

"I wonder if Nargis is back or if she is still in Rawalpindi?" Suri remarked.

"How did you know I was thinking of the day we came to the wedding?" Rumi said. "You looked so beautiful in your orange and gold sari, just as you do now…"

Rumi's mother had given her an orange colored sari, and she had quickly taken in the blouse, as it was quite loose. Rumi's mother was as plump as Ammi and with the gentlest eyes in the world. Rumi had inherited his mother's dreamy eyes.

"That was a long time back, Rumi."

"No, it was only a year back. Don't you remember?"

"It was an eternity ago…" Suri did not want to continue talking about the past. It hurt too much.

"Hiru said that all the Bengali officers who were in West Pakistan are interned in camps with their families, pending repatriation. There is already ongoing talk of swapping prisoners between Pakistan and Bangladesh."

"Swapping? With the ninety thousand POWs?"

"I think it will be figured out!"

"Then why did your leader not give us a chance to choose if we wanted to remain in Bangladesh or go to Pakistan?" Suri challenged Rumi.

"They should have. Listen…there is something I want to tell you…"

"What is it? You know about Abbu…?"

"No, no!" Rumi said. "When I was in Mirpur with Hiru, he took me to the police station, which was serving as their office, and I overheard some officers talking…"

"What were they saying? "

"They were talking about some girls they had taken out for themselves. One was teasing the other of how much better looking his girl was."

"Maybe they were just talking about their girlfriends or something?"

"No, they were specifically talking about girls from your area."

"Oh my God…they have Naima and Ghousia. We left her sister by the wayside…" So the Bangladeshi soldiers were just as capable of using women of the opposite side as booty.

"Your neighbor, Naima?" Rumi asked.

"Yes…she was taken that night from the quarters we were in and she did not come back."

"What quarters?" Rumi was perplexed. "Were not all of you in your homes?"

"No, first the soldiers came to our house in the night and…and please do not ask any more…I don't remember…"

Suri did not want to give him all the details. Maybe one day she would.

The rickshaw dropped them off in front of the Intercontinental Hotel. There were many people sitting around the assorted green upholstered sofas in the lobby. Suri walked up to the front desk and asked if he could tell her if some foreign reporters were staying in the hotel. The man asked why she was asking about them. Suri said that she wanted to talk to them about "that night"; she was sure he would take "that night" to mean the March night when the Pakistan Army attacked Dacca. He eagerly informed her that three reporters from the foreign press were having tea in the lobby at that very instant and he could take her to them. Suri thanked him for his offer but said she would manage since her brother was with her.

Suri and Rumi approached the three reporters.

"Excuse us! Can we speak to you in private?"

"What is it?"

"Listen," Suri said, "I need to tell you of something that has happened in the first week of February with my people…"

"You look familiar!" one reporter said. "Were you on the jetty in Narayanganj?" Suri nodded in agreement.

"So it was you? You disappeared…"

"Yes! That is what I want to tell you about, but not in public."

"Should we go up to my room?"

"Can we come as well?" The others wanted to hear the story of what had happened.

Once in the lift, Suri introduced herself and Rumi. Then in the ochre and cream hotel room Suri narrated the events of the February days when Abbu and Sami had been taken away on the bus, and she, Ammi, and Munni sent to the camp. She asked if they could help get the others out of the camp and find the men.

"There is a representative of the Red Cross in the hotel. He can help. I will go and get him."

"We were told you were Bengali women who were raped and violated during the nine months and were being taken to shelters," the reporter told them, "and they said that it would not be appropriate for us take photographs. But I was skeptical after one young woman came up to us and said they were from Dacca." He pointed to Suri. "You said that you all were from this city."

"I know what they told you," Suri said, "but now will you investigate and write the truth?"

A tall, thin man entered the room and introduced himself as a representative of the International Red Cross. From his accent it was clear he was French.

"Can you tell me where the camp is?" he asked.

Suri told him that she could not." We were taken to the camp on a steamer, and Rumi brought us back by road."

Rumi said he could show them the location of the camp on a map. After some discussion, Rumi and the Red Cross representative believed they knew where Murapara mansion was by the Sitalakhya River. It could be accessed by going toward Rupganj on the Dacca-Chittagong Highway.

One of the reporters exclaimed, "I know that place! There is a strange lore about it. It was built by a man called Ramrattan with money he was able to squeeze out of a bereaved English indigo grower who wanted to leave when his little daughter died of malaria…"

"Hey! Stop, this is serious business…" the other reporter intervened.

"Sorry. So should we go to the mansion to check…"

The Red Cross representative promised to take up the matter of the women, interned in Murapara, with the authorities.

"Look," Suri told him, "more than getting them food get them out of there…they do not belong in a camp. Why were we put there in the first place?"

"I know you are angry, but we cannot become involved in it. This the reporters can do…" the Frenchman replied.

"At least identify them for who they are, not Bengali women violated by the Pakistan Army but women violated by the soldiers of Bangladesh."

"The first thing we need to do is register them as inmates of a refugee camps," the Frenchman explained, "and then they will be entitled to all the facilities that refugees are given through international laws. It will also establish them as needing resettlement…"

"But they are not refugees. Their homes are here!" Suri insisted.

"Listen, I understand your point. But we will look after them while they are in the camp. Only the government can give them their homes back. I think they will be held for repatriation."

"Repatriation?"

"Yes, to Pakistan."

"But Bangladesh is their country."

"Not any more," the Frenchman said.

"Why not?"

"It seems that since Bangladesh was made for the Bengalis, and all those who are non-Bengalis are automatically not its citizens."

"But Sheikh Mujib said that everyone who lives here are our citizens." Rumi told him. To this Suri added, "How about those people who want to live here?"

"I think that is not going to be a choice if they have been removed from their homes to refugee camps. But first, let us see if we can get the government to admit that they have removed people from their homes and what is their intent."

Rumi signaled that they should leave now. After making one more appeal to the men in the room to help her people, Suri followed Rumi.

"You are very brave." The reporter to whom Suri had whispered her identity on the jetty in Narayanganj complimented her. Suri did not answer.

Ammi asked Suri when she returned if she had been able to get help to Gurhiya and the others. She told her that the Red Cross people did not even know that people had been removed from their homes. But now maybe they would get some help.

The magistrate informed Rumi's father that indeed hundreds of men were brought to the City Jail in the first week of February. They had all been registered by the prison warden as political prisoners and would be tried as such by the government. Who would defend them? No one had really thought this through. The magistrate had asked if there was anyone in particular that Rumi's father was interested in. Rumi's father asked him to see if a Matiur Haq was on the list. The magistrate got back to him some hours later and informed that a man named Haq was on the list. His first name was not indicated. He added that this Haq has probably been charged with collaboration and providing information to the Pakistan Army against Bangladesh.

"Things are confused right now," Rumi's father told Suri when he got home that evening.

"At least we are sure that Suri's father is there," Rumi said. "What about Sami?"

"I did not ask. But if Haq sahib is there, then Suri's brother must be with him as well."

"Are you sure that the person called Haq is Suri's father?" Rumi asked. "You said there was no first name."

"We can probe further. I will ask the warden to give Suri and her mother a pass to visit him. The warden is known to me from some cases that I worked on."

"Baba, I will go with them, so please get a pass for me too."

"Rumi, do not expose yourself so much," Rumi's father cautioned. "You know how dangerous it is. But what you can do is ask Hiru if he can send someone with them? I think this will be good security, and the warden will not be accused of bias or anything."

Hiru agreed to send a lieutenant along with them when they went to the City Jail. He would probably have to lie to the officer and tell him the prisoner was a Bengali arrested for siding with Pakistan. "Make sure no one speaks Urdu," he instructed Rumi.

More than a week had gone by, and Sadi had not yet contacted them. Rumi went to the university every day. When Suri asked him about Shelly, he said he had not seen her. And Najma? He had not met her either. Most students had come back to classes, but none who were Urdu speaking had returned. Rumi made sure he did not call them "Biharis" after Suri's outburst earlier. He told her that there were some skirmishes already between ex-fighters and students on campus. A chasm had also arisen between those who joined the Liberation Front and those who seemingly went about their daily lives during the nine months. So there was always tension in the air. Besides, there were a large number of weapons in the city since no one had done anything to recall them. There was unease that the weapons were being used for criminal activities.

Rumi's father was able to get three passes. Hiru arranged for a lieutenant to meet them in the warden's office. He was told that Abbu was a Bengali who was incarcerated because of his loyalty to Pakistan. The City Jail was located in the old town, about ten minutes away from the memorial to Lal bhai. The lanes overflowed with hawkers selling kamala-oranges grown in the Hill Tracts, boiled eggs, sliced cucumbers, and all kinds of knickknacks. The rickshaw puller had his thumb permanently on the bell to part the jostling crowds. It seemed impossible to get through, but the rickshaw managed to reach the gates of the prison.

The grey high wall surrounding the City Jail was covered with a thick layer of moss and greasy carbon. The main gate was heavily barred with black metal rods, and behind it a heavy wooden gate led inside the prison compound. The two policeman standing guard at the gate looked at the passes and then looked the three over.

"Who are you going to meet?"

"My father," Suri answered.

"What is he in for?"

"They have arrested him mistakenly."

"They all say that...Is there some *bakshish* for us, eh?" He was asking for gratuity for letting them in.

"Yes, we will give it to you when we come out."

The policeman signaled someone inside gate by rattling the bars. The guard examined the passes and gestured that they be allowed in. A sign showed that the warden's office was on the left. Ammi began to pray under her breath. She had been told not to speak, for when she was nervous she forgot to speak Bengali. A young man in starched khaki sitting in front of the warden's desk asked if they had come to meet a Mr. Haq. When they affirmed they had, he introduced himself and said he had been sent by his commander to accompany them. The warden took them to the visitor's room and asked them to wait while he got the prisoner. Suri asked him about Sami. The warden had instructions to let them meet only the prisoner called Haq.

What if this was another Haq. Please let it be Abbu? Suri prayed silently. And please let Abbu not speak Urdu, please, please let him talk to them in Bengali or English.

The prisoners were to meet their family members through iron bars. No one would be allowed to sit across a table as Suri had hoped. A man was escorted to the other side of the bars. It was Abbu in a dirty lungi and vest. He was not wearing his glasses, and his beard had grown. His wavy hair was matted. When he came up to the iron bars with childlike enthusiasm in a singsong voice, he intoned, "My name is Hoq. What is your name?"

"It is us, Abbu—Suri, Munni, and Ammi," Suri told him. "We have come to see you..."

"My name is Hoq. What is yours?"

"Abbu, it's me, Suri."

"My name is Hoq…what is yours?"

Abbu kept scratching his head as he peered at them. Without his glasses, he was practically blind.

"Ji, what have they done to you?" Ammi forgot that she was not supposed to say anything. "Please talk to us properly."

Suri quickly checked to see if the lieutenant had heard Ammi. He was standing at the door and out of range of their voices.

"Abbu, is Sami with you?" Suri asked.

Abbu scratched his head and turned away mumbling, "I will go on this bus…baba, you will go on that bus! I will go on this bus… baba you will go on that bus…*joi*…victory…victory…"

Suri put her hands through the bars and clutched his shoulders, but Abbu did not stop.

"Abbu, please come back," Suri called out, but there was no response.

Abbu disappeared to the far side. Ammi covered her mouth with the ends of her sari and began to weep. Suri stood by the bars disturbed and upset by Abbu's rambling. She again called out to him. This time her voice was almost a scream. But there was no response, and she could not see him anymore. They waited for him to reappear.

Maybe Abbu was in shock! He could not bear the deprivation. He craved cigarettes, and his lack of them was driving him crazy. All this could happen to people when they were put in such extreme circumstances. Maybe now that he had seen Ammi, Munni, and Suri, he would calm down and regain his senses. They will come back tomorrow. Sami will remind him of them. That would shake him out of this condition.

The warden did not know why Abbu was behaving this way. There were five busloads of prisoners delivered on the evening of the fourth of February, and he was asked to put them in the cells. Suri was surprised. She had counted six buses leaving Mirpur. Maybe the warden was mistaken in the number of buses that arrived at the jail.

Suri asked the warden if the prisoners got regular meals and water to wash. Abbu looked so dirt ridden and smeared, and there was a terrible smell emanating from his body. There were not enough washrooms, the warden told them. As for the food, Haq eats what the rest eat. What is that? Rice with lentils in the afternoon and rice gruel in the evening! The jail was overflowing and there were not enough funds. What about Sami? The warden had no idea. The lieutenant probably felt sorry for them and requested the warden to help find him. The warden promised that early the next morning he would ask for Sami when making count of the prisoners. Can we send clothes and food? He was not a criminal but a political prisoner. The warden was not too happy with the suggestions, but with the lieutenant there, he agreed that he would try if they brought a few things only. When will he be sent to court? The warden shrugged and ended the visit. Suri knew that the judge would set Abbu free as soon as he appeared in court. Of this she was sure. Rumi's father would appear on his behalf.

The ride back in the rickshaw was long. Ammi wept, and Suri tried to calm the turmoil in her head and think of what they could do. The image of Abbu getting ready for office every morning kept coming back to her. Each and every morning, Abbu shaved using the two-edged sharp shiny safety razor blade, placing the blade with its middle slit carefully in the rectangular seat at the end of a tube. The top of the seat was opened with a twist of the tube, and after the shaving was done, the blade was taken out, washed, and placed in the paper cover to be used again the next morning. He then slicked back his thick wavy hair that had first attracted Ammi to him with a dab of cool white hair lotion, Brylcreem, scooped up from a white tubular container with a red top that was as deep as the container. In winter, Abbu wore suits and, in summer, pants and long-sleeved shirts with cufflinks and ties and tie pin, all in keeping with the English tradition of appropriate attire for work. However, winter or summer, as soon as he came home he changed into the very comfortable lungi. Suri's heart ached at the image of Abbu unwashed and dirty. Perhaps this is what was making him behave so strangely. Suri shrugged and forced herself to think of what to do next.

Now that they had seen Abbu they must find Sadi.

"Instead of going home why don't we go and see Sadi bhai and tell him about Abbu and Sami being in jail." As usual, Munni had come up with the right suggestion.

But was Sami in the prison they had just visited? Now Suri was not so sure. The warden said five buses were brought to his jail. And why did Abbu keep repeating, "baba, you will go on that bus, and I will go on this bus"? Was he referring to Sami? Was he not with Abbu? Suri did not share her fear with Ammi. For now, it was her burden.

XXIII

The gentle face of the "imam of the time" smiled above them as Suri, Ammi, and Munni sat in the drawing room of Pippi's house in Scout Colony. The elaborately gold-framed photograph hung on the wall opposite the main entrance to the room. Pippi's mother greeted them warmly. Although Sadi and her son were good friends, the families had never met.

"We have come to see my son, Sadi. He came to stay with you on the first of February."

"You are Sadi's mother?"

"Yes, and these are his sisters. Is Sadi here with you?"

"He came to us but stayed only one day or two days and went back home," Pippi's mother replied. "Did he not return home?"

"No, He did not..." Ammi's voice began to quiver.

"The roads were closed, so he must have turned back!" Suri said.

"I don't know," Pippi's mother responded. "He did not come here. Maybe he met Pippi in the shop...you know we have reopened after many days. There has been much loss..."

"But is there another place Pippi can let him stay?" Suri asked.

"I don't know, but there is another friend of Sadi's who came to our house with him many times. What was his name...now? He was Sadi's roommate in the hostel...nice tall boy and so well mannered."

"That is right. Kabir…you may know him as Tutul," Suri told her. "He and Sadi have been friends since they were together in Dhanmandi Residential School. Maybe he went to his house. Can we talk to Pippi? He must know where Tutul lives."

"Pippi is at work…"

"Can we call him at work?" Suri asked.

"The telephone in the shop never works." Pippi's mother sounded vague. "But I have your number…that boy left it with me last week. What was his name…?"

"Rumi," Suri told her.

"Yes, yes. Who is he?"

"His family is very close to us, and we are staying with him," Ammi told her.

"What about Sadi's father? Is he still in Mirpur?"

"No, no…we were taken away…" Ammi began to tell Pippi's mother of their ordeal but Suri interrupted her.

"Yes, he is," she said, "is it okay with you if we come back in the evening to see Pippi?"

"No don't come. I will ask him to call you."

Now where would they to look for her son? Ammi was bereft. All this time she had thought he was safe with Pippi. That day there were so many soldiers about. Sadi must have seen that something was up when he saw the bulldozer blocking the road and turned back. All evening they waited for Pippi to call. Ammi asked Rumi to see if he could locate Tutul. Sadi had told them that Tutul had not come back to campus after that March night! Did he return after the war? Rumi would find out about him.

The next day Suri and Ammi went to the jail with some food and clothes. The warden had not been able to learn whether the boy was with his father.

"Could you get the clothes and food to Abbu?"

"I'll try!" The warden was noncommittal.

"Can we see him?" Suri asked.

"Come back next month. These political prisoners are allowed one visit a month."

One set of kurta and pajama, belonging to Rumi's father, one new vest, one packet of cigarettes, two packets of biscuits, one loaf of sliced Nabisco bread, and some puffed rice were handed over to the warden. There was a set of clothes for Sami, from Rumi's younger brother, in the bundle as well. Could they come back with more food tomorrow?

"No, I am doing you a favor by allowing even this." The warden was annoyed at Suri's insistence. "Go now and come back next month."

Was there anyone else they could approach for help? They knew so many people in Dacca. Suri asked Rumi as they sat in the moonlight on the roof. It had become a ritual to sneak up to the roof whenever they could, when the others were busy or Rumi's parents were out. The roof's high parapet walls shielded them from prying eyes. The branches of a mango tree dominated the roof on one end and a *jamun* plum tree the other. It was March, and both the trees were on the verge of bursting into blossoms.

Suri would have much preferred to sit on the patio with Rumi what with the sweet peas on the trellis in their final bloom. But they had to stop sitting there. The neighbors were curious and prone to gossiping. Rumi's mother had told them that Ammi was her cousin from Chittagong. The neighbors wanted to know if there was some liaison between Rumi and Suri. They said that they saw them sitting in the dark every night in the patio. They study together for their exams, Rumi's mother told them. Suri is also studying law. Then why does she not go to her classes like Rumi does? She studies in Chittagong University. She was in Dacca for her mother's treatment. One lie led to another and another.

On the roof, in the dark, they would hold hands and kiss. Rumi assured her again and again that everything would be okay. Soon he would graduate, and they would get married. What about her studies? She could start again when things settled. First Abbu and Sami have to be brought out from the jail, and Sadi had to be found, and those in Murapara had to be helped. Of course, all that had to be done, but they could still plan their future. Rumi was resolute. Suri told him that the burden of his family's generosity lay heavy on Ammi.

"How long can we live with you?" she asked.

"For as long as it takes for things to become normal." Rumi's gentleness soothed Suri. She did not ask Rumi to define normal.

What about money? They must have money to survive. How long could they keep taking money from Rumi's family?

"Ammi has a box with some jewelry in the United Bank on Jinnah Avenue," Suri told Rumi.

"The avenue is now called Bongobondhu Avenue after the Sheikh, you know."

"I know," Suri said. "Ammi says she also has the deeds to our Mirpur house in the locker. The key are lost with the rest of our house, but the box is in Ammi's name."

"I will ask Baba to think of a way to get to it."

Rumi's father obtained an affidavit saying that their house was looted by miscreants on a date that showed that the robbery happened during the nine-month gestation of Bangladesh. When they took the affidavit to the manager of the bank, he was suspicious of their identity. Did not the address show that they lived in Mirpur and that was the area where Biharis lived? Suri told him that they were one of the few families there who were Bengalis. The manager took out the two sets of jewelry, some gold bangles, and the deed for the house out of the locker and asked them to wait in his office while he made a record of the items. When they got home, they handed Rumi's mother the folder the manager had given them, so she could sell the jewelry. One set of jewelry was missing. The manager apparently felt that the favor he was doing them deserved some reward.

Ammi held on to the house papers. At least it proved that they lived on the soil of Bangladesh even though their house was now in possession of some local League leader. Nuru's family had been allowed to stay on temporarily until the leader's family moved in. Nuru refused to go back to Mirpur, and Rumi's mother let him work for them, running errands to the bazaar and cleaning the garden. Bit by bit, Ammi got information about all her belongings. Everything that could be sold was taken away within a couple of days of their leaving the house. The television, the refrigerator, the radio, and the furniture were carted away by Nuru's father and his friends. The books were sold to the ragman by weight. She asked him about their large collection of photographs, the images of her children as babies, as toddlers, her pictures with her husband and friends, Abbu's graduation picture that she was so proud of. These were thrown in the garbage dump, Nuru said. So their past was now in some large pile of rubbish!

Rumi found out that after the liberation, Tutul, who had performed heroic deeds against the Pakistan Army, had been given a job by the government, but no one knew where he lived.

"Ammi thinks we should go and see Pippi in his shop in the stadium," Suri told Rumi.

"That may be a good idea," Rumi replied.

"When Sadi worked with him last summer, he said they sold electrical goods."

"There is just one large electrical goods shop in the stadium market, so maybe that is Pippi's," Rumi said.

When Suri and Ammi reached Jinnah Avenue to look for Pippi's shop, they could not recognize the place. Hundreds of makeshift shops had sprung up around Gulistan Cinema, all selling saris and ready-made blouses. These saris were not the ones woven in Bangladesh: the exquisite jamdanis, the colorful Tangail saris, the fine muslin saris or even the silks from Rajshahi. The shops were selling Indian saris, and hundreds of women were thronging to buy these. The area had a festive look.

Ammi and Suri crossed the road, entered the stadium shopping area, and were able to find the electrical goods shop quite easily. The shop manager informed them that Pippi had left for Khulna. When did he leave? Last week. When will he be back? They had no idea. Was his friend with him? Which friend? Sadi! He worked with Pippi during last summer. Maybe!

Ammi and Suri quickly headed to Pippi's house.

"Why did you not tell us that Pippi was leaving for Khulna?" Ammi asked Pippi's mother.

"I did not want to say anything until Pippi was out of Dacca."

"Why?" Suri asked.

"Because my son is to leave for Pakistan from there…I did not want anyone to know that."

"For Pakistan?" Suri was incredulous. Suri knew that one could get to Jessore from Khulna and then the Benapole border to Calcutta. Shelly had told her. But that was India. So how did people get to Pakistan sixteen hundred miles away? India and Pakistan had not yet resumed diplomatic relations after the December War. The POWs were still held in India. So how was this to happen? Suri asked Pippi's mother.

"Yes! There is a system that we have worked out," Pippi's mother said.

Ammi was not interested in all this, and she interrupted, "Can you please tell me if my son was with him?" Ammi's voice trembled.

"I don't know," Pippi's mother answered. "But I can tell you this. We all want to leave because we don't know for how long we will be safe here. Besides our business has suffered…"

"Please can you ask your son about Sadi? Please ask," Ammi pleaded. "Please I beg you…"

"I will ask him when he calls. The trunk call lines are not very good."

"Please, sister, please call…we will come again tomorrow."

"No, don't come," Pippi's mother answered firmly. "I will let you know if I hear from Pippi."

They left in utter confusion. No one had told them definitely if Sadi was with Pippi. They should start making more of an effort to see if Sadi was with Tutul. At least they knew where Sami was. Ammi was comforted by this thought. Was the warden mistaken about the number of buses that reached the jail that evening? Of course, he was. So, Suri thought, there was really nothing to worry about.

Should she tell Rumi about this new information that people had already started to leave for Pakistan? Pakistan had not even recognized the state of Bangladesh yet. So how were people going there? Let this be a secret for now. She would only tell Rumi that possibly Sadi was in Khulna.

One evening late in March, Rumi insisted on sitting with Suri on the patio in spite of what the neighbors would think. She asked him about her friend Shelly. "Will she come to see me?"

"I do not know if she can face you." Rumi said.

"But my friends had nothing to do with my situation."

"I know," Rumi responded. "But there is such a thing as collective guilt. Each time I meet Shelly, she says, 'This should not have happened to your family!' I'll urge her to come and see you."

"But you told me you did not meet her," Suri said.

"I did not want you to be upset that they were on campus and you were not," Rumi explained. "Next time I see them I'll tell them to come here to meet you."

"No, don't force anyone. If they want to, they'll come. If they don't, then what can I do?"

"Don't think about it too much. Everything will be resolved sooner or later."

"Maybe I should look for a job, and we can wait this out," Suri said.

"What kind of work could you do?"

"Teach in school or something…"

"Where are your certificates of matriculation and from college?"

"In the garbage dump most likely."

"It will take a while to get duplicates," Rumi told her. "And once you apply and they see that you had taken Urdu, they may not give you the certificate."

"Maybe I'll work as a maid, cleaning people's houses. That seems to be the only thing I am fit for now," Suri said bitterly.

A soft breeze sent the fragrance of mango blossoms towards them and Rumi wished her happy birthday. That was why he was sitting with her so late, waiting for the midnight hour.

In the morning Suri decided to give herself a birthday present. She would meet her friends on campus. Everyone would be at the Teacher Student Center at lunchtime, and she would surprise them. Around noon, she walked through the main door of the dining hall. The ache that had begun in the area of her heart at the time she took the rickshaw to come here had by now settled like a brick in her chest making it hard to breathe. The krishnachura trees were on the verge of budding, the flowers stretching to break out. The Arts Council stood sedate and silent. Set up by the artist Zainul Abedin this council was the repository of his sketches documenting the man-made famine of 1943 when more than three million Bengalis had starved to death. When the Teacher Student Center came into view, Suri felt her heart race with anticipation. She stood at the door and looked around at the boys and girls gathered there for lunch. All the girls wore saris. No one looked familiar. She waded into the room and walked around the tables when the sound of a familiar laugh made her turn to see Shelly sitting there. She was wearing a turquoise blue sari and sleeveless blouse laughing her full-throated laugh with her head flung back, her thick braid of hair lying over her shoulders. The sound was so sweet. Suri wanted to rush over and embrace her dearest friend. The next instant she caught Shelly's eyes. Their eyes held, and then Shelly looked away. Suri turned back and ran out.

Rumi railed against her trip. She had set herself up for disappointment, he told her.

"Shelly did not recognize me. Have I changed so much?"

"You have not, but she has…and it's not her fault either."

"What do you mean?"

"Look, there are spies everywhere looking for the so-called collaborators. If Shelly had recognized you and hailed you and someone had pointed out that you were…"

"I am what? That I am a Bihari! A speaker of Urdu!" she exclaimed.

Rumi was really angry. She could never again go to the campus. It was too risky. That evening Suri waited for Shelly to call. They would weep, and she would ask her to stay with her and tease her about Rumi. She never did.

Rumi reported that the krishnachura trees had blossomed in all their glory. Had her favorite tree in front of Sakura also blossomed? Suri asked him. Especially that tree! He told her. So it was time once again to visit Abbu.

"Take a detour through Mymensingh Road so you can see the blossoms," Rumi suggested.

"I don't want to," Suri replied. "I would rather get to Abbu and Sami as quickly as possible."

"I only want to make you feel happy."

"I know. I'm sorry, Rumi."

Rumi was trying to cheer her up, and she was being so reticent. But what did the changing flowers and trees matter when she still had to visit that awful dingy City Jail? But then it was spring, the harbinger of new life, so maybe this time they would meet Sami as well. They waited in the dark smelly visitor's room for Abbu and Sami to appear behind the bars. Again Abbu was alone, more disheveled and dirty than the last time. Munni ran up to the bar and grabbed Abbu's hands.

He asked her, "Have you brought my sweets? I want sweets… have you brought me sweets? They told me that you had brought me *mithai*….give it to me quickly!"

"It's me, Munni."

Ammi took Munni gently by the shoulders and told her it was okay. Abbu was unwell.

"Ji, how are you?"

"Where is my *mithai*?" he whined. "They said someone has come with sweets for me. Where is it?"

"I have the sweets in the box. But Ji, where is Sami?"

As soon as Abbu heard Sami's name mentioned, he began to intone, "I will go to this bus, baba, and you go to the other bus, *Joi*…I will go on this bus, baba…you will go on the other…" exactly as he had done on the previous visit. Abbu abruptly turned, walked to the back, and disappeared. They expectantly waited for him to return, but he failed to do so.

In the warden's office when Ammi wanted to express her suspicion that perhaps her husband and son were not getting the packages left with the guard each week, Suri signaled her to be quiet. She asked the warden about the trial preparations. The warden laughed, "Ha! Who cares about these wretches? When the time comes, everything will be sorted out."

Suri thought maybe they should get used to life without Abbu, Sadi, and Sami for now. But they would have to find a way to talk to Tutul. He was the only one who could tell them where Sadi was. How long could they stay in Rumi's house? Suri often wondered. Not that anyone made them feel like they were unwelcome in any way. They were all too good for this. But it had become cramped in the house. They had taken over Rumi's room so his friends could not come, and none of the relatives visited. Rumi's older sister came from Chittagong with her husband, and she had to stay with her in-laws in the old neighborhood of Dacca. Lal bhai's son had come once and left as soon as he saw Suri. Rumi's mother said she would explain everything to him, so they should not worry.

One morning soon after the April jail visit while reading the *Morning News*, a news item caught Suri's attention. The UN High Commissioner for Refugees was in Dacca to deal with the issue of the return of Bengali refugees who had fled to India after the Pakistan Army crackdown in March. The Commissioner was staying in a government rest house not far from the Intercontinental Hotel. The High Commissioner, Prince Sadruddin Agha Khan, was an uncle of the "imam of the time" whose picture hung in Pippi's home. Maybe they ought to tell him of the camp in Murapara and of the rape and killing by the Bangladeshi soldiers that had descended on their people, Suri thought. There was no way of finding out if what she had told the Red Cross official had helped the women in the camp. Rumi's father, however, had heard that there had been some reporting in the foreign media about the transfer of people from places like Mirpur to internment camps. Maybe this was due to the information Suri had given the white reporters. They should try to meet the Commissioner, she decided.

"The man will not meet us. How will we approach him?" Ammi asked when Suri told her of the plan.

"Let's go to the rest house around noon," Suri suggested. "Maybe he comes back for lunch, and we can stop his car and talk to him. We have to do something," Suri expressed her feeling of helplessness. "I will go mad just sitting in the house."

"We promised that we would help Gurhiya and Sekina. I feel so bad every time I think of them," Ammi remarked.

The white semicircular building of the state guesthouse was located in a cul de sac. The gate and a curved driveway overlaid with red brick chips led to a wide veranda. At the gate, they were stopped by the guards. However, when they told him that they were there to inform the Commissioner of the treatment meted to them by Pakistani soldiers, he eagerly called out to the white uniformed doorkeeper that he should inform the secretary that there were some important people here to see the Commissioner. A stocky man dressed in white pants and cotton safari shirt came out to see them. He had a pronounced paunch and thick eyebrows.

Suri asked him in English, "Are you also from the UN?"

"No, I am a personal aide to His Excellency."

"Are you of his community?" Suri wanted to ascertain, although from the tone of his voice she could make out that he was from Bombay.

"Yes! But what is it to you?"

"It does matter who you are," Suri responded, "because we are not who you think we are. We have been dispossessed from our home in Mirpur, and my father and brother are in jail, because we are Urdu speaking. We are who they now call Biharis," she added.

"Please, can we see the Prince?" Ammi pleaded in Urdu. "We too are refugees, and he must do something for us."

The aide was taken aback at this request, but he looked concerned. To persuade him further, Suri told him that her older brother's best friend lived in Scout Colony for Ismailis, and Abbu had several Ismaili friends in Narayanganj, and that they had set up a school together. The aide said his uncle helped in setting up an English school there. So maybe he knew Suri's father. Now the aide was convinced of their bona fides. He took them to a waiting room and told them that he would see what he could do about meeting the Prince. After about ten or so minutes, he came back and asked them to follow him.

"The Prince has to be at a lunch at the French Embassy, and he has agreed to put it off for fifteen minutes to see you. I have told him who you are."

Suri, Ammi, and Munni were ushered into a drawing room where Prince Sadruddin, the UN Commissioner for Refugees, was waiting for them. He stood up when they entered, and when they had introduced themselves, he asked them to sit on the sofa next to him and tell him about their dilemma. He was tall, fair, and balding. In his grey suit, white shirt, and blue tie, he looked distinguished, and his eyes revealed his compassionate nature. He patiently heard their tale and seemed quite concerned.

Did he know of the Murapara internment camp up the river? He did, but was not sure who was interned there. Suri, Munni, and Ammi gave as much detail as they could in the fifteen minutes allotted to them. The Prince understood some Urdu, since his father Sir Sultan Aga Khan III was a Pakistani born in Karachi, so Ammi was able to relay her ordeal to great effect. The aide came in to tell the Prince that the car was waiting to take him to lunch.

"Wait until I finish talking to the ladies," and turning to them, he said, "Now tell me how can I help you all personally."

"Get our father and brother out of the prison," Suri responded.

"I cannot. I have no jurisdiction."

"You do!" Suri said. "They have been taken collectively and falsely charged with political crimes." Suri pleaded with him to talk to the authorities and even to Sheikh Mujib and tell him of how this act was against the rights of people as envisaged by the UN that the Prince represented.

"I can do that, but this will not help you directly!"

He looked thoughtful. Then he took out his card, wrote a few sentences on it, and handed it to Suri.

"You know the head of my community here?" the Prince asked Suri.

"We do know some members of your community."

"Ask whoever you know to take you to the head of the community in this city and give him this card. He will help you."

"Help us how?" Suri asked.

"In whatever way he can," the Prince replied. "And I will ask the President about this situation with political prisoners. What is your father's name?

"Matiur Haq and our brother's name is Sami. They are both in the City Jail, and we do not think there will be any trial or anything."

"What happened to your house?"

"We do not know. We were forced to abandon it on the fourth of February."

"Do you feel your life is under threat here?"

They told him that as long as they spoke in Bengali they were safe.

"But this is not our land anymore," Ammi added. "The people of Bangladesh do not want us here. We want to go to our Pakistan."

This was the first time Ammi had said that she wanted to go to her country.

So this was the beginning of the end of their life in Bangladesh.

The Prince assured them that the community leader would help them, and after shaking hands with each of them and wishing them luck, he left for his luncheon engagement. The card had the words "help this family on my personal request" written on it.

Suri thought that the best way to contact the leader of the Ismaili community in Dacca was through Pippi's mother. So the three headed to Scout Colony, and before Pippi's mother could reproach them for not waiting for her to call, they handed her the card. She looked at it, and her face changed several shades, and her eyes opened wide.

"You met the Prince?" she asked incredulously.

"We did," Suri responded.

"He gave this to you personally?" Pippi's mother asked.

"Yes!"

"You talked to him."

"We did."

This line of questioning was perplexing. Did she not believe them?

The sheer ecstasy of holding an item touched by the uncle of the "imam of the time" was exciting Pippi's mother. When she heard that they actually shook hands with him, she did something quite peculiar. She took each of their right hands by turn and pressed it to her eyes. The imam's bloodline was divinely sacred.

"Were you able to talk to Pippi yet?" Ammi asked Pippi's mother.

"No, but I will call him today." Pippi's mother became very friendly. Their meeting with the Prince had made them special.

"Can you call now?" Suri asked impatiently.

"I will book the call, but it might take a long time to get through."

"We will wait," Ammi said.

"Sit here. I will get you all some tea," Pippi's mother offered.

"Thanks. That will not be necessary," Ammi responded. "Please just make the call."

"Can you help us meet the head of your community?" Suri asked.

"I will tell him of what the Prince has said, and he will call you immediately." Pippi's mother seemed excited.

"Can you get us an appointment?"

"I will do better that that," Pippi's mother replied. "I will go with you."

"Okay."

The phone rang and Pippi's mother picked it up.

"Yes, Yes, please connect...Malika...Malika...where is Pippi?" she shouted into the phone. "Okay...okay...is Sadi with you... Pippi's friend Sadi? No...Can you tell Pippi to call me? How is the baby? Okay..."

Apparently, the connection was not good.

"Malika says Sadi is not staying with her..." Pippi's mother addressed Ammi.

"Oh God...my son...my son...where are you? Please God protect him."

Munni gave Ammi some water to calm her down. Pippi's mother suggested that maybe Pippi put Sadi in the rest house instead of his sister's house. When he called, they would know for sure.

Early the next morning, there was a phone call asking if they could meet the head of the Ismaili community that afternoon. He lived in the more upscale settlement in a lane adjacent to Suri's school on Bailey Road. Of course, they would come to his house. Pippi's mother was already there gushing with concern. The community leader met them in the drawing room of his large posh apartment. The heavy curtains, the sofas, the crystals, the ornate gold-framed painting of the "imam of the time," the flower arrangements on the tables all bespoke of considerable wealth.

He addressed Ammi, "As soon as your husband and son are out of prison, come and see me. I will arrange for safe passage for your family out of here."

"But how do we get them out of prison?"

"That is something I cannot help you with. I can offer you a place to stay until you leave Dacca…"

"But maybe we don't want to leave," Suri said.

"Listen," he turned to Suri. "There is no room here for romanticism. You are not accepted in Bangladesh and will have to leave."

He suggested that if they have relatives they could go to Pakistan or that if they have relatives in India that too can be arranged. "Is there a third option?" Suri wanted to ask but kept quiet.

"I can offer you a flat in Scout Colony to stay in while we arrange for your passage to Karachi, but for couple of months at the most. We cannot risk giving a family charged with conspiracy against Bangladesh to live in the colony for long. There could be reprisals against my people if some miscreant finds out."

"But we are not criminals…" Ammi told him.

"Look, I know all that," the community leader answered. "But the reality is that all of you are branded as Biharis and worse still Pakistanis, so try and get out. Contact me as soon as your family decides to come and live in the colony, and then we will try to get you out of Bangladesh to Pakistan."

"We will…" Suri replied.

"Do you have any money?"

"Not much, but we have a house in Mirpur!" Suri told him.

"What about relatives in Pakistan? Will they help?"

"My older brother lives in Karachi, and of course he'll help," Ammi responded. "But how will we contact him?"

"We will work all this out."

That evening when Suri told Rumi of what had transpired that day he did not want to accept that there was no other way. "We will think of something. I cannot let you go."

Suri did not answer.

XXIV

Ammi and Suri discussed if they should contact others who could help. What about Abbu's colleagues in the telephone department? Not a good idea. The fewer people involved the better. God knows how an individual would react, especially if someone from his family had been killed, injured, or raped during the nine months. What about Doctor Wahid? He was a good friend of the family. That was a possibility.

Doctor Wahid had not yet come back from Narayanganj, but his wife, with her ever-present red lipstick and red flower in her hair, was surprised to see Ammi and Suri. She had heard that Urdu-speaking residents of Mirpur had been relocated, and had assumed that they were in India as POWs.

"No, we are still here, and we were in an internment camp," Ammi told her. "And my husband and son are in jail, and we cannot find Sadi. Is there any way Doctor Wahid could help?"

"He would surely find a way out for you," the Doctor's wife assured them. "Wait for him and have dinner with us please. We had so many good times together."

"You are the Sheikh's neighbor and must know him," Suri said.

"We have no contact with him," the Doctor's wife replied.

"Does the Sheikh and his family still live in his house next door, or have they moved to the President House?"

"He spends time in both places."

The absence of policemen and guards meant that he was not there on that day.

When Doctor Wahid came home, he was shocked to see the state they were in.

"I am glad that you came to me," he said. "But there is nothing, absolutely nothing I can do about Mr. Haq and Sami. That was a huge black hole that no one had access to."

"Then what should we do, Doctor sahib?" Ammi asked.

"Perhaps the only help to be got is from the government of Pakistan. You have your brother there, Bhabi. He can help I think."

"How?"

"If they asked after their people stranded here..." Doctor Wahid said.

"But we are not stranded here," Suri replied. "We have lived here all our lives..."

"Look," Dr. Wahid explained, "I know that you all have been put in the mix so to say, but really, the only way out is if the governments negotiate...at least for the people who worked for them. Haq sahib is an officer of the central government, so he should be given that status..."

"They don't care! Why should they?" Ammi said bitterly.

"That is the thing. When they negotiate the release of the POWs, then they should also talk about you."

All this sounded so vague and confusing and utterly out of their control.

That night Suri and Rumi sat on the roof discussing the events of the day. She finally felt totally helpless. If they had to wait for negotiations between Pakistan and Bangladesh to take place before Abbu and Sami could be freed, then there really was no hope. They might as well give up!

They heard Rumi's sister calling from downstairs. "Rumi bhai, there is someone at the gate asking for you."

Rumi went down to see who it was. Suri stayed on the roof. She was so lost in thought that she did not realize that an hour had passed and Rumi had not returned. She went down and asked his sister if she knew where Rumi was. She said he had gone out with the boy next door. Rumi's mother was a little worried for Rumi was not friendly with that boy. There were rumors that he was involved in some gang.

When Rumi did not come back by eleven, his father called Hiru to see if Rumi was with him. He was not. Hiru told them not to worry. He would look for Rumi. Maybe he was studying with someone. Another hour went by, and there was still no sign of Rumi. His mother went next door to inquire if their son was at home. He was not, and they said that he was often out all night.

Rumi's parents were anxious now. Suri went up on the roof and kept vigil. Rumi would be there momentarily. She saw Hiru's jeep stop at the gate, and her heart soared. Rumi was back. But only Hiru got out and conferred with Rumi's parents. His mother was by now a nervous wreck, praying and weeping by turns.

"You have to find him, Hiru," she cried. "I have a feeling that something very bad has happened to him."

"Stay calm...I will look...he must be with some friends," Hiru assured Rumi's mother.

Hiru knocked on the neighbor's gate and asked the father where his son was. Suri heard some altercation between the two. Hiru was furious at something. He quickly got into his jeep and sped off. Half an hour later he was back, and this time Rumi was with him. His shirt was torn, and the side of his mouth was bleeding. Suri ran down to meet him but stopped at the drawing room door. Hiru was berating Rumi's mother, who was by now hysterical. "He is such a fool. I told him so many times to be careful, but Rumi does not listen. I managed to get to him in the nick of time. They were going to shoot him."

"Who was going to shoot my son? What has he done to anyone?"

"I have taken care of things for now," Hiru's was almost shouting. "But that boy is accusing Rumi of siding with Biharis and accusing him of harboring them in his house...this means that Rumi could be accused of collaborating with enemies of Bangladesh and arrested. This situation cannot be allowed to carry on. It has to be taken care of."

"How do they know?" Rumi's mother asked.

"That is what I asked him as well," Hiru replied. "He said that he had seen Suri many times before in your house, so how could she be from Chittagong…"

Suri did not wait to hear any more. She had put Rumi in danger. They had to leave. She could not endanger Rumi and his family. Early in the morning, they would leave. But where would they go? For now the only place they could go to was Doctor Wahid's house. He would give them sanctuary for old time's sake. She would not tell Rumi where they were. He must not be seen with her anymore. It was too risky. He could be arrested for harboring collaborators. Suri could not allow this to happen to her Rumi.

Early the next morning, they said good-bye to Rumi's mother before the others were up and thanked her for all that she had done for them. She wept and said that she did not want this to happen but was now helpless. They assured her that they had a place to stay and she should not worry. Suri was determined not to let Rumi know where she had gone for he would surely come to see her, and someone would find out.

Doctor Wahid had already left for Narayanganj, but his wife said they could stay for a few days until some other arrangement was made. When the Doctor returned in the evening, he agreed with his wife that Suri, Munni, and Ammi could stay with them. Then he asked Ammi if she had the deeds to their house in Mirpur. Also would she give him power of attorney to sell the house? That way they would have some money to rent a small place. Ammi gave him the deed, but since the house was in Abbu's name, they would have to get the power of attorney signed by him the next time they visited him.

The Doctor's wife gave them the room at the back next to the kitchen. This was the only empty space she had at the moment and could Ammi help with the cooking. Of course, she would.

XXV

May in Dacca was hot and humid. Thunderstorms lit up the skies and cyclones formed in the Bay, but that year none made land fall. When they went to the City Jail, Abbu behaved in the same manner. He looked even more emaciated, and he coughed and wheezed. His hands were scrawny, and his eyes seemed to be glazed. This time Suri made sure they did not ask him about Sami because then he would make the same excuse about the buses and disappear. They had brought some jaggery for him and told him that if he signed the paper they had brought for him they would give him sweets. It seemed so callous, but what else could they do? They had to sell the house. There was very little money left from the sale of the jewelry. When Abbu signed the document giving power of attorney to the Doctor, Suri's eyes filled with tears. His signature was as crisp and flowing as it had been before.

The warden again said he had no idea where Sami was.

On the ride back to the Doctor's house, they passed the martyrs memorial and the Officer's colony opposite New Market and Green Road. Did she really ever live in these places? Suri wondered. That was in another life. This was their reincarnation as refugees and household help. Why did she hope that Rumi would guess that it was time to visit Abbu and he would come to the jail? But they did not go on specific dates, so how could he know? Thank God Rumi had forgotten about her. It was too dangerous. He had already done so much for them, for her. Maybe when she

271

got to Karachi, she would write to him. But there was no communication between Bangladesh and Pakistan, so how would she get the letters to him? She willed her mind to stop wandering. Here she was thinking of the future when the past had not yet been resolved.

Doctor Wahid was happy that they had trusted him enough to give him the papers. Of what use was the deed to them anyway? Ammi said. Owning a house was no proof that you were of Bangladeshi soil. He commented that he really liked Ammi's cooking.

Yes! Suri thought, Ammi had come a long way since those first days in East Pakistan and her first encounter with cooking fish. Her voice would gurgle whenever she told them about it.

"We were living in Sylhet. Your father went off to office. The office clerk brought over some fish saying that sahib had sent these to be cooked for lunch. So I washed the fish with two tumblers of water from the drum. We did not have taps for water?"

"No taps! Then where did the water come from?" one or the other children would ask.

"All the water was brought in from the pond in front of the house and stored in a big drum, and we took out the water in tumblers to wash…"

"Did you drink water from the pond? And you had said it was used by men and women to bathe in!"

"Yes, it was. But we drank water from the tubewell. Every morning your father would fill a pitcher with water, pour it into a pan, and swish a piece of alum in the water. This caused all the sediment to settle at the bottom. I would then pour the water into the pitcher running it through a muslin cloth. The water from the pitcher was quite good, in fact, and really cool. Your father would bathe in the pond but not me. I used the water from the drum to bathe indoors."

"Okay so what happened with the fish?"

"I washed these and then fried some onions in a pan, put in some spices, you know the usual, turmeric, chilly, cumin, and coriander, all of which I ground on a stone slab, and put the fish in whole, covered these with water, and let it cook. Can you imagine the stink? I did not realize that the stomach had to be cut open and the insides taken out and the scales removed. Then your father taught me how to clean the fish with the large curved knife, the *baithi*. I had to pin it down with my toes and run the fish over the sharp edge to remove the scales. I had never used such a knife before. It was like the meat cleaver that the butchers used to cut meat in Poona." Suri smiled as she recalled Ammi's anecdotes about her life as a bride.

The Doctor also thanked Suri for helping with the house chores. His wife added, "A young man had come asking for you. I told him that you had gone out and that he should come back tomorrow." It must be Rumi! It had to be. Oh Rumi. He knew that Doctor Wahid was the Sheikh's neighbor, and he must have figured out that they had nowhere else to go. Oh my love. But she should not meet him, and she should send him away. But how could she? As soon she saw him, she knew she would throw caution to the winds just to hold his hands and kiss him. No, she could not do that. Oh, Rumi, you came…you came.

That night while they lay on the mat in the room next to the kitchen, Munni suddenly got up and excitedly shook Suri. "Apa…Apa…I know where Sadi bhai's friend lives," she uttered breathlessly.

"Where, Munni, and how do you know?"

"Remember, Sadi bhai said that when he had gone to see Tutul bhai's mother on Eid day he met a singer there and said she lived next door to Tutul…"

"Yes, yes, I remember," Suri racked her brain. "She is a famous singer, but what was her name…?"

"Her name is Ferdousi Begum." Ammi piped in. The singer's song for the Urdu film Talaash made in Dacca in 1963, "*Kuch apni kahiye, kuch meri suniye…*You tell me about yourself and listen to what I tell you about me…" had been a great hit not least because it starred Rahman and Shabnam. Both Bengali film stars now lived in Lahore, starring in Urdu films. Shahnaz Begum, a beautiful young Bengali singer from Dacca, had also set up house in Karachi where she sang a famous song, *Jeevay, Jeevay, Jeevay Pakistan*… Long live Pakistan," written by the Urdu poet Jamiluddin Aali. None of them showed any signs of coming back to the golden land.

"Ferdousi Begum is famous so many people must know where she lives. But I recall he also said there was some sort of a lodge in the lane…what is it called?"

Munni had no idea about any lodge.

"Yes, yes, I know the name…it's on the tip of my tongue…" Suri said.

"What lodge?"

"Munni, let me think…It was the freemason lodge…yes that's it. Both the singer's house and the lodge should be easy to find. I'll ask the Mrs. Wahid tomorrow. Munni, you are brilliant. I love you!"

A prolonged rumble of thunder woke Suri the next morning. The sky was overcast, and lightning lit up the dark clouds at regular intervals. When she opened the door of their room to cross the courtyard and go to the servant's toilet, the Doctor's gateman called out to her that there was someone at the gate wanting to see her.

It was Rumi. He had come to her.

She ran to the gate, and there he was. Her heart skipped a beat, and she felt as though that day had dawned just for her. She quickly took him with her to their room at the back of the house.

"Rumi, it's not safe for you to come here."

"Why did you not tell me before you left?"

"I did not want any more trouble for you," Suri replied. "Your mother and father would begin to hate us if we stayed and exposed you all to…to…all the hate that exists for my people."

"You should have let me find you a place." Rumi looked perturbed. "Not this. You are in a servant's room…My God, I don't believe this…the Doctor is such a bigot…Do you work for him as well?"

"No, Rumi, we just help around the house…Ammi cooks and we help her clean…"

"Has he hired you as maidservants and your mother as a cook?"

"No."

Suri tried to calm him. "They are very nice, and this way no one guesses who we are and he has even offered to sell our house so we can live elsewhere on rent, but Rumi, you must not come here,"

Suri pleaded. "I will call you, and we will talk on the phone. Please, Rumi, we are okay. Now go."

Suri forced him to leave. Her heart broke as she saw him walk along the narrow corridor between the house and the compound wall that separated the Sheikh's house from the Doctor's. The Sheikh rarely came here, and whenever he did, the place was filled with soldiers, cars, and policemen.

That day while dusting the Doctor's bedroom Suri asked his wife if she knew of any freemason lodges in Dacca.

"Why do you want to know? Are you going to join them?" the Doctor's wife asked. The Freemasons were fraternal organizations viewed with suspicion as anti-religion and not allowed to hold meetings openly. The advent of freemasonry into the Indian sub-continent could be traced to 1730 when officers of the East India Company held their meetings in Fort William in Calcutta.

"No! Just asking...do you all also have clubs that you can meet in?"

"What do you mean?"

"I mean, you are Qadianis..." She wanted to put the Doctor's wife on the defensive by questioning her Qadiani faith that believed that their imam was the promised messiah of the Muslims. Most Muslims believed that the Qadianis were a cult, like the freemasons, and were thus unacceptable within the faith.

"No, we just have our own mosques. Not lodges," the Doctor's wife replied.

"But the freemasons have lodges. Do you know of any lodges here?"

"There is one big lodge on the corner of Purana Paltan Road, beyond the United States Information Services' building. And yes, there is a smaller one in one of the lanes nearby. But these are all locked and abandoned, and they cannot help you."

"I don't want them to help us," Suri replied. "I was just curious. We used to go to the USIS and always wondered what that big building was. It was always locked up."

Tutul's house, Suri reckoned, must be in a lane as there were not many residential houses on the Purana Paltan Road, so it must be near the smaller freemason lodge.

Next day Suri and Ammi got down from the rickshaw in front of the General Post Office opposite Baitul Mukarram mosque at the end of Jinnah Avenue. They must get used to calling Jinnah Avenue Bongobondhu Avenue now, Suri told Ammi. They tried to figure out where the lodge could be. The day was hot and sultry, and Ammi was bathed in sweat. Suri realized how thin and worn out she looked. The twinkle in her eyes had faded, but as soon as Abbu, Sadi, and Sami were with them, it would return. Of this Suri was sure.

The lodge, which was shuttered and looked abandoned, was right at the entrance of the first lane opposite the Secretariat building. They asked a passerby where they could find Ferdousi Begum's house. Next to it was Tutul's house if what Munni remembered was correct. As usual, Suri cautioned Ammi that since she forgot to speak in Bengali when she was nervous, she was not to speak in front of other people. Suri would do the talking.

Tutul's single-storied house looked deserted. They knocked on the gate, and a woman came out.

"Is this Mr. Kabir's house?" Suri used Tutul's formal name to inquire about him.

"Whose house did you say?" The woman had no clue as to who Kabir was. So Suri asked again using his *daaknaam*. "Is this Tutul bhai's house?"

"Yes! But he is not here."

"When will he be back?"

"We do not know when he will be back."

"Is his mother in the house? Can we see her?" Sadi had said that Tutul's mother was a really nice person.

"What do you want?" Tutul's mother asked as soon as they entered the drawing room. "So many people come asking for favors. How much can my son do?"

"No we just want to ask him if he knows about my brother's whereabouts."

"Was he with Tutul in India?"

"No, he studied with him in the university."

"What is his name?"

"Sadi."

"You are Sadi's sister?"

"Yes, and this is my mother."

"I remember Sadi. Tutul was very fond of him." Tutul's mother's voice became soft. "He came to see me on eid. He was the only one who came,"

"We do not know where he is since February. He came to the city to meet his friends. Tutul bhai is his good friend we thought maybe he was with him," Suri explained.

"Are you still living in Mirpur? And why are both of you in such a ragged condition? Sadi always dresses so well."

"No, we are in the city now."

"Tutul has gone with the Sheikh on a tour. He is a security officer, you know. When he returns, I will ask him about Sadi. Don't worry."

"When should we come again?" Suri asked.

"Come next week. He will be back by then, and my son is so dutiful…as soon as he comes back, the first thing he does is come here to touch my feet to show his respect and seek my blessings."

Luckily Doctor Wahid also subscribed to the *Morning News.* So reading it every day was the one routine that remained unchanged. When the month of May was nearly at an end, the newspaper reported that due to overcrowding in the City Jail it had been decided that prisoners who had not been charged yet would be released as well as some old people. Suri asked the Doctor what this reprieve meant, but he had no clue. Rumi's father would know. No harm in making a phone call. No one will know whom it was from. Suri dialed Rumi's number and waited with bated breath to hear his voice. When he answered, she could not speak for a few seconds.

"I have called to ask you for another favor."

"Nothing I do for you is a favor, Suri," Rumi said. "So don't talk like that."

"Sorry. Rumi, can you ask your father if he knows of any details regarding the release of some prisoners from the City Jail due to lack of space?" Speaking rapidly, her voice quivering with anxiety, she continued, "Criminals who had been sentenced could not be released nor could those charged with murder and theft. So maybe they were going to release those that they could not hold without trial, and since there had been no trial or anything, maybe Abbu and Sami were to be released. Right? Right?"

"Hold on, Suri! Let me ask Baba if he can find out anything about this. I'll call you later."

"No, let me call you tomorrow."

"Is there some restriction on your receiving phone calls?" Rumi asked.

"Not really! But you never know," Suri replied.

"It makes me so mad to think of how they are treating you."

"It's okay. Maybe it is for the better. This way the neighbors think they have hired some servants."

"Please, Suri, don't say such things. It upsets me too much."

Rumi's father agreed that what Suri was saying was logical, and he would see what it was all about.

Yes! Rumi's father got the information that many prisoners were to be released in a general amnesty. Who and when was uncertain.

How would Abbu know where to go once he was released? That he would be released she was sure of. Suri decided that starting early the next morning she would wait outside the jail gates, even though it was uncertain when the prisoners, and which ones, were to be set free. She would wait every day outside the jail for as long as it took.

Doctor Wahid thought it would not be a good idea to bring Mr. Haq to this house once he was released. Maybe they could now take up the offer of a flat in Scout Colony made by the Ismaili community leader. But Ammi requested that the Doctor should look at him as soon as he was set free. God knows the state of his health. He was so emaciated and he coughed and wheezed. His mental condition was also not normal for sure. He had not recognized them or said anything coherent the three times they had visited him. Doctor Wahid cautioned that the reprieve may turn out to be false hope. Nonetheless, for old times' sake, Haq sahib could be brought to his house and could even stay for a couple of days until a more suitable place was found. Had a buyer been found for their house? Not yet! But hopefully soon!

XXVI

The lane leading to the jail entrance was, as usual, choked with rickshaws and people. Ammi would not think of letting Suri go to the prison alone. She got up at daybreak and did the day's cooking so the Doctor's wife would not be inconvenienced. They reached the jail at eight and waited outside the locked gate with the crowds jostling around. Their armpits and backs were bathed in sweat.

A couple of hours later, the gates opened and some old men appeared. Each of them carried a small bundle. Some were greeted by people waiting outside like Suri and Ammi while others wandered off. Then except for officials arriving and leaving, there was not much activity at the gate. They were unable to meet the warden because they did not have passes. Suri went up to the gate and asked the guards if they knew who was being released. The policemen looked her up and down and with a sneer. "Who is inside?"

"My father and brother…"

"What are they in for?"

"We don't know," Suri replied.

The guard spat on the ground. "Everyone says they don't know. Where does this riff raff come from? Get going."

They decided to wait until at least the evening. There was no place to sit on the road. So they went into one of the narrow lanes and, for lunch, ate some cucumber slices bought from a hawker. That evening more people came out, but this time too, Abbu and

Sami were not among them. When it began to grow dark, they went back to their quarters on the banks of the lake.

On the seventh day of the daily vigil, Abbu finally appeared at the gate. He wore threadbare grey lungi and a dirty blue shirt that was askew in front having been buttoned the wrong way. He squinted as he came out into the sun and looked around, uncertain of what he should do. Suri ran up to him and gently led him to Ammi. Abbu asked if she had brought him any sweets. Ammi took him by the arm and guided him into a lane. Suri stayed by the gate for Sami and spotted their neighbor from Mirpur, Mr. Doja. His son who the soldiers had beaten up the night before the fourth day of February was not with him. There was no one to receive Mr. Doja. His family was probably still in Murapara camp. Suri went up and greeted him.

"Beti, where is my family?" he asked.

"They are in an internment camp…"

"Oh my God! Are they okay? Oh God, please have mercy on us.'

"They are safe there."

"Why are you not with them?"

"A friend of Abbu's got us out," Suri replied.

She asked him about his son.

"When they were putting us on the bus, they separated the young and the old," Mr. Doja said. "They brought us here, and I waited for the bus with my son to arrive. It did not. At that time, the soldiers told us that they have been taken somewhere else…"

"Was Sami on that bus?"

"He must be. All those who were young were put on one bus."

Suri's heart sank. It was true then that only five buses reached the City Jail.

"How will I get to my family?" Mr. Doja asked.

"I do not know," Suri replied. "Maybe you could go to the Red Cross people and they will help."

"Look at what has happened to all of us, Beti? Haq sahib began to blabber from the moment we got here…he had screamed and shouted at the soldiers for not allowing Sami to sit with him, and they hit him viciously with the butts of their rifles, and his temple was bleeding when they pushed him into the bus." Abbu had high fever and was quite delirious for a week. Mr. Doja and others used water compresses to bring the fever down. "When the fever broke, he kept blabbering *joi...joi...*Then Haq sahib wanted everyone to give him cigarettes. No one had any to give him. Then he demanded sweets." Mr. Doja explained, "We all want something sweet to eat. It must have been the constant stale salty rice gruel that all the prisoners were given to eat."

Suri gave Mr. Doja some money, "Go to the Intercontinental Hotel where there are some Red Cross people. They can help you."

"Where are you going?" Mr. Doja asked.

"We have a place to stay," Suri replied, "and thanks for helping Abbu."

As she turned to go to Ammi, a hand on her shoulders stopped her. It was Naima's father. Suri's heart froze. What would she tell him if he asked about Naima?

"Beti, where are Naima and Gurhiya? Are they with you?"

"No, they are in a camp many miles from here. The Red Cross will take you there. Go with Doja sahib." Then Suri asked, "Where is Harris Bhai?"

"I don't know. He was in the other bus. The soldiers said they are being taken to a better place than us!"

When the jail gate was closed, Suri joined her parents. Ammi had bought Abbu some sticky puffed rice and jaggery ball from the vendor, and he seemed happy to lick it. They hired two rickshaws, one for Ammi and Abbu and the other for Suri. As usual they went past Lal bhai's memorial, past Azimpur Colony, past the New Market, and then a large swathe of Dhanmandi. All the while Suri dwelt on what Doja sahib had told her. Sami and the other boys and young men had probably been taken to another jail, but where? Hiru would have to find out. She will go and see him. But she decided not to tell Ammi. Let her nurse Abbu back to health.

Rumi was appalled to hear that the soldiers had separated the young and old in Mirpur that February day. "Why would they do this?"

"Rumi, maybe Hiru knows where the bus has taken Sami and the others. And please could you ask him if he knows anything about Sadi?"

"Why? Are you convinced that he is not in Khulna with Pippi?" Rumi said.

"Probably he is not there! We have not been able to talk to Pippi and his mother is so evasive. When we went to Tutul's house…"

"What! You went there?"

"Yes! I went with Ammi," Suri replied. "He was not there but his mother remembered Sadi and…"

"You are taking too many risks, Suri. Let me do the investigations…"

"No one guesses that I am Urdu speaking. I speak Bengali quite well you know!"

"That is true. Listen I'll go to Hiru right now and ask him about Sami. Can you call me later?"

"Yes! I'll call tomorrow," Suri said. "I don't think the Doctor's wife likes me using the phone so much."

"You have to get out of there. It's a shame how they are treating you."

"Let it go, Rumi. We will talk later."

Hiru had known all along that everyone had not been sent to the City Jail. Some had been taken elsewhere. He advised Rumi that it was better not make further inquiries.

"But surely you can tell me," Rumi said.

"No, I cannot even though you are my best friend."

"Have they been taken to a jail somewhere else? Please tell me.'

"I don't know," Hiru replied. "Be grateful that Suri's family is mostly intact!"

"What do you mean mostly? Someone in the family is dead?"

"I did not say that, but who knows what happened that February day when our soldiers got the chance to avenge the injustice of the nine months."

"What are you telling me?"

"Look, there was a mass burial in Mirpur of the men who were killed in clashes with the soldiers. But who knows who they were?"

"When did the burial take place?"

"On the sixth I think?"

"But Suri told me that the clash took place on the first of February when the goons from Alshams and Albadr rode around brandishing their weapons!" Rumi exclaimed, so there were people killed after you took over! Why did you not prevent it?"

Rumi felt utterly betrayed by Hiru. He should have done something to stop the bloodshed and reprisal that had surely taken place, "I am so ashamed. I cannot tell Suri what you have revealed."

"I'm sorry I could not do more."

Rumi informed Suri that Hiru did not know anything about those February days.

"Then who do we turn to for information?" Suri asked.

"How do I know?" Rumi banged the phone.

Why was he so angry? Suri was perplexed. Maybe we are getting on his nerves!

Ammi did not want to remain in Doctor Wahid's house for longer than a week. They had to find a place to stay. The leader of the Ismaili community had offered them a flat in Scout Colony, provided they were prepared to leave Bangladesh.

"But we have no option," Ammi said. "Let us take it and then we will see."

"See what?" Suri asked.

"When we find Sami and Sadi we will have to leave," Ammi replied emphatically. "There is no place for us here except as maids and cooks. And I refuse to submit to this servitude. This is not our destiny."

Pippi's mother consulted with the leader of the community, and he offered them a small two-room flat in Scout Colony rent free for two months. He made sure they knew that the largesse was due to Prince Sadruddin who had asked the Ismaili community to help them. Suri and Munni packed the few clothes they had. The Doctor's wife gave them some old sheets and towels. She was sorry to see them go. Everyone loved Ammi's cooking she said. Doctor sahib had not been able to get a buyer for their house. He was so busy. Rumi's mother sent a kerosene stove, plates, and pots and pans for the kitchen. Pippi's mother sent over some mattresses before she left to visit her daughter in Khulna.

They were the only non-Ismaili residents in Scout Colony, but the people were nice. Shireen, their next-door neighbor, was a single woman who ran a beauty parlor in Dacca and lived with her old parents. The two families ate dinner together, and all Ammi could contribute to the meal was lentils and some vegetable curry. Shireen made sure that they had chicken and meat every other day. She was also planning on moving away from Bangladesh, as were most of the families in Scout Colony. Some would return to Bombay, but most were to move to Karachi.

XXVII

Rumi came to see Suri every day, often bringing food sent by his mother. In Scout Colony, no one knew them so there were no prying eyes. They sat in the balcony at the back overlooking the bazaar and talked of the day's events. It was bleak in the flat. It rained every day and sometimes for hours on end. The trees drooped under the weight of water, and the crows, sparrows, and shalik-myna birds fluttered their shiny wings in vain attempts to dry out and perched wherever they could get a claw hold under the ledges of the buildings. On the ground, rivulets of muddy water intersected the landscape. Ginger pye-dogs wandered around on the roads with bedraggled tails carefully treading the pools of water that gathered in every dip and pothole.

The days were spent hoping for some news of Sami or Sadi's whereabouts. Suri and Munni helped Ammi with cooking in the morning. They slept in the afternoon, walked around in the small ground in front of the building in the evening, and chatted with Shireen when she came back from work. Abbu mostly slept.

Once a week, Suri went to City Jail with food and clothes for Sami that Ammi sent. She had not told her of what Mr. Doja and Naima's father had said. After leaving the packet with the guard at the gate, she would go to Tutul's house to see if he was home. After several visits, one day she saw some activity at the gate. A new jeep was parked in front, and guards and soldiers were milling around. Suri was afraid, but there was no recourse but to see if

Tutul knew about Sadi's whereabouts. When the guard at the gate asked her why she wanted to see the chief, she gave him the tale of that March night when the Pakistan Army had commenced its massacre of Bengalis in Dacca. She hoped doing so would elicit sympathy. Sure enough he let her in.

Sadi's friend, Tutul, now an advisor to Sheikh Mujib because of his role in the liberation struggle of Bangladesh, sat on a sofa surrounded by men seeking favors. He seemed to recognize her. But she had changed, become thinner, and her sari was faded from multiple washings. She did not introduce herself and went straight to the point.

"Do you know where Sadi is?" Suri asked.

"Who are you?" Tutul looked surprised with this direct question.

"I am Sadi's sister, Suri."

"Suri, I did not recognize you. You've changed. What happened?"

"Well! What can I say?" Suri did not want to talk about her plight in front of the others, so she asked again, "Do you know where Sadi is?"

"I will talk to you later. I am busy right now. Why don't you wait for me inside?" Tutul's demeanor suggested that he understood Suri's hesitance.

After an interminable wait, Tutul finally came to the inner room. The expression on his face was soft and full of concern.

"I'm sorry I could not talk to you in front of the others."

"That's okay."

"What happened with Sadi? I told him to go away to Karachi. Why did he not go?"

"Why would he?"

"Because after a revolution, this is what happens!"

"But we were on your side."

"I know, but that does not matter. When was the last time you saw Sadi?"

"February first."

Disturbed by her reply, Tutul said, "That is the day we decided to launch an operation in Mirpur! What time did he leave?"

"He left early that morning in our car. His friend Pippi, or rather his mother, says he went back the next day. But he did not come home. And then on the fourth, my family was made to leave our house…"

"There were soldiers surrounding your area, so Sadi could not get into Mirpur."

"Then where is he?" Suri asked.

"He does have a short temper you know! It is entirely possible he got into an argument with the soldiers. I can see him do that… God knows what took place, but the soldiers were under orders not to let young Bihari men get away…"

"So maybe they arrested him?"

"Maybe, but I don't think so," Tutul replied. "It is possible but…!"

"But what?"

"You know what!"

Suri stomach began to churn, and the vice around her temple tightened. Sadi was a hothead. Tutul asked if there was anything he could do for her.

"Get me a rickshaw please…"

How could she tell Ammi that Tutul had no information about Sadi's whereabouts? Perhaps, he was arrested. Is that what Tutul had implied? Maybe he was in some prison like Sami. But Tutul had said that this was unlikely. Let Sami be found then she would tell Ammi about Sadi, Suri decided.

It was raining heavily that evening. Suri went to the kitchen to make tea for Rumi.

He followed her. "Listen, Suri, I want to tell you why I am so angry with Hiru…"

"Yes, I wondered about that. He has been so helpful to us, arranging for our return from the camp…Rumi, I could not have survived another day there. I would have drowned myself in that river…"

"Please, Suri, just listen to what I need to tell you about your brother…"

"What about him?" Suri's heart fluttered uncontrollably.

"Hiru says that one bus was taken away...I think it was the bus with the younger men, and Hiru says he has no control on those bent on revenge..."

"What are you saying? Doja sahib did say that the young and old were separated and that they had been taken to another prison. At least that is what he thinks."

"I think what Hiru meant was that the passengers of one bus may have been done away with..."

"What do you mean?"

"I mean they might not be alive..."

"How do you know? That cannot be true..."

"It could be true, Suri," Rumi said. "That is why I am so angry with Hiru. Why did he not make sure that such a thing did not happen? Why did they separate the young and old? It was the soldiers who did it, and he is an officer of the army...he should have taken care..."

"Please, Rumi..." Suri was trembling. "Tell me even Hiru is not sure..."

"I think he is."

"Please, Rumi, don't say that...he cannot be...did he see what happened with his own eyes?"

"There is a mass grave in Mirpur."

Three hundred souls must rise from each grave!

"No, he said it is possible...very possible that some bent on revenge diverted the bus and..."

"But there were six buses the next morning..." Suri was whimpering by now.

"You have to understand that this is a big possibility..."

"It is not...Rumi, please do not tell Ammi this. She will die..."

"But we have to tell her..."

Suri's heart felt that it was about to burst. A massive lump in her throat threatened to choke her. Rumi sat next to her, saying nothing. It was still raining. Rumi held her hands. Then she told him about her conversation with Tutul and that she did not believe that Sadi had just disappeared from Mirpur on the first of February. Rumi put his arms around her shoulders. She shrugged them away and said, "Go away...just go."

"Please, Suri, I am ashamed of all…"

"Just go away and never come back," Suri began to shout at Rumi. "I don't want to have anything to do with you."

"Please, Suri…"

"You cruel, horrible people…you killed my brother and…"

Rumi left.

Ammi walked into the kitchen and asked, "Why are your eyes so red?"

"I was just upset about Abbu and everything," Suri replied.

"Did you find out anything about Sami?"

"No! No! No! And stop asking. I don't know anything about Sami. Where can I look? Why could not Sadi do all this? He abandoned us…Why me?"

Suri ran to the room and lay face down on the mattress, blanking everything out, willing herself not to remember Sami, her brother's love for cricket, his adoration of Tonto, his curly hair—all gone—rotting in some ditch or thrown into the river. Was he shot in the head, or was he bayoneted like the four men in the public meeting, each thrust missing the heart so that death did not come quickly? Was he lying with his face on the green grass, and did his blood cake the white flowers? Did the odor of dried blood linger in the air? And Sadi who argued with her every single time she said something…Sadi, who was a charmer and charmed every girl he met…Sadi's wavy hair, just like Abbu's…Why could you not keep your temper in check!

Why should she bear this alone? Everyone else must know, but Ammi will die if she is told. How will we handle that—how will we bury her? Will we bury her in the graveyard by New Market? Will the earth here take her in, or will it spit her out?

Munni coaxed Suri to eat a few mouthfuls at meal times. Rumi came twice a day for a few minutes each time but did not come into the house. He would call Munni to the door and ask her about Suri and leave. Ammi by turn scolded Suri and cajoled her. On the seventh day, Suri got up and announced that they had to leave Dacca as soon as possible.

"What about Sami and Sadi?" Ammi asked.

"Well! I don't know."

"What do you mean?" Ammi was perplexed at what Suri was telling her. "Look, Ammi, we have come to a dead end. Maybe the Red Cross will find him and let us know. We will leave an address with them or something."

"It's not like you to talk like this. What is the matter?" Ammi suspected that Suri was not telling her everything.

"I want all this to end." Suri began to weep. "I cannot take it anymore…I need to get away from this hell. Didn't Pippi's mother say that her people have arrangements to take people like us across the border?" Suri continued as if demented, "We can pay them when we reach Karachi…"

"Of course, as soon as we find Sami and Sadi, we will leave," Ammi told her.

Suri did not hear what Ammi said and continued, "They have everything worked out and have been doing this since the war was over. Shireen gave me all the details. They take people through the Benapole border. They have arrangements with the security there to smooth things over.

"We will stay a few days in Khulna in the Ismaili Colony," Suri continued, "then take a taxi to Jessore and cross over at Benapole and on to Calcutta by bus. From there, we will take the train all across Bihar to Rexhaul at the Nepalese border. We will cross over into Birganj and then take a bus through the mountain roads to Kathmandu. Here we will go to the Pakistan Embassy and get our travel papers. I think from there we will have to go to Bangkok as there are no direct flights to Karachi from Kathmandu."

Ammi listened patiently and then asked, "How will the embassy accept us?"

"Well, your brother will have to vouch for us. He also works for the government, and the embassy can contact him. Maybe he will even send us tickets and money."

"Of course, he will. But we have to wait until we find Sami and…" Ammi tried to interject.

But Suri continued, "Shireen says they arrange everything for a fee of ten thousand rupees per person. That comes to forty thousand rupees for crossing the borders. Maybe we can get a discount because of the card we have from the Prince. Either we pay them here or give them collateral and pay them once we reach our destination. We will have to arrange our own tickets from Kathmandu to Karachi. Do you think Mamoo will send us the tickets?"

"Stop, Suri! Why forty thousand? Are Sadi and Sami not going with us?"

Suri could not contain the secret anymore. There had to be a way to tell Ammi. There was a knock on the door. It was Rumi.

"Why are you here?" Suri challenged him.

"I just wanted to make sure you are all right."

"I am…Rumi, we are leaving!"

"When do you propose to leave?" Rumi voice betrayed his pain at the mention of separation.

"Today if we could," Suri replied.

"We will leave when we find Sami and Sadi," Ammi interjected.

"Suri, you have not told her?" Rumi realized that Ammi did not know about her sons.

"No!"

"But you have to…"

"What is this, tell me what?" Ammi asked.

"Sami is dead, Ammi…Sami is dead…they killed him…the bastards killed him…" Suri shouted.

"No! That is not possible. That is not…" Ammi fainted and fell to the ground.

Suri screamed, "They destroyed us…they took everything from us…Sadi is rotting somewhere in the earth or in some prison…"

Ammi had said she could not live without her sons! What about us Ammi, your daughters? Suri pleaded to no avail. Ammi died of a broken heart, killed by the golden land that had snatched away her sons.

Azimpur graveyard by New Market received Ammi's body. Rumi's mother arranged for the funeral. It would not have been possible otherwise. Only people of the soil can bring their martyrs to the graveyard where Lal bhai was buried with his fellow martyrs to Bengali. When Ammi was nervous, she forgot how to speak in Bengali.

"Will you accept us now that we have buried three, no four in your soil?" Suri asked the skies over Dacca.

No! Your mother was not born here, came the reply.

"But my mother is buried here and my brothers, and don't forget a little sister as well, she is said to have gone to heaven.

Not enough. Not enough.

To hell with all of you! I don't want to live in your golden land anymore.

Pippi's people have to make do with the promise of thirty thousand rupees to be paid on arrival in Karachi. The Doctor does not remember where he has kept the deeds to the house that Ammi gave him, so the Prince's card with his words to help Suri's family will do as collateral.

February in Bangladesh is the month of martyrs to the mother tongue and girls in red bordered yellow saris offer marigolds to them.

August in Pakistan is the month that people cross over to the land of their faith, even after twenty-five years had passed since the cleaving, and at that time no one asked anyone about their mother tongue.

And in the golden land lie buried a mother and son, perhaps, two sons, killed in the golden land for their mother tongue.

Perhaps, Rumi will come to her.

Perhaps, he still loves her although she had spurned him. This was his land as well, was it not? A land for those of the faith!

Rumi, my Rumi, nothing is permanent in the cycle of history.

Nothing except February, the season of martyrs and marigolds!

Glossary

The following relationship terms are used throughout the text to denote, more often than not, mark of respect for an older person, in both Urdu/ Bengali:

Apa – older sister
Bhai – brother
Bhabi – brother's wife
Chachi – uncle's wife
Sahib – the Urdu/ Bengali equivalent of 'Mister' ['Begum' prefixed to the word connotes the wife of the sahib and 'Bhai' prefixed means older brother.]

The following Urdu/ Bengali terms used in the text mean:

Abbu – Father
Ammi – Mother
Anchal – the untucked end of the sari or dupatta
Beti – daughter
Beta – son
Dupatta – long stole worn by women around the shoulders and sometimes used to cover the head.
Kurta – Long shirt worn by men over pajamas or lungis
Lungi – Sarong worn around the waist by men
Mamoo- maternal uncle
Nani – maternal grandmother
Qameez – shirt worn by women
Paratha – fried flat wheat bread

Roti – unleavened flat wheat bread
Shalwar – loose pants worn by women
Some Urdu/Bengali terms are self explanatory in the narrative.

Acknowledgements

This novel is dedicated to the countless Urdu-speaking Pakistanis who were massacred and dispossessed in East Pakistan/Bangladesh in 1971/72. The survivors live in Karachi. Many came here via Nepal, others through Rangoon and still others when repatriation took place following the Simla Accord in 1973, and recognition of Bangladesh by Pakistan in 1974. Thousands of so-called 'Biharis' still languish in camps in Bangladesh.

Of Martyrs and Marigolds began to be written after I pointed out to my daughters, Saima and Sahar, in Central Park, New York City, in 2008, that George Harrison had sung his song for Bangladesh there. This led to discussions of my life in East Pakistan, from birth to twenty years of age, and their insistance that I put it down on paper.

To my daughters I owe everything good in my life.

My husband, Masood, whose cousin-in-law, Safiur Rahman, is one of the 1952 martyrs to the Bengali language, stood by my use of details of his family's relationship to the Bengali Language Movement. To his friendship and love I owe my life.

My sister Perween, who is my spiritual touchstone, filled in many details that my memory had blocked out.

My brothers, Khurshid and Anis, still bear the scars of being born in a land that did not want them, and are an every day reminder of the events of 1971/72.

Masood's cousin and my friend, Saquib, precisely recollected the events that took place in Chittagong during 1971/72. To his power of narration is owed deep gratitude.

My friend H. Agha survived the massacre in Ispahani Jute Mill, and had no one to listen to her painful tale.

Masood's childhood friend, Maj. Gen. Ashraf Hussein [late], then a Major in the Bangladesh Army, previously a Captain in the Pakistan Army, rescued my family from the depths of hell. To him we owe our deepest gratitude.

Zubeida Mustafa, who spent her childhood in East Pakistan and went back for several visits as an adult, urged me to include details of the bigotry with which the West Pakistani bureaucrats treated the Bengalis of East Pakistan.

Hillel Black, my editor, for his invaluable advice that the role of the novel is ultimately to tell a story.

Jenny Legun, my consultant at Createspace for her help in putting together a great package.

The Createspace Project Team 1 for taking care of all my technical and non-technical queries promptly and efficiently.

Above all my parents who taught us love for country and fellow human beings regardless of faith or ethnicity.